International Praise for *The Folded Earth*

"A gently perceptive story, half comic and half poignant, of a woman's struggle to forget her sorrows in new surroundings."

—*The Sunday Times*

"Tight with life . . . Roy's attention to individual words pays off as she conveys the full texture of experiences. . . . Even minor characters are evoked with inventive idiosyncrasy." —*Daily Mail*

"Pure pleasure, that old-fashioned sort of novel in which one can immerse oneself; an absolute treat." —*Businessworld* magazine

"Eminently readable, a literary novel that feels timeless and authentic."

—*DNA*

"[Roy's] novel offers a vivid evocation of North India. She conjures up striking images with the lightest of touches." —*The Tatler*

"A jewel of a story." —*Deccan Herald*

"A perfect treat . . . Roy brings her characters vividly and amusingly to life." —*Country and Town House* magazine

"There is a gentle perfection to the way Roy writes. . . . A beautiful love story . . . about people who love and long—impossibly?—and love again." —*The Hindu*

"[Savour] this work. . . . I hear echoes of Anita Brookner and Edna O'Brien and other writers like them as Roy brings Maya and her travails to life." —*Biblio*

"A book you will hold close to your heart long after the last page is turned." —*First City* magazine

"[A] deeply unsettling but beautiful novel . . . utterly enrapturing."

—*For Books' Sake*

Praise for

An Atlas of Impossible Longing

"Refreshing . . . [Roy] defines her characters quickly and skillfully, she has a keen eye for landscape, and she knows how private lives can suggest the larger shape of the public world." —*The New York Times*

"Set in mid-twentieth-century India, this debut novel spans generations and political upheavals, [chronicling] both the strength of domestic bonds and the wounds that parents and children, and husbands and wives, inflict on each other." —*The New Yorker*

"Epic . . . [a] gorgeous, sweeping novel." —*Ms* magazine

"Impressive. . . . With her rich imagination, vivid descriptions, and skillful handling of events Roy weaves a tapestry of family life in India. . . . The story and characters stay with the reader for a long time. Roy is a writer to watch." —*The Seattle Times*

"Roy's prose soars with a lyricism that can take your breath away. . . . From her whirlwind opening sentences, readers know they're in for a ride." —*Star Tribune* (Minneapolis)

"A novel to convince us that boldly drawn sagas with larger-than-life characters are still possible in a relentlessly postmodern world. . . . A sprawling epic of love, class and ambition." —*Denver Post*

"An incandescently evocative debut novel filled with wrenching tragedy as well as abiding passion." —*Booklist*

"[Roy] is a fabulous storyteller with a true gift for transporting the reader right into the heat, smells, and sights of India. . . . A poetic novel easily read again and again. A complete success and an excellent choice for a discussion group." —*Library Journal*

"Impressive . . . the sounds, smells, and feel of Bengal come vividly to life. Cultures may differ, but longing and love are universal."

—*Publishers Weekly*

"In *An Atlas of Impossible Longing,* Anuradha Roy bravely explores love, the caste system, and familial lines in a vivid portrait of war-stricken twentieth-century India. This absorbing story defies prediction. Roy's grace and mesmerizing language stayed with me long after I closed the book." —Katie Crouch, author of *Girls in Trucks*

"A novel of beauty, poignancy, and gut-churning suspense. . . . A lyrical love letter to India's past—an India of innocent child brides and jasmine-scented summer evenings. Poetic and evocative, Roy's writing is a joy." —*Financial Times*

"A story to lose yourself in . . . this tale of three generations of an Indian family, set over the span of the 20th century, is brilliantly told . . . intensely moving." —*Sunday Express*

"Roy's novel is engaging from start to finish and difficult to put down."

—*Sunday Sun*

"Recalls classics from *Great Expectations* to *The Cherry Orchard*. . . . Roy's prose is luscious." —*The National* newspaper

"Now here is a perfect monsoon read: an exquisitely written first novel. . . . You might find yourself unbearably moved by her delicate probing of the fragility of love and longing." —*India Today*

Also by Anuradha Roy

An Atlas of Impossible Longing

Anuradha Roy

THE FOLDED EARTH

Free Press

New York London Sydney Toronto New Delhi

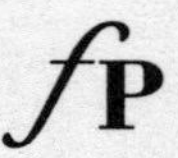

Free Press
A Division of Simon & Schuster, Inc.
1230 Avenue of the Americas
New York, NY 10020

Map by Anuradha Roy
Originally published in Great Britain in 2011 by MacLehose Press

First Free Press trade paperback edition April 2012

Manufactured in the United States of America

1 3 5 7 9 10 8 6 4 2

Library of Congress Cataloging-in-Publication Data
Roy, Anuradha.
The folded earth / Anuradha Roy.
p. cm.
1. Women teachers—Fiction. 2. Social change—Fiction. 3. Himalaya Mountains Region—Fiction. 4. Psychological fiction. I. Title.
PR9499.4.R693F65 2012
823.92—dc23 2011044146

ISBN 978-1-4516-3333-7
ISBN 978-1-4516-3335-1 (ebook)

For my mother, with whom I climbed my first hill

And for Rukun and Biscoot, dedicated non-climbers

TRISHUL
NANDA DEVI
ROOPKUND
Qureshi's Garage
SADAR BAZAAR
ST HILDA'S
CHRISTIAN CEMETERY
Jam Factory
CHURCH
REGIMENT HQ
Post Office
Meghdoot Hotel
Chauhan's house
SHOPS
MALL ROAD
KNOCK FIERNA
OAKLEY
Police Station
GENERAL'S RETREAT
WESTVIEW HOTEL
THE RANIKHET OF THIS NOVEL
Army Area
Stream

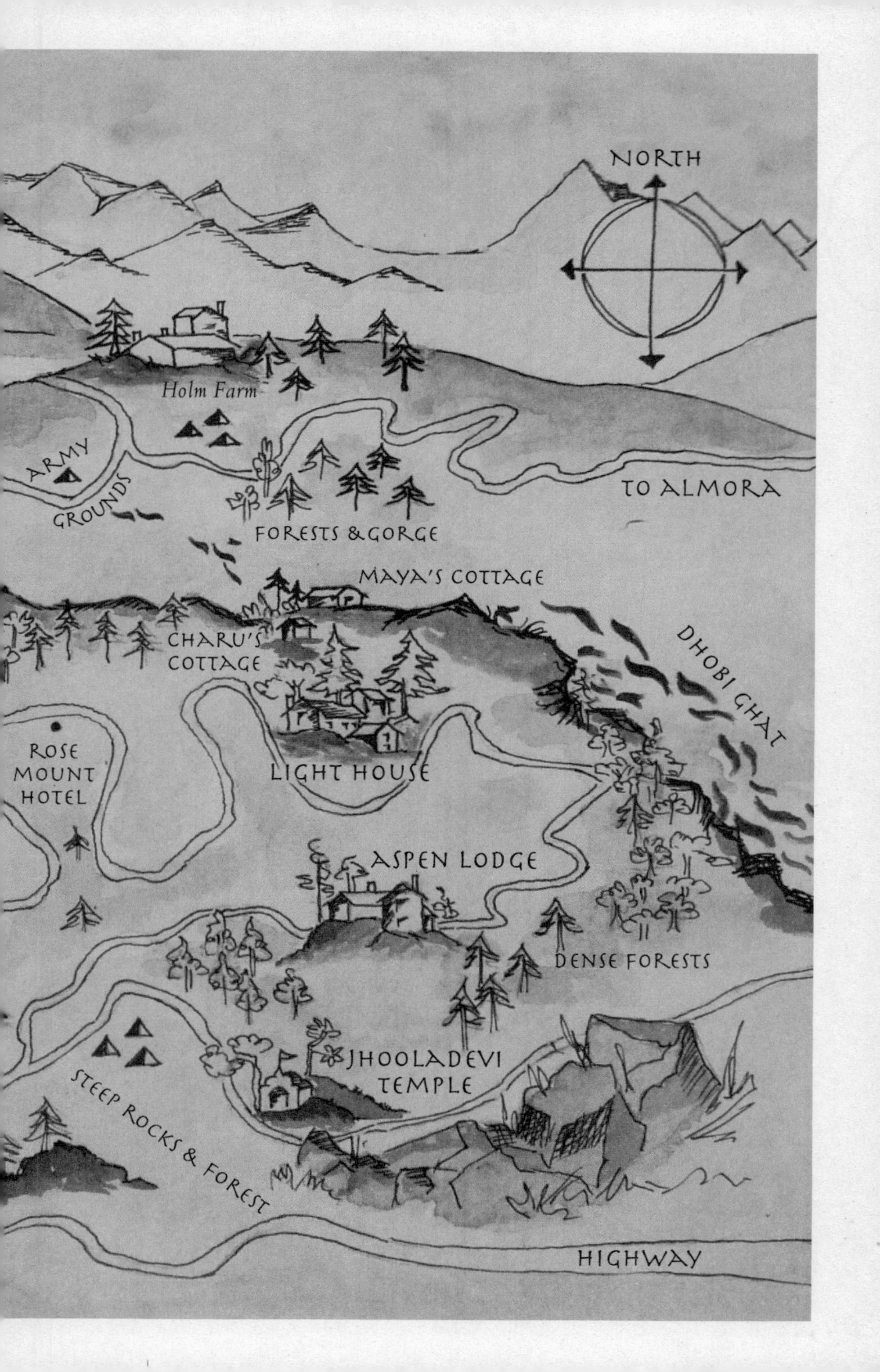
NORTH
Holm Farm
ARMY
GROUNDS
TO ALMORA
FORESTS & GORGE
MAYA'S COTTAGE
CHARU'S
COTTAGE
DHOBI GHAT
ROSE
MOUNT
HOTEL
LIGHT HOUSE
ASPEN LODGE
DENSE FORESTS
JHOOLADEVI
TEMPLE
STEEP ROCKS & FOREST
HIGHWAY

PART I

ONE

The girl came at the same hour, summer or winter. Every morning, I heard her approach. Plastic slippers, the clink of steel on stone. And then her footsteps, receding. That morning she was earlier. The whistling thrushes had barely cleared their throats, and the rifle range across the valley had not yet sounded its bugles. And, unlike every other day, I did not hear her leave after she had set down my daily canister of milk.

She did not knock or call out. She was waiting. All went quiet in the blueness before sunlight. Then the soothing early morning mutterings of the neighborhood began: axes struck wood, dogs tried out their voices, a rooster crowed, wood-smoke crept in through my open window. My eyelids dipped again and I burrowed deeper into my blanket. I woke only when I heard the General walking his dog, reproaching it for its habitual disobedience, as if after all these years it still baffled him. "What is the reason, Bozo?" he said, in his loud voice. "Bozo, *what is the reason*?" He went past every morning at about six thirty, which meant that I was going to be late unless I ran all the way.

I scrabbled around, trying to organize myself—make coffee, find the clothes I would wear to work, gather the account books I needed to take with me—and the milk for my coffee billowed and foamed out of the pan and over the stove before I could reach it. The mess would have to wait. I picked up things, gulping my coffee in between. It was only when I was lacing my shoes, crouched one-legged by the front door, that I saw her out of the corner of an eye: Charu, waiting for me still, drawing circles at the foot of the steps with a bare toe.

Charu, a village girl just over seventeen, lived next door. She had every hill person's high cheekbones and skin, glazed pink with sunburn. She would forget to comb her hair till late in the day, letting it hang down her shoulders in two disheveled braids. Like most hill people, she was not tall, and from the back she could be mistaken for a child, thin and small-boned. She wore hand-me-down salwar kameezes too big for her, and in place of a diamond she had a tiny silver stud in her nose. All the same, she exuded the reserve and beauty of a princess of Nepal—even if it took her only a second to slide back into the awkward teenager I knew. Now, when she saw I was about to come out, she stood up in a hurry, stubbing her toe against a brick. She tried to smile through the pain as she mouthed an inaudible "namaste" to me.

I realized then why she had waited so long for me. I ran back upstairs and picked up a letter that had come yesterday. It was addressed to me, but when I opened it, I had found it was for Charu. I stuffed it into my pocket and stepped out of the front door.

My garden was just an unkempt patch of hillside, but it rippled with wildflowers on this blue and gold morning. Teacup-sized lilies charged out of rocks and drifting scraps of paper turned into white butterflies when they came closer. Everything smelled damp, cool, and fresh from the light rain that had fallen at dawn, the first after many hot days. I felt myself slowing down, the hurry draining away. I was late anyway. What difference did a few more minutes make? I picked a plum and ate it, I admired the butterflies, I chatted of this and that with Charu.

I said nothing of the letter. I felt a perverse curiosity about how she would tell me what she wanted. More than once, I heard her draw breath to speak, but she either thought better of it or came up with, "It has rained after three weeks dry." And then, "The monkeys ate all the peaches on our tree."

I took pity on her and produced the letter from my pocket. It had my address and name, written in Hindi in a large, childish hand.

"Do you want me to read it for you?" I said.

"Yes, alright," she said. She began to fiddle with a rose, as if the letter were not important, yet darted glances in its direction when she thought I was not looking. Her face was transformed by relief and happiness. "My friend Charu," the letter said:

How are you? How is your family? I hope all are well. I am well. Today is my tenth day in Delhi. From the first day I looked for a post office to buy an inland letter. It is hard to find places here. It is a very big city. It has many cars, autorickshaws, buses. Sometimes there are elephants on the street. This city is so crowded that my eyes cannot go beyond the next house. I feel as if I cannot breathe. It smells bad. I remember the smells of the hills. Like when the grass is cut. You cannot hear any birds here, or cows or goats. But the room Sahib has given me is good. It is above the garage for the car. It faces the street. When I am alone at the end of the day's cooking, I can look out at everything. I get more money now. I am saving for my sister's dowry and to pay off my father's loan. Then I can do my heart's desire. Send me a print of your palm in reply. That will be enough for me. I will write again.

Your friend.

"Who is it from?" I asked Charu. "Do you know someone in Delhi, or is this a mistake?"

"It's from a friend," she said. She would not meet my eyes. "A girl. Her name is Sunita." She hesitated before adding: "I told her to send my letters to you because—the postman knows your house better." She turned away. She must have known how transparent was her lie.

I handed her the letter. She snatched it and was halfway up the slope leading from my house to hers before I had closed my fist. "I thought I taught you to say thank you," I called after her. She paused. The breeze fluttered through her dupatta as she stood there, irresolute, then ran down the slope back to me. She spoke so quickly her words ran into each other: "If I bring you extra milk every day . . . will you teach me how to read and write?"

TWO

My rival in love was not a woman but a mountain range. It was very soon after my wedding that I discovered this. We had defied our families to be together, and those first months we were exultant castaways who had fitted the universe into two rented rooms and one narrow bed. Daytime was only a waiting for evening, when we would be together. Nights were not for sleeping. It took many good-byes before we could bear to walk off in different directions in the mornings. Not for long.

It began in little ways—silences, the poring over maps, the unearthing of boots and jackets stuffed into a suitcase under our bed—and then the slow-burning restlessness in Michael became overpowering. He was with me, but not with me. His feet walked on flat land but flexed themselves for inclines. He lay at night with his eyes open, dreaming. He studied weather reports for places I had never heard of.

Michael was not a climber; he was a press photographer. Through a school friend whose father was an editor, he had found a job with a newspaper when we got married. We could not afford more than an annual trek for him in the mountains and that one trek was what he lived for all year.

Michael's yearnings made me understand how it is that some people have the mountains in them while some have the sea. The ocean exerts an inexorable pull over sea people wherever they are—in a bright-lit, inland city or the dead center of a desert—and when they feel the tug there is no choice but somehow to reach it and stand at its immense, earth-dissolving edge, straightaway calmed. Hill people, even if they are born in flatlands, cannot be parted for long from the mountains. Anywhere else is exile. Anywhere else, the ground is too flat, the air too dense, the trees too broad-leaved for beauty. The color of the light is all wrong, the sounds nothing but noise.

I knew from our student days together that Michael trekked and climbed. What I had not known was that his need for the mountains was as powerful as his need for me. We were far away from the high peaks: we lived in Hyderabad. The journey to the foothills of the Himalaya took two nights on trains and cars and it took many more days to reach the peaks. No hills closer at hand would do. Not the Nilgiris, nor the entire Western Ghats. It had to be the Himalaya—it would be impossible for me to understand why until I experienced it, Michael told me, and one day I would. Meanwhile, each year, the rucksack and sleeping bag came out and his body left in the trail of his mind, which was already nine thousand feet above sea level and climbing.

One year, Michael decided to go on a trek to Roopkund, a lake in the Himalaya at about sixteen thousand feet. It is reached by a long, hard climb toward the Trishul, a snow peak that is more than twenty-two thousand feet high. For much of the year, its water remains frozen. A park ranger stumbled upon the lake in 1942 and it has been an enigma ever since: it contains the bones and skulls, preserved by the cold, of some six hundred people who died there in the ninth century, some say the sixth. Many of the skeletons wore gold anklets, bracelets, necklaces, and bangles. Six hundred travelers at that altitude, in that stark wilderness—where were they going? Impossible to tell: there was no known route from Roopkund to Tibet, or to anywhere else. How did they die? Archaeologists think they may have been caught in an avalanche or hit by large hailstones: there are tennis-ball-sized dents on many of the skulls.

The bones were stripped of their jewelry and most of them were left where they were. And there they have remained, although memento-seekers have carried off bits and pieces as trophies. Even now, each time the lake melts during the monsoon, bones and skulls float in the water and wash up at its edges.

Michael had tried to reach Roopkund once before and failed because of bad weather and lack of experience. This time, he had better equipment, he said; he was timing it differently, he knew what to expect. Even so, I felt a cloud of dread grow and darken as the day for his departure neared. I found myself looking at him with an intensity I had forgotten over six years of being married to him. The smell of him, which I breathed in deep as if to store inside me; the bump on his nose where it had been broken when he was a boy; the early lines of gray in his hair; the way he cleared his throat mid-sentence and pulled at his earlobes when thinking hard.

He knew I was worrying, and the night before he left, as I lay on my stomach and his fingers wandered my tense back and aching neck, he told me in a voice hardly more than a murmur about the route: the trek was not really difficult, he said, it only sounded as if it was. His fingers went down my spine and up my neck while an iron ball of fear grew heavier inside me. Many had done it before, he said. The rains and snow would have retreated from that altitude by the time they reached it; there would be wildflowers all over the high meadows on their route. His hands worked their way from my legs to my shoulders, finding knotted muscles, teasing them loose before he returned to my back. The boots, sleeping bag, tent, would be checked, every zip tried, every rope tested. The bulbs and batteries in his headlamp were new; he would get himself better sunglasses in Delhi. It was as if he was running through a list in his head.

Each item he mentioned reminded me of things that could go wrong. I did not want to know any more. I touched his always fast-growing stubble and I think I said, "By the time you're home you'll have a beard again, like every other time." My fingers held the inch or two of fat he had recently grown at his waist. "And you'll have lost this. You'll be thin and starved."

"Completely starved," he said. "Lean and hungry." His teeth tugged at my earlobes. He stretched over me to switch on the shaded lamp by our bed and traced with his eyes every curve of my face and the dimple in my chin. "Why did he marry this girl?" he said in a voice that imitated the stereotypical older relative. "Why did he marry this stick-thin girl, as dark as boot polish? All you can see in her face are her big eyes." He ran his fingers through the tangled mass of my hair. "Almost at your waist, Maya. Where will it have grown to by the time I'm back?" I could smell onions frying although it was almost midnight. On our neighbor's radio, a prosaic voice reported floods, scams, train accidents, cricket scores. Michael's hand wandered downward till it reached my hips. He said, "Your hair will be here—or maybe longer? This far?"

I switched the light off.

* * *

The news came to me by way of my landlord, who had a telephone. They had found Michael's body after three days of searching. It was close to the lake, I was told, he had almost made it there when the landslides, rain, and snowstorms came and separated Michael from the others with him. His body had a broken ankle, which was no doubt why he had not been able to move to a less exposed place. And the face was unrecognizable, burned black by the cold.

They brought him downhill to a tiny village on the route and cremated him there. They saved the backpack they had found beside him, and the mountaineering institute sent it to Hyderabad along with Michael's ashes, which they had put into an empty ghee can. I tried going through the contents of the backpack, but after taking out the first two sweatshirts, with the scent of him still in them, I found it too painful to unpack further and locked it into the suitcase it had come from, below our bed.

The day the backpack came, I went down our alley to the little paan shop, which had a tin box of a phone booth tacked to one side of it. We used to be regulars there. A small group of people hung around, smoking, chatting, waiting for their paan to be made, for their turn at the phone. I waited too. Eventually my turn came. Conscious of curious ears all around me, I murmured my questions into the phone. The mountaineering institute was in the hills, hundreds of miles away, and it sounded as if we were speaking through a wild storm. "What, what?" the voice at the other end yelled. I spoke louder, then louder still above the crackles and echoes. "What? Who is it?"

the voice still demanded. I began to shout: "My husband has died in that accident. Could you give me more details?" The crowd at the paan shop edged closer, stared at me without blinking. The tiny booth oozed the thick scent of old chewing tobacco, cigarette smoke, and incense. An old woman patted my shoulder, said, "Paapam, paapam," in pitying tones. I pushed her hand away. Finished explaining all the facts to the distant voice, its unfamiliar Hindi-accented English. "Madam, I am not authorized," the voice said, "hold one minute." After a long silence another voice arrived and in cautious tones began, "Am I right, madam, that you are—" Again I repeated: "My husband died on that trek. Tell me what happened, I need to know what happened." The second man's voice ebbed and flowed into my ears; the storm on the line intensified. I could hear nothing. I could no longer see or speak for tears. I thrust the telephone into the nearest hand and stumbled away from it.

I could not face the thought of another crowded call from that booth. The next day, I started a letter to the mountaineering institute instead. "Dear madam or sir," it began, "I am writing to find out . . ." I put it aside, then picked up my pen again a week later. I needed to know how Michael had died. How, exactly? I had a hundred questions. Could I get answers? I stared at the white, unlined sheet of paper. Faces frozen black with cold appeared before me. I heard the crack of bone as Michael's ankle snapped. Set aside the pen again.

I lay back on the bed and saw that the ceiling was hung with sticky cobwebs in that corner that only Michael could reach with the broom, if he stood on a chair. The spiders would live there in peace now. I knew that at the back of the cupboard there were letters from an earlier girlfriend of his. I would burn them without reading them. Had he loved her as he had loved me?

I was afraid to know. I needed to not know.

I never finished my letter to the institute. Nor did I telephone again. A terrible restlessness took hold of me. I began leaving our rooms at daybreak and scouring the city as if I might run into him somewhere. I felt compelled to do it. At night I wondered why my legs ached, or why my clothes were sweat-wet, and it took me a while to remember that I had been out all day on scorching streets, walking at random, getting onto buses without looking where they were going, pausing at parks, shops, then walking on, until shops shut and traffic thinned, and the streets grew too empty for a woman alone. Once I ended up at the ruins of Golconda Fort, where, by some miracle of acoustics, the sound of hands clapping at the gateway can be heard—after a few moments' pause—at the distant ramparts of the fort. Michael had laughingly said when we were there together not many months earlier, "What if I clapped my hands and then, the next second, dropped dead? You would still hear the echo of that clapping. Ghost clapping."

"What rubbish you can talk," I had said crossly. And then held his hand to my cheek to reassure me with its un-dead warmth.

I was alone. I had no contact with friends: I had lost them over the years of being wrapped up in Michael. I had in effect no family although my parents did live in the same city. My father had made a great show of formally disowning me when I married. A son-in-law of a different religion was abhorrent. My mother was too intimidated by him to do more than steal out for occasional trysts with me at a temple. She had no way of getting news of me unless I contacted her. I did not. Not yet. What was I to say to her? The pain would extinguish her. I had a job, but it did not cross my mind that I needed to inform my office why I had stopped coming to work. A tin with ashes lay in my bed where Michael should have been. I was twenty-five years old and already my life was over.

THREE

I cannot remember how many weeks I wandered the streets this way, or why I decided that the first person I had to talk to about Michael's death was his priest, Father Joseph. I waited for the bus that had always taken me to work, and sat beside the girl at the third window who used to save a seat for me every day. She talked about her fiancé again: "my Would-be" is what she called him. They were to be married that year. He wanted to arrive for the wedding on an elephant, but she had since girlhood pictured her groom on a white horse, as she had seen in the movies.

"Are there any elephants in Hyderabad?"

"Maybe not," she said, smiling. "But my Would-be feels higher up is safer in traffic." She spoke close to my ear to be heard over the sound of honking cars. I tried to make sense of what she was saying, but her words were obliterated by the panic my own thoughts unleashed: Michael was gone forever. I would never in my life—my days, nights, or evenings, never at meals or in bed or on the street—I would never be with him again. What was this city to me now, without him? He *was* this city. He was the meaning of its buildings and streets.

We were passing the minarets and lawns of the Hyderabad Public School, an old, long, sprawling mansion that might have been a palace. The girl clutched my hand to draw my attention, and pointed at it. "Actually what my Would-be wants is to light up that building, and have the wedding there," she laughed. "He wants me to feel like a princess."

I thought of the very few people who were at my wedding: all strangers to me. Our families had stayed away, loathing each other's religion with a passion. Michael's parents had refused even to meet me. Only two rebellious young cousins of his came and took photographs—each one a different grouping of the four of us—plus the marriage registrar, whose droopy mustache and drowsy eyes gave his face an all-in-a-day's-work expression. After the paperwork, we had gone with the cousins to a biryani house in the Charminar area. An aquarium framed by panels of beige satin covered most of one wall. It was filled with murky water and plastic ferns, but there were no fish. The bill for our food came to 378 rupees. In all, our wedding cost us under five hundred rupees. It was nothing compared to the opulent weddings of my relatives and friends, but I had cared only for the happy light in Michael's eyes, the scent of the flowers in the garlands he had brought for my hair and my neck, and the way he had pressed against me in the cramped seat of the rickshaw on our way to our newly rented two rooms.

My sari was a dark-green silk that had belonged to my mother. She had given it to me the night I ran away from home. She had not said a word, but had kissed my hair and then my face, staring at it as if she might never see it again. She took off her emerald earrings and twisted them into my earlobes. She draped a corner of her treasured sari over my head to see how I would look in it. For a long minute she stared at my half-veiled face, then put a finger to the kohl in her eyes and smudged its blackness onto my forehead to protect me from evil spirits. We spoke in gestures and were careful not to make a sound; we knew my father was somewhere in the house, alert to every rustle, every whisper.

From the day my father had found out about Michael, he had become as watchful as an animal waiting to pounce. He prowled all over the house, somehow soundless despite the stick he always carried as a crutch to compensate for his shorter left leg. He said nothing, but no longer allowed me to leave the house, not even to go to college. I was only nineteen then, an undergraduate who needed to go to classes. He told everyone I had chicken pox and was too contagious for visitors. He cooked up a doctor's certificate for my college principal. He put a stop to friends, outings, telephone calls. At times, I felt his cold-eyed gaze traveling over my body as if he were trying to gauge which parts of it Michael had touched. But I was his daughter. Before my fall from grace, he had done his best to train me to follow his example: to be ruthless in getting what one wanted, to take calculated risks. His efforts must have yielded results. I escaped him within a fortnight, knowing I would never return home.

My companion in the bus that morning reached her stop, still chattering of Would-be. She said, smiling, "Tomorrow I'll bring you a card; you must come for my wedding!" I got off two stops later, and walked toward Father Joseph's office, feeling disembodied, weakened and sleepy, as if I would be compelled to sit on the pavement and then not know how to get up again. I found myself outside a hotel painted pink and yellow, and walked through its gates to a swimming pool at the back. There was a sheltered staircase next to the pool. I sat on one of its steps, before the shining blue emptiness of the water, the stretch of green tiles around it, the damp towel discarded on a chair. There was a line of plate-glass windows on the other side that produced mirror images of everything I saw. A bird passed overhead, low enough for its shadow to ripple across us. At the other end of the pool, a little girl was being urged by a swimming coach to plunge from the diving board. She shouted, as if in a movie: "Let me go! I want to live! I want to live!" My eyes blurred and I began to see human skeletons and bones at the edges of the pool, on the green tiles: skulls, clavicles, fibulas, tibiae, and femurs. Mandibles and ribs, foot and hand phalanges with ancient silver toe rings and gold finger rings on them still. Necklaces of gold beads intertwined with vertebrae. I saw skulls at the bottom of the pool, turning their blind gaze this way and that in the clear water, magnified by it. They bobbed to the surface. One of them splashed to the edge of the pool, next to my feet, and the face streaming away from it in dissolving ribbons was Michael's.

The windows, the towels, that screaming child, the green tiles, the fire-blue sky with its shadow-birds, retreated. The step I was sitting on crumbled and I began to fall dizzily through a vast sky, as you do in dreams. It was only when a face rose from the water close to my feet and in a French accent said, "Are you alright?" that I realized my face was wet with tears, my nose was running, my hair was disheveled, and I was late for Michael's priest.

I ran up the stairs to Father Joseph's room and burst in without knocking. I stopped and held the back of a chair to steady myself. A house with a trident-shaped peak framed in its window, Michael had said, a house that looked out at the Trishul, and at its base Roopkund, the phantom-lake. He had seen such a house once; he had told me where it was. He had dreamed we would live there and wake each morning looking at the Trishul emboss itself on the sky as the sun lit its three tips one by one.

"Father, find me work in Ranikhet. Please," I said. "I can't stay on here a single day longer."

* * *

Four months after Michael died, I climbed into the train that had taken him away from me. It went from Hyderabad to Delhi, a northward journey that took a day and a night. One more night on a different train brought me further north, to Kathgodam, where the train lines stopped and the hills began. It was another three hours by bus over twisted, ever-steeper roads to Ranikhet, a little town deep in the Himalaya. In my bag was the address of the school in which Father Joseph had fixed me a job. I was going to be two thousand kilometers from anything I knew, but that was just numbers. In truth the distance was beyond measurement.

FOUR

The sky over our heads here in the mountains has not the immensity of the sky I grew up with in the Deccan, where it spans the entire planet, broken only by the building-sized boulders that sit here and there on the open flatland of the plateau as if a giant's child had collected them from the giant's river and dropped them like marbles on a playing field. In the hills the sky is circumscribed. Its fluid blue is cupped in the palm of a hand whose fingers are the mountains around us. We too are cupped in its palm and while there is a feeling of limitless distance, we have at the same time the sense that here on our hill is where life begins and ends. Here is where sky begins and ends, and if there are other places, they have skies different from our sky.

Our town spans three hills. It is far away from everywhere and very small. If you look at it from the other side of the valley at night, you see darkness dotted here and there with yellow lights half-hidden by trees. On every side there are mountains and forests, stretching many miles, interrupted only by tiny hamlets and villages so small that they might have just five houses and nothing but a foot-beaten path connecting them to the main road miles away. To the north of our town is the high Himalaya: ice-white peaks on the other side of which lie Tibet and China. On clear days, eastward, you can see the five pyramids of the Pancha Chuli, which are at Nepal's door.

When you come up to our town from the plains, the dust-gloomed, table-flat land begins to slope upward at Kathgodam, folding itself into hillsides, and in less than two hours the trees change from banyan, mango, banana, and sal, to pine, oak, cypress, and cedar. Everything looks sharper-edged in the clear air, as if your bad eyesight has been inexplicably cured. Ferns fountain from rock faces, flowers blossom on stone. In fertile areas, the hills are terraced into green-and-brown circles of wheat fields with squares of white, where the peasants' slate-roofed cottages are. The disheveled small towns are soon left behind, and then you pass gushing mountain rivers and barren cliff sides pincushioned with cacti, deep forests, and still gray-blue lakes. By the time you are in Ranikhet, you have traveled from the tropics to temperate lands.

This was the town to which I came after I lost Michael. Father Joseph used his network to get me a job at St. Hilda's, a church-run school. I found a cottage to rent, on an estate called the Light House because it was so situated that the mansion on the upper grounds caught the first rays of sun on its eastern windows, and the last of them on its western lawns. My landlord, whom everyone called Diwan Sahib, lived alone in the crumbling mansion. Down the slope there was a set of brick and mud rooms clustered around a beaten-earth courtyard and cattle sheds. Charu lived here with her grandmother and an uncle, Puran, who was often called Sanki Puran because he did not seem to have all his wits about him.

My own cottage, close to theirs, had once been stables where herders were housed in a room above the stalls for horses and cows. The cottage now had two whitewashed rooms of stone, one above the other, and a small veranda. The wooden planks of its floors creaked and shifted with age. The kitchen and bathroom, tacked on later, stood at odd angles to one another and to the house. None of the windows or doors fitted well. Icy drafts surged through the gaps in winter, and in the monsoon insects took up residence in the corners of the rooms: slow-moving black scorpions, confused moths that banged into lights, green-eyed spiders whose legs could span dinner plates.

My cottage was at the edge of the spur on which the Light House stood. When I lay in bed, what I saw framed in the window was the Trishul. At its base, invisible at this distance, was the lake where Michael had spent his last hours. Nothing but miles of forests and wave upon wave of blue and green hills between us.

FIVE

St. Hilda's is not really a convent, but since people think of convents as places where their children will be taught good English, that is what the church that owned it had decided to call it. The children would come to learn English, they reasoned, and would be taught a little bit about Jesus, which they could keep or cast aside as they pleased.

Charu had been one of my students. She was twelve when we met, and came to school pigtailed, face shining, hair reeking of mustard oil, in navy and white, scrubbed clean, exercise book and pencil in hand—and she daydreamed in class all day. She barely learned to write even the alphabet. Many days of the week, she simply did not come. Later, walking home in the afternoon I would spot her grazing her grandmother's cows. Or I would hear her high voice from across a hill, calling one of them, "Gouri! Goureeeeee-ooo!" In the summer months I could be sure of spotting her navy skirt halfway up a kafal tree and if I called at the tree, "Why weren't you at school?" she would clamber down, thrust at me a handful of red, just-plucked kafals, and vanish into the forest.

One late afternoon in my first year in Ranikhet, I saw Charu's grandmother sitting outside their house, sunning herself on a mat. She was a bony woman with hollow cheeks, her skin raisined by years of hard labor in the sun. Her eyes had a quiverful of lines at their corners. Everyone called her "Ama" and she was renowned for having been the most beautiful woman of Ranikhet. She was not afraid of anything or anyone, and had thrown Charu's father, her younger son, out of her house for being drunk every day and beating his wife to death in a drunken fit. She would bring up her grandchild alone, she had said, they did not need a man around the house if it was a man like him. He still visited, a weedy fellow with a ravaged face, and a beedi tucked behind each ear. He sat glumly in the courtyard and smoked while his mother scolded him about keeping a mistress and demanded money for his daughter's upkeep. Meanwhile somehow she fed and housed yet poorer relatives who arrived without warning from remote villages and stayed for days, sometimes weeks.

Ama had a voice that could carry across several valleys and a laugh I could very often hear from my own house nearby. From here and there, she had picked up English phrases and words with which she seasoned her talk. If I had a cold, she would insist, "You must breathe in steam from water boiled with Eucalipstick." Every time prices rose, she said, "Does Gormint care if we live or die?" Government was a person who lived far away and grew fat while her cheeks hollowed with too much work and too little food. "One day," she said, "I will find a Gormint babu for Charu to marry and then we'll kill a hen to eat every day." As she said this, she shook with laughter at the improbability of her dream.

Whenever she sighted me, her eyes, already creased from years of battling sun and wind and cold, creased up more, and she smiled a mouthful of stained, brown teeth and shouted, "Namaste, Teacher-ni!" That is what she called me, tongue-in-cheek: Teacher-ni. Everyone else called me Maya Mam.

"Why do you pay the fees if you can't make Charu come to school?" I had asked her that afternoon. "Why not send her to the government school? It's free."

"I can put grass before the cow," she said. "Can I make it eat? But it is still my cow, so I have to feed it, don't I?"

"Charu is hardly a cow," I said. "She is your granddaughter. And I am not fodder."

The old woman laughed loud and long. "I know who Charu is," she said. "Now, you tell me, what can I do? I get her ready every day, I send her off, and then—where she goes—how can I stop her? Should I chase her with a stick all the way to the school? She will learn when the time comes. A girl learns what she needs to know."

I gave up on Charu after a while, and stopped scolding her about her truancy. She did not altogether stop coming: on the days when she felt her uniform needed an airing or she wanted to see her friends, she would turn up, smile angelically at me, settle down at her place on a bench, and draw five-petaled flowers throughout the class. On some evenings she came to my veranda, which had a smooth red floor, to play gitti, her pebble game. Often she brought with her two girls, Beena and Mitu, twins who lived down the hill: neither of them could speak or hear, but we managed. They had shy smiles, light-brown hair, and improbable blue eyes: Ama said their mother, Lati, also deaf and mute, had slept with a wandering firanghi who had eyes as blue, and here was God's punishment: two girls. "Deaf and mute as well!"

Charu taught me her game: it involved five pebbles that you had to do dexterous things with, throwing up one, scooping up the others, then catching the one in flight before it hit the ground. I was new to the town; I hardly knew anyone, and had nothing very much to do apart from the school. Many evenings she and I sat with the twins, playing with the stones, watching evening fires being lit outside nearby hutments as the neighborhood dogs were called back from creeks and bushes before leopards slunk out from the shadowed forests to feed.

I could have chosen differently. I could have found a better-paid job elsewhere. I could have returned to my own family. It had been a source of bewilderment to my mother why I did not go back to my old life at home after Michael's death. The edge of my father's anger was blunted now that Michael had left my life. All I had to do was to tell him that I had been wrong and misguided, and beg him to trust me again. My mother was tearful and imploring. I did not need to teach in a school, so far away, hard up, all by myself. We could be together again as before.

My mother died two years after Michael, uncomprehending to the end about my stubborn refusal. In one of her reproachful letters, she accused me of being as unforgiving as my father: how could a girl punish her parents and reject her home this way?

But I *was* at home. I had got used to thinking of Charu, her grandmother, her half-witted uncle Sanki Puran, and my landlord Diwan Sahib as my family now. I could no longer imagine living anywhere else. Though I cannot know precisely when it happened, a time had come when I became a hill person who was only at peace where the earth rose and fell in waves like the sea.

SIX

It was six years after I began to live in Ranikhet: I remember it was a December afternoon, about three o'clock, the sun already too weak to warm anything, and I was on my way back from work. As every day, I went first to my landlord's house. Unusually for that time of day, he was not alone. I found him with a man I had never met before and they were so engrossed in conversation that they hardly noticed me as I laid a bundle of newspapers on the grass and stood behind Diwan Sahib's chair.

It was a daily ritual. On my way back from school I picked up the newspapers from Negi's tea stall on Mall Road and walked home with them to Diwan Sahib's. His man Friday, Himmat Singh, would make tea for us and we would sit and read the papers together. Diwan Sahib got the *Statesman* for a column it had of odd news from around the world. Once he told me of a woman in Texas who had to be detached by surgeons from a toilet seat she had sat on for two years. Her boyfriend had humored her and served her meals in the bathroom for all of that time. "I have been told women take forever in the bathroom!" Diwan Sahib said. "But I didn't think they took this long." He had the habit of chuckling for ages over such nuggets of information before making neat clippings of them with his nail scissors and gluing them into a bulging leather-bound diary.

Afterward, if Diwan Sahib had made some progress with his biography of Jim Corbett, he gave me the additions to his manuscript, and I would type them up on his chunky Remington. I had by painful degrees grown used to his long-limbed scrawls and learned to make sense of his arrows, brackets, lines between lines, looped scribbles. I had learned a great deal from the manuscript about the hills in which

I now lived, for before Corbett turned writer and naturalist he had been the Kumaon's most famous hunter, an affable-looking man in khaki shorts and sola topi whose particular skill was the slaughtering of man-eating tigers and leopards. Over his several drafts, I thought I had become almost as much a scholar on the subject as Diwan Sahib, and if I felt brave enough I ventured comments on the book that, on the whole, he ignored.

Diwan Sahib regularly rethought the structure of his book. The first draft, which I had typed three years earlier, began with Corbett's ancestor Joseph, who was a monk, and Harriet, who was a novitiate at a nearby convent. They met, broke all their vows, and married. I thought this a good romantic prologue for their descendant's life, which, by contrast, was all celibacy and hunting. I had typed fifty or so pages with great care. We had scarcely reached the young Corbett's first hunting exploits as a child, however, when Diwan Sahib changed his mind and began to organize the book thematically. In the new plan, the chapters were entitled "Scholar Soldier," "Tiger-Killing," "From Gun to Camera," and the narrative moved back and forth in time within each chapter. The nun's and monk's story was abandoned. We were now on our third attempt, a plain chronology beginning with Corbett's birth in Nainital, which was only two hours away from us. Bundles of discarded typescripts lay about the house. The "a" and the "s" keys on the typewriter had worn away long ago. Nobody in Ranikhet knew anymore how to repair a typewriter so the manuscript looked as if it were written in code.

That afternoon, as I stood behind his chair and listened, Diwan Sahib was sitting with the stranger under his weeping spruce, and talking about the Nawab of Surajgarh, whose finance minister, long years ago, he had been. The Nawab had kept beautiful Arab horses, Diwan Sahib was saying. They were his passion. He spent more time with them than on his royal duties. He loved wildlife and went off on horseback for long days to the jungles, where he slept on machans with no more than two servants to attend to him. Although he disapproved of hunting, he was a very good shot. He believed in keeping his guns oiled, and his finger and eye steady. He had been schooled for a world in which every self-respecting warrior had to be capable of firing an accurate shot in all situations, even when startled from deepest slumber. Every night, an alarm clock was set for five o'clock the next morning, and hung on a wall, or placed on the head of a stuffed tiger some twenty paces away across the room. The instant it rang, the Nawab sprang up, and "with one eye still asleep," as he liked to boast, he aimed his revolver at the clock and fired at it to stop it ringing. In twenty-five years, he had never scarred the wall around the clock, or singed a whisker on the tiger's head, and had slaughtered some fifteen brands of clocks: imported wooden and gold ones—Ansonias, Smiths, Junghans—as well as clocks locally made. He had shot wall clocks and small brass timepieces. He had once executed a Bavarian cuckoo clock, Diwan Sahib said, and got the cuckoo itself when it popped out the third of its five times. On one occasion, when he had run out of alarm clock supplies, he had made a khidmatgar wait in the room all night. At exactly five, the shaking man had had to hold a wristwatch at head height, ringing a brass bell with his other hand so that his master could shoot the watch.

After his morning shot, the Nawab returned to snooze for five more minutes with his head under a velvet pillow, and then he got out of bed to go to his horses. He had five favorites, whom he had named after Mughal kings and queens: Noor, Jahangir, Babar, Humayun, and Mumtaz. When Surajgarh fell to India at Partition and the Nawab realized he had picked the wrong side in the years before, he lingered for some months, then went into exile in Paris, parted from his palace and possessions and lands. He could not take his horses with him and they became an all-consuming worry over his last few days in India. He did not trust anyone else to look after them well enough. The day before his departure, he went at dawn to their stables, rode each of them for a few minutes, patted them, brushed them, watered them, whispered to them, and then shot them with his hunting rifle, one after the other.

The man sitting with Diwan Sahib did not look like one of his usual visitors; he seemed neither a local nor a scholar. He was wiry and long-limbed, too restless to sit still for long. He had a hollow-cheeked, cadaverously handsome face, and close-cropped steel-gray hair. I had to keep myself from seeming curious about his oddly deformed left ear, and a missing finger that I noticed whenever he wrapped his hands around his mug of tea, to warm them. Every time I stole a glance at him, I found his intent, gray-brown eyes on me, and unlike other people who look away when they are caught staring, he did not. He let his eyes linger, then float away to something else, and return again. If I interrupted Diwan Sahib's story with comments on guns and shooting, from my recently acquired knowledge of Corbett, the man listened with great seriousness. He said very little himself, but when Diwan Sahib silenced my interjections in the acid tones he reserved for ignorant experts, I felt something like a current of sympathy pass between us, leaving Diwan Sahib out.

Now the man spoke. "I can understand the Nawab perfectly, I would have done the same myself."

"Shot the horses?" I said.

"I'd rather kill something I loved? Than think of it belonging to someone else?" His statements ended in a question mark. A whisper of California rippled through the accents of his English. He did not smile and signpost a joke as he spoke. Instead he looked away with a slight frown, as if a troubling memory had poked its foot through a door in his head. He got up from his chair with such abruptness that it fell, and said, "It's been too long since I came back here. Is my room still OK?"

Diwan Sahib introduced us at last. "This is Veer," he said. "I know we are related—not sure how, but I know we are—maybe a nephew via some roundabout route? Veer, this is the love of my life, Maya, and I would certainly shoot both her and myself if she so much as threatened to leave my house for someone else's."

* * *

Diwan Sahib's house was a higgledy-piggledy mansion built on many levels. It had doorways that turned out to be cupboards and cupboards that led into other rooms; it had attics, trapdoors, a basement. It had staircases that disappeared into darkness and so many rooms that

I had not been inside all of them; nobody admitted it, but I think even Diwan Sahib thought the further reaches of the house were the domain of ghosts and spirits better left alone.

He used for the most part only two central rooms on the ground floor, and these he kept warm with a small fire and a basic bar heater. The roofs leaked and many of the chimneys were blocked. He was too old to be bothered to repair anything, he said. A neighborhood handyman was called in to patch up whatever was absolutely necessary and the rest was left to the elements and the monkeys that danced on the roof each afternoon. In the monsoon, buckets, tubs, and even gilded soup bowls from a fine porcelain dinner set were planted all over the house to catch dripping rainwater. In winter Himmat Singh, who was only a little younger than Diwan Sahib, tottered about blocking broken windowpanes with pieces of cardboard, as a result of which the inner rooms were as dark as night in the daytime.

I had heard that before my time here, Diwan Sahib used to drive around in a temperamental blue Morris Minor that passersby were accustomed to pushing to revive the engine when it lost interest. One afternoon, when it stalled thrice, he got out of it, gave it a parting kick, and left it to tip, handbrake-free, over Ranikhet's steep western ridge. You could still see its rusted ruin trapped in the rocks below. Foxes lived in the shell. Mr. Qureshi, the man who owned the town's garage, and had repaired it for all of its life, could not stop mourning its brutal end. "That is no way to say good-bye to a car that has served you faithfully, to the best of its ability," he said, and Diwan Sahib scowled, "Its best was appalling." Mr. Qureshi muttered, "Diwan Sahib is not himself after a few . . . Allah was wise to forbid alcohol." Yet I often saw them together in the garden on folding aluminum chairs, Diwan Sahib squeezing lemon into gin, and Mr. Qureshi holding a steel cup with both hands, sipping cautiously, as if it contained hot tea. He had a kind, bald face as round as a pumpkin, and as on a pumpkin all its lines radiated toward its center, which was his small, cherry-like nose. The cherry grew redder as he sipped, but he persisted in deceiving himself that nobody could tell what he was drinking.

Diwan Sahib's drinking sessions were his durbar. The table next to him had a bottle of gin on it before lunch, and rum if it was evening. Next to the gin on an old walnut-wood tray stood a bottle of bitters, a saucerful of lime quarters, a glass jug of water covered with a beaded white napkin, and a silver cigarette case. Diwan Sahib no longer smoked, but the cigarette case had been his constant companion for decades and he liked having it nearby. The case was shaped as a Rolls-Royce Silver Ghost, with every detail of the car intricately worked into the metal. The only moveable part, other than the wheels, was the car's hood. Instead of carburetors and pistons, what was revealed when the hood was lifted was a compartment for cigarettes. Mr. Qureshi coveted the case like a child, but Diwan Sahib would not part with it. His only concession was to allow Mr. Qureshi to use it whenever he came. Mr. Qureshi would place five of his own cigarettes within it as soon as he arrived. He would click the bonnet open when he wanted to smoke one, and quite often even when he did not. Diwan Sahib disliked the strong, filterless cigarettes Mr. Qureshi smoked and would wave the smoke away saying, "I'm not going to let you use that case after today. Never."

Diwan Sahib looked royal: his worn, brown dressing gown was his robe, and the woolen cap Charu had knitted for him his crown, while his immense height, his great age, and the whiteness of his hair and beard made everyone around him deferential. In the morning, if he was in a good temper, he allowed entry to visitors, and in summer they were frequent. Apart from Mr. Qureshi and the elderly General, who lived on the next estate, scholars of Indian history and wildlife made the long journey by train and road up from the plains to meet him and ask him questions about the princely state of Surajgarh. Where the Nawab had wanted Surajgarh to become a part of Pakistan at Partition, Diwan Sahib had opposed it, even getting into clandestine negotiations with political high-ups in Delhi to make sure Surajgarh fell to India's share. Eventually he was jailed by the Nawab for treason. He described this as "enjoying the hospitality of the Nawab."

The scholars asked him questions about his Surajgarh years, but in fact the lure for their trips was not Diwan Sahib's reminiscences. Early in 1948, the Mountbattens, Edwina and her husband, went to

Surajgarh for a state visit on which Nehru accompanied them. It was rumored that Edwina and Nehru had written each other notes during the week they spent there in rooms at opposite ends of the palace, or stranded at separate dining tables. The notes were thought to have been stolen by a member of the palace staff, and ended up in the Diwan's possession. Historians hungered for them. Dealers came for them too: their passion was not in the cause of biography; it was because of what the letters would fetch if sold. I was not sure the letters existed, but if they did, Diwan Sahib appeared to have no plans for them. He was contented enough in his dressing gown all day, drinking his rum and gin.

Because of Diwan Sahib and the rumor of those letters, I met many scholars and writers. I never knew who they were, but he gave me a summary after they left. "That man's a fraud, he does nothing but plagiaries." Or: "That woman sits in Chicago all year and then produces authoritative work on Indian villages after two weeks of fieldwork." If he approved, he called them "good boy" or "good girl." "That was Ramachandra Guha," he said once, of a tall, distracted-looking man in glasses who had addressed him as sir throughout. "He's a good boy, but he didn't have a single drink."

"Those letters should be in the Nehru Memorial Library, sir," Ramachandra Guha had told him. "They should not be at the bottom of a trunk."

"They are safer at the bottom of a trunk than in any Indian library I know of," Diwan Sahib had said.

Diwan Sahib was brusque enough with visitors to acquire a reputation for being outright rude, and none of his acquaintances were allowed to grow into friends. Although he could not do without seeing me every day, he could become cantankerous or quarrelsome in minutes. But with his newfound relative, he was transformed. He hovered, he stood waiting as Veer looked around the house, he said in tones of apology that it needed repairing and cleaning up. Veer wandered from room to room as we followed, occasionally stopping and saying, "Where's the walnut-wood chest that used to be here?" or "There was surely a desk in that corner."

"If you come and live here," Diwan Sahib said vaguely in Veer's direction, in a voice so hesitant that it did not sound like him at all, "I would prod myself and get some repairs done."

I lingered with them that evening and watched Veer stow his things in one of the unused bedrooms. He cast an appraising look around it as he unhitched his backpack and changed his walking shoes for slippers. It was clear he intended staying for a while and I could tell that the predictable temper of our days was to change. Himmat Singh staggered in with a bundle of wood and coaxed a fire out of it. "Very damp room, Chote Sa'ab," he said to Veer. "But it will be better with this fire." He had known him "this high," he told me in the kitchen. In those days, Veer would often come during his school vacations and even then the semicircular room with bay windows and prints of rearing tigers on the walls was his room. Himmat Singh began to work through a pink hillock of onions and set eggs to boil. Because Diwan Sahib himself ate very little in the evenings, there was hardly any food to be had. Now dinner had to be conjured up out of nothing and Himmat Singh bustled about with a self-important air. "Ah, the old times were so different," he said. "Visitors every evening and the kitchen busy from morning till night. I had an assistant just to chop and cut and clean. You should have seen how much Chote Sa'ab ate. My own stomach would feel good and full to see him licking bowls clean, and at the end he sighed like this—*fuuuuf*—and he said, 'Himmat Singh, there is nobody who can cook like you in all of the Kumaon.' "

That evening, Diwan Sahib grew merrier and merrier, drinking twice the amount he normally did. When I left them, Veer was pouring him a fourth generous measure of rum and Diwan Sahib was saying in approving tones, "A man's inner nature is revealed by the size of the drinks he pours."

My little house was cold and dark from being locked up all day. There was a power outage by then. I found my way by flashlight to the cupboard that hid my bottle of rum. I laid the bundle of unread newspapers beside me on the floor and leaned back in my chair, taking long sips. It was this solitary drinking that gave me the deepest satisfaction, as if it were an affirmation that my time was my own at last, after a whole day's effort with other people. It pleased me that if anyone—other than Diwan Sahib, who supplied me with the rum—had known that I drank alone, I would have been labeled a "Bad Woman." This thought alone was usually enough to restore me to tranquility.

But tonight I was restless and unsettled. I huddled in a shawl, hardly tasting the rum. I put off warming up my food or lighting candles or drawing my curtains. The squares of cold glass in the windowpanes had frozen the stars in the black night's sky. I breathed on the glass and wrote the stranger's name in the immediate mist. Veer. Where had he been all these years? Why had Diwan Sahib never mentioned this nephew before?

Diwan Sahib was fiercely private. I was the only person he ever allowed close: to argue with, confide in, joke with, or scold. Once, in passing, he had said in his acerbic way that seeing how I haunted his rooms, I might as well abandon the cottage I rented from him, and move into his house. We had smiled at that, and I had left, knowing that he now wanted to be alone. He was not the kind of person who could share his life with anyone else. He had been single all his life and it was plain he disliked constant company. But the arrival of his nephew had changed everything in one afternoon. He had not fed me my daily diet of odd news from around the world. He had not even thought to ask for his precious *Statesman*. I could not remember the last time he had forgotten about the paper. It was what he waited all morning for; it was his link with the world he had renounced.

I fell into a troubled doze in my chair and woke aching and cold more than an hour later, when the power returned and the harsh white lightbulb overhead snapped to life.

SEVEN

Life changed for Charu that December. It began in one of the old estates of our town. Like the Light House, other estates of the kind in Ranikhet had quaint British-sounding names like Oakley and Knock Fierna, which was all that had survived of the British who built them in colonial times. The one where Charu often went to look for pasture was called Aspen Lodge. It rambled over many acres of hillside and had deodar and oak forests, a stream, and several ruined peasant huts. The big bungalow was made of stone. It had French windows; a deep, pillared veranda going all the way along its front; five chimneys; and a flat expanse of land around it that must once have been a lawn. Fruit trees twisted with age stood at the edges of the flat part, and below them were terraced slopes that in the monsoon were restless with pink swathes of cosmos.

It was a puzzle to outsiders why of all houses this one should lie buried in tall grass and bushes, almost in ruins, when it cried out for tended lawns, people, parties. The locals knew why it was derelict: a woman called Molly Mispeller had hanged herself from a roof beam in the dining room in colonial times and ever since it had been haunted. Anyone who lived in the house thereafter came to grief: all sorts of bad things happened to them and their families. It had been hurriedly abandoned by the last two families who scoffed at the ghost and had sunk good money into the estate.

That winter, a rumor had meandered its way around Mall Road, idly at first, then with energy, that there was one more aspiring unbeliever: the house had been bought by a hotel chain that planned to start operations elsewhere in our town. The hotel's manager was to live in Aspen Lodge. "He will be driven out in a week," it was declared. Mrs.

Mispeller would see to that. She was said to walk about the house at night, sitting occasionally to play a ghostly piano.

Charu knew nothing of Mall Road rumors, nor did she believe in ghosts, so she often brought her cows to graze at Aspen Lodge. In the rainy months, she had come every day and cut tall grass from those slopes with her sickle, looking like a bush with legs as she carried enormous bundles of it home on her head. On this sun-browned winter morning, she loosed her cows on the grass that had survived the cold and sat on a boulder to fiddle with a flaming-orange sweater she had been knitting for weeks.

The cows grazed on the slopes; her goats scampered about, brass bells tinkling at their necks. Charu's dog Bijli scurried up and down the slopes, the russet of his coat merging with the pine needles on the forest floor. The cows lumbered away, shaking their horns at him. He trotted back to Charu, parked himself next to her, and wedging his bottom against her for warmth, nibbled his paws one by one.

Charu hummed a tune that she interrupted at times with a yell to stop straying cows, then returned to her wool and knitting needles. The December sun and the soft weight of Bijli on her feet made her drowsy with the comfort of being warm after her cold day's work milking cows, filling water, and washing clothes. Usually her uncle Puran shared the chore of grazing the cows, but the last few days he had been subdued and withdrawn, disappearing into the forest, smoking grass, hardly eating. Charu was used to Puran's eccentricities and made excuses for him to her grandmother, but it tired her out doing his share of work too. Her eyelids dipped and the sweater-in-progress subsided on her lap.

For once, however, the Mall Road rumor turned out to be true. Sometime in the night, when nobody had been looking, the hotel manager had moved into Aspen Lodge. And now a tentative voice above Charu told her she needed to take her cows away.

"And never bring them back," the voice went on, sounding a little more determined. Flowers were to be planted now, Sa'ab had ordered. The garden was to be protected from all cattle.

She looked over her shoulder and stood up. She squinted at the boy speaking to her. The sun was in her eyes; she had to shade them with her palm. She saw that he was tall and had curly hair. His eyes had the color and shine of the horse chestnuts that fell from trees in the autumn. When she frowned, he smiled at her in apology. It was a lopsided smile. His clothes were what anyone wore, but his face looked to her as if it had come off the pages of those magazines that were hung with clothespins at the newsstand.

She felt herself smiling back and stopped, with some difficulty. He pleaded, "It's not me, I have to tell you what Sa'ab says. I am only the cook."

His voice, though young, was richly rounded and deep. She felt she could roll his words on her tongue like smooth river pebbles and taste them. Just like those pebbles, the voice had faint rough edges that her tongue paused against to feel their grain.

She said, "You are not going to cook your Sa'ab the grass, are you? Or has he brought cows with him from the city?"

Like most hill girls, Charu could be tart when crossed and did not take kindly to being told what to do. The boy stammered, "This morning I found a very nice patch down the hill with grass. It has a stream; the cows will have water as well as food. I'll show it to you, and you can take them there."

She shrugged in scorn. "You don't have to show me any grass patches on these hillsides," she said. "I know them all. The way down to the stream is too steep for cows. But I have many other places. I don't have to bring them here."

For two days she stayed away. But on the third or fourth day, something made her leave her house again after she had tethered her cows in their stall. When her grandmother asked her where she was off to, she said she had to take the goats grazing. She skipped light-footed through the forest to the area below Aspen Lodge and made her way down the steep path to the old Dhobi Ghat. At places where the pine needles on the ground were thick and shiny she let herself slide downward. Her braids thumped her shoulder blades as she jumped from rock to rock, past the two tiny white Muslim shrines draped with tinseled cloth, and the cave where a leopard was believed to have its lair. Then she was down beside the stream. Its chilled, clear water ran over mossy boulders. At the stream's edge there were low stone alcoves that washermen had used half a century ago. She sat on one of those and watched her goats feeding. She was sure he would come.

He did not, not that day, nor the next, but on the third day he was waiting there, and on the fourth, and every day after that. Charu's grandmother asked her why she did not graze the goats closer to home, but she tossed her head and said she was tired of the old places and liked washing clothes in the stream. "I get two jobs done at the same time," she said. "I should always have been going there." Every time she went, she made sure to take a bundle of dirty clothes and return with the washed ones that she hung out ostentatiously in their courtyard.

* * *

I have been to the Dhobi Ghat once. You need to be agile: the descent to it is through pine forest and for feet not used to them the needles that cover the ground below the trees can be treacherous. I had to calculate every step so that I did not lose my footing and hurtle down the hillside. Around me the forest stretched for quiet miles, uphill toward Aspen Lodge, which was quite close, though hidden by trees, and on the other side it descended to a valley, which could be crossed for a shortcut to the town's bazaar. At the heart of the forest, I felt as if nothing and nobody existed apart from my own panting breath and aching knees. I kept going, having decided I must. When I reached ramparts of thorny bushes and slippery, mossy rock I hesitated, but at the thought of the steep ascent that was the only way back, I beat down the bushes with my walking stick and pressed on.

Near the end of the steepness, I heard the low gurgle of rushing water. Where the path met the stream there was a flattening, a stretch of soft grass, an opening fringed by trees. There were boulders to sit on, over pools of clear water into which feet could be dangled. Time passed idly down the stream, as I daydreamed, watching insects slide and swoop at the edges and dead leaves flow by.

Because it was so inaccessible, Charu never came across anyone at the Dhobi Ghat when she went down with her goats. This became their most frequent meeting place, though there were others. She told the boy the names of all her goats. She told him of her five cows, especially of the black and white Jersey cow whom she called Gouri Joshi. Gouri had come as a large-eyed, timid, sweet-faced calf when Charu was a girl and whenever she was troubled or scolded by her grandmother she still ran to Gouri and buried her face in the cow's warm flanks, breathing in its comforting scent of dung and straw and milk. Gouri's eyes were dark pools of patience and had lashes that were a mile long. She never kicked, however long Charu held her. The only difficulty was that she was inclined to wander far off and then had to be searched for throughout the forest, and begged to come back home.

"Like you," he said. "A wild thing."

He was half-Nepalese, as she was, a child of the hills as well, but from a low-lying small town, so the sounds of the forest did not speak a language he understood. Over the next months she showed him which of the yellow berries that studded the bushes were edible and which ones were poisonous. She showed him how to find the best kafal trees and blackberry bushes, and which persimmon trees could be raided without fear of watchmen. She pulled sprigs of wild oregano from the forest floor and crushed the leaves between her palms and made him breathe in the fragrance. Martens should be chased away, Charu told him, they raided birds' nests and hen coops. Foxes could be ignored, but you had to protect your goats from jackals.

He listened faithfully to her lectures, but when it came to a thorn deep in Bijli's paw, it was he who pulled it out with no fear of the dog's low growls, and Charu thought she had never known anyone so brave. And once at dusk they saw a leopard slink through the trees into the gorge below. They clutched each other's hands for reassurance and did not let go long after the leopard had vanished. Charu thought it a kind of magic how neatly her hand fitted within his and how, when she was with him, her shyness left her and she became a chatterbox—as if all the words inside her had been readying and ripening for him.

One day, about a month later, when he was not at the stream, she waited and waited, growing annoyed, then anxious. She was so angry she told herself she would never see him again. The next minute, she was clawed by the worry that his city feet had slipped on the way down and he had fallen somewhere, bones broken, not able to cry loud enough for help. She clambered up the hill, leaving her goats unwatched. Where the slope met the flat lawn of Aspen Lodge, she hid in the bushes and peeped through the scrub at the edges of the lawn. She saw that the place was full of people: men and women in fine clothes, holding glasses, laughing and talking. White tables and chairs were set out under umbrellas bigger than she had ever seen. Two bearers with trays went from one knot of people to the next, waiting to be noticed and for something from their trays to be picked out and eaten. One of the bearers was the boy: hers.

Later she giggled and said, "When we are married, you will do the cooking and look pretty, and serve me food when I come home. I'll go out and earn the money."

He did not smile back. He turned away without a word. He went to where the stream disappeared into trees as if he had seen something there. He bent down and picked up a stone, which he flung into the water. She called his name: "Kundan," she said, "O Kundan Singh!" and broke into more giggles. But after a few more minutes when he looked away still unsmiling and pretended she was not there, she ran up to him and tugged at his clothes and pleaded, "Don't you know when I'm joking?"

EIGHT

The principal of my school, Miss Wilson, had realized soon enough that I was not much good as a teacher. She thought my classes undisciplined and chaotic; I thought of it as a happy noise and could not bring myself to silence the children and impose the order that was required. Miss Wilson stormed in from time to time and imposed order with one bellowed *"Quay-it!"* and a stinging rap of her cane on the desk, after which the class and I stood in meek disgrace waiting for the angry speech that usually followed. Charu was not my only failure; there were others who had gone through my classes for two years or more, playing truant and then failing examinations. At staff meetings, looking pointedly in my direction, Miss Wilson said, "Some people think teaching is a job anyone can do. No, madam, no, it needs dedication, discipline, love of Jesus Christ Our Lord." She addressed me as "madam" whenever she wanted to take me down a peg or two.

Miss Wilson was a Catholic from Kerala. Somehow, any sari she wore became an untidy roll of cloth around her, making her an animated bundle. Her austerity was renowned: she ate only two brisk, salt-free meals every day and for jewelry wore just a silver crucifix. Her thick, black-framed glasses slid down her bump of a nose every few minutes and she was always pushing them back up with a stubby forefinger. During her First Communion and First Confession, she had "heard the voice of Jesus, as clearly as yours or mine," she liked to say. In her teens, she joined a convent wanting nothing but to be a nun. She was sent for a year to teach in a church school, attend Mass, recite novenas. During the time there, she, along with other girls, was under observation: were they fit for the religious life? Miss Wilson was fervent enough, but in the end the church did not allow her to take orders. She would not say why, only hinting at convent politics, but this was the great tragedy of her life and she held the world responsible for it. Whenever someone annoyed her, she would say in her grating voice, "And it is for this, *for this* that the Lord sent me out to serve the world when I wanted to be His bride in prayer and solitude!"

It was a canny move for her to make me manage the modest jam-making cooperative the church owned: the revenues from it went into the school's coffers, and I ran it well, quickly expanding its operations. She nevertheless made it seem a favor. "You need not take the afternoon classes," she said. "There are other teachers more experienced. You sit with the girls in the factory." After a year or two the factory began to make good money, as well as acquiring a reputation for providing occasional employment to village girls and a ready market for the local fruit harvest. Miss Wilson took credit for it when visitors came to be shown around the factory, making sure not to introduce me to any of them.

In a way it was a grim irony. Miss Wilson pointedly made comments about how ungrateful, unloving progeny deserved the suffering that came to them; I just thought it coincidence that while my father owned several pickle factories I worked in one for a small salary. My father's factories had never been planned. My father's father, whom the entire neighborhood called Thataiyya, or Grandpa, was a landowner who made a fortune out of growing rice and sugarcane along the Krishna River, renting out tenements, and selling arrack (though by my father's time we were too genteel to admit to any of this). He built a big stone-flagged house, surrounded it with mango orchards, and trees of amla, tamarind, chikoo, and guava. By the time my father was a young man, the mango trees fruited, laborers were summoned to pick the fruit, and vast vats of pickle were made out of the green mangoes, which were a prized variety. The pickle and other fruit were distributed among the larger family—until my father sniffed a business opportunity, and began supplying a few shops. By the time I was twenty, and already cast out for marrying Michael, my father owned three factories across Andhra Pradesh, which pickled every conceivable thing from ginger to gongura, from lime to bitter gourd. The labels on the bottles said that they contained an ancient and secret mix of spices handed down the generations. I knew it had been concocted by Beni Amma, our plump, flirtatious, bright-saried cook, who had had a child by my middle uncle.

As a young girl I used to play at being shopkeeper. I weighed fallen fruit on a toy balance made of two tin plates and string, making my father's workers buy hard green mangoes from me for ten paise each. It was much the same now, baskets and gunny bags of fruit all around me. Diwan Sahib said he could tell the month from the way I smelled when I came back from work every afternoon with his newspapers. "If you smell of oranges, it must be January," he would say. "If it's apricots, this must be June."

* * *

Charu was one of our best workers. Like many of the other girls, she worked part-time, but unlike the others she was methodical and hardworking. She was so good at solving problems and so decisive that when I saw her at work, I often wondered why she had been such a disappointment at school.

That year, however, she was different. It was February, marmalade season, and where Charu's slicing of the orange rinds was usually even and thin whether she had two kilos to do or ten, for no reason that we could determine she began slicing the rind too thick, or did not shave off enough of the pith. When adding the pulp, she let through so many seeds that the work had sometimes to be done all over again. She spoke less than usual, smiled to herself more, and when her friends asked why, she said it was a funny story she had just remembered.

"Come then, tell us the story."

"No, this is time for work." Her silver nose stud sparkled as she shook her head.

She started again on the orange rinds. She would not look up for a while. Then the secret smile returned to its lodging at the corner of her lips.

The room was scented with oranges and smoke from a brazier filled with pinecones and wood. Our windows overlooked the valley. Just outside was a small stone courtyard where village women sat sorting through great orange slopes of fruit. On these February days it rained often, sometimes with sleet and hail. A bitter wind blew over us from the north, rattling windows, blowing early blossoms off the plum and peach trees, and chilling us to the bone. Then the women worked inside, close to the brazier and the gas stoves on which the marmalade boiled in giant pots. Their hands grew shriveled and cold as they sorted, washed, cut fruit. Every hour they needed tea to keep them going. I made it thick and milky, with quantities of sugar and ginger, spiked with cardamom. I had a tape recorder in the room, on which sometimes I played the news, sometimes hymns in Hindi. I was not Christian, but certain that Miss Wilson would disapprove, I would not allow frivolous music. I knew the girls switched to film music the minute I turned my back. Sound carries in the hills, especially on clear, birdless winter days, and from faraway slopes I could hear mournful songs of longing: "I have erased that name from the book of my mind, but I am still the prisoner of my love."

Charu, who had laughed at these songs before, now hummed them under her breath. It was so cold that the water in buckets left outside grew skins of ice overnight; yet she washed her hair every few days, and I frequently saw her sitting in the yard outside their house, drying it in the milky winter sunlight. It no longer went uncombed till evening. She began to tuck flowers into it: a small pink rose from a wild bush, an iridescent plastic carnation.

One afternoon, there was a cry of pain at our workshop and I ran in to see a chopping board bright red with blood. Orange rinds need sharp knives and Charu and the other girls who had the work of slicing were picked for being dexterous. Accidents were very rare. But this time the knife had gone deep into her ring finger. She was standing there, clutching it, looking dazed. The others had wrapped a dishcloth around the finger and one of them was exclaiming, "She's in her own world these days, never looks where the knife's going." The blood dyed the white cloth red in seconds and by the time we stopped a passing jeep-taxi and got her to the Civil Hospital for stitches, she looked as if she was going to faint. The smell of blood was strong, metallic, and frightening.

The next day Ama insisted Charu stay at home and before she could utter a word of protest, Ama had yelled toward her son, "Enough idling. You take the cattle grazing alone today, Puran. And count them when you bring them back. If there's one goat or cow missing I'll smash your head into so many pieces you won't find one bit of it again." She shook her walking stick at Puran.

But Charu stole out in the afternoon when her grandmother dozed in a patch of sun near their radish patch, and went down to the Dhobi Ghat. She held up her finger like a trophy and unwrapped the bandage to show Kundan Singh the stitches. As expected, he took the finger into his hands and stroked it around the stitches. And although that tenderest of touches was agony for the swollen finger, she kept herself from wincing so that he would not stop.

Only two months had passed since Kundan Singh had come to Ranikhet, but his presence had become air, water, and food to Charu. She had to see him every day. If he was late she worried, if he left early she sulked. She hid keepsakes from their meetings in the cowshed: a blue and white feather from the long tail of a magpie, a stone from the Dhobi Ghat stream, a bead necklace he had bought her that she could not wear for fear of Ama's questions. She could think of nothing but him all day and if he had asked her to come to the Dhobi Ghat at midnight to meet him, she would have run down the night-shadowed, leopard-smelling slopes without a thought.

What would happen when Ama and other people found out about them? Charu confided her fears, desires, and hopes only to Gouri Joshi when milking her each morning. With the rest of the world she was as secretive as was possible in a small town where everyone came to know everything, sooner or later.

NINE

Our town has two distinct parts. One part is the crowded Sadar Bazaar. In the other part, the cantonment, where the Light House is, most of the estates are at a distance from each other, and stretch for several acres across valleys and streams. The houses were built in the nineteenth century by the British, without architects or building plans. They made enormous stone mansions with chimneys and attics, fireplaces and mantelpieces, but also deep verandas and tin roofs. To the extent that it was possible in distant India, they re-created their remembered Scotland. Ever since, Ranikhet has been made up of memories and stories: of trees laden with peaches the size of tennis balls, of strawberry patches and watercress sandwiches, of the legendary eccentrics who lived here. There was the scholar-dancer who lived alone tended by a village man whom she had taught to recite Hamlet's soliloquies. In her eighties she employed an impecunious artist to illustrate a book on dance and posed for him day after day in full Bharatnatyam costume, frail and bony, and relentlessly scathing about his ineptitude. He crept out one night, braving the darkness and his fear of wild animals, and escaped her and the town, leaving his sketches behind on his bed as a tidy heap of shredded paper. Then there was Angelina, the Goan visitor who fell in love with our retired General, who was old enough to be her father. He was smitten by her cropped, floppy hair, her careless beauty, and her brisk disregard for propriety. They married, and she wandered the town in flamboyant dresses, flowers tucked behind her ear, intercepting tourists and telling them the Forest Lodge had ghouls that drank blood on particular nights.

Our town has a private history that is revealed only to those who live here, by others who have lived here longer. Ama had a daily story for me both about the dead and the living, talking in the same breath of Janaki on the next hill who made bhang and charas out of the marijuana plants that grew wild all over the hillsides, and of unmarried Missis Lily, who had fallen pregnant forty years ago by the judge of the local court. When I went to the Christian cemetery, where I had buried Michael's ashes, I recognized the names on the other tombstones from stories I had been told over the years. In the older part of the graveyard was Charlie Darling beneath a gravestone with winged angels. He had been dead since 1912, of syphilis, I had been told, after too many visits to Lal Kurti, where pretty Kumaoni women earned extra money from soldiers stationed in Ranikhet's army barracks. The fiery Angelina was a few feet away, beneath a marble slab with carved roses. She never came out of anesthesia after some minor surgery at the hospital. The General, now in his nineties, had been mourning her for decades. He came to her grave every week with Bozo, and if we met there, he gave me a ride home in his old Ambassador. Bozo would sit very straight in the front, staring solemnly ahead, while I had to make do with a corner in the back that I managed to free of clutter and dog things. From behind, the big German shepherd was a head taller than the General, who—in his prime no taller than the army's mandatory five foot five inches—was shrinking every passing year. He held himself as high as his five remaining feet would allow and as he drove he alternated between humming songs from old Hollywood musicals and holding forth on the anarchy in the country. "It's going to the dogs," he would say, and immediately apologize to Bozo: "Not you, dear boy, not you. You would rule with an iron paw . . . ," and in the same breath to me, "June Allyson, my girl, did you ever see June Allyson? No, of course not . . . too young—"

These were the people I was telling Veer about one afternoon when he had fallen in step with me, as he often did these days when I was on my way back from the graveyard or when I took the shortcut through the woods and across the stream to the bazaar and St. Hilda's. Once he held out a hand to me on the steep bit in the forest path to the bazaar where tumbling boulders made footholds precarious. I had been so taken aback that I had taken his hand, forgetting that I clambered down those stones all by myself every day.

"But what about you?" I said. "You came here in your childhood, you probably know all this old gossip. Himmat says the house was full of people in those days, and parties. I can't imagine Diwan Sahib throwing parties. He is such a solitary person."

"Oh, the old man was very different then. He was very handsome, straight and tall and strong looking. He had a romantic, heroic aura. People said that once he put his own life at risk to save one of those tribal lion trackers. That long scar he has all the way down his left cheek? That's from the mauling he got."

"He told me it was barbed wire," I said.

"Ah, he did, did he?" Veer said. "That's strange, he used to boast about it when he was younger. Maybe . . . anyway, he had a famously glad eye—you should have seen his entourage and the adoring women—army wives and daughters, and all those summer visitors who arrived from upper-class Lucknow and Delhi. Virtually every year there would be a new—invariably very beautiful—woman who would be introduced as a friend of the family, but everyone knew she was the flavor of that year. I only came for vacations. So did he, because he lived in Surajgarh at that time, and came here for the summer. He traveled in one of those first-class carriages, the old ones, all teakwood and gilt mirrors—and his dogs traveled with him."

I knew about the dogs because on one of the walls above the fireplace in Diwan Sahib's drawing room was a black and white photograph of four fringe-tailed golden retrievers on an open field. Each dog was backlit, its coat glowing in white outline from the sunset. That line of light transformed them into ethereal beings with floppy ears and panting tongues. One of the dogs had a happy smile as it looked up at Diwan Sahib. His hand had intruded into a corner of the picture. A fine riding boot was visible too.

"Parties, booze, love affairs, music on the lawn and singers he invited from Benares, meat slow-cooked on wood fires, machines for hand-churned ice cream that always tasted slightly of salt," Veer was saying. "He had no time for grubby parentless boys parceled out between relatives for boarding-school vacations. I was left to fend for myself. The only thing that made him take an interest in me was if I asked questions about wildlife. So I thought of something new every day. Why does the woodpecker peck a tree trunk? How does the magpie fly with such a long tail? Where did all the tigers of these hills go? And then he'd give me five minutes—undivided attention—whatever he was doing. Sometimes he would do those imitations of his: birdsong, tiger calls, barking deer. After that I would be alone again until I caught the train back. All I did was eat, ready to be the school's fatso again when the school break was over."

The bitterness in his voice startled me. His face suddenly appeared thinner to me, worn out with remembered pain. He turned away as if he did not want me to see it. I knitted my fingers one into the other and held them behind my back so that I would not give in to my impulse to reach out for his hand. When Veer turned to me again it was with a smile, and a question about something inconsequential. We discussed his difficulties in setting up an e-mail connection and the hide-and-seek his mobile phone's signal played. We did not mention Diwan Sahib again that day.

Veer had by now shifted base to Ranikhet. He was a climber, a professional whose work it was to take other people on climbs and treks. He was starting a new trekking company here and was busy setting up: laying in equipment, computers, looking out for an assistant to hire. When I saw the sophisticated, expensive things he came back with from trips to Delhi, I was wracked with compassion for Michael's ill-equipped attempts, armed with little more than his passion for the mountains. Those thick-soled shoes, that plastic tent, his windproof jacket with its twice-repaired zip—they had seemed so invincible then, so flimsy, cheap, and makeshift now. It would have been a natural point of conversation for Veer and me. Yet I could not bring myself to say a word. The contrast felt too painful, the comparison almost disloyal to Michael.

Veer was away so often I might not see him for days at a stretch. We had never talked about anything personal until that afternoon. Yet every encounter with him left me feeling as if I had swallowed five cups of strong coffee at one go. A swarm of bees took up residence inside me as soon as I saw him, and they buzzed crazily, knocking against each other. I was unable to sit still, even at the factory. I was restless, and confused about the reason for it. I knew I mentioned Veer in conversation far too much but could not stop myself. I had noticed Diwan Sahib raise his eyebrow at me when I did, with a "yet again" look on his face.

That afternoon was not the first time I had felt an overpowering need to touch Veer. Not long ago, at dinner at the Light House, he was seated opposite me, telling us about a trek he had taken his clients on the year before. It was a long story involving routes, tents, altitudes, and crevasses, and Diwan Sahib stopped him often for clarifications. I had heard barely a word. There was a trace of spinach clinging to Veer's lower lip. I was mesmerized. I noticed the exact shape and line of his lips and the cleft in his chin. I tried looking away from it, could not. I had to sit on my hands to stop myself from reaching out to stroke the scrap away.

I stared into the bathroom mirror that night, clutching a comb, forgetting it was in my hand. I did not notice the icy breath from the tiles that was freezing my toes and traveling up my legs. I remembered another time before a different bathroom mirror, moments after news of Michael's death reached me. Water was trickling off my face that day. There were no tears. I did not know why I was in the bathroom or why I had flung handfuls of water at myself. If my body had been turned inside out at that moment, there would have been fire and drought in place of veins and muscles. My face should have been ravaged, burned away. And yet it looked as it did every other day: the same bush of dark hair around the same coffee-colored face, the same spectacles on the same pointed nose reflected in the same stained and cracked mirror that the bathroom had come with when Michael and I rented the place. We had never got around to replacing it. Parrots quarreled over the fruit on the rain tree that overhung the terrace adjoining our two stuffy rooms. I was conscious of the birds' screeches, of children in the house next door practicing the song they did at this time, the echoing cry of late afternoon from the flower seller who circled those warm Hyderabad neighborhoods on his jasmine-laden bicycle. Each daily sound had seemed heavy with a meaning I could not understand. The toothbrushes—two because Michael had left his behind—the soap dish, even the steel tap, looked as if they were more than ordinary, utilitarian objects. Two of his shirts hung in the cupboard unwashed. I had made him leave them that way so that I could bury my face in them to breathe in his smell while waiting for him to return. The new camera bag his office had given him for assignments lay on the bottom shelf of the cupboard, unused.

It had taken me all these years to claw my way back from that day to some kind of normality.

I had lost my taste for adventure, my impulsiveness. I wished Veer had never come, to fling a stone into my calm pond.

TEN

It was in March that I met Charu's Kundan Singh for the first time, when the imminence of spring spurred the hotel manager to throw a party at Aspen Lodge. There was still rain at times and sometimes knife-edged gusts of wind, but the pewter of last month's light had taken on a pearly translucence and one morning I opened my door to find two hopeful pigtailed infants waiting there for me to discover the little heap of pink, white, and red blossoms they had deposited on my doorstep. I returned inside to get them small change to buy sweets with, as was the custom. Living alone I lost track of these things. Now I remembered that Phooldeyi, springtime's flower festival, was not far off.

I realized when I went for the party that the hotel manager had intended to invite only those he considered people of consequence. As a penniless teacher I was out of place among the generals, brigadiers, bureaucrats. Even Miss Wilson had not been thought grand enough for the occasion. But the manager had found me with Diwan Sahib when he came to ask him, and could hardly avoid including me. "Just a few friends," he had said, "nothing much," and I had pictured five or six people around a sunny table in the garden.

When I reached Aspen Lodge, I stood for a few minutes at the edge of the lawn, looking at the crowd and considering a quick retreat. Silk saris shimmered past. There were men in tweed jackets and lamb's-wool pullovers. The lawn was full of people I had never seen before. My fingers plucked at my clothes. I wished I had not arrived straight from work. I had put on my best kurta that morning in honor of the lunch, but it was hidden beneath my thick, many-colored winter shawl, which Diwan Sahib always said would do nicely for a rug. My hair was probably dusted with white chalk from writing on blackboards.

I took shelter behind a wide-trunked chestnut tree, plucked out the striped pencil that held my untidy bun in place, and ran my fingers through my hair. I neatened my shawl, rubbed the dust off my shoes with a handkerchief, and before I could change my mind and leave, I made my way toward the nearest person. It was the Subdivisional Magistrate, who was talking to Mr. Chauhan, the administrator, congratulating him on the educative slogans he was putting up all over the town. Our host, the hotel manager, stood by looking deferential, as was politic before our town's two highest-ranking bureaucrats.

"The messages are very good, especially for the young," the Magistrate was saying to Mr. Chauhan. Mr. Chauhan looked down at the glittering toe caps of his shoes. Ever since he had been posted to Ranikhet, about six months before, he had been writing slogans, which he then made his staff paint on rock faces, or on boards that were then nailed to trees all over town. You could no longer take more than a few steps without meeting a sign.

"It gives a certain distinction to the place," the hotel manager said. "Such educative signs."

Early in his time in Ranikhet, Mr. Chauhan had brought a school exercise book to share with us when we invited him to St. Hilda's to give away prizes on one of our sports days. The book had a bright, hard cover that showed a magenta-cheeked baby with large eyes, holding a pen in dimpled hands. The cover said "Apsara Single Ruled for your Writing Pleasure." In the slots for "Name/School/Subject," he had written, "Avinash Chauhan/Administrator Ranikhet/Signs for People Betterment." When Mr. Chauhan held the exercise book toward me and Miss Wilson, I had noticed a tremor in his hands. For a moment, he had looked very much like one of our students.

"I have not shown these to anyone before. Please give me your honest opinion, Mams," he had said.

Inside the exercise book were line after line of slogans, written in blue ballpoint:

Get Fresh on This Footpath
Keep Your Side, Don't go Wide

Forest is Poor Man's Overcoat
Enjoy Thrills of the Hills
Mountains are Fountains of Joy
Walk in Nature Zone, It is Health Prone
Be Careful of Flying Balls

"The last one is for the army golf course," he had said, noticing my nonplussed look. And then: "My teacher—in Ranchi, you know, that is where I grew up—my teacher told me I had real talent. I won all the essay-writing prizes. Once I wrote an essay on a picnic to Dasham Falls and he said: 'You have real talent, young Avinash,' that is what he said."

"Yes of course you do, Mr. Chauhan," I had said. "You must not waste it."

But today Mr. Chauhan seemed not to remember who I was. He spoke only to the manager and the Magistrate, pursing his lips and saying, "A little guidance at the right time is very valuable." He had a small, officious-looking mustache, and though he was otherwise skinny, a paunch the size of a watermelon pushed out his navy-blue pullover. The bazaar gossip, which Mr. Qureshi reported to Diwan Sahib daily, was that Chauhan had made enough from kickbacks in his six months here to build himself a three-story house in Lucknow.

"It is also good that you are going to replace the parapets. These old stone ones are so untidy, grass and wild plants growing out of them," the manager was saying.

"I am putting benches also," Mr. Chauhan said in the Magistrate's direction. "You will see. Ranikhet has to become the Switzerland of India. Or at least it must be another Shimla. I am making a View Point. With telescope. For one rupee anyone can worship Nanda Devi-ji through zoom lens. And furthermore I am getting many roads relaid." After each of Mr. Chauhan's statements, which came with stately pauses in between, the manager murmured, "Point taken, sir. Point well taken."

"The roads, that's urgent," said the Subdivisional Magistrate. "Has to be done on a war footing." He looked well-informed and important.

A uniformed bearer hovered by his elbow holding a tray laden with little samosas. The Magistrate paid him no attention at all.

"Will the metaling of Mall Road go so far as our properties?" the hotel manager inquired in a hesitant voice. "You know, tourism is ruined by bad roads. This road was last repaired ten years back, I hear, but now—"

"Not this time, not this time," Mr. Chauhan said. "I would like all of Ranikhet to have smooth roads, but this time our budget allows repair of only one part of Mall Road, for administrative purposes."

I cleared my throat and said, "If only you could repair the road going to St. Hilda's! Our children have a hard time."

The Magistrate and my host noticed me at last. Together they said, "Madam, you must be—"

"Maya Mam," Mr. Chauhan said, beaming at me in an unlooked-for burst of bonhomie. "A teacher at the convent. A valuable citizen! She teaches her children to make jams and jellies."

"They do schoolwork," I said. "But they need practical skills too."

I opened my mouth to expand on the topic, but the men had moved on already to another: who would be the candidates for the elections coming up? The two main contenders for the Nainital seat had already begun campaigning. Surely the BJP would win—the time was ripe for Hindus to govern their own country, show the world, they agreed. "Will the minister change?" the manager said to the Subdivisional Magistrate, who replied, "I am a mere servant of the people and have to humor whichever minister I get." They laughed together and raised their glasses in a mock toast. The hotel proprietor, unsure of lunchtime protocol in a new town, had served no alcohol. They had to say their "cheers" with plain Coke and Kissan orange squash. His wife was in Delhi still, he said to me, apologetic. "That's why things are a bit disorganized." She would come in a month, when it was a little warmer.

I looked around for Diwan Sahib, whom I spotted sitting at a plastic table under a plum tree snowy with blossoms, tipping his hip flask into his glass, making no attempt to be discreet. He had come in a dark-blue shirt against which his white shock of hair and beard looked whiter and more disheveled than usual, giving him a raffish air. He threw a twisted half smile in my direction and nodded to me to come across. The wives of the other guests, who sat in a separate group further away, sipped their squash and darted exasperated looks at him. One said as I was passing, "We must have more lunch parties, but only for *select* people."

They looked around the relaid garden and admired the geometric precision of the flower beds. Within the beds, segregated by color and type, were the plants that would flower in summer. Several flowers already bloomed in the martial lines of tulips, lilies, and carnations, staked and tied with string so they could not stray. Some of the women got up from their chairs to examine the flower beds closer too, so as to show off their saris. When one of them bent down to sniff the tulips, her companion broke into giggles and exclaimed, "Oh, Mrs. Sood, those flowers have no smell! They are tulips. They come from Holland. I went there once on a Thomas Cook tour! Whole fields of tulips, as if they are wheat or rice—this is nothing."

I sat down next to Diwan Sahib and he said, "Had enough of the Burra Sa'abs?" His eyes twinkled and his wrinkles deepened when he smiled. I felt immediately at ease. I stretched out my legs, swiveled my ankles, and rested my head against the backrest of my chair.

"Why come," I said to him, "if you will not meet anyone?"

"I am happy enough meeting only you," he said. "But I never seem to see you. Even when you come in the afternoons you hide behind a newspaper."

The General began talking at us as he advanced, tap-tapping the Naga spear he used as a walking stick, although it was much taller than him. His voice had long ago acquired the ability to reach the last row of soldiers in a parade. "I never read the papers. And look at my eyesight, perfect! Still driving. Why? Because I never read anything smaller than the headlines. Nothing but anarchy, I say, bombs and terrorists everywhere, waste of time reading about it. 'Improve your Eye Sight, Never Read or Write': I told Chauhan to nail that one to a tree—right next to the Central School."

"Don't come anywhere near our school," I said. "It's hard enough as it is, getting the classrooms filled."

He frowned at me. "What? Who—ah, it's you, Maya. Better off empty, I say, those classrooms. You're ruining those pretty village girls by teaching them to read. Social misfits." Though his head was just about level with mine, the General was confident of his authority. He held himself very straight, and like a cartoon general, he had a thick, white mustache that was curled at the tips. He adjusted the Kumaon Regiment cap he invariably wore and looked at the empty chair beside us.

Diwan Sahib held his flask out and said, "Sit down, General Sahib, I know why you're interested in my company all of a sudden."

The General lowered himself into the chair and held a glass out toward the hip flask. "Where's that boy of yours? Hasn't he come? Heard he lives here now."

"He's gone off somewhere. Wandering. Trekking, he calls it," Diwan Sahib said, concentrating on his pouring of careful drops from his flask into the glass.

"Strange to see him after all these years, our young Veer. Don't mind me, Diwan Sahib, he's your nephew, of course. But—Maya, I knew this boy when he was just this high, and even when he was a little child he was like a grown-up. You know? I'd make jokes—every other child would laugh his head off, but this boy? Nothing. Not a smile even. Couldn't get a word out of him." The General gave a loud laugh after his first sip of rum. "Takes after his uncle, doesn't he? Yes, Diwan Sahib?"

Ramesh ambled across and patted the General on the shoulder. He was the only man in Ranikhet who would take such a liberty. "I say, General," he boomed, "you have named your house General's Retreat, but generals should never retreat, they should always advance." His face turned pink as he chortled with merriment. Ramesh was a retired economist from Harvard whom everyone called Professor. He told people to their faces what others did not dare to say behind their backs. He got away with it because of his unquenchable good humor. Now he settled down with a sigh, helped himself to Diwan Sahib's hip flask, and said, "Next time we should meet at home. I brought lots of Kingfisher beer from Delhi. And I have a new recipe for mutton biryani."

"I didn't know you cooked," I said.

"Oh no, Maya, of course I don't cook." Ramesh waved his hand grandly as if to gesture at his battalion of cooks. "I will make the biryani only in the way that Shah Jahan built the Taj Mahal."

The Brigadier stood at the far end of the garden with an earnest-looking woman, who seemed to be an outsider. She was asking him, "What happens when a soldier has doubts about war, sir? What if they don't want to fight?"

"We call such people bullshitters," the Brigadier said. "That's what we say, damn bullshitters!"

The woman mustered courage and said, "Sir, what about all this we hear, of army men raping and molesting women in the Northeast—and in Kashmir—"

The Brigadier interrupted her in a sharp voice that we heard across the lawn. "One rotten fruit here or there, madam, doesn't make a bad basket. We deal with deviants, we do it more swiftly than anyone else."

The hotel manager tried drawing the woman away. "Ah, Kusum-ji," he said in arch tones, "now why don't you have another samosa? And look, all those ladies at the flower bed there want to show you something. You remember the rule, Kusum-ji, parties and politics don't ever mix, isn't that what they say?"

Mr. Chauhan thumped a table and said, "That I will put on a signboard right away! And also, 'Politics before Food, Does your Digestion No Good.' In fact, this I may prepare and send you for display in your hotel's lobby."

The once-desolate bungalow was painted and polished. Its once-dislocated windows sat squarely within their frames; its roof shone red with fresh paint. The hotel manager's profession had trained him in setting up a pretty home: the tablecloths had frilled edges, vases sprouted fresh flowers, wrought iron lampshades hung from the trees. There was a new terra-cotta birdhouse, too small for the long tail of the magpie struggling to enter it. Huge striped canvas umbrellas shaded the tables. Two bearer boys went from person to person with trays of drinks and pakoras. One of them held his tray out to me. I was intrigued by his face, which had the startling beauty of young boys in the paintings of Renaissance Italy.

I said, "You are new here, aren't you?"

He was taken aback at being spoken to. "I travel wherever Sa'ab goes," he stammered. His voice was a mismatch, too deep for his slight, young body. He gave me a smile that showed a mouthful of crooked teeth. "I am Kundan Singh," he said. "I am not really a bearer, I am the cook."

Ramesh, sitting beside me, spoke before Kundan Singh could say anything more. "You know, once I had a cook who was not really a cook. In Lucknow when I was teaching there. His name was George. Anglo-Indian fellow—they all used to join the Railways then, but George was a cook. So one day I asked him, 'George, how did you become a cook? Why didn't you join the Railways? You're an Anglo-Indian,' I say. And you know what he said?"

"Tell us," I said. Kundan lingered with his tray, stealing a fearful glance over his shoulder in case his lingering was noticed.

"You know what he said? He said that for most of his life, he had been an engine driver." Ramesh slapped his chair's arm, roaring with mirth. "At least that explained why his cooking was so third-rate. But that is not the end of it, my boy"—Kundan had shown signs of leaving—"that is not the end of it. He was an engine driver for fifteen years and then the railways sacked him. He was very puzzled, you know—they told him to leave after so long in service. Why? On one medical checkup they had found that he was color-blind. The railway people said an engine driver had to know the difference between red and green—for the signals, you know—but George was very upset. He said to me, 'Sir, I understand that an engine driver must distinguish between red and green, but as life is all shades of gray, and as for fifteen years I could tell red's shade of gray from green's, I ask you, sir, what does color-blindness mean to those who can see what's what?' But this was really too much! So much philosophy from an engine driver I could not take. Besides I realized why his food tasted so bad—the man didn't know when he was putting chili and when turmeric or cumin into food! All the spices looked like blue powder to him."

Ramesh picked up a pakora from Kundan's tray and said through his munches, "Beta, what were you before you were a cook? You didn't drive a bus, or write poetry, did you? One never knows." He waggled his head sagely in my direction.

Kundan opened his mouth to answer. But then noticed something. He hurriedly put his tray down on the table and ran toward the far end of the garden.

Three cows and two buffaloes were browsing at the edge of the lawn, quite close to the Brigadier. The bells around their necks tinkled as they reached for leaves just above their heads. I recognized Gouri, who let out a bellow as Kundan Singh reached her, slapped her rump, and shouted. Gouri gave a dismissive shake of her head, seeming to know at once a man who had no notion of herding cows. Kundan Singh looked around for the gardener and the chowkidar, who knew how these things were done, but they were nowhere to be seen. The second bearer came to help move the cattle away from the people and the food, but now there were two amateurs, shouting to little purpose. One of the cows ambled down the slope, while a buffalo lumbered toward a laden table, scattering the captains and majors sitting at it. A few goats paused inquiringly at the edge of the slope and then skipped onto the lawn, eager to join the party. I spotted the delicate, long-legged little kid that Charu had named Pinki and necklaced with a red rope and bell.

"Quite a dairy industry here, Chauhan," the Brigadier said with a dry laugh. "So what if Ranikhet lacks other industries."

Mr. Chauhan looked around with agitated swivels of his head for the cowherd responsible. I could see the culprit at a distance: it was Charu's uncle, Sanki Puran, half-asleep in a sliver of sunlight on a warm boulder far down the slope that led away from the house, smoking a beedi, which was very likely spiked with dope. The forest around Puran was stabbed here and there by the first scarlet explosions of rhododendron and there was a white cloud of plum blossoms not far from him. Those patches of color apart, his clothes merged so perfectly with the green and brown of the foliage that nobody else had noticed him. Puran wore the same khaki and olive army camouflage uniform all year, never taking it off save to bathe a few times when the summer grew too hot. Summer or winter, he also wore an army-issue leather-patched olive pullover, his elbows glistening through its holes. He had trousers that ended five inches above his ankles and a woolen cap that covered half of one eye.

By now, much of the party had converged in the center of the lawn, looking as if they had never seen cattle before. The goats scampered about making for the discarded plates on the grass, chewing pakoras and paper napkins with gusto. Pinki executed perfect twirls and leaps near the birdhouse, to the delight of the children who had been watching TV inside all this time. Kundan scoured the valley for Charu, and when at length he sighted Puran, he clambered down the hillside toward him in relief, shouting, "Arre O, Puran-da!"

Puran came to life at last. Something was the matter—he grasped that—and he clambered up toward us yelling his herding calls. Alarmed and confused by clashing shouts from Kundan and Puran, the cows and buffaloes began to blunder off in different directions. Then I saw a flash of purple streaking uphill at great speed from far away: Charu.

The Brigadier sidestepped a buffalo and said to his flustered host, "Difficult proposition having a lawn, eh? You need more staff—and fencing, you need fencing. What's the point of signboards saying trespassers will be prosecuted? Can you prosecute a cow?" He gave everyone a wide smile and Mr. Chauhan said, "Well put, sir, well put."

Ramesh said, "No, no, Brigadier! Cows are—holiness apart—natural lawn mowers. Best way to use resources, I say! Two for the price of one—they get food, you get a neat lawn."

Puran's exhortations were more effective than Kundan's, and the cows began to head for the valley where Charu now stood. Puran clicked his tongue against his teeth, urging them on. The Brigadier, the hotel manager, and Mr. Chauhan stood aside, pretending they were not flat against the garage, trapped between thorny rose bushes on one side and the garage door on the other. Diwan Sahib observed them with a savage smile and muttered, "Perfect," under his breath, while the women cheered to encourage the cows. The smell from unbathed Puran made the Brigadier put a napkin to his nose, and two or three others followed suit.

"Why is this cowherd in fatigues?" the Brigadier asked Mr. Chauhan over the sounds of laughter and mooing. "Where did he get them? Are the army stores secure? Must look into it." He had turned away from the cattle toward Mr. Chauhan as he spoke, and did not notice a young cow aiming a kick at him as she passed. The Brigadier yelped and sprang away, and then, ashamed, said into the middle distance, "Pahari cows! It's only hill cows that kick like this. Nervous beasts." He glanced around to see if anyone was laughing at him, but everyone, all at once, had gone quiet. The hotelier stared at the cattle with a fixed gaze of horror, shredding a paper napkin into tiny pieces. Bits of white tissue paper settled on the lawn around him.

Mr. Chauhan lost his composure. "Enough!" he shouted toward Puran. "Enough is enough! I'm going to lock you up! With your damned cows and goats!" He noticed people staring and lowered his voice. "Every single day since I've been posted here," he said to the Brigadier, "I've seen this madman sitting on Mall Road in that dirty uniform, feeding stray dogs, and I've said, 'Is this the way? Can this be allowed?' I pitied him because he is poor. No more, sir, not another day! I will tackle this with immediate effect."

Puran shuffled past them, uncomprehending. Touching his woolen cap in an improvised salute, he said, "Namaste, Sa'ab," in a hoarse voice that sounded as if it came from the depths of a barrel, then shambled after his cows and goats, retreating bit by bit until we could only see the bobbing top of his cap.

Charu was still in the valley below, miniaturized by the distance. She was looking up the hill in our direction, at nobody but Kundan Singh as he struggled with Pinki, who had remained there to chew one last napkin. Before Kundan came into her life, her uncle Puran had been her closest friend. He was as defenseless as a child; he had always been.

He could talk to animals, but people left him confused and mumbling. He gave dead bats and birds tender burials and allowed monkeys to pick lice off his head. People might think him mad but Charu stood up for him if anyone harassed him or called him crazy.

Now she was shaking Puran by the shoulder and scolding him for dozing when he should have been watching. The clear mountain air carried her words to us. "They're right to call you mad if you can't even manage a few cows! I told you they were not to go to that garden anymore!" She walked rapidly off into the valley, then up the slope on the other side, swatting Gouri Joshi with her stick. I had never seen her strike an animal before.

ELEVEN

About six kilometers downhill from the frayed glories of the cantonment is the commercial center of our town, the main bazaar. Houses are stacked five deep up the slopes of the bazaar hill, tumbling down on each other, threaded through with narrow, dirty alleyways and stinking open drains. The ground floors of the first row have shops with wooden shutters and shelves knocked together out of cheap plywood. Through the doors of the shops, you can see a cobbler stitching soles, a picture framer measuring glass. There is Bhim Singh, who sits walled in by steel and copper in his shop all day, selling everything from saucepans to nails and hammers. There is the one-eyed old Gopal Ram, who repairs watches; Jewel Tailors, which always ferrets away bits of our cloth. There is the rheumy-eyed drunk in a beret who darns with such skill that old and new cannot be told apart. There are rows of villagers on the road in front of the shops; they sell their produce from gunnysacks and handcarts. One man has a sack full of onions, another just has tomatoes, or misshapen oranges. Coolies trudge up and down between the cars and crowds, bent double under gas cylinders, crates, and metal trunks that they carry on their shoulders. There is a gas pump, Mr. Qureshi's car workshop, and Bisht Bakery, with its "We Bake Memories" sign at the entrance. At the mandi, vegetables are sprinkled with water to make them seem fresher than they are. Its concrete floor is slippery with rotting peel and water. The two butchers' shops are behind the mandi, and people hurry there for the marble-eyed heads of slaughtered goats, the cheapest meat you can buy.

Our school's jam factory is in the grounds of the church in the cantonment area, but St. Hilda's itself is in one of the back lanes of the bazaar and I walked there almost every day of the week for staff meetings and the classes I still took for the very young children. When I went in through the gates one morning soon after the hotel manager's party, I found Miss Wilson in heated discussion with two young men who had parked their cars within the school compound.

"It's not safe for the children, this is their playground," she was saying in her strident voice. "You, Deepak Bisht, you were a student here, you should have more sense than to park in a school playground."

"Only till the elections, Agnes Mam," the man called Deepak said in a tone half-playful, half-pleading. The elections were still some months away, but this time, because there was a contender from Ranikhet, campaigning had begun early. "Please, Mam, there's no space on the road," he said. He gestured outward as if to point to the obviousness of it. A bus and a jeep that had come from opposite ends were at that moment conclusively stuck side by side, paring each other's paint off if either of them attempted the smallest movement. Behind them, on both sides, for as far as we could see, the narrow road was a choked cacophony of cars, motorbikes, scooters, and trucks, honking and beeping to hurry things up although it was clear that nothing of the sort was possible. The air was sooty with diesel fumes.

"What is all this 'please, please,' Deepak?" the other man said, shouting above the noise. "We have to park these cars, and that's the end of it. She can't do anything to stop us."

"Today there are two cars, tomorrow there will be twenty, and how will I stop them?" Miss Wilson wiped her face with a folded hanky and tucked it back into her waist. She shook her head. "Take them away, take them away now," she said, gesturing for me to come with her and not interfere. She began to walk off before the argument went further along its futile path. She appeared afraid and aggressive at the same time. She knew she would not get her way. Like all of us, she was wary of the anarchic power of party workers in the middle of a campaign, when our small town, where everyone knew everyone at least by sight, was invaded by outsiders with microphones and motorbikes. In Bihar, we had read in the papers, small-time political goons commandeered any vehicle they fancied and did not return your car or scooter until the elections were over or the car ruined.

The other man slapped Deepak on the shoulder. "Sisterfucker," he said amiably, "you've never told us you went to a Christian school. We should throw you out of the party." He laughed. "You're a guy to be watched. We never know with you, the direction of the wind changes your color from saffron to green."

Miss Wilson's back stiffened and she stopped in her tracks. I turned back to the men and said, "Half your party's from schools just like these. What's your problem? Hypocrites," I muttered, loud enough for them to hear. My heart thudded and my breath grew short. I never picked fights. I did not know what had got into me.

The laughing man turned toward me with an expression of mock amazement. When he spoke, his voice was lazy and salacious. "Madam, why are you getting into something that shouldn't bother you? You're not even one of them."

I began to sweat despite the cold. My hands had gone clammy. I could see my face in his reflecting sunglasses, distorted, small, windblown, scowling. Defenseless.

Deepak gave me an apologetic look and tried to propel the other man away. He patted his companion's shoulder and said, "Let's go, we're late. We have all those banners to put up." The other man turned to go, but flung a last look in my direction, growling, "They're schoolteachers, they're women. So I'm letting them be. No son of a . . . picks a fight with me."

Miss Wilson, who had been standing a few feet away, shook her cane at some blue and white uniforms she spotted in the grounds and shouted, "Inside, *inside,* children! There are *cars* here now, you can't play! And you, Maya, ring the bell, the chowkidar has forgotten and it's past nine o'clock. What's wrong with all you people?"

* * *

All through my childhood, I was my father's pet. He had put aside his disappointment at not fathering a son, and had begun to take perverse pride in me, his only child, the girl who won all the prizes in school, his bright-eyed, adoring devotee. When he came back from work, mine was the name he called from the door, and despite his bad right leg, he scooped me up and swung me in the air when I was little enough, saying, "Now tell me, my princess, which giants have you killed today?" When I was a little older, I went with him on his rounds of our factories and once, when I was no more than seven years old, he pulled me out of the chalk grid of a hopscotch game and introduced me to some visiting grown-ups with a flourish: "Meet the princess of Begumpet Pickles! One day she will become the first female industrial magnate of this country." He spoke to me only in English because he considered it the language of success, even though this excluded my Telugu-speaking mother from our conversations. From infancy, I was made to understand I was the heir. Once when my mother protested, "She will be married, she won't be your daughter anymore, she'll have her own life and she may want other things," my father snapped at her. "She'll live here and run the business, and I'll arrange a husband for her who lives with us. Why am I earning all this money if not for my grandsons?"

He continued the practice of calling for me until well into my teenage years—his car would stop; I would hear his step on the staircase and then hear my name. I would put aside whatever I was doing and run to the front door to open it and hand him his glass of fresh coconut water. It was only during my senior school years, when extra classes began to keep me away from home, that this routine began to be disrupted. Finally it ceased altogether.

I can see now that my father sensed even then that he was losing me, and everything he did was an attempt somehow to corral me, to reclaim our lost days of easy happiness when I was a willing disciple and he my unquestioned master. He insisted that I spend hours with him on the factory's accounts after school. Holidays were to be spent going to work with him and learning on the job. "Nothing like learning on the job," he would repeat, tapping his silver-headed stick on the floor. "Get your head out of the clouds, Maya, life is not lived on a cloud." Twice, when I was still a pigtailed teenager, he made me sit behind his big shining work desk—I needed a cushion to reach the right commanding height—summon a wretched employee, and inform the man that he was being sacked. If I knew something of this kind was in the offing and tried to hide from him, he forced me out of the house and into his car. "You don't become a businesswoman unless you learn to be tough; you have to be steel inside," he would say. On the drive, he would lecture me all the way: "Business is all about decisions that are taken in the larger interest, with a long-term plan. That man you sacked was serving no purpose anymore. His salary was a waste of our money. It had to be done. Do you think I like sacking people? See this as your management degree, Maya. This is teaching you more than any business academy."

After these encounters, I would retreat to a corner of our orchard, where, under a chikoo tree, a stray dog twice had puppies. I brought food for the bitch, milk for the puppies, and sat with them for long hours, letting the puppies nip my hands, feeling myself restored limb by limb, muscle by muscle, by their bemused joy over a dead leaf or a mound of soft earth they could dig.

I despised myself for not having had the steel to stand up for Puran during the party when Mr. Chauhan had threatened him. Ramesh had protested; why didn't I, when Puran was part of my "family"? My two worlds had never intersected this way before and when for once they did, I had not measured up. With the men who had threatened Miss Wilson today, I wondered how brave I would be if I faced real, physical danger when just their suggestion of violence made me so afraid for myself.

That afternoon, I went to the tea shack by the Jhoola Devi temple. The temple was laden with thousands of tarnished brass bells, big and small, decades old, heavy with wishes. They were everywhere: they hung from ceilings, windows, doors, railings, walls, tied to each other with bits of wire, string, fading red-gold cloth, tinsel. It was an ancient temple to which people came when in need, and tied on those brass bells for their wishes to be granted.

None of the bells were mine, but this temple had replaced the chikoo tree of my childhood. Its surrounding forests of oak, chestnut, and rhododendron were so dense and dark that when I walked through them, the sky narrowed to a road-shaped ribbon overhead. I liked the little temple's blue pillars and flower-filled courtyard and was friends with the priest's daughters, who sat outside knitting in the sun. One of them worked in our jam-jelly unit. There was the temple dog whom I fed batashas; I waited to hear him howl in tune with the priest's conch. The sound of the conch reminded me of a temple I used to go to with my mother in Hyderabad. She and I would meet there, unknown to my father, after I left home. We would sit together in the stone courtyard outside the temple and she would buy me a string of orange flowers from the vendors by the gateway and pin it into my hair, saying, "Be strong. The moment you have a baby, he will not wait a day, he will want you to be his daughter again." Each time, she brought me a piece of jewelry from her box and thrust it into my hands, without a word.

The boy who ran the tea shack at Jhoola Devi made me instant noodles topped with fried onion and chopped green chilies, and a glass of gingery tea. While I ate, he pottered about, giving me the latest news on forest fires, the water supply, leopard sightings. He claimed every time to have seen a leopard, sometimes families of them. "Just before you came, not five minutes ago!" When average leopards seemed too run-of-the-mill to boast about, he said, "I know they say India has no black panthers, but I have seen one sitting here, in the middle of this very road, coal black but for a white patch on its tail, with green, shining eyes. There is another I have seen—not once but twice—it comes up from the forest on full-moon nights, and this one has square markings instead of round."

He had to raise his voice to make himself heard that evening. Songs relayed by a microphone drowned his voice. The singing did not come from our temple, but from one further away, where a godman had taken up residence. Jeeps drew up and off-loaded fresh platoons of acolytes who marched up the hill to his temple. The way to it was festooned with banners and garlands.

"It's started early this time," the boy said, when I asked him what the noise was for. "It's not for a religious festival—the Baba has come for the elections. He'll be here for the next six months." The boy's smile was wide and untroubled. "It's great for business, as long as it lasts!"

TWELVE

Sanki Puran had no recollection of his cow having aimed a kick at the Brigadier, but Mr. Chauhan's neck throbbed with stress each time he allowed his thoughts to return to that party. He had tended, since that day, to encounter Puran at every turn: smelly, slovenly, a disgrace. What was more, he grazed his animals on precisely those slopes where Mr. Chauhan had planted signs both in Hindi and in English announcing fines for illegal grazing. Puran was not acquainted with the alphabet in either language, but he welcomed the iron signboards because the posts they stood upon provided sturdy places to tether cattle.

Throughout his working life, Mr. Chauhan had despaired over the lack of discipline, civic sense, and hard work among his fellow citizens, but what he saw around him in the hill country beat everything he had ever been exasperated by before. It was as if people were on vacation all the time. Apart from getting drunk or gossiping around the peanut seller's charcoal brazier, Mr. Chauhan did not see the men doing anything at all. And of all the men he saw, Sanki Puran grated the most. "Not only is he a shiftless rowdy," he told his wife, "he is shiftless and rowdy in an army uniform. But I have decided what I need to do, for a start."

His wife saw that familiar gleam in his eyes and smiled. He really did know how to change things. She remembered the time when they had been posted in a cantonment town in Uttar Pradesh, where too he was administrator, "responsible for everything from light in a bulb and water in the tap, to keeping the cantonment clean and green." His notion of "clean" included reforming the morals of the young. He came up with a novel scheme. He sent the police around to all the public parks in the cantonment area and wherever they came upon romancing teenagers, the policemen frightened them out of their wits by taking their pictures, demanding their names and addresses, and threatening to inform their parents of—as Mr. Chauhan put it—their "extracurricular activities." "This is when you should be studying, not being obscene in parks," Mr. Chauhan had thundered at a cowering couple on the first raid, one that he had personally conducted to show the staff how to go about it. Mrs. Chauhan narrated this story of her husband's innovative thinking to many people in Ranikhet and told them she was sure he had thought of something similarly novel and exemplary for the insane cowherd.

What happened a few days after the party later became a frightening haze in Puran's head. It was around midday. He had been sitting at the edge of the slope next to his cows. He had tied Gangu, the skittish young one, to a tree; spoken some sense into the wobbly, large-eyed new calf that was unable to draw enough milk from its mother; and then sat back on his haunches, smoking grass. Charu was at some distance, high up in a tall oak tree, cutting fodder with her sickle. She saw the four men approach Puran but returned to cutting oak leaves, not for a moment imagining what they were going to do.

Without warning Puran felt rough hands on his shoulders, harsh voices in his ear, giving him instructions; he could not tell what. He saw nothing but a blur of laughing faces. They thrust him into a jeep. He responded with keening, terrified, animal sounds to its unfamiliar rolling motion as it charged off, taking bends and slopes at high speed. The men slapped him around the ears and shouted, "Arre yaar, shut up! Chootiya! Donkey!" Then they stopped the vehicle, pushed him out, stripped him down to his threadbare underpants, and thrust him under a roadside tap. The icy water clawed at him. They threw a bar of bright green soap toward him. He shivered at the unexpected feel of open air on his near-naked body. It made him ache with the cold. He clutched the soap not knowing what he was expected to do with it.

One of the men who was kinder than the others tried telling him something, then, getting no response, rolled up his sleeves, took the soap from his hand, and lathered him all over while the other men screamed with laughter and slapped their thighs, shouting, "Mammi, Mammi, give him a good wash!" Puran's knees knocked and he clasped his hands over his crotch. A small knot of people had gathered by this time, some of them waiting with empty canisters and buckets for their turn at the tap. Nobody dared raise a protest against the men, among whom they recognized Mr. Chauhan's guard, driver, and chowkidar. Some of the gathered people thought it was a joke. Some said, "Good thing, that crazy Puran really needed a bath."

After it was over, Puran found himself in an unfamiliar yellow shirt, red pullover, and overlarge blue trousers. He babbled in his hollow-sounding voice and darted for his own clothes, which had been flung to the verge in an untidy heap. Before he could reach them, one of the men picked up the clothes on the end of a stick and tossed them into a heap of twigs and leaves and pinecones he had set fire to at the road's edge. The shoes followed. The flames leaped and crackled; the fumes from the burning rubber made people draw back with choking coughs.

Puran let out a strangled yelp. He thrust his hand into the flames to rescue his clothes. The man who had scrubbed him with the soap tried pulling him away, but Puran's small frame was possessed with a new demonic strength. Charu, who had clambered down from her tree and cut across the valley to catch up with the jeep, saw him put his hands into the fire and screamed, "Chacha, Puran Chacha!" and tugged at his new yellow shirt, but she was not strong enough to stop him.

His hands were as charred as the clothes by the time he had retrieved them, but he tore off the yellow shirt and replaced it with his tattered and still-smoking old uniform. Some of it came apart in his hands, but he managed to get it on, though one of its arms and a part of the collar had burned away.

Ama gave me a theatrical account of what had happened, but I did not see Puran for several days after the incident. He took to hiding in the cowshed and whimpering in a corner there, refusing to graze the animals. He slept huddled in the straw, holding a goat kid for warmth. Charu took him food and water and wheedled him into eating, then left to graze the cows and goats alone. Puran only dashed into the forest at dawn to shit when everyone was still asleep. One such morning, he came back, holding an animal in his arms.

He set it down in the courtyard. It stood there, only a little higher than the very tall black rooster that waggled its head at the intruder and circled it, pecking at the ground around its hooves. It was a fawn, exquisite in its delicate beauty, its long eyelashes fencing in pools of brown that took up most of its pointed face and big moist nose. Puran knelt next to it, and groaned and cooed and slapped the sides of his thighs in delight. The fawn would not let anyone else come close. If they did, it moved away with careful dignity. But when Puran cooed, it turned its head in his direction, took a step toward him and even allowed him to touch it, which he did with infinite tenderness. He gathered the creature in his arms after we had inspected it, and disappeared behind the stand of bamboo that blocked the cow stalls from our view. He made the fawn a soft, cushioned bed with piled pine needles and dry grass. He named her Rani, because she was queenly in her disdain and because she was a deer from Ranikhet.

Over the next weeks, we grew accustomed to seeing Puran carrying the fawn like a baby when he went to the forest, her legs poking quill-like out from beneath his arms. He fed her milk in an aluminum bowl and muttered to her day and night. She listened to him with the distant patience of a diva before an acolyte. After a while, having had enough of his adoration, Rani would get up and walk away to nibble at grass. The clerk said, "Puran has a lover at last, a princess no less, and she's playing as hard to get as any pretty woman." Everyone laughed, and shouted, "O, Sanki, shall we arrange a wedding?"

I thought it a rare thing, almost otherworldly, that this barking deer's fawn had come to live among us. I waited every morning to catch a glimpse of her when Puran carried her down the hill for a constitutional before he left with the cattle, which he was now grazing again. It made me late for school some days, I said to Diwan Sahib, but I felt as if my day had not begun until I caught a glimpse of Rani's liquid eyes and languid legs.

"Do you know what drew me to Corbett?" he said to Veer and

me after he had heard me out. "That is, apart from the fact that he habitually described springs with 'gin-clear' water? There's a man after my own heart. Imagine mountain springs gushing gin!" Diwan Sahib poured himself a hefty measure of Bombay Sapphire.

"His tall tales?" Veer said in a tone so caustic that Diwan Sahib looked at him in surprise.

"Oh, come on," Veer said. "That story where he kills a man-eater in a gorge with a gun in one hand and two nightjar eggs in the other? A tiger that munched dozens of people for dinner is killed with one shot, and the eggs survive!"

"You're losing the wood for the trees, Veer," Diwan Sahib said, sounding stricken. "Every adventure story has its exaggerations and embroidery. That doesn't mean all of it is untrue. Look at Corbett's jungle craft, his love of nature."

"If I want fiction, I'll read novels," Veer said, and left the veranda for his room. We heard him banging and thumping inside, then a bellow. "Where the hell does that fool put my laptop charger? Himmat Singh! Himmat! A different place every day. It's just not possible to run an office in this madhouse."

Himmat Singh scuttled past us toward Veer's room as fast as his creaking legs could manage. Silence for a moment or two, and then Veer snapped, "Behind that curtain? Which hiding place will you think of next?"

"I won't be back tonight," he shouted from his room. "Going to Bhimtal for dinner. Sick of Himmat's food. Greasy chicken curry and rice every bloody day." After a pause, we heard a door bang and the fan-belt screech and whine as he started his jeep.

Himmat went past us on his return journey, now with an impassive face. He would not look in our direction but muttered, "All these years nobody could cook better in the Kumaon than Himmat Singh. And now the chicken is greasy. Just from this morning."

Diwan Sahib was crestfallen. "What's the matter with Veer?" He fiddled with his drink, trying to recover his temper. He sounded thoughtful when he began to speak. "Look at Veer, he's the opposite of Corbett," he said. "He climbs the high Himalaya, the mountains give him his living. Yet with all this climbing and walking, what does he know of the forest or mountain, its wildlife or its plants? There's no sense of wonder in him. Lost. Gone, entirely. It's a—what do you call it?—*macho* thing for him: how high, how fast, how many peaks? The other day I pointed out the dog roses to him—the first flowers this year—and he hardly even looked up."

"Maybe he was preoccupied with something else," I said.

"Come, come," said Diwan Sahib, "you aren't the world's most avid botanist, but you noticed those blooms before I said anything to you."

We were quiet for a while, silenced by a shared memory. I knew we were thinking back to my first spring in Ranikhet when Diwan Sahib had found me imprisoned in the dog rose creeper that ran wild along a wall at the Light House. My clothes were caught in the briars, my fingers bleeding from efforts to take out thorns. The more I had tried to move away, the more stuck I had got. There was no help at hand. By the time he came upon me I was almost in tears of annoyance and self-pity. "Damsel in distress," he had said, "and no knight at hand."

Diwan Sahib had extracted me thorn by thorn while I babbled embarrassed explanations: I had merely been trying to smell a flower and pick a few for a vase and get a cutting to plant in my own patch of green and I did not know how or when . . . After a while he had said in the impatient tones I came to know so well, "Could you stop chattering for a minute please, so that I can get you out of here and not be crucified too?" But his eyes were kind and the care with which he took each thorn out made me think, for the first time since Michael's death, that I might one day feel less alone.

Now Diwan Sahib was speaking again, his voice dreamy. "I've always thought about the dog rose that it was wild, unglamorous—the scent is light and a bit sharp, and there are more thorns per flower than on almost any other rose. It is the quintessential beginning rose, no breeding, almost no color, stitched probably by birds a thousand years ago. And yet when you see it, as on that outer wall of this house when it is in full bloom, holding those half-broken stones together—they remind you what is imperishable, real beauty."

He stopped as if taken aback by his own eloquence and said in his everyday tones: "Where was I? Yes, Corbett. Corbett understood the jungle by looking, and he could tell you its story from the sounds he heard. If he heard a chital far off, he would know whether it was calling its young or calling to warn other animals of a tiger. He walked the forests barefoot when he was a boy. He understood the fall of every leaf and the meaning of a cloud—would it bring a hailstorm or rain."

He suddenly seemed to remember it was his nephew he was discussing, and not very favorably. "Who am I to criticize?" he said, finishing his gin in one long swallow. "I taught him nothing when he was a boy. I could have."

"But he said you taught him birdcalls and animal sounds and answered all his wildlife questions," I said. "So you're wrong on both counts. He *is* interested in nature, and you *did* teach him things."

"No, it's different. His interest in nature—it's not what it seems. He is a complicated man, our friend Veer."

Diwan Sahib stopped up his caustic words with another slug of gin and changed the subject. "Corbett was one of a kind because he never lost sight of the humans—and I mean the poor, the hill peasants whose cattle and kin were in danger from wild animals. In my days in Surajgarh, in the Nawab's court, I saw many feudal lords and white colonials who knew a great deal about animals. They could read the jungle almost as well as Corbett. But they couldn't have—wouldn't dream of it—sat and gossiped with peasant women as Corbett did, answering all their nosy questions. None of them stayed up nights with a gun, guarding their crops from rats and birds. Why do you think they called him Carpet Sahib and adored him all over these hills? He would have understood Puran in a second." He laughed bitterly. "He'd have understood that poor idiot's grunts and groans and whimpers and made sense of them. He'd have talked to Puran in his own language."

The afternoon deepened and grew more mellow. A large family of pale-furred langurs alighted on the deodars. Their tails painted elliptical loops in the air as they swooped from tree to tree; the branches swung low with their weight as they landed. The monkeys disagreed with each other, now in soft chatters, now in screeches. Some of the mothers held tiny, ancient-faced babies to their breasts. Dogs barked at them in a frenzy and strained at the chains that tethered them to doorposts. The langurs knew the dogs were tied up and paid them no attention, but when they noticed us they turned their black, human-looking faces toward us, trying to decide if we were a danger.

Until humans came and made anthills out of these mountains, Diwan Sahib was saying, looking up at the langurs, the land had belonged to these monkeys, and to barking deer, nilgai, tigers, barasingha, leopards, jackals, great horned owls, and even to cheetahs and lions. The archaeology of the wilderness consisted of these lost animals, not of ruined walls, terra-cotta amulets, and potsherds. Only now and then did we catch a glimpse of the distant past of our forests, when the shadow of a barasingha's horns flitted through the denser woods, or when a leopard coughed at night. It was extremely rare, though not unknown, for wild animals to trust human beings, Diwan Sahib said. Why should they, when we have destroyed their world? Puran's affinity to animals was a lost treasure. Puran was the sanest of us all, because animals knew whom to trust. They were imbeciles themselves who called Puran half-witted.

THIRTEEN

Veer returned at the end of the month from Dehra Dun and Delhi. He had been away for a fortnight, getting things organized for the next trekking season, which he was going to run from Ranikhet. He came back laden with gifts. There were exotic southern edibles for me: yogurt-marinated chilies, murukkus. He had even brought me a bottle of pickle, made from whole baby mangoes—the kind I had been used to in Hyderabad and had only dreamed of ever since. Had I told him about my past? I flipped through our old conversations, which I could recall virtually down to the last detail. The bottle remained unopened on my table for several days as I tried to get used to it. I picked it up every now and then, my heartbeat quickening each time I examined the label, which said, "Begumpet Pickles: Traditionally Made from a Secret Recipe Handed Down for Generations." I was reminded of the day my father had put one of his palms over my eyes as he led me to a thick-trunked mango tree in our garden to show me my new tree house. I must have been seven years old. A little red ladder led up to the house, and its inner walls were painted with butterflies. It had a toy telephone with a bell that rang. One morning my father had called me down from the tree house saying in an absurd telephone-operator voice: "Hello, hello, phone call for the princess of Begumpet Pickles. She must come down at once to see the new labels on our pickle bottles!"

For Diwan Sahib, Veer had brought an expensive illustrated guide to India's birds that had just come out. I began leafing through it as soon as Diwan Sahib let go of it, to look up a bird I had seen that very morning, when I turned a wooded corner so loud with harsh screeches of magpies that it sounded like the playground at St.

Hilda's when the bell rang at the end of the school day. I had crept closer to see what the birds were agitated about, and a slow, large, brown shape had detached itself from a shadowy branch and sailed off toward a nearby tree, with the magpies in outraged pursuit. It was an enormous owl, made eyeless by the sun. It sat immobile on the second tree, submitting to the screeching and pecking of the many magpies, like some ancient nobleman resigned to his suffering. The prince of darkness, reduced to nothing when his time was past, I told Diwan Sahib in an unthinking attempt at cleverness. He raised an eyebrow, and with a rueful smile murmured, "How true." He reached for the book again, opened it to the right page, and returned it to me. "Maybe this one?" he said. There it was, in glossy color, my owl: a brown wood owl. I snapped the book shut, triumphant. The caption said it was usually almost two feet tall.

"It was exactly that height, it hardly even looks like a bird," I said.

"'After variations in color, form, and melody on a million birds, he was cast on earth, an afterthought.'" Diwan Sahib spoke in the voice he kept for quotations. "Maya, do you know that poem about the owl? And then how did it go? 'When stars their voyages fulfill, attired in light from east to west, cloaked in night he moves to kill' . . . no, I think I missed a verse."

Veer had also brought alcohol: two cases of superior rum and gin. Until Veer came, Diwan Sahib had bought humbler alcohol, a bottle at a time, via the General, who had access to subsidized army supplies. Despite his grand past, Diwan Sahib was no longer wealthy. He had rented out the two cottages on his estate for extra income, but he ended up taking no rent at all from Ama, and for the past two years he had left my own rent checks uncashed. If I protested, he said I was paying him rent in kind, by running his errands and typing his manuscript. He lived an austere life and his bare house contained nothing but worn essentials. I rejoiced now to see him surrounded by creature comforts: a new heater; an imported, feather-light duvet; thermal socks; and good gin and rum. Veer saw to it that Diwan Sahib had the best, and plenty of it. But since Diwan Sahib in turn passed on a bottle or two to me, I had nothing to grumble about.

For himself, Veer had brought a new wristwatch. If you pressed any of the tiny knobs that ran down each side in a row, it turned from watch to compass, altimeter, thermometer, or barometer. The needles that told the time swung up and down to inform us that in the cantonment we were at about 6,100 feet, while St. Hilda's, in the bazaar, was at 5,600 feet. Veer could not stop fiddling with the watch, but when I teased him, saying he was like a child with a new toy, he protested. "This is survival for me. It's work. It's like having a phone or a computer. It'll be my lifesaver in a blizzard on some glacier far from help."

The rhythm of my life changed whenever Veer returned. My days became changeable. I could not tell if he did it on purpose, but very often he drove up the hill from the bazaar just around the time I walked up from St. Hilda's to the factory. His jeep would stop beside me, a look would pass between us, and I would get in. Sometimes he paused to buy hot samosas and we took the longer, more isolated route back home, stopping on the way for a brief picnic. I could talk to him in a way I could with no one else. I knew I would be understood, and knew exactly the conversation we might have when, for example, I said, "I wonder if mules too wear horseshoes."

Our road had been blocked by a line of sweet-faced, slow-witted mules. They were being urged on with much shouting and prodding by their herdsmen. Some of the mules, living up to their reputation, simply refused to move despite being pushed from behind.

"*Do* mules wear shoes or not?" I said. "And what about elephants? Do they wear horseshoes? And if they do, what are the shoes called?"

"A topic most worthy of research," Veer said. "The field could be extended and deepened. What decides it? Is it soft-footedness or hoofedness? Is it the distance traveled, the load carried? Shall we propose it to my uncle as the subject of his next book?"

"What about bullocks? They have to walk miles. Dragging heavy carts."

"Not to forget camels," Veer said in a parody of a formal, professional voice. "And yaks. Have you considered yaks? Nilgai? Zebras? Other than research, I see definite business possibilities here. Maybe you should give up your school and get into making shoes for animals? Might they have standard shoe sizes? Should you outsource the manufacturing to China?"

Once a new teacher at St. Hilda's was in the jeep with us when Veer and I wandered into one such nonsensical conversation. She had wanted to visit me at home—to test out the possibility of a friendship, I suppose. She looked out of the window throughout the drive, saying nothing, and after five minutes I forgot that she was there. After Veer had dropped us off at my door and driven away, she walked through my two rooms picking up this and examining that while I made tea. She paused before the pictures of Michael on my desk, and of my mother, and wanted to know about Michael, about when my mother had died and why I did not return to my father to be with him in his solitary old age. When we had settled down with cups of tea on my veranda, she said, "You talked very funnily with that gentleman in the jeep. Like you're a mad child. And the way he replied—as if you're both eight-year-olds. Are you friends? Or is he a relative of yours?"

She gave me a searching look. I changed the subject as soon as I could. Neither she nor I mentioned a next visit when she left.

One evening soon after coming back from his Delhi trip, Veer unveiled his slide projector. With the first slide, the far end of Diwan Sahib's disused dining room, usually a bare expanse of rough whitewash, turned gold and blue and a sigh went across the room. It was the high-altitude desert of Leh: barren gold earth in moon-surface formations beneath a vast sky. The land looked as raw as on the day of creation. In its folds you could see the shifting of continents, the breaking away of the Indian peninsula from Africa, and hear the cosmic boom as it crashed into Asia and thrust the Himalaya out of the ocean.

Another click and we moved to blue goats somewhere on a mountainside, and traditional stone and slate houses that had stood intact through earthquakes when new concrete structures had tumbled into the dust. Then the wall turned indigo with water and a gasp went around the room. Slopes of snow rose out of the liquid and clung to a very blue sky. "This is Pangong Lake," Veer's voice said from the back of the darkened room, "in Ladakh. I took a group of Swiss bird-watchers there a few years ago." A whir and a click lit up another view of the lake. Ama said, "That's one place in the hills where water won't ever run short," and there was a murmur of laughter until Veer said, "It's salty water." Ama came back with, "No need to spend on salt then, just boil the vegetables in it straight."

The room was dark, crowded with shadows of people: all of the hillside—Charu, Ama, and their three visiting relatives from a remote village, the deaf-mute twins Beena and Mitu, the clerk from the water board and his young son—had assembled to watch the magic of pictures from Veer's just-unpacked projector. Ranikhet had only one battered cinema. It cost money. A free slideshow was a novel treat.

"We went by motorbike from Manali to Ladakh—through the Rohtang Pass, the Baralacha La, and we could even see the Karakoram." The slides moved almost too quickly for us to register details as Veer showed us pictures of prayer wheels, exotic Buddhist dwellings, and the monasteries of Shey, Thikse, Alchi. It was remote, spectacular, and unfamiliar for those of us who had only seen such great heights from a distance. Another click: a view from the Ladakh plateau of barren land far below. Veer said, "That is China; half of Pangong Lake falls in China. Nobody is allowed up that close to the boundary, but I knew someone in the army. We left our motorbikes and trekked all over Ladakh and reached here in the end."

"So if we start walking today in Ranikhet, one day we will reach China?" This was Ama.

Diwan Sahib said, "You'd get a bullet in your head when you crossed over." Diwan Sahib had no patience with Ama's garrulity and what he called her "animal husbandry department." Every so often he had futile arguments with her over her goats lunching on the lilies and marigolds that still survived in his garden.

"Arre, Ama," the clerk said, "your forefathers and mine walked to China many times. That's what my great-grandfather told me. He went twice with some firanghis in the time of the British."

There was a babble of voices. "Your great-grandfather was a coolie," Ama said. "What was he doing in China?" Himmat Singh gave a series of phlegmy coughs and struggled up a thought: "I have heard they eat tigers in China. And dogs. They also eat dogs."

"Aah, but then what do the leopards in China eat if the people eat the dogs?" the clerk wanted to know. They laughed. Charu, who had not spoken so far, said, "I would kill any leopard or Chinese who laid a finger on my Bijli."

"That useless dog has a magic life," Ama said. "So many dogs get eaten. But this one roams all over in the dark and next morning he's sitting right there, by the stove, waiting for a roti to fall."

I sat back, warm in my shawl, feet tucked into it, a woolly bundle listening to voices eddying over me. Diwan Sahib began to talk about the Great Game—the intrigues and spying, the explorers sent in disguise over the undiscovered massifs, passes, peaks, and ravines of the Himalaya by the Russians and the British looking to gain control of them. The names of early travelers fell from his lips like those of old friends: George Moorcroft crossed the fast-flowing Sutlej on the inflated skins of buffaloes and traveled disguised as a Hindu sadhu to search for the goat whose wool made pashmina shawls. Nain Singh Rawat surveyed the Himalaya to map it accurately for the first time. He was a pandit from our region, the Kumaon, said Diwan Sahib, and he reached Lhasa, Xinjiang, Nepal, and China not once but three times in the 1860s. His brother Kishen Singh Rawat went to Lhasa too. At that time nobody even knew exactly where Lhasa was.

How did they do that, Charu said in wonderment, on foot? To which Ama replied, impatient, "That is what was his bijniss. Other people run shops and offices; his work was to measure distances. Just like us: don't we walk up and down the hills after cows day after day in rain and sun and snow? Can a city person do that?"

"You illiterate woman," Himmat Singh said. "Walking Ranikhet's slopes is not like walking through the mountains to China."

"They could walk for days," Diwan Sahib said. "Look at Corbett. When he was hunting the Chowgarh tiger, he went without food for about two days, and he was quite comfortable sleeping in the forks of trees."

"Maybe he thought an underfed man would be less appealing to a hungry tiger," Veer said. "And a lighter weight on the forks of those trees."

I thought Diwan Sahib would lose his temper this time. Why was Veer attacking Corbett again? It was childish, the way he tried to antagonize Diwan Sahib. But Diwan Sahib went on as if Veer had not spoken and I relaxed in my shawl again. "Those people were made differently from us," he said. Nain Singh Rawat had to use exactly two thousand footsteps per mile, using a rosary with a hundred beads to keep count. Because the Chinese would have executed him if they found him, he traveled dressed as a lama, turning his prayer wheel, in which he had hidden a compass.

For the moment everyone was too busy talking to remember they were in the middle of a slideshow and that there were many more slides to see. Veer was behind me, at the back of the room. If I turned an imperceptible fraction, I could glimpse him outlined against the faint light that came in from the veranda through a murky old glass pane, could sense his eyes upon me in the darkness. I curled deeper into my shawl, my arms holding my shoulders close. He had bought the murukkus because he had heard me saying how much I missed them—I had said it only once, in passing. But he had remembered—and the pickle, which by some miracle was from my father's factory. I wished the room were empty and his show for me alone.

Veer fiddled with the projector, and a new picture flickered on the wall, turning it gray and white and very cold. My eyes, half-shut with daydreaming, snapped open. The slide showed a woman looking up into a camera pointed at her from above. She was bent under the weight of her rucksack and her face was etched with pain. Snow had settled like white trim on the purple of her anorak's hood. The snow-covered slope she was climbing fell behind her into gray-green water half covered with splintered sheets of ice. Flakes of snow were sprinkled all over the photograph. Icy slopes rose out of the water on the far bank.

Veer was saying, "It was freezing and windy that day. This woman almost slipped and fell into the water just after I took this photograph.

She was already feeling ill and the altitude made her worse. It's over sixteen thousand feet. People can start bleeding from the nose. Their skin might peel off. They get terrible headaches and frostbite. My ear and missing finger—that's from frostbite. Frostbite means your blood has frozen—literally."

Every head in the room swiveled toward Veer as if they had not noticed his deformed ear and missing finger all these days. He changed the slide to turn them back to the wall.

I did not stop Veer to ask him the name of the place. I did not need to. I knew it was Roopkund. That was the water beside which Michael had frozen to his death. I scoured the pictures that snapped onto the wall one by one. A different angle each time: close-ups, long shots. Water and ice, ice and water. Lead-colored sky. Sheer sides of brown rock and white snow rising from sheets of ice. I examined every inch with frantic concentration in the seconds before one picture made way for another. I had never seen Michael's dead body. His death felt more a disappearance, still unreal, leaving behind a smoke-like vestige of hope. He was there on those slopes. He had to be. I waited for Michael's blue and red-hooded jacket to appear. Then he would step away from the wall and into the room.

Long ago, when I was a little girl, I used to believe that radios contained people. No more than a few inches tall, but in every way human, those people were forever imprisoned within the big brown and black radio that stood on my father's desk. It had a large dial, and round, serrated knobs for switches. When it was turned on, the panel inscribed with frequencies glowed with a yellow light that made the radio look like a little house. If someone took it apart, the singers on *Binaca Geet Mala* would step out onto the table and talk to me.

I felt icy winds curl around my fingertips, my toes, my face, even my heart. I was trembling. I thought I would cry out in pain and fear. I buried my face in my shawl and stopped my ears under it. My throat had wound itself into a tight knot.

"What is that, is it a waterfall?" someone in the room, who still had a voice, asked. Someone else said, "See how the falling water has frozen!" I inched out of my shawl again. The scene had changed to a herd of white sheep on a meadow enameled with flowers. Veer muttered, "Wrong sequence," and then there was another stretch of water on the wall, a glassy expanse that reflected the sides of the gorge within which it flowed away into the horizon. At the banks were the frilly white edges of waves frozen in mid-surge. Charu went excitably to the wall to get a closer look and everybody shouted to her to get out of the way as the immense shadow of her head, caught in the projector's beam, obscured the ice-sheeted river and its frozen waves.

Something snapped into place in my head. Roopkund was not a river. Roopkund was a lake. Lakes did not have waves. Lakes did not flow. I found my voice at last and said to Veer, "This sequence of pictures, it's not—it's not Roopkund, is it?"

"You obviously haven't heard a word of my long-winded commentary. Why do I bother? It's the Zanskar River. In Kashmir. Why would you think it's Roopkund? That's a lake, not a river." He closed a box with an irritable snap.

The spell was broken; people began to stir. Beena and Mitu scrambled up. They were to leave early the next morning for Varanasi to start a new life at a convent. Diwan Sahib waved them toward him and placed rolls of money in their hands and closed their fists. He patted their heads when they dived downward to touch his feet. "Enough, go now, go," he said. "Himmat Singh, refill my glass. From the new bottle Veer Sahib brought from Delhi." The clerk scurried after Himmat into the kitchen in the hope of a stolen drink.

Ama stood up with an abrupt push of her chair. "Traveling is all very well," she said. "But it's for people with money to burn and nothing better to do but eat, drink, and idle. Why go walking up and down hills for pleasure? We do that every day for work. Charu, come on, we have to go. Puran will have set fire to the cowshed by now."

* * *

That night, after dinner, Veer collected his flashlight and stick to walk me to my cottage. At the front door we saw that the light outside the veranda was falling in a shower of tiny golden drops. He went back in to find his umbrella, big enough for two in that kind of rain. My cottage was not far—maybe five hundred yards—but the slope was thick with trees, and leopards sometimes lay in wait for stray dogs or forgotten goats; it was not wise for me to walk down alone so late in the evening, he said.

We walked slower, I knew, than we needed to. By the time we reached my door, the drizzle had stopped and every night scent was deeper and muskier in the dampness. We stood outside, chatting of this and that in voices softer than usual. Apart from a faint television noise from the postman's house and a pressure cooker that hissed once every other minute, there was hardly a sound. Above our heads the huge ivory trumpets of datura glowed like dimmed lamps in the starlight. We were swathed in their heavy scent; the flowers were so low that they brushed my face. Veer touched one of the flowers, then looked at me and said, "So beautiful."

I felt something leap inside me. "And deadly," I said. "Just like those pretty foxgloves. Never go by appearances."

I could not see his face clearly in the starlight alone, but he seemed to frown and turn away. He switched his flashlight on again, as if he were about to leave.

"It's what Diwan Sahib says: we saw valleys covered in foxgloves when we went for walks before," I said, not ready to confront my empty house yet. "I wanted to pick them because they were so pretty, and he told me how poisonous the prettiest plants and mushrooms in the hills can be."

Not far from Ranikhet, Diwan Sahib had said, during one of those long walks he and I went on in my first two years, a woman and her child were poisoned by wild mushrooms cooked at home. They ate the mushrooms around a table with five others. Nobody could later remember which of them had eaten the dish with the mushrooms, and which had not. That night, the child's face turned blue and he began to shiver and vomit. When it was almost dawn, he had a shuddering fit, his muscles relaxed, and he stopped breathing. The mother became bloated as if she had been dredged out days after drowning. She would have exploded if pricked with a pin. They lived in a remote hamlet, and the roads connecting it to the world had been washed away in monsoon rain. No hospital could be reached, though she lived three days more.

Why was nobody else at the table poisoned by those mushrooms? Diwan Sahib said it reminded him of a curious, very old man at the Nawab of Surajgarh's court, who had been there since the Nawab's father's time, and who wore brown clothes and a green pugree and had a face as cavernous as a starving man's. He walked long hours in the forest and came back with cloth bags full of plants that he disappeared with into his laboratory, which was a quack's den filled with glass flasks and Bunsen burners and test tubes and vernier calipers, and where, in the instant when the door opened a crack as he slid in, the smells that trickled out were of a kind that existed only in hallucinations and nightmares, so that when he shut the door you wondered if you had imagined them. It was rumored that he manufactured poisons in that den, and the rumor was strengthened by the inexplicable decline or death from time to time of people at the court who had fallen foul of the Nawab. The Nawab had claimed that the man made medicine, Diwan Sahib said, but the line between medicines and poisons is finely drawn, and this very foxglove, so poisonous and so beautiful, in the correct quantity, produced digitalis, which was medicine for troubles of the heart. "Not devastated hearts," he had said, laughing, "like yours or mine, Maya, for that there is no medicine but death, which too the foxglove can provide."

By now, despite the chill of the spring night, we were sitting on the steps that led to my front door, inches apart. I could feel the warmth of Veer all along my legs. Twice, by accident, our shoulders touched, and he did not move away. The scops owl began its low, periodic call, a sound so muted that it emphasized how quiet the hillside had fallen. The pressure cooker had stopped hissing. The clerk's television had been put to sleep. I saw a curtain flutter at Charu's house. It was sure to be Ama, eavesdropping. "It's late," I said, getting up. "I have been talking on and on. You should go." The clerk too could see us from his cottage. They would exchange notes tomorrow, while grazing the cows or filling water. "That Teacher-ni . . . ," Ama would say, before she began embroidering her tale.

Veer saw me looking at Ama's windows. "Yes, it's late, and the Ranikhet town crier is busy collecting material." He got up as well and, to my surprise, put an arm around my shoulders and gave me a quick hug. His chin briefly came down and rested in my hair. And then he was gone, the beam from his flashlight flickering and leaping like a large firefly as he walked away. A few nights before, when he and I had been walking downhill just as we had today, we had seen five dancing fireflies a few feet away and stopped, flashlight switched off, and for a time that was both as long as eternity and as short as a second, we had stood gazing at the tiny globules of light racing each other, being snuffed out by bushes, then appearing again.

I wrapped my shawl tighter and strolled around my house, brushing past geranium leaves that unloosed clouds of lemony perfume. I thought back to the morning that Michael had left on his last journey. I had gone with him to the station to see him off and we stood on the platform, our hips touching, our shoulders touching, as long as he dared, until departure was announced and the chaos of people on the platform emptied into waving arms, and the train began pulling out. I said, "Go, go, you'll miss it!" He held me close for an instant, kissed the top of my head, then loped off into the train. That was the last time I saw him, and the last time any man had touched me—until this evening.

The humps of hills all around the spur on which I stood were shadows. After a while, the lights at Ama's and at the clerk's went off. In the absolute darkness the sky felt larger, the stars came down, the trees grew blacker. The lopsided half moon was trapped in a cage of branches. Now that I was alone again, a corner of the terror I had felt during the slideshow edged its way back. That woman's pain-filled face, the ice, the green water—it was not Roopkund, it was a river in Kashmir, but how different could Roopkund be? I felt a shiver go down the back of my neck from some fear I could not define. I was reminded of the way Corbett said he sensed the presence of a man-eating tiger even if he had not seen one: "I felt I was in danger," he wrote, "and that the danger that threatened me was on the rock in front of me. The fact that I had seen no movement did not in any way reassure me—the man-eater was on the rock, of that I was sure." I had typed three of Diwan Sahib's drafts in which those lines appeared and they were engraved on my mind. Corbett's words had never felt so palpable. Now I understood what he meant, and the apprehension was all the more powerful for being illogical.

I looked up at the stretching limbs of the deodars. The trees were vastly high. Only eagles reached their very top and they told nobody what they saw from there. Each fringed branch was almost large enough to be a tree on its own. For a dizzy moment, it felt as if I were the one human left alive, glued by gravity alone to the edge of a spinning globe, only just keeping myself from being flung off.

FOURTEEN

That night, I had a vivid dream in which skulls rolled down white slopes and fell into pools of green water. I saw a woman hooded in an anorak, clawing her way up a snow slope. Someone was photographing her as she struggled, saying, "Smile, say cheese?" The voice was Veer's. Then the woman's face turned into Michael's and suddenly he was falling, toppling over the edge of the slope, and as he fell through the white space toward the water, I felt myself falling too, flailing, unmoored, weightless, helpless, until I woke up sweating under my blankets.

It was long past the time for the army bugles. The sun was blazing through the window. It was a holiday. I could hear children playing and the clerk's boom box pumping out music with a bass beat that resounded across the hillside. Ama's side of a conversation was taking place in shouts just below my window. Someone had wound barbed wire around my head and set fire to it. I staggered down to the kitchen to make myself coffee. How much rum had I drunk the night before? One at Diwan Sahib's. And did I have one, or was it two, after Veer left?

I sat at the dining table with my coffee and a painkiller, and noticed a familiar piece of paper on it, weighed down with a jam jar: Diwan Sahib's electricity bill. He had asked me to deal with it—that was a week ago, and now it was late, so there would be a fine. How much? I looked at the bill—an extra thirty rupees. It was not a lot, and I missed the due date almost every month. But today it made me feel as if someone had just tightened that wire round my head. I covered my aching eyes with my palms and felt them dampen with tears. I was always in trouble with Miss Wilson, my students failed their exams, my house was a mess of old and useless things because I could not bring myself to throw anything away, every month I paid late fines out of my tiny salary because I put things off. The two people most precious to me, my mother and Michael, were dead, and my father was growing old alone in that vast, echoing house in Hyderabad while I was alone in mine, thousands of miles away. Yet he and I, equally implacable, could not find a way back to each other. I put my head on the table and broke into sobs.

After a while I picked my head up, swallowed my mud-cold coffee, and decided I would visit Michael's grave. If I went to his grave and talked to him I would calm down and the knot in my throat, which had come to live there since the evening before, would dissolve. I would pay that overdue bill on the way.

I walked down to the electricity office by various shortcuts past the backs of people's houses. Past Tiwari, the plumber, who raised his hands in a namaste; past three lumbering olive-green army trucks, each one as big as my bedroom; past the sign that said "Military Area, You May be Questioned"; past the soldiers who stood at attention all day at the gates of the officers' mess; past Mr. Qureshi, who rolled down his car's window and told me a long story about how he was driving around house-hunting for relatives who had been given an eviction notice. "It is impossible, there's not even a tin shed to be found, Maya. You'd find gold hidden under a tree in Ranikhet more easily than a place to live in." I tried to hurry away from Pande, the hobbling old advocate, but he stopped me and said with a worried look, "Where to, Maya Mam, where to? Tell me, did you know there is a London in Canada also? Do you think that somewhere else in the world there is another Ranikhet? What is real in this world, Mam, can you tell me? Till last week I thought Timbuctoo was not a real place. Then my grandson—he is only seven, you know, and this little one already knows much more than me!—he says, 'No, Dadaji, it's a city in China!' Child is the grandfather of man, I feel it truer every day."

By the time I had paid the bill, reached the low wall that crumbled around the graveyard, and walked under the stone archway toward Michael, my headache had turned into hammer blows. I reached the grave in a mist of pain, hardly able to open my eyes or see straight.

I thought I had walked by mistake to the wrong grave and began to stumble away, when I stopped and looked at the headstone again. It was the right one, of course—low, dark, square, inscribed with Michael's name, and the words "ever after"—a modest stone with no decoration. At this moment, it had one broken bottle on it and another empty bottle propped against it. Shattered glass lay all around the grave. The day lilies I had planted had been dug out and thrown aside, their long leaves wilted, their light-starved tubers helpless under the sun. Some of the plants had buds on them, some had shriveled flowers.

The day I buried that tin of ashes there and planted the bulbs, I had had nobody for company but Miss Wilson. She had not thought it worthwhile to summon the church gravediggers for my small tin, so she had stood by, reading aloud from her Bible, her dull voice reducing the beautiful words to monotonous rubble as I dug with a kutala, an implement whose curved blade I was then unused to. It had been a cold day, with a clammy, gray wind that swept through the pines around the cemetery. The earth was frost-hardened. Nearby was a nettle bush that set my skin on fire if I brushed against it. Miss Wilson interrupted her reading occasionally to say, "Deeper, deeper. At least three feet." Her double chins wobbled, and the large mole under her right eye, which sprouted hair, seemed to twitch. She sucked on her buckteeth, making a kissing sound as she read. Though I knew she was there out of compassion and was trying to help, I felt a concentration of hatred for her such as I had not felt before for anyone. The burial had taken more than an hour—she had noted the time on the round gold watch she wore on her right wrist. It had belonged to her maternal grandfather from Kozhikode, she told me that morning; he was once the collector and this was his retirement present. At intervals she said, "It is eleven. This watch has never been wrong in *six-tee* years. You have taken half an hour already. We should have brought the gardener with us after all. I thought you'd be able to dig a simple hole. I would do it faster." But she did not once offer to take over the digging.

In a heart-stopping flash the thought crossed my mind that the tin with Michael's ashes had been dug out and flung away as the lilies had been. It must have rusted by now, or disintegrated altogether. What if vandals had thrown it down the valley? I went this way and that in a panic, looking for the tin, then decided I was being irrational, that the tin must still be where I had put it: three feet down, as Miss Wilson had insisted. The vandals had not dug so deep, I could see that. I began to gather the lily bulbs from all around the grave to replant them.

* * *

On my way back from the graveyard, when I reached Mall Road, I saw Mr. Chauhan standing at the fork of the road leading down toward the Light House. I was tired and aching; my clothes were filthy and my fingernails black and split from returning the lily bulbs to their places with my bare hands. Mr. Chauhan did not seem to notice my disheveled condition. He was studying one of his signs, which said, "Don't Drive Rash, You Will Crash." The yellow paint still glistened wetly on the dark rock face. He swayed back on his heels and tilted his head for a different view, caressing his thin mustache with a smile of satisfaction. I had not noticed the purple birthmark by his ear before. It was shaped like Australia.

When he saw me, he smiled. "Ah, Mam, as you see, I'm doing what I can for our town. I think it has potential, but nobody has known how to tap it. This could be a great tourist destination. I am going to beautify it from top to bottom before the Regimental Reunion in November."

"What needs beautifying is the graveyard," I said. "Have you ever been there?" I knew I sounded short, but could not help my tone.

"These signs, you see," Mr. Chauhan went on, as if I had not spoken. "Daily you will pass them, without thinking you will read them, and slowly—what will happen?" He smiled in triumph. "They will start altering your mind. You will begin to think differently. I don't mean you, of course, you are a good citizen. I mean all these . . ." He waved an arm over all the landscape. "All these wretched villagers, their dirty children . . . they have to learn." The grass along the side of the road was strewn with plastic cups, beedi wrappers, and deflated foil packets that had once contained fries and gutka. He poked at the rubbish with a stick and said, "No civic sense, I tell you, none. This road was swept only last week." Then he spotted Charu at a distance, slapping the rump of a cow to make it move. Instead it raised its tail and let out great dollops of dung that steamed in the cool air.

"That is *exactly* what I mean," Mr. Chauhan said. "Disgusting, disgusting! Is this what an army cantonment should be filled with? Dung?"

Charu threw us a guilty look over her shoulder, as if she had overheard Mr. Chauhan, and harried her animals to make them go down the hillside, out of sight. She gave me a quick, apologetic smile as she passed us and tugged at Bijli's collar to make him follow her. He had other plans.

"I went to the graveyard," I said, trying to control the tremor in my voice. "And not only was my husband's grave vandalized, I saw that the wings of the angels on one of the colonial graves have been broken—smashed deliberately. Many of the graves had garbage on them. The wall around the graveyard is broken."

Mr. Chauhan said, "Do you know what I think the real problem of the Indian state is?" He paused for effect. "We are too soft, far too soft on everything. Just as we are with terrorists. They keep dropping bombs here and there and what do we do about it? Nothing. And here? Same thing, different situation. All antisocials. These cows, dumping dung, is anyone able to stop them?"

He was startled into silence by a voice exclaiming in a foreign accent, "Oh *look*! Another foraging party!" We had not noticed the bearded man who had stationed himself on the grassy slope below, with binoculars round his neck. He was pointing them skyward at a flock of passing birds. A backpacked woman stood next to him, staring up through an identical pair of binoculars.

Mr. Chauhan lowered his voice to a hiss. "What sort of impression does the tourist get of Ranikhet when he arrives expecting a neat and clean army town and sees all this garbage? In foreign countries I have heard people have to pick up even their dog's . . . waste from roads."

"Mr. Chauhan, I am trying to tell you something," I said. "A genuine problem."

Maybe I was shouting, because he said in a soft, dangerous voice, "I heard you, madam, please do not raise your voice. People throw rubbish everywhere, it is a big problem in Ranikhet, not only Ranikhet, all of India. I have seen it in Lucknow, Bareilly, Dehra Dun—wherever I have been posted. Foreigners rightly remark that India is a country ruined by us Indians. We requisition trash cans, but nobody uses them. As for the old graves, and angels' wings, even stone has a lifespan, and these are two hundred years old. And your late husband's grave? I will send someone to check. We will look into it. We have correct procedures for everything."

I was about to retort with something acid when a pleased expression spread over his face. The army band had just struck up. The first notes of brass music were rolling over the hills. Sounds of instruments being tuned reached our ears. A baritone voice joined them, with a line from a sentimental Hindi film song. *"Ek akela is shahar mein, raat mein aur dopahar mein,"* the voice warbled mournfully. "Alone in this city, all alone, at night and through the afternoon."

Mr. Chauhan stood with his eyes closed in pleasure until the song was interrupted by the General's barks. The General rounded the bend, thwacking Bozo with his Naga spear in an effort to stop the dog from tugging at his leash to get at Bijli, who was growling back from a parapet across the road. "What is the reason, Bozo?" the General demanded as he pitted his wispy strength against his dog's muscle. "I fail to understand. *What is the reason?*" He glimpsed the bird-watching couple and called out to them: "Hello there! Spotted anything yet?"

"Before the regimental reunion," Mr. Chauhan said, walking toward the General with a wide smile, "I will make it all new. This town will be the star of the hills, that is my promise."

* * *

I gave up on Mr. Chauhan and headed for the Light House. I was earlier than usual and Diwan Sahib, expecting no visitors at that time, was sitting in his garden practicing birdcalls. Once a year, he went to St. Hilda's and put on a performance, educating the children about forest sounds and signs. He had done so for the past sixteen years and it was now part of the school's Annual Day celebrations. The assembly hall would ring with his leopard and barking deer and owl calls while the children sat in rows on the floor, shrieking in delight and terror. He had got the idea from Corbett, who used to put on similar performances at schools in Nainital. I was not able to make sense of it in someone as irritable and solitary as he was, but he took it seriously and began practicing months ahead, so I stood still, waiting for him to finish. After a long while he noticed me, and stopped a chital's call midway with a frown.

I handed him the receipt for his electricity bill, and his newspaper.

He looked at the receipt and said, "Today? You were supposed to pay it two weeks ago. It's long overdue, there must be a fine."

My knees and fingernails were sore. The cloud of my headache hovered as if it would return at the least inkling of distress. Diwan Sahib's tone made my head throb. "Not two weeks ago, one," I said, and then, for no reason that I could think of, I lied. "I did pay it then, just forgot to give you the receipt." Diwan Sahib raised a skeptical eyebrow.

"It's paid, isn't it? That's all that matters."

I turned away to go, without waiting for tea or our newspaper session. He said, "What is it? Why do you look as if you walked into a tree?"

Diwan Sahib could be perverse. When you least thought you would find sympathy he could be kindness personified. Yet when you felt battered, afraid, uncertain, he might turn it all into a joke. It was with some reluctance that I told him what had happened at the graveyard. A mocking smile began curling his lips before I had finished.

He said, "A few drunks go berserk and you report it as if the end of the world has come. They must have been college boys, looking for a lonely place to go wild in . . . and the bazaar booze shop is down the road from that graveyard."

"It is not down the road from the booze shop, the bazaar is two kilometers away."

"What is two kilometers these days? Boys have motorbikes."

"It's not a few drunks," I said. "Don't you read the papers? Haven't you noticed how missionaries are being threatened and beaten up? I told you how those election workers threatened me and Miss Wilson. The poor woman was terrified."

"The poor woman! You're constantly complaining, 'Agnes this, Agnes that, Agnes needs her vocal cords changed, no wonder Jesus didn't want Agnes Wilson for His bride.'" Diwan Sahib spoke in high-voiced imitation of my own. "So why is your heart bleeding for her now?"

"That's different. This is serious, I'm sure this is another way of giving the Church a message." I was stumbling over my words in my anger and tried to slow down. "I've noticed things going wrong there over the last few months. Most of the old gravestones have chunks missing. Some of the writing on them is wiped off. That beautiful angel on little Charlie Darling's grave is headless."

"Why have graves, is what I say. The man's dead and you hold on to his bones. It's all molecules." Diwan Sahib looked sullen and obstinate. "Throw the ashes into a fast-flowing river. Or scatter them in the air. Much more poetic."

"That's neither here nor there," I said in as sharp a voice as I dared. "That graveyard is sacred to some people."

Diwan Sahib refused to take me seriously. He poured himself another drink, topped it carefully with an equal amount of water, and flung himself back into his chair. "Chandan and Puran and Joshi and Tiwari," he said. "I suppose they're all hiding country bombs in their haystacks and shops and cowsheds to go and attack your precious school and church and jam factory, one of these days. And your chaiwallah at the temple, who spots a leopard for every cup of tea he sells? He may be manufacturing gunpowder boiled in leopard blood as we speak. Look for another job, Maya, while there is time. And go back to your maiden name."

FIFTEEN

By the end of April the peaks were hidden behind a dust haze that rose from the plains, and on the rare early mornings when they became visible we could see bald gray stone on ridges where snow should have been. Down in the plains, we heard, the hot winds had begun to blow. Here it was cool in the evening, but the grass was yellow, the earth dusty far too early in the summer, and the sun was so intense that it tore through layers of clothing like fire. Water ran dry in the pipes, garden plants wilted. If the sky showed signs of clouding up, Ama cautioned Charu not to bring in the washed clothes from the line or the red chilies that were drying in the sun. Her notion of rain was that it was a sentient creature that enjoyed wetting things put out to dry. It would lose interest and saunter off if the clothes and the chilies were moved to a sheltered place.

Charu and Puran began to go further and further afield with the cows, having exhausted all the grass closer to home. Despite the heat, Puran neither bathed nor changed out of his sweater and cap. When he passed, the air around him hung with a sour unbreathable smell that was a putrid compound of sweat, hay, milk, and cattle. These days I moved away if I saw him approach.

Charu and Puran would leave the house early and come back late in a flurry of cowbells and dog barks. Bijli was still an overgrown puppy more inclined to play than shepherd. He leaped before the goats, his front paws slapping the ground, tail furiously wagging. If the goats approached to butt him in response, he took it as encouragement and raced around them barking, sending them up slopes in bleating disarray. Charu's grandmother said, "This is not a dog, it's an ass. How will it ever look after the cattle? Even the leopard thinks it's not worth eating."

I had heard a leopard calling the night before, a hoarse sound much like the sawing of wood. It was very close to the house—I smelled its scent, like that of burned hair, and buried myself deeper in my pillow. I wished I had never read Corbett. The leopards in Corbett's stories were all natives of our hills, and short of opening locks on doors were able to enter almost any house at will, with the kind of intelligence and stealth that nobody imagined animals possessed. Had I remembered to lock the doors downstairs? Were the windows properly bolted? After tossing and turning I got up and checked and then tried to return to sleep again. The next day I heard that the General had almost lost Bozo to the leopard; miraculously, the dog had escaped with a gash on its shoulder.

The day after that I heard Charu's call for Gouri coming and going, growing louder, then fainter, louder again, hopeful, questioning, despairing, as afternoon purpled into dusk. She wandered up and down every slope that I could see from my windows. The brass bells on the other cows tinkled as they came homeward from the valleys, but Gouri did not appear.

By dusk, a knot of people had gathered outside and the clerk shook his head and pulled on a beedi saying, "Call the girl back, it's no use." He bent over the fire outside his house and poked at it. "Take every care you can, but when the leopard wants something he gets it."

"What do you expect?" Ama said. "We live in the middle of a forest."

"The other day," the taxi driver said, "we were standing by the road—at just this time—four of us. And Lachman's dog was sniffing about right there, two feet from us. Before we knew it, a leopard had come out of the bushes and snatched it away. We chased it with sticks, we shouted and screamed, but it was too quick."

"And?"

"And, what do you know? It dropped the dog! But by then the dog had died—maybe of fright—but it had a deep wound, dripping so much blood, the road went red. Half its fur and skin was torn off; you could see right down to its bones near the head."

"That Lachman had paid five hundred rupees for it. And he'd been feeding it a boiled egg every day for the past year. Said it was a valuable guard dog."

The other man smirked. "The bastard didn't have money for his wife and children, but he made sure the dog got a boiled egg each day!"

"Boiled!" they said again, and held each other, shaking with laughter. "Not even raw, boiled!"

Ama snarled, "Why don't you get out and help the girl hunt for her cow instead of sitting here telling silly stories?" She hitched up her sari and creaked down the slope with a long stick in her hand, shaking her head at them and muttering.

Charu found Gouri at dawn the next day, in a deep gully. The cow had fallen in awkwardly. Two of its legs jutted at such an odd angle they were certainly broken, and it had a deep wound near its neck. It was alive, but it lay with a still, glazed look, not making a sound. The bell at its neck was red with blood as were the white patches on its mostly dark body.

Everyone gathered around the cow. Charu held out torn pieces of roti to it, eyes streaming tears, saying, "Gouri Joshi, eat something." She tried to stem the flow of blood from the wound on its neck by stuffing her dupatta against it, but the cloth was soaked in a moment.

"We should call the vet," I said. "I'll go."

"That animal doctor will be no good now; it's too late," the clerk said. There was a general murmur of assent.

"If anyone can get it out of there, it's the Ohjha," Ama said. "Send someone to call him. But will he come?"

Just three days before, Charu's grandmother had been holding forth to me about how the Ohjha loathed the new vet. The new vet was a local man who spoke a Pahari dialect, and this had won people's hearts—the earlier vets had all been strangers from the plains. The new man had cut into the Ohjha's livelihood. Unlike the vet, the Ohjha was not employed by the hospital. Unlike the vet, the Ohjha had fulminated to Charu's grandmother, there would be no food on his plate or drink in his glass if sick animals stopped being brought to him.

The government paid the vet every month, regardless of how many animals he treated, but who paid the Ohjha? He had to make his way in the world by his own devices. "There he was, sitting in the middle of all the junk at the Kabariwallah's," said Ama, "shaking his trident and screaming into his glass of booze, 'I'll kick that crazy bastard, the vet, I'll kick him in the balls!' I told him, 'Forget all that, old man, your bijniss is going to go *thup,* your days are numbered.' I laughed at him. He won't come now for me."

"Why won't he come? He needs the work," the taxi driver said. He got into his cab and drove off to Mall Road to spread the word: anyone who saw the Ohjha was to tell him to come at once.

Ama said, "You don't believe any of this, Teacher-ni, you city people, but someone's put a spell on that cow, or an evil wind is blowing curses over it. Or else why did it wander so far this time?"

"Yes, only the Ohjha can do something," the clerk nodded in somber agreement.

I said, "Don't let Charu stay out there all night, it's too cold and too dangerous." But her grandmother, realizing it would be pointless, did not try calling Charu back home. That evening, she took down a stack of rotis for the cow and food for the girl, helped her make a fire, then hobbled back up. She would do all Charu's share of the work herself and ask her no questions, however long the cow remained alive; and who could tell, perhaps Charu's devotion would work a miracle.

The Ohjha came the next afternoon. He lit a fire near Gouri Joshi and threw all kinds of things into it. Little boys from the neighborhood were made to run up and down the hill many times to cater to the Ohjha's demands: Ghee! Turmeric! Some uncooked rice! A lemon. Green chilies! A piece of yellow cloth. And so on. He waved his peacock feathers over the cow, chanted, swayed, and shrieked again and again, shaking his head so hard it looked as if it would snap and fall off his neck. Then he went still and quiet. After an interval when everyone waited, respectful and expectant, he gave his verdict: "When the time comes to return to the world of ghosts and spirits, nobody can stand between death and life." He shook out his robes and feathers, picked up his trident, and walked away. By then, he had deposited charms all over the hillside, eaten three meals at Ama's house, and pocketed twenty rupees.

Charu remained with the cow all the next day and the day after that. During the day, between grazing their other cattle, Puran came and sat by the cow, stroking it, pressing his own concoction of ground-up herbs to its wounds, and muttering his gibberish into its ear. For some of the time that Puran was there the cow's eyes appeared to flicker with a suggestion of life, its pain seemed briefly soothed. Then it sank back into a stupor.

Charu had another visitor too. Every evening, when there was no danger of other people, Kundan Singh came stealing down the slope to the forest and sat with Charu till it was time to serve dinner at Aspen Lodge. He collected wood to make a fire near her to keep leopards away. He bought noisy little fireworks from the market to frighten off animals. He went away at mid-evening to resume work and then, after he had served dinner, and his duties were done, he came back with a flashlight, down the dark slopes, weaving between tree trunks and brambles. He brought whatever food he had been able to squirrel away from the hotelier's dinner and laid open steel lunch boxes for her to eat from. He wanted Charu to have the best bits, things she had never eaten: meatballs the first day, chicken the next, then fried rice and egg curry. After eating, they held each other close by the fire, wrapped in a blanket thick enough for the chill of summer nights. Only when sunlight crept up over the ridge did he leave to serve the hotelier and his wife their bed-tea and Marie cookies.

Kundan Singh thought he might never be as happy again, despite Charu's tears, the gasping sobs that interrupted her numbed silence, and just below them, the pain-filled eyes of Gouri Joshi, which on the fourth day clouded over and closed.

SIXTEEN

My house was very small. It had two rooms, and a tiny kitchen with two doors. One of the doors opened toward a rock face that in summer was covered with wildflowers. There was so little space between the rock face and the door that you had to walk between them sideways. The larger room, on the ground floor, led out to a north-facing veranda where I had hung geranium overhead that trailed pink and red when it flowered. Every afternoon, after I finished with the school and factory and had had my tea with Diwan Sahib and read the papers with him, I would come back and sit in my veranda, waiting for the sun to set over the snow-peaks.

I was not a good housekeeper, but I could not bring myself to employ someone to clean up. I did not have the spare cash, and besides I had never liked people going through my belongings. The only time someone—a childhood friend—came to stay with me in Ranikhet, she was lecturing me by the second morning: "Maya, for heaven's sake! You're never going to use that broken lamp again! And this ancient toaster? Has it ever worked? Why don't you throw out that ugly tin trunk and get a proper side table? And, *my God,* look at those cobwebs!" When I told her cleaning cobwebs had been Michael's department because I was not tall enough, she gave me an exasperated look and climbed onto a chair with a broom in her purposeful hand. She kept picking clothes out of my closet, holding them up for display between a finger and thumb, and saying, "Hey, there are flood victims who would turn this down if you donated it to them!"

Sometimes I did have cleaning fits, but just as I was about to throw something out, I would be held back by a memory: that's the chipped blue ceramic bowl Michael and I bought when we set up house, that patched and darned sweater I never wear is the one my mother knitted for me, and that's the toaster Diwan Sahib gave me during my first month in Ranikhet—it fused in a blaze of sparks the very next week and resisted all attempts to repair it, but still. Over the years, the clutter had become part of the comforting topography of the house, and after I had locked up at night and drawn the curtains and sat down with my glass of rum, I felt the house sighing with me, as if it were unwinding as well.

The cleanest part of the house was the earthen courtyard around it, which Charu swept every morning as if it were an extension of her own yard. She would come early with a broom, her hair and mouth covered with her dupatta, sweep and rake and sweep again, and leave in a cloud of dust and dry leaves. She would return a minute later and sprinkle a mug of water before the door to settle the dust, and when the smell of damp earth reached me inside the house, I would know she had finished.

In the days after Gouri Joshi died, Charu did not come. I did not expect her to: her grandmother said she was moping and hardly managing her chores. Then she did begin to come once more, but the sweeping was haphazard and the leaves remained unraked in many places. I watched her listless movements and was reminded of Mr. Chauhan's despair over the filth in the cantonment and his promise to turn Ranikhet into a Switzerland. He had said he would do something about the vandalism at the graveyard where Michael was buried, but he had done nothing that I could see. The lilies had struggled back to life, however, and no more damage had been done.

Charu disappeared for long hours with—and sometimes without—the other cows and goats. She often left Bijli behind too, tied to the doorpost, indignant and restless, barking all afternoon. She left Ama to do all the work in their vegetable patches. When she ate at all, she poked at the rice on her plate, pushing much of it away. I heard her grandmother's strident voice shout at her. "You think food grows on trees? Half your rice is thrown into the cow's feed every day. You need to starve a day or two and then you'll know what food is about."

I did not know it then, but Charu did: Ranikhet appeared to be a dead end to the hotel manager and he had decided to move back to Delhi. With him would go his cook, her Kundan Singh. Charu had never been to the city he would go off to; she had no way of picturing his future life far away. What unimaginable lures and temptations did it hold? She did not know if she would ever see him again.

Later, when things fell into place, I was able to understand what I had seen that summer when I went deep into the forest one afternoon. I had followed my usual route to the temple until, near Westview Hotel, I decided I would walk along the stream instead, to see where it led. I went down a low slope and with every step seemed to leave a little more daylight behind. There was a path of sorts, beaten by human feet for some of the way, then the undergrowth grew dense and thorny bushes began to catch on my clothes. Somewhere I could hear a whistling thrush. Its piercing, clear song cut its own path through the forest, each surge of melody punctuated by a few seconds of rustling quiet.

I had not thought of it for years, but the air, the trees, the aquarium-green light all around, took me back to a forest near Hyderabad where I had once gone with Michael. It was a wilderness with a half-dry stream somewhere in it and we had chanced upon it during one of our joyrides on Michael's motorbike. He had been teaching me how to ride it, seated behind me, putting his hands over mine on the handlebars to guide me. For several days we had had nothing but painful falls, collisions, and quarrels, but that day I had finally got the hang of it and was speeding down the empty road, jubilant, when Michael suddenly said, "Stop!"

The sound of the motorbike died down, I parked it at the edge of the forest, and we walked into it, hand in hand, as if we were children in a fairy tale entering an enchanted wood. Broad-leaved trees, stacked close and deep, blocked out the sun, their green looking black in the shade. There was dark earth and mulch underfoot, and a drumstick tree with a furry blanket of caterpillars over its trunk. The air was sweet with the dense scent of the tiny white flowers of wild curry leaf plants. I picked up a dead branch to use as my machete, but it broke in half with my first swipe at the brush. I plucked a red wildflower and stuck it behind my ear. We laughed a lot. I felt beautiful. My hair was loose; it fell to my waist. We found a small, dead bird on our path. I mourned for the loneliness of its mate. Michael had a smile in his eyes when he said, "The mate is happily mating with a newer, bluer, larger bird."

"If I died," I had said, "you would find a newer, bluer bird within a week, men are like that."

And Michael had said, "You wouldn't wait for me to die to find another man, look at the dozens humming around your ears like butterflies on a flower." He had stopped walking then and kissed me everywhere, his urgent hands inside my clothes.

* * *

I was summoned to the present by the call of a fox. It was some distance away, invisible in the undergrowth. Its cry made the forest seem quieter and more deserted than I had noticed, the road very distant. The canopy formed overhead by the trees hid most of the sky. In the stillness, I heard voices, and then saw them: Charu and Kundan Singh. They were a little way ahead, in a clearing, the sun giving their hair golden halos as if they had stepped out of a painting. I stopped, hardly daring to breathe. I noticed every detail: his white and blue shirt, his mop of hair, the way his eyebrows overhung his deep-set eyes, her dupatta, the green of a tender new leaf, his young man's Adam's apple, the brass amulet tied to his neck with a thick black thread, the sparkling green glass studs in her earlobes, the look on her face of desperation.

Her back was against a giant chestnut tree. He stood facing her, barricading her between his arms against a tree. I heard him saying, "I will be back, you're not to worry, I will be back. You must wait. I'll write to you."

She said, "You'll write!"

"Yes!" he said, fervent. "Every week. Every day."

She turned her face up to him and I could see tears in her eyes. In a mumble so quiet I could hardly hear it, she said, "But I can't read. I can't read or write. I never learned."

He looked flummoxed for a second. Then in a pleading voice he said, "I'll do everything else. You just have to learn to read and write. Or find someone to read for you."

She laughed despite the tears. "And how will I get someone else to read out your letters? What will you write about? What you cooked for lunch, what the manager said to you?"

He buried his fingers and then his face in her hair. "I'll write in riddles," he said. "It is only you who will know what I am saying." He twisted the studs in her ear and said, "Give me one of these, and when we meet again, it'll be back with the other. It'll be our lucky charm."

It was about a fortnight later, early in May, that Charu came to me for the very first letter from her friend "Sunita" and asked me to teach her to read and write.

PART II

ONE

It was early one morning that summer, Diwan Sahib still rumpled with sleep, holding his mug of tea, and I on my way to school, cutting through his lawn. A distant humming sound that came closer every second had stopped me in my tracks and brought him out from his bedroom in his night clothes.

The sound resolved itself into an olive-green helicopter and I said, "It's just a helicopter." As I started on my way again, Diwan Sahib said, "It may not be *just* a helicopter. Not in an army town. Have you any idea what goes on here? This is a town that lives by secrets. State secrets. Army secrets. Grubby little personal secrets."

He looked more ill-tempered and bleary-eyed than was usual for his early mornings, and looked set to embark on a long story I would not be able to interrupt. I quickened my pace and shouted over my shoulder at him, "It *is* just a helicopter, and I'll see you after school."

That day however, the helicopter noise was insistent, and there were two of them: circling the forests, first coming down very low, then swooping away in another direction, chopping up the sky with their blades. Was it a general visiting, or did a forest fire needed monitoring? Each time the sound approached, people paused in whatever they were doing to look up and puzzle over it.

The restless sound echoed through the skies all day. By midafternoon we noticed dark plumes of smoke in the distance, and some people claimed they had heard an explosion. At Bisht Bakery, both customers and bakers were agreed that the army was trying to find a Chinese spy who had slipped in through the northern border. By the time I reached Negi's tea stall, the consensus had changed: an escaped terrorist was on the run and had set fire to something important.

On my way back from Negi's, at about three o'clock, I saw Veer's jeep turning a bend. I paused, waiting for him to stop and pick me up to drive me to the Light House, with a long detour for samosas. This was our ritual when he was in town. But today he drove past without even a wave. The road was empty. It was narrow. I had to stand aside to let him pass. He was close enough for me to see that he was wearing his dark glasses and a white shirt, that his backpack was on the seat next to him. I stayed where I was, sure he would realize his mistake and slam on his brakes further down the road.

The sound of his jeep died away. Once the cloud of diesel fumes cleared I resumed walking. I made myself focus my attention on the orange creeper that climbed a nearby pine, the yellow-throated marten that was making its way up a tree trunk, the kalij pheasants scuttling in the undergrowth, the mysterious fragrance that always hung over that particular curve on the road—all the while pushing away the thought that Veer had seen me and had not stopped.

When I reached Diwan Sahib and gave him his newspaper, I waited as long as I could, sipping my over-sweet tea, before asking with elaborate casualness, "Where's Veer disappeared to?"

"He left all of a sudden," Diwan Sahib said. "That boy's a mystery to me. He was sitting here, staring at his computer, when his phone rang and within five minutes he was out of the house and in his car. Without a word to me. All he said to Himmat was that he would be away for a few days."

"Do you think it has anything to do with—" I looked up at the sky.

"What? Do you mean with this business of the helicopters?" Diwan Sahib said. "As far as I know, our young man has nothing to do with the army or with helicopters. But I'm the old fool, the senile drunk; I'd be the last to know anything." He looked as bad-tempered as he had that morning. After a minute's silence he threw me one of his unexpected questions.

"How old were you during the Bangladesh war?"

I tried to remember when the Bangladesh war had been, without giving my ignorance away, but he knew me too well. "Nineteen seventy-one," he said in a voice that could have cut glass.

"Do you know Michael and I had the same birthday?" I said. "Once we added up our ages and had a cake with forty-four candles on our birthday. It was a chocolate-cream cake and it had two white sugar mice with pink eyes, I remember. I ate one of them and the tail got stuck in my throat because it was made of a dried noodle." I giggled at the memory.

Diwan Sahib was looking at me as if I had lost my mind. Then he dismissed me with a you-foolish-woman shake of his head and I resigned myself to the story that had been postponed since that morning. During the Bangladesh war, one of the intriguing political figures was Maulana Abdul Hamid Khan Bhashani, Diwan Sahib said, a man he remembered from pre-independence days. He was a largely self-educated villager who had turned fervent socialist. He threw himself into every revolt that came his way in British times, from the Khilafat movement to the non-cooperation movement. In the last days of the British Empire, it was rumored that he had come to Surajgarh for a secret meeting with the Nawab to plot the state's secession from India, but that was the time the Nawab had put Diwan Sahib in jail for plotting the opposite, so the Maulana and the Diwan had not met.

By 1970, Diwan Sahib went on, the Maulana was ninety, but still an incendiary demagogue, now fighting for Bangladesh's independence from Pakistan. Although he was violently against India, like most Bangladeshi political leaders he took refuge in this country when the war started. He was a frail old man of volatile temper, given to making provocative statements. He had to be kept out of the public eye, far away from the newspapers. Which place was secluded and secret enough? Naturally, Ranikhet, Diwan Sahib said, a town whose secrets were kept by the hills, by its remoteness, by the army.

The Maulana hated the mountains. He kept urging the Indians to give him a few acres of land nearer Bangladesh, in Assam, where his son was buried. But he was not allowed to leave Ranikhet until the war was over.

The helicopters drew closer again and louder. Diwan Sahib shouted over the noise, brandishing a book at me. "And do you know when I found out about this? Yesterday. From a book! Here was this walking archive, lodged maybe a mile away from me in one of those army houses, and I had no idea." The sounds died down as the helicopters circled away and Diwan Sahib shook his head irritably at them. "Nothing makes you as irrelevant as retirement, Maya. There was a time when Nehru and Patel trusted me with secrets. All these bloody generals in Ranikhet used to beg for invitations to this house. And now?" He withdrew into scowling silence.

That evening, I sat on my veranda with a cup of tea, staring absently at the spot in the sky where the peaks would have been if the heat haze had not rubbed them out. I thought of the ninety-year-old Maulana hidden away in Ranikhet's silent hills, longing for his familiar rivers and swampy heat. My reasons for coming to Ranikhet were strangely similar to the Maulana's, I thought; we had both been on the run.

My thoughts turned to Veer. From all he had said in passing over the last few months I had constructed a story in my head about his reasons for moving to Ranikhet. He had been an orphan looking for his home, and in his childhood he had found one, after a fashion, in the Light House. Diwan Sahib's affection had been understated, but combined with the force of his personality it had been enough to make an impact on the lonely child. Veer was a man in search of a father figure and had found one in Diwan Sahib. Nothing else could account for his rough-edged tenderness toward the old man. He was short-tempered at times, he could be brusque or impatient, but when he sat listening for a whole evening to Diwan Sahib's reminiscences of Surajgarh, or when he came back from Delhi with just the book his uncle had been looking for, it was clear their bond was a deep one. I saw them walking around the garden together sometimes, their heads level with each other, one white-haired and the other dark, each man tall and spare, uncanny in their similarity from the back, and it was oddly moving, as if Veer was a younger version of Diwan Sahib.

I had no doubt about it, Veer had come to Ranikhet to tend to Diwan Sahib in his last years.

When I once tested out this hypothesis on Ama, her response was succinct by her garrulous standards, and enigmatic: "Cares for his uncle, does he?" she said. Then added, "Cares for his uncle's things, he does, the way he cleans up his papers, more than Himmat Singh has done in years." Veer had in fact been dusting and sorting shelf after shelf of Diwan Sahib's work papers in whatever little leisure time he had. In my eyes this made him more considerate than even his gifts of rum and thermal socks.

Now I wondered if there was more to Veer's presence in Ranikhet. Was he somehow involved with the army? Was the trekking a front for something else? Was he here merely to position himself as Diwan Sahib's heir? Or like all the others, had he come after the letters of Edwina and Nehru?

I pushed away my teacup—and with it my suspicions. They were too far-fetched and too petty. Veer often had to leave town in a hurry because he had work in other places. He had never seen the need to explain his every action. There was no more to it.

In a day or two we forgot the helicopters and the Chinese spy, and the terrorist on the run—it had been another of those things the army needed to do in its secretive, military way. The only person upon whom the helicopters appeared to make an impact was the clerk, whose son Gopal was preparing for trials to join the army. Every morning, if I was awake that early, I heard the bugle that summoned the army cadets: four blasts at dawn, at intervals of two minutes in order to awaken them. For many months now, the bugle had been followed, moments later, by a light at the clerk's house. Gopal woke with the cadets. On cold mornings, he emerged hunched in the mist of his own breath, crunching the frost-glassed earth in hawai chappals. At the baked-mud clearing outside his hut he did push-ups followed by at least forty sit-ups, a hundred sometimes. Once there was more daylight he did short sprints up and down the hill, and exercises that he had observed the cadets doing in their training area. Gopal had dreamed of being in the army for years. Since his childhood he had watched soldiers in rows of khaki and green, hair sheared above their ears, marching down roads, carrying the gear of the day, anything from bedrolls to brooms, buckets, and guns. The soldiers looked at other people as if some invisible but impenetrable barrier cordoned them off. Gopal dreamed of being inside that magic cordon, marching with them.

All this time, his father had been proud of his martial son and boasted that his boy would retire as a captain—at least. The mystery of the helicopters and the smoke made him take fright. He quarreled volubly with his son for several days. He now wanted the boy to join the water board instead: they would give him a safe clerical job, he knew they would; a father's job often passed to the son. "What's good enough for your father is good enough for you, you fool!" I heard him shout. "The army is not fun and games. You'll thank me when you see your friends being sent off to die!"

One inexplicable consequence of the helicopters was that the mail did not come for a week. Perhaps the two things were not connected; later we came to know that a postal strike had begun in the plains the same day. But rumbles began after the second day without the mail and we heard that our letters were being looked through for clues, that the postmaster was involved in the trouble, and that the post office was the terrorists' next target. I was unconcerned, but Charu grew more anxious with every passing day. The postman arrived in the late afternoon, sometimes in the evening; ours was his last call because he lived across the stream from us. Charu hovered nearby as the time of his homecoming approached, waiting for him to go limping past. She did not dare ask him if there was a letter. She had only received one letter, in May, soon after Kundan Singh had reached Delhi. Since then, there had been silence. Charu behaved as though an eternity had passed.

TWO

"How are you? How is your family? I hope all are well. I am well." So began the second letter Charu received, which arrived when she had all but given up hope.

I had brought a Hindi primer from school, with the alphabet and brightly colored pictures, and some exercise books. After I read out the letter from Kundan, I opened the primer and made Charu find each letter he had used. I made her write the simpler words from his letter into an exercise book. His spellings were often not correct, but at that stage I did not pause over spelling. She sweated and muttered and pushed away strands of hair in her effort to concentrate. She had only the foggiest recollection of reading and writing from her classes of long ago, though there were unexpected shafts of clarity. Charu's delighted giggles at such times were so infectious that we sounded more like two teenage conspirators than a teacher and her young student. These occasions were not frequent. She had forgotten much of the alphabet; it was coming back, but slowly. She had forgotten all her numbers.

I drew her cartoons of the letters as people and animals. I made her write them again and again. I brought back different books of nursery rhymes and stories from the school's library cupboard every few days. I made her read the larger print on cookie packets and soap bars. I was possessed by my task: it had become a mission. I had failed with Charu all those years ago when she was a little girl in my class. This time it would be different! I let no opportunity pass. Once Mr. Chauhan came upon us when I was trying to make her read one of his Hindi signs as she grazed her animals, and he exclaimed overjoyed, "I knew it, Mam! I knew it! You have a velvet fist in your iron glove. That day when I told you the peasants need education in civic sense, I thought you were annoyed. I thought you walked away in anger. But no, you took my words to heart. Mam, you have given me a fresh lease of life! Now I will charge ahead with my mission—on a war footing."

Charu applied herself to this new chore in her life with resolve, and often, when I saw her pressing a piece of chalk to a slate I had bought for her, her skin glowing in the honey-colored sun of evening, she looked to me less an ordinary peasant girl and more a heroine from a folktale, even if her battle was not with fabulous monsters and wicked witches but only with the alphabet and absence. I would see her sitting in her courtyard with an intent look in her eyes, chin resting on knees, tongue sticking out, writing on the ground with a twig as she waited for the evening fire to catch or the hens to come in. She swore in frustration if, despite retracing the letters in the dust with her own fingers, she could not tell what they added up to. The "ba" and "ka" and "pa" confused her. The lines wobbled and dissolved and swam into each other. The letters flipped over as if they had a life of their own. She had to stop herself from tearing the page up in her fury at her own slowness. But still, evening after evening, she came back for her lessons.

* * *

"I have to go every afternoon to Sa'ab's hotel," Kundan's second letter said.

> *They do not like eating hotel food. They like daal-roti-sabzi, food from home. They like it hot. So every morning I cook it and then pack it all in a special lunch carrier that keeps it hot. Then I cycle with it to the hotel. It has been built very recently. Your eyes would be dazzled by the hotel. It is like a magic palace. I am not allowed to enter it. I have to go to the back entrance and hand the food to someone. But when I pass the main door I can see how shiny everything is. It smells different. Music comes out of there when people go in and out. I saw a pool of totally*

blue water. People swim in the water, with hardly any clothes. You would laugh to see them. Mostly the people are dressed like kings and queens. But none of them look as beautiful as hill people. I think of my parents in Siliguri. But more than that I think of Ranikhet. Send me something from the forest.

Your friend.

When I finished reading a letter, Charu would ask me to read it again, sometimes three times, and listen carefully, frowning, as if trying to memorize it. Then she would take the letter from me and hide it in her clothing. Charu's living quarters were so cramped she could not find a place to hide the letters there. Ama, Puran, and she had two small rooms, one of which was partitioned in half: one half was their kitchen, the other had bright blue walls and a black-and-white TV covered with a crocheted cloth. A vase with pink plastic roses stood on top of the TV and on the wall was a picture Charu had painted, of purple and blue flowers that might have been irises. There were two chairs and a bed and a trunk made into a table. Through patterned plastic curtains you could glimpse the second room, which had a bed. Of course, Charu did not have her own room or cupboard; it was sufficient if she found the same corner every night to sleep in. After two near misses, when Ama very nearly lighted upon her letters, Charu now put them in a plastic bag and tucked them into a rafter in the cowshed, along with her magpie feather and bead necklace.

It was a problem finding the time for her lessons. We were both busy. Charu was forever rushing back and forth between her chores at home and her part-time job at the factory. Even when she managed to come to my house, she had to leave if her grandmother yelled for her: "Where did you put the spade?" "Run to Mall Road and buy some oil." "Who do you think will put in the hens?" "God knows where the girl is, or her dog. Charu!"

I had to divide my time between taking classes at St. Hilda's and overseeing jam making, bottling, and accounting at the factory. May and June were our most crowded months: all the soft fruit of summer—plums, peaches, apricots—arrived from distant villages, baskets and crates of them together, and they had to be dealt with at once. Some days, neither Charu nor I got home from the factory till after dark. At times it was late afternoon when I reached Diwan Sahib for my newspaper session and on the rare days that he decided to work on his book with me, I was lucky if I returned in time for the sunset on my veranda.

I would sit there with a cup of tea, waiting for Charu, watching the blues and greens of the hills darken range after range. When the farthest ranges were smudged into shadows, and the flying squirrels began skittering up the deodar trees, Charu would appear, bounding down the slope, not bothering to look where her feet fell, tossing from hand to hand two warm potatoes her grandmother had baked in the embers of their cooking fire. They were fluffy and tender inside, steaming with stored-up warmth, the charred skin smoky and delicious. Since I hardly ever managed more than an egg and bread or instant noodles when I ate at home, I was as grateful for the potatoes as Charu was for her lessons.

She came for her lessons when her grandmother was unlikely to need her, and she thought she had covered her tracks well, but Ama was too shrewd a woman for Charu's efforts at subterfuge to go unnoticed. Although she could not put her finger on it, she knew something about her granddaughter was different. She had sensed currents of gossip too, from which she was being excluded: she had heard Charu's name in conversations between drugged-out Janaki and the clerk's wife, which dried up the minute Ama came within earshot. She smelled a rat and so came one day to my house and settled on the bottom stair of the veranda to find out where the smell might lead. "Did you hear," she asked me as she sat, "of Rosemount Hotel's cook?"

I knew that the cook was probably not why she had come to me, but I said no, I had not.

"He was riding pillion on a scooter when he was hit by a speeding car—a Delhi car, of course," Ama said. "He fell from the scooter. But thought he was fine. And then—then he looked down and he had no right leg! It had been sliced clean off. There it was, still in shoe and sock, lying in the pine needles. They wrapped it in a shirt and carried it to the hospital with them, but nobody could stitch it back on."

"That Puran," she began next, still not ready to come to the point. "He's as senseless about his deer as about everything else. Lunatic fool giggles and whispers to it like it's his lover, and feeds it all the grain I store for the hens. Between his deer and Charu's useless dog, I am losing all the money I earn from selling milk."

I murmured and waited. After a brief pause, unable to hold herself back any longer, she demanded, "Why is the girl with you all the time? People are talking."

"She is learning to read," I said. "I have told her she must."

"She missed school all those years when I was paying for her, what is this new hobby for?"

"It's never too late," I said.

"Why?" Ama said, narrowing her eyes. "I never learned to read a word, and has it been a problem for me?"

Before I could argue, she appeared to reconsider and said, "No, it's a good thing. She won't be as helpless as her poor dead mother. She won't let a man get away with treating her badly. But don't teach her too much. Girls who study too much are no good for anything—she won't get a husband and she'll have all sorts of silly ideas about herself." She continued in a heavy voice, "I'm growing old. She is such a worry. I have to find her a groom, but my son is such a drunk—everyone knows it and stays away. These last few months his face has gone black—did you see him when he came yesterday? Just comes to me to demand money, as if I grow rupee notes in the field. As thin as a stick and lies about all day in a daze. That woman he's taken up with is a born witch." She shook her head. "How long will I live?" she said. "Every day I feel closer to death. My heart feels as if it has slid to my stomach sometimes. And who will look after Charu if I am dead? Sometimes I think it's a curse that she's pretty. How is an old woman to keep her out of trouble?"

Her wrinkles deepened and darkened. Her fingers were callused, dry, and chunky like small yams from overwork. The strap on one of her slippers was held together by a safety pin. I felt a deep pang of guilt and worry at what I was doing behind Ama's back. I said, "You mustn't worry about her. I'll look after her."

Ama shook her head and smiled in the ironical, all-knowing manner she adopted with me at times. Usually it annoyed me, but this time I thought her attitude was justified; even to myself, my words sounded like a tall claim. How was I planning to look after Charu?

In a rush, as if I had planned it all along—although the thought had not crossed my mind till that minute—I said, "She's my responsibility too, I've known her since she was twelve. And . . . everything I own will be hers." It was suddenly self-evident: who better to inherit my savings bank account, the bits of jewelry my mother had given me over the years, and the furniture I had collected? I had been told that my chest of drawers, bought secondhand from people moving house four years ago, was an antique.

"You!" Ama exclaimed. Her thin body shook with mirth. Her long teeth, stained from chewing tobacco, were black and yellow. She noticed my offended look and stopped her laughter. "How are you to look after her?" she said. "You can barely look after yourself, far away from family, all alone."

I started shuffling the pile of books beside me. I could not tell why my thoughts turned to Miss Wilson's watch, the round gold one that had belonged to her grandfather, the collector of Kozhikode. For the first time in sixty-five years, it had stopped working, and she had, with the greatest reluctance, left it for repairs at a watch shop in Haldwani. But last week she had heard the shop had burned to the ground, taking her watch with it. Agnes Wilson had been distraught. Her face had crumpled and her glasses had misted with tears. She could do nothing else but speak of her grandfather: how he had adored her and thought her capable of great things while for the rest of her family she was an unwanted fourth daughter, dark skinned and ordinary. Her grandfather had dreamed he would see her installed as collector, or even district commissioner, and that was what he had whispered on his deathbed, when he handed her that watch. "Not one of his dreams for me came true," Miss Wilson had said in a broken voice.

"And on top of everything, I couldn't look after his dying gift." The other teachers had found her grief over an old watch comical. One of them had even done a flawless imitation of her overdone distress. But to my surprise I had felt a pang of sympathy so strong that I had almost reached out to give her hand a squeeze. I had sat with her in silence that afternoon, as if I were on a condolence call, listening to her rambling memories as long as the lunch break allowed. I found my own behavior mystifying. I had said nothing about it to anyone, not even to Diwan Sahib, knowing he would unleash the full force of his amused sarcasm if I had told him how Miss Wilson's solitary grief haunted me.

Distracted by my own thoughts, I had not heard a word of what Ama was saying. I scrambled back to our conversation. By now, her tone had turned conciliatory. "You are doing enough for her, Teacher-ni," she was saying. "But Charu can't work in that jam factory forever. She has to have a normal life: marriage, children, her own home. I have to marry her off before I die."

THREE

Ama had left without looking at me again, as if conscious she had been tactless. The next day she sent across a bowl of kheer made from the milk of her cows. But I found myself dodging her and turning away from the skeptical look that said it knew everything there was to know. Her presence began to feel intrusive, even overbearing. And then, as if by malicious intent, the mail brought me two letters from college friends, both with reports of new babies, thriving families, holidays. "Busy, busy, busy," said one of them, "I don't know where the days go. And how are you?"

Charu sensed something was wrong, and wordlessly brought me gifts the whole week: first a white rose made out of crepe paper, followed by a lumpy papier-mâché Ganesha that a friend of hers had made, then a vase she had fashioned out of reeds. She cleaned my courtyard with rediscovered concentration. She brought water on her head from a far-off stream when my taps ran dry.

By now five letters had come. I realized I had begun to wait for the postman as expectantly as Charu and it seemed silly for me to keep up the pretense that I did not know who the letters were really from. After the third one came, I said to her in a casual tone, "There's a letter from Kundan Singh for you." A look passed between us, I turned to go and fetch the letter, and she knew she was safe. She never mentioned her friend "Sunita" again. She began to interrupt our lessons with unexpected nuggets about Kundan Singh: how he had been with her every night of her vigil when her cow was dying, how they used to meet every afternoon at the Dhobi Ghat, how they had once stolen away and gone to a fair at the army grounds together and he had bought her a bead necklace. She told me about his parents, his job. It was as if, by talking to me, she was reassuring herself that he was real.

I found myself thinking about them in the middle of my working day, creating sagas out of her stories. In my mind's eye, I saw her and Kundan haloed in the sunlight of the forest clearing the time I had observed them unseen. From there it took only a minute for me to slide into that afternoon in Hyderabad's forest reserve when Michael had kissed me and held me against a tamarind tree.

It was not all daydreaming; I was anxious too about Ama's reaction. She was venomous without restraint about other transgressors, such as Janaki's teenage daughter. "Shameless hussy!" she had spat. "Doesn't care that everyone knows she's carrying on with that boy at Liaquat's medicine shop. He's not just a different caste, no—he's a *Muslim*!" What would she do when she came to know of the secret life her own granddaughter was leading?

I thought back to that fortnight when my father had virtually imprisoned me at home after he spotted me with my arms wrapped around Michael, as we drove past him on the motorbike. I was in the middle of laughing at something, my chin on Michael's shoulder, my hair streaming behind me in the breeze, when I had noticed my father, limping from the opposite direction, stopping to stare when he noticed us, his head turning to track us as if following a ball at a tennis game where not a stroke could be missed. His eyes had locked into mine as I passed, and for that long moment we were tied together by a thread stretched more taut with each turn of the wheels, which snapped in half when he receded too far into the distance for me to see him any longer. I would never forget the horror on his face that day. Michael's parents were second-generation Christians, and my father was contemptuous of all Christians—even though he was happy enough to send me to St. George's Grammar School for Girls on the first rung of his grand plan to turn me into an industrial magnate. I had stopped early in life trying to make sense of my father's paradoxes, as had my mother. He was the natural born lord of all he surveyed; he needed to explain nothing. He ruled over factories and fields and two younger brothers. He spoke little and to the point. He was a short square man, with a bald head that shone in the sun. His bad leg ensured that his silver-headed stick never left his side. It may have been this stick, or his lazy right eye that wandered so that you never knew precisely what he was looking at. They combined to create a subtle suggestion of violence, which nobody wanted to test. By the time I grew up, I was as afraid of him as his brothers were.

The summer nights grew warmer. I could not fall asleep however long I lay in bed, however tight I shut my eyes. I sat for long hours looking at the forest fires outside my window. They happened every summer and they could go on for weeks. When beaten down, they would go underground and travel unseen below the thick matting of pine needles, to spring out in another part of the forest. I could hear a faint crackling. At some distance down the slope, there was a glowing orange line as if someone had flung a long necklace of flames into the forest. Beyond it was another such ring and further away, another still. In the blackness beyond the arc of light from my table lamp, I could see the shadows of soldiers as they raked paths to stop the flames spreading. To the left I could see one of the fire-lines creeping up toward the clerk's cottage.

As the summer wore on, the air turned heavy with smoke. It gave everyone colds and coughs and Diwan Sahib's breathing made a sound like rustling leaves. A chir tree near my house had been burning for three days. Flames leaped out from a hollow halfway up its long straight trunk. Its resin oozed down the trunk and made the fire burn more fiercely. There was no water with which to douse it.

I stayed up those nights correcting school homework. I circled words in the grubby exercise book before me: "Ashu was quite," Guddu had written. "It was quiet cold"; "The mouse in the house sat very quite." He got it wrong each time. In the next exercise book, Anil had flipped every single S, B, and P to face the wrong way, as he always did. I pushed the books aside. My head sank between my hands onto the table.

In the dark hours my thoughts took a form I would not have recognized in the daytime. If I slept at all, I woke from contorted dreams in which, night after night, Veer held me till I slept, or insistently kissed me awake, or crushed me to bloodied pulp with his jeep, or drove away saying not a word. Sometimes Charu appeared, and sometimes even Kundan Singh. But never Michael. If I shut my eyes and tried to visualize Michael, the elements of his face refused to coalesce into anything recognizable. I discovered I could no longer hear his voice in my ears, or the sound of his laugh, or the way he cleared his throat every few sentences when speaking.

I sifted through my mind for whatever I could retrieve of him, reconstructing our years together: the way I pretended to sleep so that he would bring tea to our bed each morning, tugging a tuft of my hair to wake me. How we would eat omelettes day after day because we had failed somehow to shop or cook.

I longed for the simple joy of being married to him, and to have him there to confirm my memories—was our cupboard black or brown? Did the neighbors really have a dog called Simona? Where was that bouldered and scrubby place we went to, the day his motorbike was delivered after weeks of waiting? He had driven very fast and we were wildly gleeful, like children who had escaped school.

I had been told that if you put your ear to a railway track, you could feel the vibration of a train many miles distant. Could Michael, wherever he was, hear me if I called out to him? I dreamed myself back to Hyderabad's long-ago summer afternoons, birds and mosquitoes falling exhausted in the scorched air, the heat-dead stillness churned by the creak of our ceiling fan. We lay on the bare, cool floor sometimes, and sometimes in the narrowness of our single bed, pillows, sheets, and floor slipping away as we tore at each other as if after days of starvation. I had to touch Michael all the time, to make sure he was next to me when I slept and was still there when I awoke. When the monsoon came that first year it had rained as it never had before. We could hear nothing but the shout of rain on the roof, on and on all night, as we slept and woke and murmured to each other and slept and woke again, as if the night itself were something fluid we were swimming through, pausing for breath, then swimming again. I would memorize Michael's face with my fingers as he slept so that I could travel its ridges and valleys through the hours of his absences: lines had been made on it by thoughts I would never know. I was jealous beyond reason of his past. If I had my way, I would not have shared his shadow with anyone else. "Was it the same for you?" I wanted to ask him now.

I was nineteen when we married, still at college. I returned to classes a week after our wedding. I would stare at the neem tree by my classroom window, and in the middle of a lecture on the Delhi sultanate I would lose myself in daydreams until at length the professor's voice once again became audible, hammering at me from somewhere far-off: "Can you repeat the assessment I just made of Qutb-ud-din-Aibak and the Slave Dynasty? I'm speaking to you. To you, Maya."

Michael used to grumble about the size of our two rooms. "It's a shed," he said, "they must have built it as a garage." The place did look smaller with him in it. The ceiling was low, the bathroom was a little box where your elbow knocked painfully against a tap if you turned. He was tall and somewhat clumsy, so he tended to bang into things. I would lie back in bed and watch him, filled with adoration as he puzzled his way through making coffee in our new kitchen, on our new gas stove. Mostly he gave up, and walked back toward our tousled bed, his eyes on me with a look of yearning so distilled, so intense, that I had to turn away for fear of its strength.

In those days in Hyderabad, if Michael tossed and turned, I got up to sprinkle water on our sheets to cool the room. If the electricity went, I would sit up, fanning us both with a newspaper. He slept through it all, exhausted by his long day at work rushing through the burning summer air on his motorbike, wherever his newspaper sent him to take pictures. I would look at his helpless, sleeping face and though he could not hear me, I whispered endearments so tender that they would have curled away and died if exposed to the light of day.

"I couldn't say them to you then, but I wish you knew," I said now, and tried to hear his voice replying. But all I heard was foxes calling to each other and pine needles sprinkling down on the tin roof, making a sound like rain.

FOUR

In colonial times, the summer months in Ranikhet meant horse races and moonlit picnics, and even now we have a "season" when the town is crowded with people who come up from the plains to escape the heat. They are everywhere for a few weeks: tourists, summer residents, day-trippers. Scholars would turn up to see Diwan Sahib. Trekkers heading for the high Himalaya paused in Ranikhet en route; all kinds of people wandered in and out of the Light House as if it were a public monument. If they found Diwan Sahib in the garden they stopped to pump him for information about the hills or to photograph him as a relic of the Raj, a bona fide old Indian nobleman. Sometimes supplies would arrive for one of Veer's trekking groups, or middlemen tasked with requisitioning porters in the Ranikhet bazaar would come and stay for hours, poring over details. There was a young assistant Veer had employed, who was stationed at the house from time to time. He hovered all day, appearing to do nothing more substantial at all.

Ever since Veer had taken up residence at the Light House, Diwan Sahib's writing had barely progressed. If I asked him for new chapters to type, he waved his hand at whoever happened to be visiting and said, "I can't write when there are so many people. I'll wait till the season ends and then we'll finish chapter seven. I'll get the book done this year, that's a promise. I don't have much more time. That Welsh poet, what was his name? We learned his poem in school—'Job Davies, eighty-five / Winters old and still alive / After the slow poison / And treachery of the seasons'—did you have to learn it too?"

"No," I said.

"You should. Good poem. I'm like Mr. Davies—worse—I'm

eighty-seven! Every morning I wake up and tell myself, 'What, still alive?' I truly don't have long."

"You don't want to write anymore," I said. "There's too much else to do." I pointed to the bottle on the table next to him. Now that Veer kept him supplied with superior alcohol, Diwan Sahib's durbar began soon after breakfast and went on long into the afternoon. He would keep postponing lunch, pouring himself yet another drink, waving Himmat Singh away each time he said, "Shall I serve lunch, Sa'ab?" Mr. Qureshi too was under the spruce tree nursing his steel glass on most days. He seemed to have abandoned his workshop to his son.

"Maybe if you wrote for an hour or so in the morning before starting on the gin?"

"What nonsense," Diwan Sahib said, and poured himself another large measure. "Don't be such a schoolteacher. My taste buds feel as if they've come back to life after twenty years dormant." He turned to Mr. Qureshi and said, "You were going to tell me something. This girl interrupted you."

"Yes, yes, Diwan Sahib, as I was saying, mysterious are the ways of man." Mr. Qureshi smiled, round faced, and red nosed, already a little tipsy. "Do you know, Maya, a car came in for servicing yesterday—a Honda City, belongs to that new doctor at the nursing home, what's his name? Sharma or Verma. Anyway, the boys started work on the car. They're strapping young fellows, foul mouthed and stoned half the time. When they opened the trunk to get the spare tire, right there, one of them almost fell over with fright. There was a head in the trunk. Long hair and all."

"A human head?" I said. "You mean a dead body?"

"Aha, Maya!" Mr. Qureshi chuckled. "Scared you, didn't I? No, when they looked again they realized it was a plastic head, a stand for a wig. There was a wig on it: long curling red hair. Even had two blue hairclips. So what do we do then? Of course we phone the doctor and we say, 'Sir, you left a wig in your car.' And the doctor shouts, 'What wig? What do you take me for? Are you trying to insult me? I have a full head of hair and it's my own, I'll come to your workshop and you can pull it if you like and see if it comes off,' he says, and bangs the phone down, so angry. There is no explanation. None, Diwan Sahib. Correct me if I am wrong, but mysterious are the ways of mankind. I have kept the head in the showroom of the workshop. Maya, you can come and see it if you don't believe me. What was it doing in the trunk? No idea."

Diwan Sahib said, "Why won't we believe you? Stranger things than this happened in Surajgarh in my time. Now let me tell you . . ."

And Corbett was filed away for another day.

One afternoon, when I came to his lawn with the newspapers, I found Diwan Sahib smoking. I said nothing, but a look passed between us. He took a long, defiant drag and after a pause blew out a lungful of smoke. He tapped his Rolls-Royce cigarette case and displayed a neat row of filter tips. If he had been a child he might have stuck his tongue out at me. He had stopped smoking with great difficulty three years earlier. He had sworn then that he was free of the siren call of addiction, and that he would never put himself through stopping again.

I marched into the house and found Veer's assistant there. He was a limp, shy young man from Dehra Dun, who spent most evenings pacing in the garden murmuring to his wife on a mobile. He was a follower of the Radha Soami sect and cooked his own vegetarian meals, minus even onion and garlic, on a separate gas stove that he had set up on a back veranda. If chicken or fish was cooked in the house, he lit incense sticks by the dozen and his face assumed a rigid expression of martyrdom. He regarded cigarette packets and bottles of gin as objects that had been planted in the house by the Devil in person. He looked horrified when I asked him how Diwan Sahib had laid his hands on cigarettes. "None of us smoke, Maya Mam," he said. "Some visitor must have left the cigarettes in the house." They happened to be Diwan Sahib's old brand too. "What's a couple of cigarettes after three years?" Diwan Sahib shouted toward us. "Do you think I have no self-control?"

That evening, when I told Ama about the cigarettes, she gave me her all-knowing look and said with a cackle of sarcastic laughter, "Life's improved for Diwan Sa'ab ever since his nephew came back! So much more to drink, and now cigarettes! The nephew will kill his uncle with trying to make him happy, just you wait and see." I pretended not to understand what she was implying and busied myself with other work. I did not want her to suppose I was encouraging malice. She had never liked or trusted Veer, and she had told me so in the early days, not thinking he would actually start living at the Light House or that he and I would become friends. She was too politic now to be open about her dislike, but sometimes the temptation was irresistible.

Diwan Sahib lost weight because of eating less and drinking more, and that made him look both younger and frailer. However his eyes, spiderwebbed with wrinkles, retained their wicked gleam. One afternoon, a buxom woman from somewhere in East Anglia arrived out of the blue, saying she was writing a love story based on the lives of Edwina Mountbatten and Jawaharlal Nehru. "It is vital to my project, sir, that I see the letters I believe to be in your possession. If you allow me a day's access to the papers, I'm willing to share my royalties with you." She came in a flowing silk sari that repeatedly slid off her shoulder to bare her cleavage, so that, Diwan Sahib later said, two roads converged in a low silk blouse, and he wished he could have traveled both.

When she met with no success the first day—she had installed herself at the Westview Hotel—she returned on each of the next two mornings. Her long black hair was in a bun crested by a red rose one day, a creamy magnolia the next. She sat very straight, adjusted the flower, and looked at Diwan Sahib, focusing her energies through her large pleading eyes. She gifted him a shawl from the local army widows' cooperative, and, the next day, a bottle of rum.

She tried to talk about Nehru, but Diwan Sahib remorselessly steered the conversation to Corbett. "Did you know," he said, "that he died the day before Einstein? Einstein stole his thunder. Was Corbett a lesser man than Einstein? If I were lost in the jungles here"—he waved a hand this way and that—"I hope you are careful when you walk around after dark? And that you know that a slow-moving snake that wriggles as it approaches is very likely a poisonous one? That is when you need Corbett with you, madam, and not Einstein—when you want someone to be able to tell from looking at scratch marks on rocks which animals have passed, how far they are from you, why the langur is calling from that tree, why the barking deer leaped away across the path. Do you follow me?"

The woman's eyes had glazed over, but she nodded.

"But who remembers Corbett now, other than a few senile ancients like me?"

It was only on the afternoon the woman was leaving and had come to say good-bye that Diwan Sahib chose to relent. "Oh, I forgot," he said, "Nehru came here to Ranikhet with the Mountbattens. He dropped in to see me too—that chair—your chair? He sat on that very chair with a gin and bitters in one hand and a cigarette in the other."

The woman jumped from her chair, stared at it in disbelief, and scrabbled in her handbag for her camera as Diwan Sahib continued, "Why don't you drive down to Holm Farm? They have a framed picture there, of Edwina, Dickie, Nehru, and Mr. Upadhyaya, who presided over the place." He returned placidly to his newspaper while she gave him a look that combined excitement, impatience, and irritation in equal measure, before rushing off to her driver to consult him about the practicalities of a detour to the Holm Farm Hotel on her way to the station.

Diwan Sahib watched the car disappear into a cloud of dust, then went inside. He poured us both a rum and we sank into our usual chairs. For a while, exhausted with talk, we did not speak. Above the fireplace was a tall vase filled with half-dead pink roses into which Himmat Singh had stuck a few blood-red Aztec lilies. It was so quiet that I thought I could hear when, from time to time, the decaying rose petals dropped onto the mantelpiece. Flames ate at a small log in the fireplace. A fire was lit in that room every day, even on the hottest summer evenings, to kill the damp and protect the books from silverfish.

"The prime minister of a newly independent country," Diwan Sahib said after a long spell of silence. "Devoted to the wife of his departing viceroy. Is it a surprise that this woman wants to turn it into a lurid romance?" He emptied half his glass in one gulp. He sighed, tilted his head back on his chair, and shut his eyes.

When after a long pause he began to speak, it was half to himself. His eyes were still shut and his voice so low that I had to lean forward to catch his words. It was a strange relationship, he said. They began to feel a closeness to each other at the end of Edwina's time in India, on the brink of her departure, and after that they could hardly bear to be parted for a single moment. Some of their letters were written when they were both in the same room, some were written moments after they had left each other; there was one scribbled across an official banquet's menu card. In the years to follow, they were rarely alone together, and saw each other only for brief snatches when one of them visited on the way to somewhere else. They were constantly among other people. Yet they wrote to each other every day for several years. The letters came and went by diplomatic bag. Each one was numbered because they were afraid the letters might fall into the wrong hands. And why should they not have feared that eventuality? So much in those letters was dangerous for people in public life. Nehru had called his friendship with Edwina a battle between convention and chemistry in which chemistry had won—more or less. It could not be allowed to win entirely. Public life is relentless, it is unforgiving, it is held together by conventions and the fear of any threat to them. "I should know," Diwan Sahib said.

His voice took on the tones of someone reciting a poem: "I lose myself in a dreamland, which is very unbecoming in a prime minister. But then I am only incidentally a prime minister." A man willingly imprisoned by his political destiny, said Diwan Sahib, separated from the woman he loved by duty, distance, necessity, even instinct. If either of them abandoned their own orbits, Nehru had told Edwina, they would both be terribly unhappy. The impossibility of their love was also what sustained it.

Diwan Sahib's brow remained furrowed in thought. He stared at the fire as if reading from it. I hardly dared say a word, never having seen him so lost to the world around him. He had not once sounded like this talking about Corbett. I could not understand it. The story was startling, of course, but surely so well-known and often repeated that it had lost its power to move anyone, especially someone as unsentimental as Diwan Sahib. You are starting to sound like a romance writer too, I would have said, if he had not looked so unlike himself.

"There were letters in which Nehru said he felt Edwina's presence like a fragrance in the air," Diwan Sahib murmured on. "She said she felt a sense of peace and happiness with him as she did with no one else. He sent her things to remind her of the country she had left: birch bark from Kashmir, leaves, stones. Edwina had even given him a ring before leaving India. When she died in her sleep, alone in Borneo, Nehru's letters were by her bed. She traveled with them everywhere. It was what she read before she slept every night."

"Why didn't you write a book on this instead of on Corbett?" I said, when his next pause grew too long.

He blinked as if he had been asleep. His face was etched with pain, but he rearranged it into an imitation of his usual half-seriousness. "Because of Edwina's dog, entirely because of her dog," he said. Edwina had a dog called Mizzen. She did not know what to do with it when the time came to leave India. Given England's quarantine rules, the dog would have had to be isolated for several months before being allowed to reenter the country. Edwina consulted Nehru and they agreed it was better to put it down than make it suffer quarantine; the dog was too old to survive it, they thought. "That did it for me," Diwan Sahib said. "All those gardens at his prime-ministerial doorstep and the man didn't offer to adopt it and let it live out its remaining years in peace? How do you think an old dog like me feels about *that*? You won't put me down, will you, if I become inconvenient?"

"Do you really have any of their letters?" I asked him. "Couldn't I see them once?" I had had a hunch all along that he had made it up to amuse himself watching people like the woman from East Anglia pay him obeisance.

"Maybe I have them, maybe I don't," Diwan Sahib said. "Maybe, maybe not. You'll find out." He had shut his eyes again. "I should chop this house into firewood," he said, his words slurring. "Too big for me, too big—"

He was drowsy now. He slouched in his big armchair, and in the dim light he looked shriveled, old and haggard, all bones and loose skin. Above him, the photograph of his dogs in silhouette was scarcely visible, but it made me think of Veer's stories of Diwan Sahib's youth: his parties, his horses, the music, his women. He was receding before my eyes, fading out of reach.

I felt the need to do something to stop him disappearing from my life. I pulled a few pages from one of the old bundles on Corbett that had emerged a month ago and said, "Tonight I'm going to type up a few of these and we'll go over them tomorrow. OK? We'll start again. We'll find out if we missed anything in the third draft."

He did not answer. He was lost again in his own thoughts, staring into the sputtering flames.

* * *

That night, I sat up with his papers, and the sound of my typewriter clacked into the night. I typed page after page, overcome by a sense of loss, which, if it had not been overpowering, would have struck me as absurd. How had I missed knowing the man who wrote those words at the time he wrote them? And if his time was short, as he insisted more and more often these days, could I bring myself to look into the abyss of Diwan Sahib's certain absence?

This is what I typed from Diwan Sahib's manuscript that night: it was his statement of purpose, his optimistic, tongue-in-cheek plan for a biography—when he had not known the project would take him forty years and still remain incomplete.

> Being petrified ever since birth of even the most minor forms of physical injury, it is conceptually difficult for me to grasp something as foolish as bravery. I can only gape in wonder at people who do not require wild horses to drag them onto a cricket pitch, at batsmen who face fast bowlers without being shackled by iron to

the wicket. I am similarly bowled over by the idiocy of people who go walking of their own free will in forests where they might be eaten by bears or be clawed by tigers whose talons can sometimes be as sharp as those of certain women I have known. Next to schoolteachers, a tiger seems to me the most terrifying thing in the world, and its immediate extinction (or at least caged enclosure) is a wild inner desire that I have to keep suppressing, given that I am writing a book on Jim Corbett. One look at a tiger's dental arrangements is sufficient to convince anyone that vegetarianism is not a notion likely to have been entertained even by its remote ancestors. In early youth I was regularly carted off into a forest by my employer, the Nawab of Surajgarh. I was informed by him that the object of these expeditions was to try and glimpse one of these beasts. After I had got over the feeling that either he was joking or lunatic, I transcended the condition of fright in which one merely sobs uncontrollably, and was restrained from the suicide I was attempting by jumping off the swaying pachyderm transporting us in the direction of Blakean fearful symmetry. The Nawab had a profound effect on my early predisposition toward being separated, via a stout iron cage, from all species of four-legged life larger than myself. In part, this accounts for my fascination with Jim Corbett, who seems to have been braver even than the Nawab of Pataudi when he captained our national cricket team. His life was years of shunting and hooting, then hunting and shooting—he was a railwayman before he became a celebrated shikari. By his own account Corbett voluntarily, even assiduously, did the very last thing I would ever do, namely "get in touch" (as he sweetly puts it) with man-eaters. As we know from his riveting tales, the man-eaters were not equally keen to get in touch with him. Once he was on their tails, so to speak, they found it hard to shake him off—which we can't either, once we get hooked to his tales. Man-eaters of Kumaon looks to me like India's third-greatest storybook, after the Mahabharata and the Ramayana. How did Corbett acquire the art of writing so brilliantly? He read James Fenimore Cooper; Jack London and Mark Twain may also have influenced him. He seems to have read fiction set in frontier territory, novels of exploration and adventure. In my book on Corbett, I want to model myself on Corbett's tales, telling a sequence of stories that provide a picture of Corbett along with glimpses of his context. I want to give a sense of original, archival fact-finding. There will be entertaining digressions that show how Corbett's immersion in wildlife was a substitute for the wilderness he suffered in relation to women because of a possessive and devoted sister. The chief source of information on Corbett is a sheaf of notes—thirteen pages dictated by the same sister (whose name was Maggie) to her friend in Kenya, Ruby Beyts, where she and Jim spent their last years. Maggie functioned for India's greatest naturalist as a mother, sister, and wife, much as Dorothy did for Wordsworth. I am starting this book today—the thirteenth of September, 1967. I plan to finish the book in two years, at most three. But will anyone ever publish it?

FIVE

Charu hovered at home around the time the postman made his rounds, pretending she had work to do there. She looked up each time she heard Bijli bark and subsided when she saw there was nobody in particular the dog was barking at. For a few days after a letter from Kundan Singh, I could hear her happy voice everywhere. She tripped down the shortcut through the forest to the bazaar with canisters of milk for regular customers, and when she returned, her face would be wreathed in smiles, although her shoulders were bent with the leaking sackfuls of rotting vegetables that she collected from the market for her cows and carried home on her head. Then as the days passed, and the gap between letters lengthened, her ebullience dwindled.

Each time a letter came, I asked her if she wanted me to write a reply and she shook her head. One day she said, "I'll write when I can write by myself." She was improving. She no longer forgot spellings from one day to the next. To begin with I was teaching her words like "hum," "tum," and "theek" that I thought would most quickly help her frame her first independent letter. Meanwhile she made me write Kundan's address on stamped envelopes once in a while and she posted him things—leaves, pine needles, pressed flowers—that I came to know about when he mentioned them in his replies.

"It is very hot here," the letter I read to her that June said.

> *You will never be able to imagine how hot. In the afternoon I can see flies falling dead out of the air. When I come back to my room my bed has dead flies on it. There are dust storms here instead of rain. The wind picks up dust from the ground and*

blows it around. It looks dark with the dust as if it's very cloudy. It stings your eyes. It is very hard to cook in this heat. The kitchen is as hot as a pot on the fire. The water in the tap is hot enough for tea. Yesterday I went to a fair after work. There were dancers like in movies. It had bright lights and a giant wheel like we had seen once in the army grounds. But I remembered that wheel and did not want to climb into this one alone for a ride. I walked around and thought of walking in the mountains. I bought earrings with red stones. They are pretty, but not as pretty as the one I have, with a green stone. I will write again.

Your Loving Friend.

Kundan Singh's large-lettered scrawl covered all three sides of his inland letters, and all the space on the flaps, as if he were determined not to waste a millimeter. His letters were in simple language, and crowded with vivid details from his days. The landscape of his life became clearer with each blue inland that arrived. He described his room: it was a small one over the garage. From it, he could sometimes hear a lion roar at night—the house was close to Delhi's zoo. Not far from the house was Purana Quila, the ruins of an ancient fortress. He had never been on the boats that sailed around in the fortress's moat, but he dreamed of doing so one day, with his "dear friend in Ranikhet."

Kundan Singh was originally from Nepal, and had a sister, for whose dowry he was saving. His family lived on the outskirts of Siliguri, a town in the plains at the eastern end of the Himalaya. His father made a sort of living as a gardener, odd-job man, and chowkidar. He had struggled all his life and dreamed that someday his son would get a government job. But Kundan Singh had skipped school and joined a local hotel instead, as a helper, from where he had progressed to his present job.

His employers appeared to be fond of him. The woman (whom he had nicknamed Jhadu because she was very thin and particular about cleanliness) often bought him clothes and gave him extra money to send home. Their house had a deep veranda shaded by chiks made of khus. I had to explain to Charu that chiks were blinds made of a kind of grass, khus, which became fragrant when dampened. The other servants sprinkled the khus with water before guests arrived. They filled tall vases with scented white tuberoses and dusted the pictures. On summer evenings, Kundan's employers and their friends sat in the veranda looking into the large old trees that shaded the lawn, with a big cooler whirring at them. The tables around them began filling with empty bottles and glasses as the evening passed. One of the frequent visitors was a woman who dressed in very short skirts and long earrings; she drank the most, and also smoked long cigarettes. "She looks like a Nepali," Kundan had written to Charu, "but she may be Chinese. She wears strange clothes. You can see her legs from top to bottom. She drinks five or six bottles of beer in one evening."

The short-skirted woman wanted one day to learn how to make mutton the way hill people cooked it. She had demanded a lesson and Jhadu had told him to be ready. Kundan, who had seen cookery shows on television, placed all the ingredients he would need—chopped, diced, ground, or powdered—ready in a line of little bowls. He had cleaned the kitchen thoroughly and cleared all the surfaces so that it looked as much like TV kitchens as he could make it. But when the guests arrived, he felt shy. "I did not want to teach anyone anything," he wrote in his letter. "I stayed in my room. Then Jhadu sent for me."

When he came into the kitchen, still reluctant, the woman laughed and said, "What, you don't want to teach me your secrets?" She stood by him and watched and took notes as he cooked the meat. She kept dipping in a spoon, blowing on it and tasting the gravy. One of the other friends took pictures of them cooking. They gave Kundan copies of the photographs, one of which he sent to Charu. It was the first photograph he had ever sent her.

I looked at it before giving it to her. The kitchen in the picture was shiny and new, like something from a magazine. The friend, a pretty young woman with slanting eyes and high cheekbones, was in a slate-gray miniskirt, very chic. Earrings dangled to her shoulders and a long silver necklace slid down the center of the low-cut, ivory-colored top she wore. She was smiling at the camera, a lovely smile. Kundan too was smiling from over the steam in his cooking pot, which had made his face shine. His mop of hair had grown and the brass amulet at his neck blazed in the light of the camera's flash.

When Charu looked at the picture she did not smile. And for the first time, she did not spring about light-footed, humming and chattering, as she usually did after receiving a letter. The next few days she went to the market with her canisters of milk banging sullenly against her legs, and on her way back with the sack of rotting vegetables on her head, she slashed at every bush she passed with her stick.

SIX

The long summer turned the hillsides to tinder, the rains would not come, and there had been no letter from Kundan since the one with his photograph. Charu was too anxious for anything beyond the mechanical performance of her chores. In earlier times she had always kept a caring eye out for Puran. She was adept at stealing grain from Ama's stores for his deer and because she knew he fed much of his own food to the animals he made friends with, she made a few extra rotis smeared with salt and ghee to give him when Ama was not looking. Now, more often than not, she forgot and Puran began to go hungry.

He did not ask anyone at home for food. Food had a way of coming to him, he had discovered, if he went up to Negi's tea stall on Mall Road. That was where Mr. Chauhan caught sight of him every other day, and then his long-nursed rage against Puran took on an inexplicable intensity. "This beggar and all these dogs! Just wait, Mam, and you will see what I mean," he said to me in a hiss one evening when I encountered him on Mall Road. At that moment, Puran was sitting on Negi's crooked bench, looking innocuous enough. At the road's edge, boys were arguing over a carrom board, and another group was cheering a volleyball game in the vacant lot next to Meghdoot Hotel. Girls in their brightest, tightest clothes walked up and down in pairs, casting sidelong glances at the boys, who stood around slapping each other's shoulders, running fingers through their hair, laughing and talking louder when the girls passed. A jeep drew up from the bazaar, roof loaded with sacks and bundles, spilling out people and goat kids and black diesel smoke. Mr. Chauhan covered his nose with a white, ironed handkerchief.

The younger Negi came to Puran with an expression of exaggerated patience. "Back again?" he said, and handed him a glass of tea and four fat slices of bread. Puran scurried away with his tea and bread across to the low parapet that ran all the way down the western edge of Mall Road, and sat on it eating in a hurry as if the bread was in danger of being snatched away from him. A ring of woolly dogs formed around him, looking up with pleading eyes and drooling tongues. Puran dropped them scraps and the dogs snarled and yelped as they fought over the food.

Mr. Chauhan turned to me in triumph and said, "See? See what I mean? Yesterday I told my secretary—we were in the car—please make a note, I said, too many stray dogs. I would like a list—all dogs' descriptions and names in one column and owners' names in the second column. Any dog that does not have a license must go. We will draw up regulations for licensing dogs and this . . . beggar? There should be no beggars in an army cantonment. We must be an example for the rest of India. I'll fix this man. That is what I said."

He returned to the door of his white Gypsy, whose bright red beacon had been spinning like an angry top all through our conversation. The car roared to life and took him away down Mall Road. Puran sat on the parapet oblivious. The stray dogs lolled at his feet, contented after their snack. The darkening mountains behind him began to swallow the blood-red sun as it turned from a disk to a sliver, slowly disappearing from view.

* * *

That night, I sat at my window in a trance gazing at the fires in the forest. What would happen to the animals that lived in the undergrowth if a wind were to fan those slow fires into a blaze? They were always in danger. One year Puran had run into the flames in the middle of the night and come back with a singed fox cub; another year he had rescued a baby monkey from the burning forest and the next morning a whole family of monkeys had appeared on our doorstep, agitating for its release in angry screeches and chatters.

I was lost in worried thoughts about Puran and Mr. Chauhan's threats to "fix" him when I heard a faint knock on my door downstairs. It was past ten o'clock; the neighbors were asleep. My light was the only one on; I was supposed to be correcting the English class test. At first I thought the knock was a figment of my imagination and applied myself to the exercise book I was working on. And then I heard it again.

Nobody visited this late in Ranikhet. My stomach gave a lurch. This was the call in the night I had known would come one day. Something had happened to Diwan Sahib and Himmat Singh had come to call me. I raced down the stairs and unlatched the front door in a panic.

It was Veer. His nose was peeling with sunburn and his face was thinner than usual from the weeks he had been away walking and climbing. His normally close-cropped hair had grown. That, and an unfamiliar beard, made him look a stranger. For a second my mind sprang to my last night with Michael when I had brushed my fingers over his clean-shaven cheeks in anticipation of the beard he came back with from every trek, when I had pinched the roll of fat around his stomach knowing he would lose it in the weeks away.

Veer was standing so close to me I could smell his sweat. His jeans were dirty and his shoes muddy. I was stabbed by a sudden, fierce need to bury my face in his shirt although it hung on him grimy with dirt. But I remembered the way he had driven away without a look at me. "You're back," I said. And then: "I've piles of work to finish."

He took his shoes off at the door and brushed past me into my kitchen. He went to the shelf where I stacked old newspapers, and extracted one, which he laid on a corner of the kitchen floor. He placed his shoes on the precise center of the newspaper and said: "See how muddy they are? All your rugs would have been filthy." He helped himself to water from the steel filter and drank it in gulps, saying in between, "Hot, hot. Monsoon delayed. But CNN's predicted rain. It'll come tonight. It's so still. You can feel the thunder."

He washed the glass and set it down with the same precision upon the kitchen counter, opened the fridge, and examined the jug of milk, cubes of cheese, and the aging lemon it contained, and shook his head saying, "Don't you ever eat real food?" He wandered into my living room and paused before the framed picture. It was a photographic panorama of the peaks visible from Ranikhet, with their altitudes written alongside. Why was he examining a picture he must have seen in every house in these hills, I wondered? Was he planning to show me the places his climbs had taken him to? Now? At this hour?

Veer's hands, resting on the back of a chair, were deep in the folds of a dusty-pink cardigan I had left draped on it. I noticed that his fingers were moving in the wool, kneading it. I knew then why he had come, even before he began to speak. "Every day on this trek I've been thinking that I've seen dozens of beautiful places in the world," he said, "and most of its mountain ranges. And I know for sure that there's nowhere else I would rather be than the Himalaya, and in the Himalaya, Ranikhet, and in Ranikhet, the corner of it that has you." He turned away from the picture and toward me with a deep breath that he exhaled in a rush. His eyes shone, half-terrified, half-exultant, when unexpectedly, he pointed to his feet and laughed. "Look," he said, "obviously you scare me more than the worst crevasse." One of his socks was blue and the other dark green.

That night a cool, moist breeze began ruffling the trees, making a sound like the sea. Pinecones clattered onto the roof. The stars disappeared and thunder boomed. Sword-blades of brilliant white light sliced open the glowing red sky. The breeze grew into a wind that howled and banged. My little house on the edge of its spur became a tilting boat. The wind blew in sprays of rain through the open windows and we closed our eyes to the mist of water as if we were not in the mountains but on a wave-thudded beach. Far below, the still-smoldering, smoking forest began to calm at last.

* * *

Mindful that gossip was almost the only entertainment in a town as small as ours, we did our best to be discreet. Veer came rarely to my house. When he did, it was late at night and he left before dawn. He never left his shoes or umbrella outside my door. When we wanted to be together, we drove miles out of Ranikhet, to one of the isolated hillsides that surround the town. We put a rug on the pine-cushioned forest floor and lay there with nothing above us but the sky in its mesh of pine fronds. It felt as if we were the only two people in all of the jagged, wild, precipitous Himalaya—until we found a goat looking at us, soon followed by a curious goatherd. Sometimes children scampering between school and village through the jungle stopped and gawped at us until I felt ready to brandish a stick at them. But I still preferred this to Ama's watchfulness, and to prevent anyone seeing us together when we returned, I got out of the jeep some distance from home and walked back by a different route, so that we arrived separately.

However foolproof our stratagems, the young widow's liaison with her landlord's relative very quickly became the talk of the hillside. Within days I felt gossip eddying around my ankles. One morning, from my window, I saw Ama in my garden, poking at the earth with her stick, apparently examining my plants. When I came outside she rambled on about the flowers on the cucumber vine, about how her beans were being eaten by pests, and about Puran's deer, which had disappeared for two hours the day before, driving him to distraction. I was growing weary of waiting for her to come to the point, when she looked skyward as if she were going to talk about the rains and said, "Do you know about Gappu Dhobi's younger bahu?"

I only knew Gappu, our local washerman. "You mean that pretty girl who grazes his cows with a baby strapped to her back in a shawl?" I said. I knew her more as a cowherd than as Gappu's daughter-in-law.

"Yes, yes, the same one. That baby . . . now that baby is not by her husband. Her husband died years ago, when she was very young, just like you. Her child from that marriage is about twelve now. Just days after the husband died, this girl—everyone calls her Gudiya, because she looks like a glass doll—she took up with the fellow's brother. That man had an eye on her even when the husband was alive, and when the husband died, the brother—they call him Vikki—he barely waited till the ashes had cooled when he began to seduce his sister-in-law.

Before they could change the sheet, the next man was in her bed. I am not making this up, the older sister-in-law told me—you know that woman who is at the public water tap every day gossiping about the universe as though she's got nothing else to do?"

"So it was good in the end, wasn't it?" I said. "The girl seems happily married now."

"Aah—but they are not married, you see!" Ama said with a cackling laugh. "No, no, Vikki is too shrewd for that. Gudiya's husband was a peon in a Gormint office in Haldwani. When he died, Gudiya started getting a fat pension—I've heard it is two thousand rupees now. You think this Vikki would let himself lose that? Oh no. He knows only widows get the pension. So he just took Gudiya to a temple and told her, 'Now before God we are married, but if any Gormint babu asks, you must say you are a widow.' And every year she goes to State Bank and has to put her thumbprint on a paper to swear she has not married. Then they release her pension for the next year. Even the bank babus know it's a lie, but what can they do?"

"So what?" I said. "Everyone breaks laws."

"How do you trust a man so greedy he wants his wife to be called a widow? Now, you look at our Diwan Sahib. He's old, he has that house and money, just wait and see, there'll be vultures circling him till he dies. People who haven't cared a bit for him. All these years, who looked after him? You did, I did, Himmat did. But you wait and see what happens. Old men without children start sprouting relatives faster than weeds after rain. It's not easy knowing who to trust. And women alone? We never know when—did I tell you about that girl in our village? She put her hand into the tin to measure out rice like every other day and before you knew it she was screaming and writhing on the floor and there was a snake—as thick as my arm—who had her hand its mouth."

Veer and Ama disliked each other equally, I realized. One evening a discussion about Puran's deer exploded into a nasty argument when Veer insisted that Diwan Sahib get rid of Ama and her family. "What purpose does it serve," Veer demanded to know, "to waste all that space for some peasants to turn it into a squalid slum and for their cattle to breed dirt and flies and destroy every inch of the garden?"

Later, when I tried to calm him down, he said, "You don't know a thing about that woman and her damned family. I've seen them here since I was a kid. They were all over the place, as if they owned it. There was that drunk of a son. He bullied me when I came for vacations, he stole from my uncle, he beat his wife to death here—ten feet from your cottage—how would you have liked that? The police came, there was a real stink. My uncle almost got charged just for being the landlord even though he was nowhere near the house when it happened. I was hardly ten, but I've never forgotten the sound of that woman screaming. I've tried for years to make my uncle see reason and make them go. He could pay them off. But the old man is such a mule."

When the poison ran so deep it was no use reasoning. I did not want Ama to be evicted any more than Diwan Sahib did, nor was I going to have an argument with Veer. "Speaking of mules," I said, "did you ever find out if mules need shoes? And elephants and bullocks? And zebras and wildebeest? Maybe we could discuss this while you walk me home?" I slipped my fingers into his and wove them together.

* * *

Ama was not the only one with barbs to dispense: everyone was discussing Veer and me. Mrs. Chauhan gave me a knowing look when I met her on Mall Road one evening and said, "Arre, Maya Memsa'ab, you are looking ten years younger! Tell me the secret, and I will buy it too!" *Maya Memsa'ab* was the name of a Hindi film based on *Madame Bovary,* in which a bored wife entertains herself with a series of love affairs. Mrs. Chauhan nudged me toward a sign that her husband had just had nailed to a tree. It said, "Fighting Fire is Our Desire." She read it aloud, gave my hand a conspiratorial squeeze, and left, suppressing giggles behind her palm. The General had a view as well. One morning, I went to the cemetery, to talk things over with Michael as I sometimes did. I sat by his headstone, chin resting on my knees, absentmindedly plucking at the grass by my feet, when the

General, who had come to visit Angelina's grave, came upon me. "Ah, Maya!" he said. "I didn't expect to see you here anymore . . . it's been long enough, you're too young to be moping over the past. Move on, my girl, move on. High time."

Diwan Sahib's response took me by surprise. I had assumed that he would be happy about Veer and me, but he became curiously resentful. One afternoon, I went to get his newspaper from Negi's shop, and the boy there said Diwan Sahib had relayed instructions that the paper was not to be given to me; it was to be delivered straight to him. I asked Diwan Sahib why he was changing such an old arrangement, and his face turned sulky. "Why not? When you forget to come every other day? I can live without your august company, but I do need my daily paper." He started keeping tabs on me and noting how little time I was spending with him. If he saw me looking better dressed than usual he would say in sardonic tones, "Where's the untidy hair, poked through with a pencil? You look like a society lady now, all shining and combed." When I wore a new kurta one day, he said to Mr. Qureshi: "Our wild Himalayan rose is turning into a memsa'ab." Another day, mellow after a long evening's drinking, he said in a thoughtful tone, "If you went climbing, Maya, you would know: unknown territories need caution. One step at a time and lots of reconnaissance."

Trekking and exploring suddenly featured a great deal in conversation. Veer said lightheartedly, when our murmurings on the rug in the forest edged toward the future: "Life's a trek too, isn't it? You meet people on the way that you like, spend days with them under tents, and then your time with them is over. But you don't stop walking the route; you have to go on. Look at you, you're the best example."

What was he trying to tell me? I was not sure I wanted to know. We were too new and fragile, too skinless to be exposed to daylight just yet. What Veer's life had been before me, I did not care about. I only knew that I could no longer do without him. Ama's disapproval was a given, of course. But whatever had Diwan Sahib meant about trekking and caution? I had no idea if he himself knew, now that he was drinking himself insensible every day.

I could think of nothing but Veer: he was with me every minute.

I became more than usually distracted in my classes. One morning, Miss Wilson slammed a wooden blackboard duster down on my table and said, "This is too much, Maya! I told you twice yesterday to inform Mr. Chauhan that the school will not be used as a voting center. Don't you hear a word I say? Now you go and handle him. He's already come with some orderlies and he's selecting classrooms." Sometimes stirring a vat of jam at the factory I would go on and on stirring while my mind and body were far away, under the lacework of deodar in the forest, until one of the girls would say, "Maya Mam?" and take the long ladle from my hand.

I had to force myself not to barge into Veer's working day, when he was immersed in his e-mails and his telephone, to suggest an expedition in his jeep. I waited for him to finish work and notice me. I waited every minute, when he was away, for him to come home.

Veer's days were unpredictable. He worked from a room in the Light House. On some days he would lock himself away in it and, apart from the low hum of his voice on the telephone, there would be no sign of his presence. On other days he did no work at all and would sit in the veranda chatting with Diwan Sahib and Mr. Qureshi, or go down to the bazaar to pick up his mail, stock up food for an approaching trek, and idle with people he met. The wool shop owner's son, who was a budding politician, had become a friend of his, and there was a hotelier in the bazaar who would buttonhole Veer to try to persuade him to bring his clients to his hotel for a few days of relaxation after their treks. Veer played along, pronouncing it a great idea, but he never did bring his clients to Ranikhet. Instead, he picked them up from the railhead at Kathgodam, from where they drove directly to wherever they would begin the trek. I had only the foggiest understanding of his work and if I asked questions about routes and clients, he would answer with a smile, "Were you thinking of signing up? The next trek is to the Pindari glacier. Leeches and high-quality instant noodles guaranteed."

Sometimes it worried me that he could disappear for weeks, when no one had any way of telling, except in the most general sense, where he was. After one of his trips to Delhi in early July, when I went into his room for something or the other I found he had left his dirty clothes in a heap on the floor next to his bag. Out of a corner of my eye, I saw that one of the shirts was discolored. I looked closer at it. The shirt's blue denim was smeared all over with blood. The large stains looked fresh, still red, perhaps still damp. I did not want to touch the shirt to find out, but I was so startled I sat on a chair in his room and studied it from a safe distance to make sure I was not mistaking ink or paint for blood.

Veer had only returned that morning and was out in the veranda. He had changed into clean jeans and a loose gray T-shirt and sat on a low chair with a tea mug beside him. His feet were bare; he was whistling "Hey Jude" and staring at the screen of his laptop. When I went out and asked, "What's all that blood on your shirt?" his face became such a mask of annoyance that I winced. Then his expression changed to one of amused tenderness. He gave me the half smile that I found irresistible and said, "I have something to confess. Will you forgive me? I killed someone." He looked around to see if there was anyone watching, then gave my cheek a quick pinch. "Look at your face: did you believe me? No, something else happened," he said. "I overnighted in a hotel in Kaladhungi. Weird place: all night they kept shifting metal furniture across the floor of the room upstairs and walking up and down, knocking a walking stick or something like that on the floor above my head. Total silence in between and then the sounds again. The dead of night in the middle of jungle—I wondered if there were ghosts upstairs. Then someone began to sing songs, very beautifully—old folksongs—but that was the last straw, I couldn't sleep at all. So I left at three in the morning. And you know that deep forest you have to drive through? You feel as if tigers will spring out of the bush anytime. Some guys were standing there in the dark, in the middle of the road, with a flashlight and a dead man on the ground—they had put a tree branch across the road to make cars stop. I thought I was going to be robbed and killed, but they just wanted my help to take the man to hospital. He was unconscious it turned out, not dead. A huge Sardar, bleeding all over. I managed to spread a rug over the backseat, but in the process of hauling the man in, my shirt . . . mustn't give it to Gappu Dhobi, he'll imagine the worst." He paused and added, "As you did."

I could not tell where the thought came from and I could not stop the words when I heard myself saying, "Where was it you rushed off to when those helicopters were circling Ranikhet? Remember? You saw me on the road, but you didn't stop. You didn't come back for weeks. Nobody knew where you were."

"What are you talking about?" Veer said. He seemed mystified by the question.

"I mean that time in May, when there were choppers in the sky all day, and you got a call on your phone and left without a word to anyone. What was that about?"

"Why do you sound so aggressive? I can't tell you everything. That doesn't mean I'm up to something fishy. What do you think I do anyway? Don't you trust me?"

"You might trust me too, and tell me what that was all about. Most of the time I have no idea where you go, what you do, who you see—nothing."

Until the moment I asked him, I had not even been aware that my suspicions about that morning were still gnawing at me. But now that I had begun, each thing I said stoked my rage.

Veer said nothing. When he clamped his lips shut the way he was doing now, and sucked in his cheeks, his face grew thinner still and grimmer, locked away. He looked at his computer screen, not at me, and said in a voice that was clipped and cold, "It was to help the army with a search they needed to do. I know that area well, and I've done chopper searches before. Which is why they called me in." He did not look up from the screen, and said nothing more.

I did not know what to say. I fiddled with a banksia creeper by the door. I looked at a goat chewing on a young plant in the garden. It had rained that morning and now every leaf gleamed in the clear, washed light. Water plopped from a rainwater pipe into a tin drum. The grass had turned a tender green, but I knew it now hid black threads that bloated into blood-gorged leeches where they found warm skin. I could feel one on my ankle and bent to pluck it off. The scab would itch for days. Bijli appeared from somewhere and wagged his tail at us and gave a few short barks to suggest a walk. I patted him and said I would take him.

I turned to go, paused, trying to form the words for an apology, but could not. As I left the veranda my footsteps slowed and I came back. "Sorry," I said, "it came out wrong." I knew I still sounded grudging, and I was filled with regret for starting a quarrel and ruining a beautiful day, especially when he had just returned after a long journey.

I waited for him to say something forgiving, but he did not look up from his typing.

One afternoon soon after, I stood looking at the mountains, which had risen out of the monsoon sky. Clouds were piled high at their base so that they floated in midair, detached from everything earthly. Something in the quality of the light made the peaks appear translucent, as if the molten silver sky were visible through them. In the next few moments, I saw an extraordinary cloud form out of nothing, gather over the peaks, and grow larger and larger, spreading a black cloak as it traveled toward me, seemingly at the speed of a rocket. In no more than a minute it reached our hills and turned afternoon into twilight. Then the rain came sheeting down.

I ran inside, and as I shook my hair dry I wondered if I should interpret the cloud as an omen. I looked around for something to do to drive the thought away. I began to pull books out of the shelves and pile them on the floor. Silverfish scuttled out from between their pages. The books needed dusting and sunning. I pulled out shelf after shelf of books, possessed with energy and purpose. I would arrange them alphabetically—or maybe by genre. I would give away the thrillers I would never read again and all those books I had bought and kept thinking I would read the next month. Why did I have multiple copies of *Man-eaters of Kumaon*? And where had this book on the arts and architecture of ancient Greece come from?

In a while, I was exhausted. I sat on the floor, and looked in despair at the tumbling heaps of books around me. I would never get them back on their shelves now.

I began to look through the ones close enough to reach without getting up: a murder mystery, a book on hill plants, *Sàlim Ali's Indian Hill Birds*. And then, between the pages of a fat collection of short stories, the old copy of T. S. Eliot's millimeter-thin *Practical Cats* that Michael had given me long ago. His angular handwriting rode a diagonal across one of the blank pages: "To my own perverse, pigheaded Rum Tum Tugger."

I pulled a cushion to me and lay on the rug, tenting my face in the opened pages of the book, breathing in its antique smell.

I would not look into the future. My life had been too cruelly overturned once before for me to think of anything but the present moment. I would negotiate each day as if I were riding a leaf in a flowing stream: enough to stay afloat. I would not ask for more.

Seven

The monsoon in our hills is a time of thunder, lightning, water, and wind so endless that it has been known to push people into fits of rage. One day, not a month into the monsoon, the tae kwon do teacher at one of the other schools punched two boys senseless because he suspected them of stealing his camera. He had come upon them peddling a similar camera in Babita Studio. He wrecked the shop too, shattering framed photographs of just-married couples with a hammer he had bought from the shop next door. The combined strength of three taxi drivers and a policeman was needed for him to be handcuffed and taken to the police station. By then the boys were bleeding, while Babita Studio was in shards—and who was going to pay for the damage? Better to occupy yourself with gossip than break each other's bones—and that is how most people spent the time, watching the rain, drinking tea, and gossiping.

When the clouds came lower and lower, to rest on our hills, they wiped away the mountains on the other side of the valley and bleached the distant trees of color, turning them into charcoaled lines on the gray-white sky. Houses felt furry with fungus and damp. Dripping umbrellas spoked pools of water before every front door. The hills were a lush, brilliant green, and wild gladioli drooped everywhere in the rain. The forest was carpeted with pretty, mauve, orchid-like flowers. Roads were reclaimed by nature as landslides buried them and waterfalls drowned them, the wind felled trees, electricity failed, and telephones died, cutting off our town. Some days, the clouds gave way to lurid sunsets, and then the curtains closed again.

That August, I wanted nothing more than for our rain-soaked town to remain untouched, cocooned and cut off from the boiling world below. Instead, the newspaper came in two-day-old bunches, the pages stuck together with damp; when I peeled them apart, they were filled with news from Orissa, every day something more brutal: churches burned; missionaries hounded; Christians driven out of their villages into refugee camps; a young woman raped, thrown into a fire, and burned alive.

I could not tell if Miss Wilson deliberately left the paper open to the page with news from Orissa. It stared at me when I sat opposite her for our daily staff meetings. The paper would be turned in my direction so I did not need to read upside-down. She began to say, "We Christians are used to sacrifices for the glory of Our Lord. We have made them since St. Thomas landed in Kerala soon after Our Lord's Ascension. Who runs all of India's good schools? Who cares for the poor?" She pronounced it as "pore" and then after a perfunctory pause, "We, Christians."

Miss Wilson had a brother in Orissa who worked for a TV channel called DivineLite, which aimed to make Christianity more accessible through stories of everyday triumphs over greed, lust, envy, and suchlike. Recent converts who looked jubilant—and prosperous—explained how Jesus had transformed their lives and urged others to find the same sustenance and joy. Every program began and ended with a feature called "Prayer of the Day" during which the entire cast of DivineLite held hands, shut their eyes, and intoned a recently written prayer. For several days now, the prayer had been, "Let us put down the weapon of hatred and violence and put on the armor of love. Let us forgive one another and ask forgiveness from one another for the wrong we have done to each other and reach out in love to each other."

One day, the TV channel's office was picketed by a bunch of hoodlums shouting slogans calling for it to be shut down. Miss Wilson told us of the incident the next day. She had tried to reach her brother on the telephone, but he was too choked with fear to talk, she said. They had even been threatened with death. She looked preoccupied and worried and whispered urgently into her mobile phone now and then.

She did not come to the classes to rap tables with her cane and shout "*Quay-it.*" Nor did she realize that the school bells were often being rung late because the chowkidar was more stoned than usual these days. Whenever I came to speak to her in her room, she shuffled papers or fiddled with something on her desk so that she would not have to look at me.

As things got worse in Orissa, the something invisible and dangerous that Miss Wilson and I had tiptoed around all this time grew in size until it took up most of the space. Despite my marriage and the change in my surname, I had never converted to Christianity. Michael's parents had said they would accept me if I converted, but Michael did not want me to, and neither did his priest. Only if it comes naturally, Father Joseph had said, only when the time is right. In the weeks after Michael's death he had asked me a few times if I would meet Michael's parents; this great grief could be a time for healing and forgiveness, he said. But I thought they might blame me more ferociously now for the years of Michael that they had lost. The time for friendship is over, I had told the father. The next week Father Joseph had relayed another request from them: they wanted something from Michael's rucksack as a memento of their son's last journey, a crumb from his final days. At that time, I was distraught enough to have handed them the entire rucksack, and all his other belongings, to stop them bothering me. But then too, Father Joseph had stopped me. "There is no hurry," he had said. "Give them something later when you are able to look through his belongings. When it comes naturally. One day you'll be ready, not now."

Miss Wilson had none of Father Joseph's wisdom. From the start she had made it clear that whereas I had a job, there were needy Christian teachers still unemployed. I was the undeserving beneficiary of Father Joseph's influence in the church and she had no option but to put up with me. Now the world beyond was making matters between us too delicate and brittle to survive much stress. And as if there was a conspiracy, this was precisely the time when the election campaign in Ranikhet charged up enough for the political parties to look around for trouble-filled pots they could stir.

* * *

By the middle of August, the bazaar looked as if Diwali had come early. The narrow main street had acquired a glittering, latticed ceiling made of orange, green, silver, and gold tinsel. Party symbols hung from it. Every day the bunting grew more ragged in the rain and wind, and the posters on the walls peeled with the damp so that the candidates' faces grew more and more lopsided.

This was a national election, especially significant for our town because it was the first time a local, Veer's new friend, the son of the wool merchant, had decided to stand as a candidate. If he won, Ranikhet would no longer be a backwater; it would be pitchforked straight into the center of Uttarakhand politics; it would get grants and attention, public money would flow in. The wool merchant's son was called Ankit Rawat. He had adopted a ball of red wool as his logo and his motto was: *"Santusth, Surakshit, aur Garam / Ankit Rawat ka hai Dharam"* ("Warm, Safe, Free of Need / This is Ankit Rawat's Creed").

The older Mr. Rawat, who had a shop in the bazaar, had hung a red woolen globe at the entrance to it; it was as large as several footballs and tall people tended to bump their heads against it on their way into the shop. All over town, there were soggy posters with Ankit Rawat's purposeful young face beaming from the center of a ball of red wool. I had only encountered him before across the counter at his father's shop, when he had sold me thermal undershirts, socks, and cardigans. "Now I will have to employ an assistant," his father said in jovial tones. "My son will be too grand for my shop." He gestured toward the sacred red circle of kumkum and rice grains on his forehead. "All God's grace, all His wish."

Ankit Rawat's supporters, mostly young friends from his college days, tore through the market and Mall Road on motorbikes, shouting his election slogan into megaphones and telling people when and where to vote. "Send your son to Delhi! Uttarakhand needs a man from Ranikhet at the center," they urged, to cheers and jokes from the shopkeepers and the people in the streets. Ankit switched from his jeans and jackets to long white kurtas and a red chadar that billowed from his neck when he thundered past with his motorbike cavalcade. Surrounded at all times by his cohorts, he acquired a pop star aura that made people want to be noticed by him. He was clean featured and tall, and when he posed next to toothless old village women or porters and farmers hunched by years of bending, people said he looked like a prince. He happened to pass by Ama's cottage one evening at the end of his monthly Ranikhet darshan, when he would meet common folk and discuss their problems. "He sat on that stool in the courtyard outside our hut, just like an ordinary man," Ama said later, to anyone who would listen. "I had nothing in the house but some batashas and tea. Mud all over me because I had just come from the fields. He told me he had never drunk such sweet tea. He promised double water supply. And the electricity will never go off."

Ankit's opponent was a man from Nainital who had won election after election promising to serve the Hindu cause. Umed Singh was said to be a battle-hardened, canny politician, and had taken to calling Ankit "chota bachha"—"little child." "Mind you, every child should be encouraged," he said, to a Nainital journalist who used the comment as a headline. "Children need to learn the ropes." Umed Singh had not yet come to campaign in Ranikhet; in the past he had never needed to. This year was different.

The Baba who had taken up residence at the temple near my favorite tea shack caused a flutter one day when he appeared in the market, where an orange and red marquee had been set up. He was greeted by singers who were bleary eyed and hoarse voiced from singing songs all night that were broadcast across the valley on loudspeakers. The occasion was Umed Singh's first campaign visit to Ranikhet. The Baba blessed them, and he blessed Umed Singh's campaign. One of his assistants read women's palms and handed out amulets that guaranteed offspring to childless women so that Hindus were not outnumbered in the coming years by those who were allowed four wives.

Umed Singh appeared next onstage. For long minutes he did not speak, letting the crowd settle and expectation build. When he began, he spoke in a ponderous voice, with measured pauses during which he gauged the temper of his audience while it held its breath for his next aphorism. He said it was time the hills were released forever from foreign imperialists who had taken them over in British times and replaced ancient temples with churches and mosques. Everywhere, he said, Hindus were being falsely accused of violence when all they wanted was to preserve their way of life against terrorism and against their own people being converted to other religions. It was time to redress the balance. This was not a task that could be left to children who had sold wool the previous week and now on a whim had set out to turn the world upside-down.

"Now what?" I said to Diwan Sahib. "Do you still think the graveyard was vandalized by boys who'd drunk too much—and not by this lot? If Umed Singh wants to, he can make lots of trouble for Agnes W. Just to add some spice to his campaign."

"It's 'Agnes W' now, is it, behind her back? To her face it's, 'Yes, Miss Wilson,' and 'No, Miss Wilson,'" Diwan Sahib said. "Your beloved principal! Be a little respectful. What do you call me when I'm out of earshot?"

EIGHT

The bazaar was not the only place to be transformed during the monsoon. Mr. Chauhan's deadline, the Regimental Reunion, was just over the horizon, and everywhere we could see evidence of his energy. Giant heaps of gravel and sand had been deposited at street corners, and in the rain they flowed onto the roads in little landslides. Some children, who found one such heap near their hut, squealed with pleasure as they pelted each other with balls of caked-up gravel. Their father rushed out with a bucket and scolded them, "Don't waste it. We might need it. Here, let's put it into this."

Laborers appeared in fours and fives instead of the usual ones and twos. Squatting by the parapets, they began to knock at them in a dispirited way with hammers. The old stone parapets, lush with ferns and little pink lilies, were to be torn down and replaced with neater cement ones. Road rollers were on their way. As soon as the rains stopped, the pitted road was going to be relaid all the way down Mall Road, past the officers' mess, and up to Mr. Chauhan's house. The tin planters that hung on the arms of cement crosses along Mall Road had long been bereft of flowers; they were now filled with fresh earth and planted with geranium cuttings. Wrought iron benches were ordered from Haldwani and placed at strategic points. Three of the benches went missing within days. One of them disappeared from near the Light House and the next morning a cantonment official arrived and asked us questions about dead trees and the branches that needed to be lopped, while he walked all over our garden, his eyes reaching into the corners and down the slopes. Diwan Sahib made him an offer of tea and said, "Sit, sit down. We may not have wrought iron benches, but we do have chairs. Shall we donate them to the army?"

Mr. Chauhan was a familiar sight on the roads now, walking under a rain-sodden umbrella held over him by an orderly who followed him everywhere getting wetter and wetter. Other administrators buzzed around in their jeeps—Mr. Chauhan told us whenever he could—"but I myself, the man in command, I need to be on the front line verifying the situation on the ground, not blindly accepting reports from juniors." He went on inspection tours. He chivvied the workers breaking down the old parapets and hammering at blocks of stone. More signs appeared, to indicate places where cows and buffaloes were forbidden, so that overgrazed trees and shrubs would come back to life.

One morning Mr. Chauhan spotted Puran, who was tying his cow to one of the metal posts on which a signboard stood. Mr. Chauhan abandoned the protection of his umbrella and snatched the cow's rope from Puran's hand. He banged the writing on the sign above them with his stick and yelled, "Not here. Not here! No cow here!" His stick clanged on the metal so loudly that Gappu Dhobi ran out from his house to see what the matter was. Mr. Chauhan flung the rope into Puran's face and shouted again, "Not here, you illiterate village fool! You'll be fined! You'll be arrested!"

Puran shied away like a startled animal and fled. His feet had been in rubber slippers ever since his army-issue shoes had been burned by Mr. Chauhan's men. His bare ankles were bleeding from leeches that settled there to feed. The slippers slithered on the wet hillside. He plunged into tall grass and gradually disappeared from view into a valley whose lush undergrowth hid stinging nettles, snakes, scorpions, and more leeches. Puran was in too much of a panic to bother about any of this. His cows and goats followed him down the valley, precisely into the area Mr. Chauhan had marked out of bounds. Their hooves flattened several new saplings Mr. Chauhan's workforce had planted there the week before.

Later, soaked and irritable, Mr. Chauhan walked into his house, and when Mrs. Chauhan said in a voice full of concern, "How did you get so wet?" he shouted, "In the line of duty! I got wet in the line of duty!" He had forgotten to take off his muddy shoes at the door. They left a trail over a new carpet as Mr. Chauhan went toward the bedroom, yanking his sopping shirt from the tight waistband of his trousers. Mrs. Chauhan gave the carpet a look and slapped her forehead in exasperation. "*Offo!* What did I say? It's become impossible to talk in this house, even a simple question." She telephoned her sister in Lucknow for solace. "This job's stress is really getting him down. Day and night, he's never relaxed, not for one minute. And now I'll have to send this carpet to you to be dry-cleaned. No dry cleaner's even seen a real Kashmiri carpet in this place or even in Haldwani."

Mr. Chauhan overheard her from the bedroom. He sat on the bed with his head in his hands. A damp patch grew around him as water seeped out from his wet clothes. He pressed his fingers on his Australia-shaped birthmark, which throbbed to the beat of his agitated pulse. He unearthed a hidden packet, lit a cigarette with a match that shook, and resolved that this time he would teach Puran a lesson he would never forget.

* * *

Burdened with her new preoccupations, Charu no longer remembered to steal grain from Ama's store for Puran's deer. He had to wait every morning for his mother to leave their rooms for the few moments that it took him to steal some of the hen's grain from her storage tin, just a little bit every day so that she would not notice. This, combined with the freshest of the rotting fruits and vegetables that Charu brought back from the bazaar for her cows, supplied the food for his baby barking deer, which had grown steadily over the past five months, and was now more body, less leg. When he took the food to the shed and whispered, "Rani, Rani," he saw her large, dimly glowing eyes turn in his direction, but she did not get up until he had set the grain and fruit in the usual place and withdrawn some distance away.

One afternoon that August, when he called to Rani on returning from grazing the goats, he saw there was empty space in the place in the shed where her eyes should have been. The shed was tiny. Even so, he scrambled around as if the deer might be hiding under the heaps of hay and sacking strewn on the floor. She had wandered off twice in the past, and both times he had rushed about the hills like a man possessed, only calming down when he had found her and shepherded her back to the shed, all the while making mewling noises of relief. When he did not find her in the shed that afternoon, he ran down to the slope where he usually took her to graze and survey the world of commoners. She must have gone off without him again, he thought. He felt his heart turn into a cold, heavy stone at the thought of leopards, jackals, foxes, dogs—all waiting to savage her.

Puran walked the slopes calling for Rani in his loud, hoarse, hollow voice, until Charu heard his calls and came to see what the matter was. She searched the slopes with him: they went in different directions, came back, met, and asked each other, "Did you see her?" and separated again. They went deeper into the valley that led to the Dhobi Ghat; they walked every path through the pine forests to the north, the oak forests to the east, and then started searching the path through the woods to the bazaar. They clambered over the boulders near the stream that cut across the shortcut to the bazaar and at the narrow bridge over the stream they encountered Joshi, the forest guard. "Your deer is at the police station," the guard told them. "You crazy fool, Puran, don't you know it's illegal to keep those deer at home? What were you thinking? It's not a pet dog or a goat, it's a deer. Chauhan Sa'ab's order: it's going to the Nainital zoo." Charu and Puran hardly waited for him to finish what he was saying. They panted their way up the slope they had just run down and then over the shortcut to Mall Road where the police station was, with the forest guard's voice in their ears: "Don't go, he'll put you in the zoo as well. They have zoos for mad people in Nainital!"

The police station was on a hillock above Mall Road, a yellow, two-roomed cottage with a red roof. It had no more than a rudimentary lockup that was occupied only sometimes, usually by drunk people who needed to sleep off their fog. The constable in charge was a tall, sharp-featured woman from the plains who had a reputation for being tough with lawless motorcyclists and water thieves. She had a tight bun; she carried a stout, polished stick to brandish at the unruly; and she was never seen dressed in anything but her khaki uniform sari that she pinned up like a neatly folded napkin.

Charu and Puran reached the door of the station gathering the courage to reason with her, and found it empty save for the chowkidar peeling onions in the veranda. Through the main room they could see the bars of the lockup and Puran ran in, despite the chowkidar yelling, "O, Puran," and getting up hastily to stop him. Puran was on his haunches before the bars in a moment.

Rani was pacing around behind the bars of the lockup. Twice, as they watched, her hooves slid on the polished floor, and she knocked her head against the wall on the other side. Puran held the bars and rocked back and forth. Something between a moan and a sob burst from him, then turned into rhythmic keening sounds.

"Let her out," Charu begged the chowkidar. "Let her out, she will die."

The chowkidar ticked them off in a loud, hectoring voice. "How dare you," he said. "This is a police station, not your house that you come in and do as you please." He yelled to whoever might be listening, "We are the police, what do you think, that we have all the time in the world for lunatic cowherds?"

Puran sat by the bars of the lockup groaning and calling Rani's name. He had some of her grain in his pockets and he scattered it on the floor of the lockup, but Rani paid no attention to him. It was as if she had not noticed him at all. The skin on her back trembled and shuddered in spasms of fright; the whites of her eyes were flecked with red. In despair, Puran pulled at the lock on the grille, banging it against the iron rods to break it. The chowkidar grabbed his arm and pulled him aside shouting, "Saala, this is government property. What do you think you're doing?"

Charu recognized that she was up against a force too powerful for her. Why would a police chowkidar—far less someone as elevated as the constable—pay attention to her? She thought of the only person she knew she could turn to. *His* words would count with the police. They would have to obey him. She ran to Puran to explain, then sped off, bounding over every available shortcut, her pink plastic slippers slipping and sliding on the monsoon-mossed rocks.

NINE

It was no use trying to finish reading the newspaper. Ama had arrived with the story of a certain Mangesh who worked for Missis Gracie long ago. He put her into one of those orphanages for old people, she said, and swindled her house away. And his wife, "that woman Asha, you've seen her, of course—tall and thin as a bamboo pole, with a voice that reaches the next valley even when she whispers, but she thinks she's pretty—she has put a spell on my cow Ratna, she gives no milk at all anymore." Ama moved a ball of chewing tobacco from one of her cheeks to the other as she spoke and sat down with a groan on the staircase leading to Diwan Sahib's veranda.

Diwan Sahib scowled at me and at Ama, and hauled himself out of his chair, retreating behind a line of dripping blue hydrangeas that separated his garden from the nettles below. I glimpsed his hands fumbling at his waist, and after a moment's pause heard the sound of trickling water on grass. All else was quiet but for the tapping of a woodpecker making its way up a nearby tree trunk, grub by grub. Ama sighed, then said: "He is half-mad. Pisses into the bushes like some common villager and they say he was a prince before. He drinks so much he keeps falling down. Did you hear, he fell down yesterday too? His shoulder has a big black mark. Himmat Singh told me."

Diwan Sahib was hidden by the bushes. I could hear thumping, as if someone was beating carpets. Then my landlord was yelling, "Arre O! Can you hear me? What are you doing?"

The monotonous *whump-whump* from below stopped for a minute, then started again. Diwan Sahib stumbled down the slope clutching his pajamas' waistband and yelling, "Leave the nettles alone, you donkey!" Now we could see him through a gap in the hydrangeas, tall, thin, teetering at the very edge of the slope, looking as if he would trip and roll downhill with his next step.

I half got up, started to call out, "Be careful!" but stopped myself. He detested what he called "clucking."

"It's only nettle," a man's voice said from below. "I'm not cutting your precious bushes, am I?" His stick hit the bushes again. I stood up to look, and saw that the man had already beaten down many of the high, overgrown nettle bushes into damp green rags. The nettles formed a barrier around the house and protected it from the road a few meters below. The more impenetrable they grew, the more Diwan Sahib rejoiced at keeping prying people out. The nettles would spring back in a month, so there was no need for an argument. But once annoyed, Diwan Sahib was difficult to reason with. He shouted back, "I planted those nettles!"

"Oh yes? Who plants nettle? Weeds—dirty, stinging weeds! He plants them he says." *Whump!* The man's stick began hitting the nettle bushes with even greater force. As the stick came down on the bushes again and again, I winced, imagining the man behind me on a lonely forest road, armed with that stick. "Useless old fool," we heard the man shout in a harsh voice. "Sanki lunatic! Says he plants nettles!"

"You aren't young yourself," Diwan Sahib yelled. "Have you seen how old you are?"

Diwan Sahib came back toward the garden. "Have you seen how old he is? And he has the insolence to call me old." His white hair stood on end, from his having torn off his cap in a hurry. His dressing gown flapped around his ankles. He had climbed back too quickly and now each gasping breath was accompanied by a whistling sound. He stooped and searched for a glass, one he must have flung into the bushes earlier that morning. He wiped it on his shirt and splashed rum into it from the bottle on the table next to him. Then he sat back in his chair and laughed until it turned into a hacking cough. "Someone's been attacking the nettle for days, and I've never managed to catch the fellow in the act before," he wheezed. "I recognized him today. He's that retired forest guard—Himmat says he's lost his mind."

Ama said, "Why wouldn't he have? He's forever grabbing our sickles and axes and taking them away. Claimed we were stealing wood from the forest. And in secret he was selling our axes in the bazaar. We cursed him, many times. So he went mad."

"Why don't you use your curses on a more deserving target—Chauhan, or that politician stirring up trouble?" Diwan Sahib said, picking up his packet of cigarettes.

"You'd better not smoke," I said. "Your performance is next week, and you can't cough all the time you're there, so don't—" I stopped as he lit up.

Diwan Sahib had been practicing for months and his day at St. Hilda's was almost upon us. Usually he talked of jungle craft and imitated the calls of animals and birds. Sometimes he told the children stories of illustrious Himalayan travelers, old and new, such as Frank Smythe, Edmund Hillary, or Bill Aitken.

"What are you going to do this year?" I asked him.

"This year—" All of a sudden Diwan Sahib became almost bashful. "This year I want to tell them how fortunate they are. How absolutely fortunate they are. I want your little perishers to understand that."

"Fortunate? Half of them don't get enough to eat," Ama said. "They won't even have a job when they finish with that school. All this studying is a waste of time." She gave me a look of concentrated scorn. The day before she had had yet another argument with Charu about the amount of time she was spending at my house on her lessons.

Diwan Sahib ignored her. "I am going to tell them," he said, "that they must put their ears to the earth and rocks and hear them breathe. Because here in Ranikhet the rocks do breathe. I am going to tell them to listen for one second on their way through the woods to their school for the sound of the sap rising through the trees, to spend one day painting the snow peaks they never bother to look at. They are like people born rich who don't understand what money is until it disappears."

"I'd rather have some money and not just the mountains," Ama said. "You can't eat mountains." She made a move as if to leave. Diwan Sahib was too deep in thought to notice her. He continued, "I want to tell them they live in a corner of the earth where predators still roam free. Where, on an evening's playing among the trees, they might hear movement in the undergrowth and see a kalij pheasant scuttling away with its mate. Where they do all these ordinary things, like lessons and tuitions and games, and then come home to the call of foxes and owls."

I said, taking care with my words, "It's natural for them not to notice owls and foxes calling. They've grown up with them. Just as city children pay no attention to car noises—"

Diwan Sahib looked at me aghast. "A scops owl like a car noise! Are you off your head?" He was overtaken by another of his coughing fits as Charu rushed in. She never spoke directly to Diwan Sahib, afraid of him or shy; today she ran to his chair and held its arm, panting, and said, in a high, trembling voice, "You have to save Puran. They have arrested his deer."

* * *

Diwan Sahib changed into a rather grand if crumpled and mothballed gray jacket and white shirt. "You can't deal with the police and that fool Chauhan in a dressing gown," he explained when he emerged in his uncharacteristic finery. We had to walk slower than usual because he coughed a lot and had to stop frequently to catch his breath. Halfway there, the drizzle thickened; raindrops were flung into our faces by the wind. Ama hitched her sari to her knees and fished out the plastic bag she kept tucked in her waistband for such eventualities. Her white hair straggled out from under the bag-cap. I rolled up my jeans. By the time we reached the police station, we were cold, soaked, bedraggled.

We charged into the police station, past the shouts of the chowkidar, to the bars of the lockup. The deer was nowhere to be seen. Instead there was Puran, caged behind the bars. He sat in a corner, whimpering and groaning, scratching his head and slapping his thighs. Tears and snot smeared his face. The room was rank with the effects of rain on his foul-smelling clothes.

The constable sat at her desk looking irritable and shouting for the chowkidar to light some incense. "What do you think? I want him here? I want to throw him out, he smells enough to make me want to cut off my nose," she said to Ama, who looked frightened and tearful at the sight of her son imprisoned. I had never before seen Ama at a loss for words. Now she slid to her haunches and half sat, half crouched on the floor, head in her hands, quite unmindful of the plastic bag that topped it like an upturned boat. Charu stood very straight, holding the bars of the lockup. Her face had frozen into anger at the constable's words and she had assumed a fierce, silent hauteur.

The constable had not invited Diwan Sahib to sit. He stood over her desk, still panting, leaning on it with both hands. He drew a wheezy breath and began to explain the situation to her with painstaking, careful courtesy. Puran was a little different from others, he said. He could not talk to people, but he could talk to animals. Animals trusted him. Foxes came to him if he called them. Injured birds arrived on his doorstep to be cured. Dogs with broken legs found their way to his cowshed. It was necessary that he be treated differently because he was incapable of understanding such things as wildlife laws.

Diwan Sahib's baritone was interspersed with fits of coughing and he searched in his long-unused trousers for a handkerchief. I passed him a tissue. The constable tapped her pencil on the table. Then she spun a five-rupee coin on it again and again like a top and waited each time till it rattled to a halt.

Puran was not raising the deer with a view to eating it, Diwan Sahib continued patiently. He had rescued it from the forest. If he had not rescued it the lost deer would have been devoured by other animals.

"That is the law of the jungle," the constable interrupted him to say. "And the deer is a wild animal."

"Of course," Diwan Sahib said, "and in every other instance you would be absolutely right. But Puran is a special case. Did you know that—"

A note of ingratiation crept into his voice. I had never seen him bend over the way he was doing now. He smiled at her as if trying to please.

The constable interrupted again. Nothing was possible, she said. She began to shuffle her papers and files. She looked Diwan Sahib up and down with scarcely concealed disdain. She had been posted to Ranikhet only a few months before, and had no idea who he was. To her, he looked like any other rain-soaked, old, small-town man—educated, no question, but she had no time for such refinement and slow civilities. She had risen the hard way, she was tough, her tongue was sharp, and as a policewoman she had to be feared and respected, not loved. All this was written on her face. No doubt, too, she could smell the rum on Diwan Sahib's breath. His big hands, even when resting on her table, shook with the tremor that we were familiar with but which she must have thought another symptom of his drunkenness. Her eyes went to his feet. He had managed a shirt, trousers, and jacket, but his feet had been too swollen for shoes and he had pushed them into purple bathroom slippers. She looked at the wet, mud-spattered slippers and back at his face. "The law is the law," she stated. "I have work to do. It is illegal for people to keep wild animals at home whether as pets or as food. He is no different from anyone else in the eyes of the law." She returned to her file and did not look up again.

Mr. Chauhan had left instructions that if Puran came after the deer, he was to be locked up until the deer was safely in Nainital's zoo, and for a few days after, to teach him a lesson. If anyone made a fuss, Mr. Chauhan had ordered, tell them this is a non-bailable offense under the Wildlife Protection Act and Puran would have to serve a proper jail term for fattening a barking deer in order to kill and eat it. "And while you are at it," he had instructed the constable, "I want those army clothes off him, and burned, this time to ashes." Having issued his instructions, Mr. Chauhan had left for Bhimtal.

* * *

Puran came home in someone else's clothes after three days. He went into his ramshackle shed and would not emerge, not even to eat. We heard from a friend in Nainital that Rani was moping and pining in her new cage at the zoo, and had refused food and water. All day she stood virtually immobile in a corner of her cage, despite the persistence of the zoo's vet. A week later, the vet advised a revolutionary step: he wanted Puran brought to Nainital. "That's the only hope," he said, "the deer might eat if he feeds it."

Mr. Chauhan's permission was sought. He slammed the telephone down, fuming. "Here I am, the ad-min-is-trator of this city," he said, emphasizing every syllable with a rap of his pen on the desk. "And they want me to give all my time to these foolish matters!" It would be the ultimate humiliation for him to have to send Puran to Nainital. He would not hear of it. He got into his jeep, its large pimple of a red beacon gleaming, and went off to inspect the site of a new amusement park, his flagship project, for which a swathe of oak forest was being cleared. It was pointless saying to tourists, "Come just for the peace and the landscape." Ranikhet was to have sights. It must generate as much revenue as Bhimtal and Nainital, Mr. Chauhan had decided, and once he decided something, he acted. This was no time for nonsense with madmen and deer. He told his secretary to say he was in meetings all day if there were more calls from the zoo.

On the thirteenth day, the deer died of malnutrition, dehydration, and grief. It became a small news item in the local paper and a journalist came to interview Puran for a "human interest" feature. Ama, frantic with excitement at the thought of her son being in the newspaper, showed him to the cowshed Puran had taken refuge in. The journalist walked to the shed as gingerly as a stork in a marsh and waited ankle-deep in mud and dung for Puran to emerge, but despite Ama's knocks, entreaties, scoldings, and curses he remained inside his shed and would speak to nobody.

* * *

On the evening of our fruitless visit to the police station, I went up to the Light House. When Veer was away, I often went there for a drink and sometimes dinner and sat by Diwan Sahib's fire before returning home to my exercise books. That day, when I entered the half-dark living room, I saw him crouched over the fireplace, feeding paper into it from bundles lying at his feet. He put in sheaf after sheaf. The fire dipped as each thick bunch of paper was added to it, and then blazed when the new lot of paper caught. I did not have to ask Diwan Sahib what he was doing. I could see it was years of work he was burning, his and mine, the many versions of his Corbett book. His hands shook as he reached for the papers and then for the fire. He was bent close enough over the flames for the room to smell faintly of singed hair. Droplets of a runny cold shone in the firelight as his nose dripped. He swiped at it once with a sleeve, then continued. When the entire manuscript was in the fire, he stood up, staring into the leaping flames. Then he seemed to remember something else. He looked above the fireplace at the framed picture of his golden retrievers. I leaped forward now, with a cry, but I was too late to stop him. He had flung it into the blaze, and the glass shattered against the logs in the fireplace. The old wood of the picture's frame caught instantly. I saw the photograph curl at the edges and melt away.

TEN

I could not account for it on a rational level, but after the death of the deer a whispering began in my head that pointed to change, an alteration so profound and yet so inexplicable as to seem more superstition than logic. It was as if we were standing before a still expanse of water and only I could sense a shark slicing through it below the surface, heading for us. On the brightest days, I felt as if the corner of a deep shadow was edging in, inch by imperceptible inch, until it was no longer a corner but a darkness that in time would obliterate us.

I grew morbidly obsessed with wondering what had happened to Rani's body in the zoo. They would call it a carcass. I remembered our neighbor's Alsatian in Hyderabad—a handsome, smiling dog with a long tail that the family never talked to or petted because they considered it a guard dog, too dangerous to touch. I used to scratch his head for him on my way to school. One day, I saw a man cycling down the road before our houses with a gunny bag trailing off his backseat from a long rope. The gunny bag cleared a swathe of dust on the earthen road as he went past. The man hunched forward and pedaled with an effort in the way people do when cycling with a heavy load. Later I learned that the Alsatian had died, and that the family had dispatched its body in a sack strung from that bicycle, to be thrown into the municipal dump.

Was Rani's body rotting in a dump along with other rubbish? Was it being torn apart by rats? Perhaps the zoo had fed her carcass to their leopards in cages. But there cannot have been much flesh on that delicate fawn's half-starved body. I told myself that the vet, who had tried to save her life, had carried Rani's body to the kind of forest she had been born in, and left it there for it to return slowly to the earth again. I tried to make myself believe that this was what happened.

* * *

On the morning of Diwan Sahib's yearly performance at our school, a gentle rain fell, dissolving into the foliage before it met the earth. It was a day or two after Rani's death. Ever since his soaking on the way to the police station, Diwan Sahib had had a cold, and I wondered if he was strong enough to last through an hour of talking and mimicking animal calls when he was breaking into coughs and sneezes every few minutes. It had been decided that Mr. Qureshi would drive us there in his car since Diwan Sahib would not be able to walk all the way to the school. Charu had been looking forward to this day, and the ride in a car, but after the death of Rani she had been avoiding us, almost as if we were to blame for not being able to save Puran and the deer, and that morning Ama said: "Charu is not well. She won't go."

At the school, the children, in order of class and height, sat on the floor of our assembly hall. The hall was blue and white and red with school uniforms and ties. The infants in the front three rows, no more than five or six years old, were my charges. They nudged each other and began to chatter when we entered the room. Two of the daring ones shot out of their places and ran to take my hand in a display of ownership that made Miss Wilson scowl. "Just you look. All this time they were sitting so *diss-iplined*! You appear and immediately there is chaos."

When the children had been calmed, the microphone tested, a bottle of water and glass procured, and Diwan Sahib seated, all eyes turned toward him. The children had bet that he would begin this year with a tiger's call. Some of them clutched each other's hands in anticipation of getting a pleasurable fright.

There was silence. A teacher edged the microphone closer to Diwan Sahib. Someone spoke at the back of the room and Miss Wilson rapped out, "*Quay-it!* We are about to begin." But Diwan Sahib still did not begin. I was worried he might have forgotten why he was there. The children started to fidget. I stepped up to him and whispered: "Start." He had shrunk into himself since his encounter with the police constable, had barely spoken since then. His shoulders had acquired a hunch, as if he were curling into himself, and his gaze, when it did turn toward me, looked as if it were fixed on something far away. He had not once cracked a joke or even been sarcastic at my expense.

And then he began to speak, but now nobody could hear him. The audio boy came up and adjusted the microphone, which settled down after a minute's whistling—"Too loud, too loud," Miss Wilson had shouted from the front row—and becoming inaudible. Diwan Sahib had carried on speaking, disregarding the microphone. His voice was low and at times he mumbled.

"I don't know how many in this room live in the bazaar," he was saying, "how many in villages further away, and how many in the cantonment. How many miles do you walk to come to school? You get up early every morning, at dawn. The older ones among you have to fill water from streams before you do anything else. Some of you have to light fires or help your mothers cook a meal before school. You have to climb up steep hillsides to reach here and you get wet every day of the monsoon during this walk. In the afternoon, you make traffic come to a stop in the bazaar when you come out of the school and stream onto the road, chattering like monkeys—"

He tried to imitate a langur, but began to cough. He drank a long sip of water and resumed.

"I have looked at your faces when you come out of school—so bright and shining and full of promise—and I have thought each time: What kind of future will you have? What will you do with your education? And what kind of world will I or your teachers leave you?

"In one corner of Ranikhet—how many of you know it?—in one corner, on the way to the Jhoola Devi temple, there is a forest path going off to the side and it leads to a knoll. If you walk down that path to the knoll, you will find a clearing on a spur surrounded by tall trees. In the time of our forefathers, there may have been Himalayan golden eagles nesting in those trees and in the rocks. They are rare, majestic birds and have not been seen here in living memory. But even now, those of you who look up at the sky will see eagles over the golf course, circling and looking for prey. These are the steppe eagles that come here each winter from the deserts of Mongolia and Kazakhstan. I used to sit on the knoll and watch the eagles; they used to roost on those tall trees."

In earlier times, this would have been Diwan Sahib's cue for giving the children a thrill; he would have said, "They are big enough to eat little children," with a smacking of his lips. But today he just said, "They are so powerful that they can kill even foxes, goat kids, fawns of deer. Yet the steppe eagle hardly ever calls and as for the golden eagle, can you believe it, their call is just a weak yelp, almost like a puppy's. Grown-up golden eagles make a two-syllable *'kee-yep'* sound in a slow, measured series. Their young call with piercing, insistent *'ssseeeeeeee-chk'* or *'kikiki'* notes."

Diwan Sahib managed both these sounds without coughing, but it was a little while before he recovered from feeling winded and could speak again.

"The spur looks at our peaks of snow," he said. "And all around the clearing, a long time ago, pilgrims planted poles with prayer flags on them. Maybe not many of you know what a prayer flag is? Well, it wafts prayers that are carried on the wind. And Buddhists had planted these flags, who knows when? They were already in tatters by the time I discovered them. And then I went there often, because if you sat still on that spur, after a while the animals would forget you and come out of the forest—"

The children sat up, expectant. Now Diwan Sahib would begin imitating each animal that came to the spur. The hall would become a joyful cacophony of squeals and screams of delight.

"But no animal comes to that spur now," Diwan Sahib said. "There are trucks that come and go, the entrance to the spur is piled high with logs from trees that have been cut from the forests all around. Have you ever heard the sound of a tree being cut with saws—coming apart at the trunk and falling?"

Still he did no imitation, but paused, as if hearing the sound in his head.

"They are building a log cabin on the spur—for the entertainment of bureaucrats. They are building grand wooden gateways out of logs from these old trees. The trees with the eagles were cut down too. Nobody knows where the eagles went when their trees were felled. That is the forest now—it is a park, it is what is called a resource, a factory. It belongs neither to the people who owned it before, nor to the animals and plants that lived in it. I had thought I would tell you how fortunate you were, to live in this part of the world where you are surrounded by rocks that breathe and animals that call to each other. You wanted me to call their calls for you—but I've forgotten their voices now. They have no voices any longer. I can't do this—" Diwan Sahib pushed his chair back and rose. "I can't do this any longer," he said.

He began shuffling to the door. He was in the corridor, coughing and panting for breath, before I could extract myself from where I was sitting, and reach him. There was an air of bemusement in the hall. The children had neither clapped nor moved. A few had been startled into silence and sat looking thoughtful. A boy from the senior section was telling everyone how good Diwan Sahib's performance had been the year before and what a dud it was today. Miss Wilson was furious. "Waste of time . . . and so many arrangements had to be made!" she protested when the audio boy came to her saying, "Where to give my bill, madam?"

"This is the last time, Maya," Miss Wilson said, taking the bill from the man. "He's too old now, he's senile. What's all this nonsense? When we call him for a purpose and make so many arrangements! He should stick to the purpose. This is not done."

ELEVEN

That evening Diwan Sahib began running a temperature. For a few days he lay in bed in a stupor that worried me enough to call the doctor, who said, "Give him fluids, but not the kind he usually drinks." I sat up nights, placing ice-cold swabs on his forehead when his fever rose. I passed my hands over his soft, sparse hair to make him sleep. He babbled in a slurred delirium about people and things I knew nothing of: "Farha . . . not Char Bagh, meet me at the Imambara . . . Farha, can you come . . . the Nawab needs a clock, he has no clock . . . The letters . . . my will . . . Veer . . . get the box, get the box, go away, take him away from me!" He had great trouble breathing and I had to raise him and massage his back to soothe his aching ribs, which he tried rubbing himself in his restless sleep. I realized he had dwindled much more than I had thought: his ribs poked out beneath his skin, his body was narrow and bony. I felt an unexpected, painful tenderness for him and quietly left his room and paced on the veranda for a while to get a grip on myself. He detested sentimentality and, fever or no fever, he would know how I was feeling from the merest glimpse of my face.

After the fever dropped away, he grew demanding and foul tempered. He refused help from those of us who were there, but he made cutting remarks about Veer's absence in times of need. "It's a talent not to be underestimated," he said when Ankit Rawat came looking for Veer one day for help with his election campaign. "The art of being away when there is tiresome work to be done for other people. The young man will no doubt come back just in time for your victory speech." He pushed aside Himmat Singh's food, said he wanted chicken stew with rosemary. I had no idea how to make it, but I looked up a rarely used cookbook and made a list of the ingredients I would need. I plucked a fistful of rosemary from the bushes around the house. I bought a chicken and whatever suitable vegetables I could find in the monsoon, when it was hard to find any good vegetables at all. The stew had potatoes, beans, and little onions that turned into translucent globes when cooked. Diwan Sahib had one mouthful and said it tasted of slop. I cooked him fish the next day and he said it was smelly. Some days I was so irritated by his cantankerousness that I did not go up to his house at all. "So busy, aren't you," he said the next time he saw me. "Huge factory to run. Quite the Madam Corporate." For the rest of the evening, he did not say a word or look at me again. I sat with him for half an hour, growing angrier each minute, then got up and left without a good-bye.

After ten days, he was well enough to sit up in a chair, but stopped coming outside to sit under his spruce tree. When I came back from work with the newspapers as before and looked in to see him, he would be at his fireplace, although it was the middle of the afternoon. He wore a sweater and even indoors his shapeless, brown woolly cap. "The older, the colder," he said, sounding belligerent.

The room he sat in was high ceilinged and dark. The walls were overgrown with dusty bookshelves filled with old paperbacks that the lightest touch might have disintegrated. Diwan Sahib sat there, nursing an "early, medicinal brandy," poking at the fire with a pair of long cast-iron tongs. We had never spoken of it, but I could not look at the fireplace now without seeing his manuscript burning there. The wall over the fireplace had a paler patch, with dust lines marking a rectangle where the picture of the dogs had been. My eyes kept returning to that bleached rectangle, as if I expected the old photograph to reappear there by magic.

The firelight carved Diwan Sahib's face into hollows. He had stopped trimming his beard, and it had grown longer, making him look like a sadhu. His eyes were still bright, however, and if he was in a good humor when he saw me, he said, "The prettiest girl in Ranikhet! Dark as coal, so she lights up my room!" To Mr. Qureshi, he said one day when I came in: "If I was younger I would warm my hands on her cheeks." Mr. Qureshi looked away quickly and busied himself searching for something he did not find.

Every evening, the rain came down on the tin roof, sometimes drumming on it and collecting in buckets and bowls inside the house where the roof had sprung leaks, sometimes no more than a soft murmur above our heads. If it stopped, all went quiet, and we sat listening to the *tup-tup* of dripping water from the rainwater drains that ran along the roofs.

Mr. Qureshi and I talked all the time, trying to fill the gloomy house with our chatter, telling Diwan Sahib the local news: Chauhan had had a little too much to drink at a party in the officers' mess and boasted about his kickbacks, and now he was trying to salvage the situation; Miss Wilson complained of sleepless nights because of Umed Singh, who was promising in his election speeches that he would make sure all the church land in Ranikhet was turned over to common use if he came to power; Bozo had got into a fight with Bijli and almost had an ear torn off, so the General no longer brought him for walks past my house; and in the last few days Puran had been heard whimpering soft endearments to an owl who had taken to roosting in his shed. Perhaps this meant he would eventually emerge from the grief of Rani's death.

Whenever there was a lull in our strained conversation, all we heard was the rain, the cracklings in the fire, and Diwan Sahib's phlegmy cough, which did not respond to any quantity of hot rum.

Every day, after those long evenings with Diwan Sahib, I returned home and sat in a weary slump with a cup of coffee, trying to stay awake and deal with my daily bundle of schoolwork to be marked and account books to be checked. I was very tired. It was the kind of exhaustion that no amount of sleep would take away. I was fed up with the endlessness of my work and Diwan Sahib's illness and his moods. I was fed up with my ironclad routine. I did not want to spend one dismal evening after another at his fireplace, going over the same old stories. Ranikhet's want of urban pleasures began to gnaw at me: why was there not one decent cinema, not a single good bookshop, not even a library? I wished I could take off in a bus to Nainital for the day—have a pizza for lunch, stroll in and out of shops, eat ice cream. But of course I could not leave as long as Diwan Sahib was ill.

This made me boil up immediately into a broth of resentment at Veer's absence. How did he manage to be out of reach when he was most required? What was the point of our togetherness if he was never there? My thoughts slid with an aching sense of loss to my mother. Even when I had no friends in my first years in Ranikhet, it was reassurance enough that she was there, somewhere—that I would have a letter from her every so often, that I might hear her voice on the telephone. It was my fault, I told myself. I had not managed to make any real friends after leaving Hyderabad. On and off there was a new teacher at St. Hilda's who made me feel hopeful because we spoke the same language, laughed at the same things, but usually they tired of Ranikhet and within a few months went away again. Until Veer arrived, I had found no one in town to spend time with.

One such worn-out night, when I was half-asleep on my table with my head on the account books, I heard sounds from Charu's house, voices I could not recognize. I switched off the light and pulled my curtain aside just a crack. Ama was outside, holding a stick and talking at the tin shed they had in front of their cottage. Someone was babbling and crying inside the shed; occasionally I heard a loud, unfamiliar, agitated voice, neither fully male nor female. The single, naked lightbulb they had outside, hanging from a tree branch, swung in the breeze, making shadows leap and subside. There was something so eerie about the scene that I felt afraid of the dark corners of my own little house.

The next morning I asked Ama, "What was happening at your house yesterday?"

"I called the Ohjha," she said, looking combative in advance. "I needed him."

Ama did call the Ohjha now and then to exorcise evil spirits from her cows or rid them of spells she thought malicious neighbors had cast on them. Not even the plainest evidence would make her see he was a charlatan. The Ohjha usually came in the afternoon, performed his rituals, sat on a stool in the courtyard smoking and drinking tea, and after pocketing some of Ama's money, bemoaned his failing bijniss. Once he was gone, Ama invariably reported miraculous change. He had not saved Gouri Joshi, she admitted that, but that was his only failure, and it had happened because the cow's time had come: Gouri's enemy had been Death itself.

"You called the Ohjha?" I said. "For the cows?"

"No," she said. "Not for the cows."

She shooed a hen away, bent to poke at something in the earth. She told me of a little boy who had fallen into an open manhole on Mall Road and come out covered in muck. She observed that while Diwan Sahib's blood relatives were never there when needed, I was looking after the old man like a daughter. And talking of daughters, had I noticed how shamelessly Janaki's teenage girl had gone off for a ride on that Muslim boy's motorbike? Everyone knew they had a thing going between them, but Janaki was too doped to care.

She did not meet my eyes when at last she said: "I called the Ohjha for Charu. Here I am, trying everything to fix a match for her and she makes things go wrong. She is in the clutches of a bad spirit." She saw the look on my face and her voice rose. "You think I'm a foolish old woman to believe in evil spirits." She shook her stick toward the flat gray sky to our north. The high peaks were lost in the monsoon mist. "If you told a stranger that there are actually big snow peaks where that sky is," she said, "would he believe you? What can he see but an ordinary, everyday sky that he can find anywhere? But you and I know the peaks are there. We are surrounded by things we don't know and can't understand." She looked at me in triumph and set her stick down. "You city people think you know everything." This was a phrase she liked using because it never failed to infuriate me.

"That's different," I said. "If Charu doesn't want to marry, it's for a real reason, not because of bad spirits." Charu's simple, unspiritual reason for turning away prospective grooms almost escaped my lips. I knew Ama suspected enough without any encouragement from me, and that this had added urgency to her efforts. Kundan Singh, a cook from the unknown east and of some indeterminate caste, would have struck her as anything but suitable. She was tapping clan networks, sizing up prospective grooms: most of these she rejected, either because the man's family would ask an exorbitant dowry, or because the man was too old, or unemployed and without prospects, or had "bad habits." I had been given reports from time to time in tones of contempt.

"They say he is about to get a Gormint job, but I know better than to believe it." Or, "They said he runs a restaurant in Almora. Lachman drove there to see. There's nothing, only a straw-roofed tea shack by the road, with two bricks to sit on and one burned pan to boil tea."

None of these dead-loss grooms had reached the point when their relatives were allowed to have a look at Charu; I had seen the process a couple of times, a troop of the prospective groom's family sizing up a girl as horse dealers might a horse. Ama had told me stories of her own long-ago ordeals when she had been similarly displayed. "Must not show a girl to too many families, that is no good," she had advised me in sage tones.

In the past few months, she had winnowed the list of possible grooms down to two. One was a clerk in a government office in Haldwani. She admitted he was dark skinned, "but who looks at a prospective groom's looks? It is his nature that matters, and this boy's nature is good." One symptom of his goodness was that he said he wanted no dowry. And her network said he had no bad habits: he did not smoke or drink, he did not chew tobacco, not even paan. An additional bonus was that his family was small, so Charu, as the daughter-in-law, would not be worked to the bone. There were only two sisters, parents, and one old granny who, she said, did not count because, "she's halfway up there already, and seems in a hurry to reach."

The boy Ama had in fact set her heart on was an assistant in a medicine factory in Bhimtal. People said he had excellent prospects; what was more he was younger than the government clerk who, Ama conceded, was perhaps a few years too old for Charu. Though the young man she favored did have a considerable paunch, her view was that it showed he was from a family that could afford to eat two full meals every day. This second possibility was also fair skinned, and from what I could see, a sharp dresser: he had sent a color photograph of himself against the backdrop of a painted Taj Mahal, posing on a red Kawasaki motorbike that the studio used as a prop.

Charu had been unconcerned about this resolute quest for a groom; the talk of it had been going on so long that she had stopped paying attention. But when the families of these two prospects announced they would come to assess the future bride, and Ama agreed to the visits, Charu began to worry.

The families of the prospective grooms came on their inspection tours, a month apart from each other. Both times, Ama dug into her cash reserves and cooked up meals that by their standards were lavish. She had even thrust some money at me one day, saying, "When you come back from work, bring a cake with pink kireem from Bisht Bakery, the small size." The Kawasaki groom's family, being from Bhimtal, "was used to city things," she said. Her homemade kheer would not sufficiently impress them.

The reason for calling the Ohjha was that all Ama's efforts and expense had gone to waste. The Kawasaki sisters had gone away suspecting Charu was feeble minded, and perhaps deaf. "That is how the wretch behaved with them!" Ama said. "They asked her simple questions and she kept staring at them as though she's an idiot and she went on squawking, 'What? What?' like a parrot." With the other groom's family, Ama had spotted Charu working up a squint when she thought her grandmother was not looking. When asked to serve the Coca-Cola that had been bought for the guests, she had limped to and from the kitchen as though one of her legs were shorter than the other, and had spilled half a glass of the precious drink on the floor.

"These things take no time to spread, I won't be able to find a single boy for her if she goes on this way," Ama cried in anguish. "I know she wanted them to go away thinking she's deaf and insane and a cripple. Tell me, what is wrong with her? Has she said anything to you? Doesn't she care about her future? Doesn't she care about my reputation?"

The Ohjha had said two or three sessions would be needed if the spirit was a vengeful and determined one, as he thought it was. He worked at night, when the evil spirits that possessed human beings were at their strongest, in a rickety shed made of corrugated iron sheets. The moment they saw a snake or a toad or a scorpion leave that shed they would know Charu was free of the possession, he had promised.

When I saw Charu the morning after the first exorcism, she looked red eyed, as if she had not slept. Her hair was disheveled and she dragged her feet as she herded the goats and cows to their grazing on the slopes below her home. But from far down the slope, as soon as she saw the postman appear and turn toward my cottage, she bounded up the hill. She was at my door less than a minute after the postman had left, chest heaving, panting for breath, bright eyed, waiting for me to tell her there was a letter from Kundan.

TWELVE

The rain had become a constant in our lives, like the damp air and fungus on our walls. It had only to pause to gather breath for Puran to plunge into the deepest forest to root around for guchi mushrooms and tender linguru. This was something he had done every monsoon for as long as he could remember because Diwan Sahib loved eating those wild mushrooms and ferns and nobody else knew where to find them. But Diwan Sahib no longer had any interest in food. He spent his nights sitting up, trying to draw one rattling breath after another—despite which, during the day he smoked and coughed and smoked again. The doctor returned, diagnosed a lung infection, and prescribed stronger antibiotics. After two days of the antibiotics, Diwan Sahib began to vomit and his feet swelled like cushions so that he could no longer stand on them.

Mr. Qureshi and I conferred, decided there was nothing for it but to put him in the hospital. Diwan Sahib vehemently opposed it, and was full of bluster that he thought covered up his fear. "Nobody ever comes out alive from that rotten hospital!" he wheezed. "In fact, nobody I know has ever come out alive from any hospital! Hospitals were made to protect healthy people from ill people. Why don't you two leave me in peace in my own house?"

"He is just afraid they won't let him drink and smoke there," Mr. Qureshi said to me as he drove off with Diwan Sahib and Himmat Singh. "The hospital is exactly what our Diwan Sahib needs at this moment."

When the car was gone I went back to Diwan Sahib's room and began to tidy up. I picked up the glasses and plates that had collected by his bedside and put them in the kitchen and sorted the medicines heaped on a trunk next to the bed. There were cigarettes hidden away everywhere: under the mattress, tucked behind books and papers. I stripped the bed and remade it so that it was ready when he came back from the hospital. I sat down on it with a tired sigh. The house was an echoing shell without Diwan Sahib's coughs and wheezes and Himmat Singh's nonstop banging about and cursing in the kitchen. I realized that in all my time in Ranikhet I had never once known the Light House empty—one of the two men was always there, creating the ineffable hum that comes just from someone else's presence in a house.

It was a long time before I managed to push my unhappy thoughts away and return to tidying up. There was scribbled-on paper everywhere, in bunches, loose sheets, fat files. With a leap of hope, I wondered if any part of the Corbett manuscript had survived the fire. I began to collect the papers and pile them on a table. I was trying to decipher Diwan Sahib's handwriting on a sheet of paper I had discovered under the bed when I heard a car in the drive again and looked up in a panic. Had they returned already? Had he collapsed on the way to hospital? I did not want to know.

I heard the car door bang. Only once. Then there were footsteps on the wooden floor of the living room, much more rapid than either Diwan Sahib's shuffling gait or Mr. Qureshi's slow amble. It was Veer, back from his travels.

"I heard on Mall Road," he said. "Negi told me. I went to the hospital first. He's better, they say it's his kidneys, too weak for those antibiotics—but it's not as bad as it looks. They've sent for a serum from Nainital. If it doesn't come, I'll go and get it this evening. He'll be fine." He looked around the room and at the medicines on the trunk and said, "You poor thing, you've had to handle the old man on your own. And it's been too long this time. Thought the trip would never end. I was starting to forget—"

He sat down on the bed, gathered me in his arms, and kissed my forehead, then my cheeks, then my lips. He got up and locked the door and came back to me. Blue-green light washed through the curtains. A long way off, we could hear Ama shouting for her rooster, which had wandered off that morning. Veer took my spectacles off and put them on a corner of the trunk next to the bed. He plucked out the long, tasseled wooden pin that held my hair in a knot and shook it loose. One of Charu's cows mooed on the lawn just outside and its bell tinkled. I had unbuttoned Veer's shirt, without thinking at all what I was doing. Somewhere I could hear the *whump-whump* sound of the madman at the nettles again. But it did not matter, Diwan Sahib could not rush out in the rain after him. Our clothes fell in a heap on the floor, next to Diwan Sahib's empty bottles, dog-eared books, discarded ballpoint pens, and shriveled orange pips. The window let in the scent of white roses from the climber that trailed over it. Veer's hands were everywhere and his tongue was everywhere, we were on the bed, then off it on the wooden floor, and then back on the bed again. I kissed his deformed ear and the four fingers on his left hand, one by one. I closed my eyes. A bird fluttered its wings beneath the stretched curtain of my skin, trying to get out. My throat made sounds I could do nothing to stop. I heard Michael's voice at my ear, saying, "You wouldn't wait for me to die to find another man."

Moments after we had prised ourselves apart, Veer got into his clothes and said, "You should go and get some sleep. You look as if you'll fall asleep standing." I left the room, but not the house, unwilling to lose sight of him so soon. I sat in the veranda, half dozing, half listening to the rustling and thumping sounds that began inside after a while. When I heard something shatter, I jumped up to see what had happened, and found Veer sitting on the floor before Diwan Sahib's open trunks, looking through them. His face was as impersonal as a stranger's. "The doctors need his medical papers and I can't find anything," he said when he saw me. And then with a frown, "Didn't you go? I thought you were going down to your own place. I need some time here. I'll come to your place later."

I must have looked startled because his expression softened. He got up in a swift uncoiling movement and pulled me to him and kissed me and murmured in my ear. He caressed me wherever he found bare skin. I was resting in his arms, my chin at his neck, soothed by his hands when, in another switch of mood, he turned briskly efficient, disentangled himself, and gave me a little push. "You're distracting me," he said. "Off you go. I have to look for that medical stuff. They have no idea about his history, they need to know the medicines he's allergic to."

That night I sat with the jam factory accounts, totting up all we had spent on bottles, labels, fruit, salaries, and what jam had been sold. I should have been lighthearted and happy; Veer was back. If he was preoccupied with Diwan Sahib's medical papers that was hardly to be wondered at; surely I did not expect him to be a lovesick teenager who had eyes and mind for no one else. Yet I was in a restless welter of confusion. I could not understand why I felt so disturbed about the changes in his moods that afternoon. I was used to it, not only in him, in his uncle as well. I had resented it sometimes, the burden of being the good-tempered one.

I tried to apply myself to the accounts, but my thoughts kept turning to what my uncle had found in my mother's room after she died. He had been so perturbed he had written to ask me about it. For much of her later life, even before I left home, my mother had stopped sharing my father's bed. She seldom allowed anyone else into her own bedroom, cleaning it herself and guarding it as an inviolable refuge, much as I did my own house now. It was only when she fell very ill that other members of the family got access to her room and uncovered all her little secrets: a tin of the chewing tobacco she had claimed to have given up, my letters to her, the album with my baby pictures that my father had wanted to destroy. My uncle said he had found there a thin, curved, lethally sharp steel knife, capable of sliding into flesh as easily as into a ripe mango. Did I know about it? my uncle had written to ask. Had she ever mentioned it to me? Why did she sleep with it under her pillow? The question haunted me still, and I would never know the answer.

* * *

Now my days became even busier, divided between hospital, Veer, school, and factory. The only constant, when I did come home, was the sight of Charu's expectant face somewhere in the vicinity: perhaps the postman had come when no one was looking and left a letter under a flowerpot; perhaps he had intercepted me on the road and given me a letter. More often than not, nothing of the sort happened. Since early August many days had passed without letters. Every afternoon Charu paced about waiting for the postman, and gave up only when she heard the shouts of other cowherds calling their animals back from deep forests at sunset. I would see her soaked, rose-patterned umbrella bob up and down as she too ran down the squelchy slope toward the stream to rustle up her herd. Summer or winter, she wore the same plastic slippers, and in the monsoon, when she returned home, she had to spend a quarter of an hour sitting on the stairs to her house, sprinkling salt over her wet feet and calves to remove the leeches that had attached themselves to her skin. By this time she had a drooping, tired air: every day began hopeful and ended with the same dull disappointment.

It was not an easy time for her. That same month Ama sold Pinki to the butcher. "I wouldn't have to sell your precious goat, if you didn't cost me so much," she had said when Charu pleaded with her. Ama had to finance the feasts for the prospective grooms, and there was the money she had to pay the Ohjha. "These goats are not pets," she reasoned. "Why do you think I keep them?" All their goats were destined for the slaughterhouse, and were sold to a butcher in the market when they reached the right size. Charu had gone through these partings before. She should have got used to it, but the pain was as new, as unendurable each time. The day the butcher came to take her goat away, she stayed inside their house, curled up in a corner with a pillow over her head, holding on to the bell she had put on Pinki's neck when the goat was a kid that delighted in leaping about, spinning in midair before hitting earth again. I saw the scrawny butcher from my window after the money had changed hands, tugging at Pinki's rope, cajoling her to move in the direction of the bazaar. He tried oak leaves as enticement and when that failed he hit her rump with a stick.

Pinki dug in her heels and pitted all her strength against his. He could not budge her. When all his attempts failed, Ama sent Puran to help the butcher. At such times she was relieved at Puran's feeble mind: he had never made the connection between the occasional disappearance of goats and the kind man who fed them fresh leaves. Upon Puran's arrival Pinki *baa*-ed with relief. I watched them walk out of sight, the goat obedient now, trotting behind Puran as if it were being taken out to graze like every other day.

The next afternoon, eating lunch with Veer, I found myself pushing away the mutton curry, bile rising within me. When I told him what had happened, he looked at me with an amused smile. Had I not eaten meat all my life and known where it came from?

"This was different," I said. "I knew the goat that had been taken away by the butcher yesterday. It had a name and a personality." Everything had changed after what I had seen: the way the goat trusted Puran and the butcher, the way it was betrayed. I'd never eat meat again, I said. Veer pinched my cheek. "You need toughening up. You're too easily upset."

Slaughtering animals was something he had been made to do by one of the uncles to whom he was sometimes farmed out for the school vacations. "The uncle thought me a coward," Veer said. "And he was right. I couldn't stomach the slightest cruelty to anything. I'd run away and hide when there were fights. I was every bully's target at boarding school. Once they paraded me in the corridors in a skirt because I was too frightened to join the boxing competition. I was the school wimp."

The uncle made him wring the neck of a chicken the first day, then skin it, clean it, cut it, and watch it being cooked. He had to eat it at lunch. The next week's lesson was a white goat kid. Veer had to bring the cleaver down on its neck. He was twelve years old. For the rest of his boyhood he no longer stayed away when pheasants and hares that had been shot on hunting expeditions were being plucked and skinned and cleaned. "And your Diwan Sahib?" Veer said. "He shot more birds than anyone. All this conservation bullshit he spouts is new."

It was two weeks since Veer had returned. He was about to leave Ranikhet again, and this was our farewell lunch, hence the special mutton curry. Veer finished my share as well. "I'll be starving the next few weeks, remember? Must eat up now," he said, as I watched him suck the marrow clean from another bone before it joined the rest on his plate.

"I've never known you to starve," I said. "And haven't you read about the goat that Frank Smythe named Bartholomew? That goat walked with them all the way up the Valley of Flowers, he was their friend, and then one day he turned into food. They began to eat him, part by part."

Veer laughed and ran his fingers through my hair as he got up, saying, "Time to leave, I can see. I'll find a Bartholomew on the way, and save one of his teeth for you." He was taking a German trekking group to the Valley of Flowers, which was at its most resplendent in the monsoon. Nobody could replace him at such short notice, so he told me when I protested that Diwan Sahib, still strapped to oxygen in the hospital, was too ill to be left. "I would pass it on to someone else if I could, really. I don't want to leave the old man right now, either, but I can't let the group down; they've planned this for a year. It wouldn't be professional. Besides, you're here, aren't you?"

THIRTEEN

It was the last week of September before the next letter from Kundan Singh came, this time in an envelope. This was only the second time he had used an envelope, which cost much more than an inland letter. This time too, he used it to enclose a photograph. In the photograph Kundan wore an ironed white shirt and was frowning so hard at the camera that he looked cross-eyed. His hair had been oiled and flattened. Charu looked for a minute at the picture and then sandwiched it between her palms. She was too shy to look at it properly, not while I was there. She would take it to one of her hideouts and study every inch of it the minute she got a chance.

She sat down on her usual chair and waited for me to read her the letter but I had other things to do, which I finished while she waited, tapping a toe on the floor. I had already told her that I would not read the letters to her for much longer, thinking this was the only way she would work hard at her lessons again—she was tending to be lazy.

I was at home so little now that unpaid electricity and water bills had collected. My chairs staggered under the weight of clothes, and the morning's milk would certainly go rancid if I did not put it to boil at once. I went about my chores and then, as I sat at my table writing checks for the bills, I became aware of a faint sound, almost no more than breathing: Charu's voice. She was whispering in a low undertone. I could hear the hisses of the sibilants, the drawn-out vowels where she halted halfway through a word trying to complete it. I sat very still, pretending to be immersed in my bills, wondering if it could be true: Charu was reading by herself! At last, on the page and in her head, the alphabet had resolved itself into words she could make sense of. I stole a glance at her and saw her squinting at the letter, her lips moving as she mouthed the words. Her fingers traced the line she was on. The quietness of the room had deepened because of her whispers. Nothing stirred. Perhaps the birds outside.

I did not move a muscle and did not look at her again, willing her to carry on, to not stop trying, but suddenly the kettle's lid began to rattle as the water for our tea started boiling. She sprang up, self-conscious. "Let me make the tea. You finish your work," she said.

We sat down with our tea and the letter. As in each of his letters, here too Kundan asked about everyone's health and informed Charu about Delhi's weather. He wrote of things that had happened at the hotelier's home, his visit to the Red Fort, an accident he had witnessed. It was only in the last page that we came to the nub of the letter. Kundan's employers had for some time been looking for opportunities abroad. The hotel industry offered plenty. They were within reach of jobs in Singapore, where they would earn five times as much and lead a better life than in Delhi. They wanted Kundan to go with them. They had told him they did not want him to lose his livelihood. I knew Kundan's employers actually wanted him because of his culinary skills; but surely it also meant that they thought him dependable and honest—a reassuring thought for me in relation to Charu. "They said many nice things to me," Kundan wrote. "I felt very happy." He too would earn a lot more, they had told him, and he would be able to pay off his father's loan much quicker, and save for his sister's wedding. He could come back once a year—it was not that far. They saw Singapore as something they would do for only a couple of years: we cannot dream of living away from India, they said. Singapore would give everyone some quick money and show them new sights. Kundan would never again have such an opportunity. He would fly on a plane. They would live by the sea. They would never feel hot, they had said, because Singapore was an air-conditioned city, which meant that even cooks lived air-conditioned.

This accounted for the photograph: it was clearly a duplicate of the one that would be stuck into his passport. Passports took a long time to be made, at least six months, so it was best to start the process right away, they had said. And of course he was free to decide not to go. He was twenty, a grown-up.

The letter did not say much more. Nothing about what he had decided or was thinking. Nothing about Charu. There were no lines of longing for the hills of Ranikhet, there was no yearning for the scent of pinewood fires or cut grass. Kundan sounded different, as if he were turning into a pragmatic, city-smart young man. It was more than half a year since they had last met.

As I read the letter, I saw Charu's face withdrawing into the expressionless immobility in which she took refuge when she was upset. She stopped me twice, to ask what a flyover was and where Singapore was. Was it as far as Jaipur or Rampur? After I finished, she got up to leave. Her head hung low and she stumbled on a rug, not looking where she was going. I had to remind her to take her letter from me. She came back for it, but as she walked away I saw her crumpling it in her fist, along with the photograph.

* * *

That night I lay awake, thinking about dreams.

I thought about Kundan's bosses' dreams of more money, change, travel, the sea; that their dreams had the power to alter Kundan's own. His family would have better lives if he earned more money. Yet his new ambitions would dash Charu's hopes.

I thought about Veer: was it only the success of his trekking company that he dreamed of—new routes, new groups to travel with, new peaks and glaciers? What did he think in the alone hours? Who did he wake up with in his head? I wondered if he ever thought of me when we were apart. He never phoned when he was away because, he said, "Once I'm on a climb, I like the sense of being on a different planet. I zone out."

And what about Diwan Sahib? He had been in hospital for almost a month now. Some days the doctor was gloomy about his vital signs and asked me how soon Diwan Sahib's relatives could reach his bedside; then he came back, wheezing, gurgling, coughing up yellow phlegm.

All the hours that he lay flat on his back the only things to look at were the cracks and cobwebs in the flaking blue and yellow ceiling of the hospital room. When he was well enough to be propped up, he stared from behind the gag of his oxygen mask out of the window that overlooked a green, serene valley. Kites and eagles wheeled around in the sky it framed.

Diwan Sahib had thrust away memories of past grandeur and lived a solitary life as the local eccentric. In his final attempt to assert authority he had been insulted by a constable who would have bowed and scraped before him in the days when he was diwan of Surajgarh. He had no children. He had burned his life's work in a moment's frenzy. Now gagged into silence by tubes and masks, he was in a zone more unreachable than Veer's. When I sat by him and talked to him, his eyes sometimes changed expression, but often he shut them and turned away as if it was unbearable to be reminded of the world outside his cage. I thought of my mother in her last days with that knife under her pillow, when she had struggled with one last letter to me. The only thing she dreamed of now, she had said in the letter's three dipping lines, was a glimpse of me, and after that, death.

I thought about Ama, who had been many times to see Diwan Sahib at the hospital. She walked the entire five miles because she wanted to save the six rupees the jeep ride would have cost. Once in the room, she perched as straight as a bamboo pole on the edge of a chair, as if sitting back comfortably would be an impropriety. She looked away when the nurse came in to turn Diwan Sahib over or attend to his oxygen mask. In that different setting, she was a stranger, a tall, bony village woman in her best going-out clothes, hair oiled and pulled back in a bun. Her expression was formal and distant. Unlike at home, she covered her head with a corner of her sari, and hardly spoke. Ama had scraped together an uncertain and tenuous living all these years, fiercely protecting her dignity and Charu's virtue in the hope of eventual respectability through a son-in-law in a government job. There was no knowing what would happen when she found out about Kundan.

And I? How far I had come from my distant Deccan home! A bright-eyed, coffee-skinned, long-braided girl with flowers in her hair, practicing Bharatnatyam in a pink and yellow half sari, and learning to grind dosa batter from Beni Amma on a great stone pestle—just for fun, naturally. A girl from a family as wealthy as mine would never have to sweat over a pestle grinding anything. What had I dreamed of then? I could no longer remember. And after meeting Michael, the fantasies—first of just a few hours alone with him, then a day, then every hour of every day. The usual thoughts of children and pets and home and work, all of which disintegrated when he died. What did I dream of now, if anything? I was afraid to find out.

FOURTEEN

There is only one way for people to leave Ranikhet: by road. Long-distance buses leave from two bus depots in the bazaar. The government bus depot has a cluster of shops around it: fruit shops, a barbershop, and small restaurants grimy from years of living close to badly sprung, rattling buses that spew out black, oily fumes. This is the more genteel bus stop, since the government bus staff do not feel the need to fight for custom: they get their salaries regardless of the number of passengers they pick up. At the other end of the market is the bus stop for private operators. This is loud, aggressive, sleazy. The staff there hustle people into their buses with all sorts of false promises: "Leaving in a minute! Haldwani, Rudrapur, Rampur, Moradabad, Delhi! Leaving in a minute!" Once you have bought your ticket and found a seat on the bus you might wait all the next hour while the driver yells out to passersby, asking them to hop in. Through that hour people harangue you to buy bananas and oranges for the journey and drunks lurch up and down demanding small change.

There are also phalanxes of jeeps and shared taxis to carry people to nearby hill towns. Charu had never traveled out of Ranikhet before, except once or twice to go to villages further into the mountains for weddings and festivals. She had never gone alone; the only town she knew was Ranikhet. How big was Delhi? she had asked Kundan Singh when he was about to leave. Was it like four or five Ranikhets put together?

At that time she had only been curious. Now it was a matter of survival. Kundan Singh's last letter had made her understand that her daydreaming had to stop. It was time for action. If Kundan was doubtful about coming to Ranikhet before he left for Singapore, she had to go to him.

Charu had no inkling of what to expect or how to find Kundan Singh if she did reach Delhi. All she had were inland letters on the back of which he had written his address. She posted him a letter, the first she had ever written in her life, telling him only the date, October 12, that he should come to the bus stop in Delhi to get her. She had decided to leave on an evening when her grandmother was away, a regular occurrence now that Ama went so often to see Diwan Sahib at the hospital. Charu picked the Friday a week away. She would have to wait till Puran was asleep, and then she would take a night bus out of town.

Every night, as Ama snored next to her and Bijli whimpered in his sleep, she lay awake, eyes open in the dark, thinking of ways to slip away unnoticed. The bus stop was a problem. Because she delivered milk in the bazaar every day, and one of her customers was Nanda Devi Sweets near the government bus depot, they knew her there. At the private depot end, there was Bimla, the Nepalese vegetable seller, from whose shop Charu collected spoiled stock every day for her cows. To dodge these inquisitive acquaintances, she had to avoid the bazaar and both bus stops.

The minute Ama left for the hospital on October 11, Charu began to look around their rooms for what she needed. She put some things from her grandmother's box into a cloth pouch that she then tied round her neck and slipped inside her kurta. Into the cloth bag that she used on her trips to the market she put the few stale rotis kept aside for the cows. She added some batashas and lumps of jaggery, a change of clothes, and a comb. She slipped in the rubber-banded bunch of Kundan's letters. As an afterthought, she put in the smaller of her two sickles. She wore her everyday clothes and her plastic slippers.

As she was getting ready to leave she noticed Bijli, bright-eyed with curiosity, wagging his tail in anticipation of a late-hour romp through the forest. He got up and gave himself a full-body shake that made his ears flap, and stood at the door, ready. Charu said, "Not now, later." She gathered a clump of his fur in her hands. She felt as if she would not be able to let go. Quickly, she locked him in. She crept up the path that led away from their house to the cow shed to breathe in their smell and to touch their wet noses one last time. In a far corner she could see the huddled, sleeping form of her uncle, Puran. Tears sprang to her eyes. Who would look after him now? How would Ama milk Ratna? Ratna only let Charu touch her, nobody else. Before Ratna looked toward her, she slipped out of the shed and ran up the slope away from the Light House and its grounds.

She kept to the forested hillsides, meeting the roads only occasionally to cross them and hop onto the next slope. In order to avoid Mall Road, where she might be seen, though it provided the shortest, safest route to the highway, she had to walk away from it in the opposite direction, past the Jhoola Devi temple, from where she could cut through the forest, down the western ridge, to the highway. She had decided it might be best if she caught a bus outside town: she would walk down the highway to Uprari, the hamlet seven kilometers away, where buses stopped to pick up passengers.

Dusk was falling. Window squares glowed in the houses above and below her, and tube lights stuttered to life on street corners. Across the airy space of the big valley, one, two, then twenty lights began to twinkle on a distant hill misted over by the fading of daylight. The roads were deserted; the evenings had grown chilly and most people were indoors by this time. Charu drew her shawl around her head and half covered her face to avoid recognition. Only a few danger spots remained: in the marigold-yellow house she was passing lived one of the girls who also worked at the jam factory; further down, where a woman was shouting for a dog, Charu knew the daughter. They had sometimes found their cows mingling as they grazed.

Soon she had left the houses behind. She began to hurry, breaking into a run. She ran past the Jhoola Devi temple, then turned superstitiously back. The tea shack next to it was shut; no one was around. She tore a thin strip off her dupatta and tied it to the railings in a knot. She could see the dimly illuminated image of the goddess through the little doorway of the temple. She touched her head to the cold steps that led inside and said, "Jhoola Devi, I have no bell I can tie, but please look after me."

She struck a match and lit a pine branch to act as a torch to guide her descent through the forest beyond the temple. It was a craggy, steep hillside beyond all habitation. Charu had never been there before and felt as if she was stepping into a land so primeval it was as if no human feet had stepped on those stony slopes. Hillock-sized boulders leaned over her. Cacti and stunted pines struggled out through their cracks. She recalled people saying they had seen animals—leopards, of course, but also jackal cubs—basking on the rocks. Somewhere on that slope, she knew, was Diwan Sahib's old blue car, home to foxes now.

Charu found the narrow trail through the forest and began sliding, slipping downhill, feet unsteady on gravel and pine needles, trees and bushes catching at her shawl and hair. She heard rustling sounds. A pair of foxes stopped and looked at her without fear, then went on their way. Her shawl fell off her head. She heard her own breathing, harsh and loud. She hoped her slippers would hold.

Her burning pine branch smelled of cozy evenings at home and for an instant she considered abandoning her wild enterprise and heading back. She had not ventured very far and would not yet have been missed. But then she spotted bobbing flames further down the path: villagers taking a shortcut through the forest after a day's work in Ranikhet. She raced after them, trying to keep the fire of her pine branch away from hair and clothes. She would walk down the hill at a discreet distance behind them. She pulled her shawl over her face again.

It must have been half an hour later, though it felt much longer, a lifetime, when she spotted tarmac snaking some thirty feet below her. The narrow highway corkscrews around the hillsides on its way down until it flattens out, straightens, and broadens where it eventually finds the plains. Like all roads in the hills, it does not have width enough to be divided into lanes. Charu could see the strong beams of a large vehicle's headlights cutting through the center of the road's blackness. The beams came from the Ranikhet end of the road and pointed in the direction of the plains. She ran down the hill, past the two villagers.

Where was the bus going? She had no idea, but the highway looked so dark and so lonely, she did not think she could walk all the way to Uprari after all. She ran helter-skelter, stopping herself at the wheels of the bus, waving it down with her flaming pine branch.

Its brakes screeched. But it was not a bus. It was a truck.

She fell back in disappointment, the pine branch dropping from her hand. The truck driver smiled, revealing a mouthful of brown teeth, and said, "Get in; wherever it is, I will take you." His helper laughed. "Ah! We get people to places they never thought of!" Their faces were half-visible, bluish-red in the light of the dials on the dashboard of the truck. They looked like plains people. Their radio played a loud, screeching song. She pulled her shawl further over her face and said, "Wait a few minutes. My father and brother want a ride also." The driver scowled. "We didn't say we would take three passengers," he said, revving his engine, and drove off.

The pine branch had gone out when it fell from her hand and she had lost the matches somewhere on the way down. Nothing was visible in the aftermath of the headlights. She closed her eyes to get used to the dark again and in a while discovered that the light of the half-moon and stars was enough for her to see where she was going.

She began walking toward Uprari. "Put one foot before another, and you will get there," she told herself. "Wild animals eat dogs, not humans." The smooth, level tarmac was a relief after her scramble through the forest. She hummed under her breath, songs from the radio at the jam factory. She changed shoulders when the bag she was carrying started to feel heavy. Her stomach began to rumble with hunger, but she put away thoughts of food, not knowing how long the rotis and jaggery would have to last. To her left, the narrow road rose into a sheer granite cliff overgrown with dry grasses and bent trees. To the right, it fell away into a valley, on the other side of which were faraway villages whose names she did not know. There was not a glimmer of light on the road. At times, cars and motorbikes charged past her, tearing the road in half with their headlights, noise, and fumes, too fast to notice anyone walking. No buses appeared.

At eight, she reached Pilkholi and sat down at the tea stall exhausted, no longer bothered that someone she knew would see her. "How much is a tea?" she asked, and was told, "Three rupees for you, four for anyone else." She asked for a glass of water, ate a lump of her jaggery with it, and then began to walk again.

Half an hour further on toward Uprari, large headlight beams once again swept toward her. Once again she stopped and wildly waved her arms, hoping that the glare of the headlights this time hid a bus and not a truck.

It was a bus, and the conductor leaped out in fury. "What do you think you are doing? Standing in the middle of the road like a cow! Who do you think will go to jail if you get killed?"

"Where is it going?" she asked, in a voice trembling with tears.

"Wherever it is going, it's not taking you. Mad girl! And there's no space."

"I can sit on the floor," she said. "I can stand." Her shoulders drooped from the weight of her small bag.

"Not in my bus," the conductor said. He put a foot on the lowest step of the bus and held the handrail to haul himself in. He slammed the body of the bus twice with the flat of his palm to tell the driver to drive on. Then as the bus revved its engines, he banged the wall of the bus again.

"What the hell are you doing? Do we go or stop?" screamed the driver.

The conductor's tone was bad-tempered and grudging, but he said, "Get in. And be quick. And pay for the ticket—no free rides on this bus."

Charu got in. The bus was going to Nainital, two hours away. They gave her a seat right at the back, and the man next to her, at the window, retched out of it all through the journey as the bus swung round the twisting and reeling and swinging and swirling hill roads.

FIFTEEN

That first week in October, I thought I could hear the earth creaking on its tilted axis, moving a little further in the opposite direction each day, toward the cold months. Very slowly, but it did move, and the wet, gray, solid sky that had come down to live around houses and treetops through the months of rain thinned to uncover an airy concentration of blueness. Standing outside the house in the mornings, I luxuriated in the sunlight and heard nothing but the chirring of cicadas. At my feet, the meadow ended and slid away into limitless forests. Far below, the forest's green was lit by bright points of autumnal red. Dinosaurs must have come up that slope once, crushing trees in their path, to sun themselves on the gigantic moss-greened granite boulders that were strewn over this part of the forest. The snow-peaks that ringed the horizon blazed; I could hardly raise my eyelids to let in their incandescence.

The golden light after the monsoon, the meadows pink with cosmos and wild lilies, and the clarity of the cool, dry air went through everyone like a live current. All around, people were whitewashing and painting and patching up their homes to undo the damage from the rains in time for Diwali. Mattresses were sunned after months of damp; women got down to the business of cutting grass to store for the winter months. In the bazaar, new election posters were plastered over the rain-sodden ones and new bunting went up everywhere. Roadworks began, and smoking barrels of tar added their acrid stench to the scent of honeysuckle. Mr. Chauhan's men were everywhere, with cans of paint and tins of Brasso. The reunion was a month away.

At the factory, we were in the middle of labeling the hundreds of bottles of jam we had made out of the summer fruit. This too had to be done before Diwali, so that the stock would reach Delhi in time for festival sales. The newspapers had forgotten Orissa's Christians and moved on to something else; DivineLite TV had once more applied itself to saving souls. Miss Wilson had calmed down. When she once more stormed into my class to rap her cane on a table and call for silence, I knew life was back to normal. In the staff room she told me after a particularly bad morning, "How long have you been teaching? Five years. Look at Joyce Mam. She only started three months ago and the students are like mice before her. Have you learned to control the children at all? Is there any progress? No. Zero!" She liked to say "zero" as a mocking "Zee-row! Zed-ee-ar-oh, zee-row!" She made a circle of her forefinger and thumb and placed it over her bespectacled eye as if she were looking at me through a monocle.

As the skies cleared, Diwan Sahib began to mend. He started asking for rum. He even wanted his Rolls-Royce cigarette case beside him again. "Since I look like a Silver Ghost myself," he explained. In a not very audible voice, interrupted by hacking coughs, he ticked off doctors and nurses, as well as me, for being too bossy. He asked for the newspaper and made me sit by him reading the oddments I knew would amuse him: that the Western Railways washed its blankets only once a month; that a Ukrainian bank robber had chosen to steal a police car for his getaway; that in Australia a pet camel had tried to mate with the woman who owned him and killed her in the attempt. His room in the hospital had turned by imperceptible degrees into an extension of the Light House. His familiar mess of bottles, books, pills, and papers collected around him.

Mr. Qureshi came every day, the General now and then. Himmat Singh lived there, and slept in Diwan Sahib's room. He had made himself a home in a corner with his own mattress and blankets. Each time Diwan Sahib made a sound, Himmat Singh clambered to his feet to see what was needed; for the rest of the day he chatted with the new friends he had made, or dozed in the sun by the window. He had smuggled in a bottle of rum from which he took slugs when no one was about; once I had caught him in the act of moving Diwan Sahib's oxygen mask aside to give him a sip. I tried going there every day to prevent such efforts; Ama went to visit him at least twice a week and sometimes we came back together from the hospital in a jeep-taxi. Already the evenings were longer, darkness fell without warning. We would hurry back from the jeep drop-off point on Mall Road to the Light House, fearful of leopards behind every shadowed bush.

On the evening of October 11, after we came back from the hospital, I had only just shut my door when Ama came out and shouted: "Is Charu over there?"

She was not. She was not in the cow shed either. We searched all over the estate for her, flashlights and sticks in hand. "Where's the girl? Has she fallen somewhere and broken a bone? Has a leopard mauled her?" Ama wailed. "When bad things start happening, they never stop." She went into her rooms in confused agitation. Puran, who had been in his shed, staggered out drunk with sleep and added his shouts to ours, calling for Charu as he would for a lost cow. The clerk heard us and came out of his cottage. He looked up toward us and shouted, "What is it, Ama, why are you waking the birds again?"

Ama's eyes fell on the wooden box that she stored valuables in. Nobody else was supposed to know where Ama hid the box or what was in it. But there it was, in plain view, its lid loose and the lock on it broken. Money was missing, as well as one piece of jewelry. This was Charu's dead mother's wedding nose ring: a bangle-sized gold hoop strung with pearls and gold beads, almost too heavy for a girl's nostril to bear even on her wedding day, but nevertheless, a ring without which a hill girl's wedding could not take place.

When Ama saw that the nose ring was gone, her finger went unconsciously to her own nostril, which a similar hoop had once pierced and left a sagging hole that was now empty of metal or stone. She rubbed it, as if in memory of all the rings and studs that had once pierced it. Slowly she put the box aside, shutting its lid so that the clerk and his wife, who had appeared by then as well, would be denied a look at the contents.

The clerk said, "I'll get Lachman, and we'll go in his taxi to look around. She must be somewhere, maybe one of her animals has wandered and she's searching for it. Arre O, Puran, go and see: are all your cows and goats there in the sheds?"

Ama was looking straight at me, with a gaze so penetrating I could hardly meet her eyes. She said, "What do you say, Teacher-ni? Should we get a car?"

"She told me she might not do her lessons today because she had to go and see a friend who is getting married soon to a boy in Delhi." I was stammering over the words. "I thought you knew." Fear was making me feel weak. I needed to sit down. I held the door for support. Charu had no notion of big cities. What had made her do this without a word to me? If she got into trouble I would never forgive myself. Neither would Ama.

"And this boy is a good boy?" Ama said after a thought-filled pause. "After all, her friend's mother would not marry her off to a rogue. In a far-off city. Eh, Teacher-ni?"

"He's a good boy, Charu told me." I tried to keep the tremble from my voice. I thought of setting off in pursuit of her. I had at least had the sense to write down Kundan's address somewhere. She must have gone to him, where else would she have run to?

"From a good family?" Ama was saying. "This friend's groom?"

"From a family that wanted nothing but the girl. No dowry, that is what Charu said. And he earns well, has a good, respectable job. His prospects are very good, he is going to travel even in foreign countries and earn five times what anyone here does."

"Arre, Ama," the clerk said, "stop going on and on about Charu's friend. She'll marry who she'll marry, what do we care? Should I get the taxi or not? I think we should go and look for Charu. It'll get too late if we wait any longer."

Ama said, "Let it be today. I think she'll be back. I think she had told me too about going to this friend's house, but I had forgotten. Our Teacher-ni, she always knows where Charu is."

SIXTEEN

The next morning, Charu woke in one of the corridors of a Nainital hospital. She had spent the night there, finding nowhere else to wait for the morning bus to Delhi. The stench of urine and disinfectant had done away with her hunger pangs and throughout the night she had stayed awake listening to ill people groaning and mumbling in the open-windowed general ward. At night her worries turned into specters. What if she never found Kundan? Had she enough money if it took time to locate him? What if he said he no longer wanted her? Why had he written so uncaringly in his last letter? What would happen to her if she had to return to Ranikhet after a failed journey? Ama would throw her out of the house with the same ruthlessness she had shown Charu's father. Ama did not forgive people; she remembered wrongdoing for years. Maybe Maya Mam would fight for her. She would shelter her for a few days. She too had married out of caste—and religion—and she had lost her family.

She closed her eyes and tried to lull herself with thoughts of Kundan. How astonished he would be to see her tomorrow. She could not make herself believe that she would truly see him again, touch him, smell the scent of his skin again, feel his lips—in a mere day, a few hours. What were a few hours after all the months they had spent apart? But these last few hours seemed to stretch longer than weeks and months.

Early next morning, as she walked by the Nainital lake soon after dawn, she noticed that you could see bubbles in the water where underground springs fed it. It did not seem right that she was at the lake without him; he should have been showing it to her. All around her was water, more than she had ever seen. She thought that the ocean on the way to Singapore could not be much bigger. There were dozens of boats moored at the waterside, bobbing in the morning breeze. "We will go right to the middle of the lake in a boat," Kundan had promised her once, after a visit to Nainital with his employer, when he had seen the lake for the first time. He had kissed the soft, tender bits behind her ears and whispered as his hands traveled over her breasts: "There will be nobody but you and me in that boat." Charu looked out across the water and imagined she and Kundan were at the center of it, on a red-and-blue boat with long white oars.

The sun was inching up the sky. Charu had lost sense of the time as she gazed at the water. She had no watch. Panic overtook her. She ran from the lakeside to the bus stop, losing her way, frantically asking one of the pony men leading out a mangy horse where the bus stop was, then scampering in the direction he pointed. Her bag thumped her hips. Her shawl flew off her head. Her breath came and went in shudders.

She reached the entrance to the bus stop. The conductor and driver had only just arrived. They were standing by the bus, exchanging notes, smoking. The early travelers had come, and were waiting for the buses to be cleaned. She ran up to the driver and asked, just to be sure there was no mistake, "Is this the six o'clock bus to Delhi?"

"Yes," they said. "The doors open after a while."

She went a little distance off and waited, eyeing the men and the bus watchfully, taking no chances. At five minutes to six, she was first at the door. Other people were now straggling in with suitcases and bags, looking drowsy. She climbed in and got herself a window seat in the second row. The windows were cracked and some of them had the remnants of blue curtains thick with dirt. Charu bunched her curtain away for a last look at the lake. She plumped her bag on her lap. She would comb her hair when she reached Delhi, and before she saw him she would try to find a place to change into the prettier salwar kurta she had packed. She would wash her face and put some fresh kohl around her eyes. She smiled her secret smile, twisting her silver nose stud to settle it better. She took out a stale roti and lump of jaggery and munched on them for her breakfast.

* * *

The journey from Nainital to Delhi takes about eight hours by road. For the first part, the bus drops down from the hills on a narrow, spiral-staired road, with jungle on either side. At times the forest breaks, and when it did Charu saw snow peaks through the gaps. The same mountains she saw in Ranikhet, here too! She leaned her head against the rattling window of the bus and let her thoughts wander.

The bus charged onward, taking the bends at a speed that made her queasy. The driver had a feverish air and a face like a skull, and he flung his shoulders this way and that as he wrestled with his wheel. He thrust his head out of the window to yell to truckers coming the opposite way: "Arre, Ustad, is there a jam ahead?" "Is the road open, should I go on?" Otherwise he laughed and sang. When he sang folksongs his voice was swaggering and loud. With romantic film songs it became a high squeak from which he emerged at abrupt intervals to yell curses at cars in his way: "Arre, saala, privaaate!" He swerved toward big cars to give them a fright.

In the rearview mirror, his eyes gleamed. When Charu inadvertently looked toward the mirror, she met his eyes, which he narrowed and winked. She quickly looked away, toward the woman on the next seat, who nodded at her over the toddler in her arms. The child gave Charu a wide, three-tooth smile. He put out a dimpled hand and clutched a fistful of her hair, pulling with all his might. Charu gasped. The woman gave the child a sharp slap and said, "I've told him, and told him, and told him, *don't* pull hair, but does he listen?" Her shrill voice rose above the noise of the wheezing bus. "What a wicked child. Not mine, or I would have taught him a thing or two; my sister-in-law's, you know, she'll ruin him with her love, a boy after three girls, so what can one do?" She pinched the child on its arm and ordered, "Say namaste to didi, you wicked boy."

Charu looked out of her window and saw they were passing a waterfall. She wished she could wash her feet in its sparkle. The woman resumed: "Sometimes he vomits because he feels sick on these hill roads. If you give him the window seat, we will all be at peace."

The child bawled, as if on cue. "He just wants to look out of the window." This time the woman sounded as if she was accusing Charu of making him cry.

Charu said, "I am used to crying babies. It makes no difference to me." She turned away. She could sense the woman's peevish looks but she was inured to such things. She leaned her head on the window rails and shut her eyes.

The bus stopped at two points for people to buy food, drink tea, and use the bushes. Charu rushed in and out of the bus at those stops, afraid of losing her seat. She ate the last of her roti and jaggery and spent two rupees buying a glass of tea. It came in a tiny plastic cup. She could hardly hold it for the heat, but the tea was thick and sweet and she felt revived by the few sips the cup contained.

Once the bus left the hills behind, it began to hurtle at high speed. The roads were wider, though still bumpy, and there were fields on either side as far as the eye could see. Charu had never seen land so flat and endless. You might walk the whole day and never have to go up or down a slope. She wondered how that would feel.

When the bus went through one of the many small towns on the way, she saw no fields, only white dust, and the sun felt as if it would burn through her skin. Every house was a grim square of concrete. Drains on the road's sides brimmed with an oily sludge. It was dirtier and poorer than the dirtiest and poorest part of Ranikhet's bazaar. How did people live like that? she wondered. Fat flies buzzed over mounds of bright orange jalebis and samosas on handcarts selling food. Dust and piss everywhere, the bus churning up black mud as it bludgeoned its way through the crowds.

Once or twice they drove through market fairs, and Charu's eyes tore at whatever they could as the bus swayed between rows of vendors who had laid out their goods on squares of sacking at the road's edge: heaps of dry red chilies, cascading mounds of tomatoes, T-shirts in a hundred colors, glittering saris, dried turmeric sticks, stacks of bottle gourd, plastic shoes. They passed tractors filled with the sugarcane harvest, bullocks being sold at a cattle fair, mangled cars and trucks left over from recent accidents, their wheels still pointing to the sky. They stopped at toll gates where boys came up to the window to sell plastic pouches of water, fried papad, roasted gram, sliced cucumbers, and coconut. Charu fished out another two of her precious rupees and bought a hot, sour packet of the gram sprinkled with raw onions and tomatoes. For some time she sat holding it, letting its aroma come to her, feeling her mouth water. The woman next to her picked some of the gram out from the packet, and tossed it into her mouth. "Good," she said. "It's good." Charu was outraged. The packet was tiny, and now a whole mouthful was gone. Before the woman took more, Charu tucked her packet out of reach, hiding it between herself and the window, surreptitiously picking out one grain at a time to suck on.

They went over bridges and through traffic jams. When they crossed the Ganga at Garh Mukteshwar, the bus slowed, then came to a stop in a traffic jam. Many passengers clamored for it to remain on the bridge so they could run down and throw coins into the holy water, but the driver threatened, "Anyone who gets off will be left behind." The woman next to Charu leaned right across her to the window, bowed her head, bumped it against the window grille again and again, and murmured, "Hari Om, Hari Om." Charu could smell the woman's stale nylon sweat. Nobody smelled like that in the hills.

The river, though very wide, looked shallow. There were people in it, and the water came only up to their waists. Low steps led away from the water to the banks, which had rows of temples as far as her eye could see. The steps were crowded with sadhus, priests, people praying. One of the temples had a clock in a tall tower, its hands stalled at five twenty. The river water below it was still as well.

"Water in the hills flows very fast," Charu said, almost to herself. "You can be washed away in it."

The woman moved away and said, "This is our mighty Ganga-ji, not a little river in the hills." Then she repeated, "Hari *Om*!"

In the late afternoon, after crawling through two traffic jams, they were in Delhi.

* * *

Charu had thought she would be awed by a big city, but already, along the journey, before they had quite reached Delhi, she had got used to tall buildings and roads that were like five rivers of cars joined into one. She felt a sense of familiarity. She had seen such roads on TV. She realized she knew big cities from films and pictures in magazines.

What she was not prepared for was the stench. It smelled of putrid things, filthy drains, sewage, burning rubber, and smoke from factories. The stench came in through the windows of the bus; it was all around and she could hardly draw breath without coughing. She had not been prepared for the sky. She had thought skies were blue everywhere, as grass was green or red roses red; but here the sky was the slate-gray color of village roofs, only dirtier. You could not see far at all, just till the next few towering pillars of buildings, which stood close together like walls with square holes. They all looked the same, and as if they would fall any moment. Beyond, there was a haze of smoke. What kind of house did Kundan live in? she wondered. One of those?

The woman sitting next to her had told her they were getting off at a place called Anand Vihar Bus Terminus. "Where do you have to go?" the woman had asked her, but Charu had ignored the question, not trusting a stranger. She kept feeling the place on her chest where her cloth bag nestled under her dupatta, with the bulk of her money and her mother's nose ring. She was now more apprehensive than she had been at any point in her entire journey. As the bus drew into the terminus, the strangeness of the new city became terrifyingly real.

Crowds of people bore down on the slowing bus. They were running alongside the bus, banging it with their hands, shouting. Some hauled themselves up by the window rods, and hung from them, pressing their faces to the windows. One face said, "Auto, auto," the other face said, "Rickshaw? Tempo? Where to?" Her eyes scoured what little she could see beyond the crowds of men at the windows and doors. The bus stop was a vast cemented area, with bay after bay for buses from various states. All the hills buses came into Bay 12, and Charu's bus too headed for it. Any minute now, she thought, she would see that loved, familiar face. He would appear, pick up her bundle, and take her home. He would hold her hand in the auto.

She got off the bus, too confused to say yes or no to the autowallahs sidling up to her with, "Share auto? Where to?" She stumbled about, trying to find a slightly empty spot where she could stand and wait for Kundan. Nearby, a transvestite in a shimmering green-gold sari and long earrings went from person to person nudging and flirting to make them give her money. She poked Charu in the waist and said, "Setting up shop?" Charu leaped backward in alarm. An old man snatched her out of the way of a reversing bus and shouted, "Are you blind?"

Charu scanned the crowd for a face that looked kinder than the others, but nobody had time to stop. All the people around her were in a hurry, either getting on buses or off them or hunting for autos, or looking for relatives or buying tickets from hectoring touts. Everyone else knew what to do and where to go. She plucked up courage and asked a woman, "Could you tell me—" but the woman pushed her aside to run after a bus that was revving its engine and leaving. There was so much noise: a vast confused mingling of horns, voices, vendors' shouts, engines. All the faces from her own bus, which had grown familiar to Charu over the eight hours they had traveled together, had melted away. She felt alone as she never had on the most deserted hillside or deepest forest.

She was standing there wondering what to do, when a man came up to her, narrow waisted, barrel chested, in black shiny trousers and a belt with studs. His shirt buttons were undone to his navel and concentric circles of shiny chains roped his neck. His hair was a puff on his head; on his wrist was a large, square, plastic watch. He looked at it, and said, "Thirty minutes. You have been here half an hour. Waiting for someone?"

She turned away. Her letter had probably got lost, she thought, and Kundan had not come. She needed to find her way to his house.

"How much?" he said.

She looked at him, startled. His lips were blackish red, the teeth smiling through them were yellow, and she could smell gutka on him. She was confused, and repeated, "'How much'? What do you mean, 'How much'?"

"Ah," he said, "I see." Then he seemed to think a little and said, "I have a scooter, and I can take you for a short distance. Not too much, not too far, but if you want to go a little way, I can drop you where you want."

Something rang an alarm bell inside her and she began to walk away from him. He followed her, saying, "What's the matter? All I am offering is a good ride!"

She half ran, and still he followed her, toward the line of autos that stood at the entrance to the bus stand. She approached the auto rank. The drivers, all in gray shirts and trousers, as if they were an army, were standing around waiting for customers. When she came up they went silent. The man following her had fallen away. The driver near the first auto asked her: "Where to?"

Charu extracted one of Kundan's letters from the rubber-banded bundle for the address. She held it out and said, "The address is here."

The man took the letter and said, "Hey, who can read this?"

The driver next to him said, "Give it here . . . Sundar Nagar."

A few of them whistled. "Rich woman," one of them said. "How much will you give? It's not cheap, you know, Sundar Nagar. It's far away."

"Whatever is to be paid," Charu replied, not knowing what to say.

"Whatever is to be paid, she says!" the man laughed, slapping his thighs. All the men had gathered around her. They looked her up and down and said to each other, "Whose is she? Who'll take her for a ride?"

In her confusion, Charu had not held tight to her cloth bag. She felt a tug and her bag leaving her shoulder. She screamed in panic and leaped in the direction she saw the bag going. A rough hand grabbed hers and pulled her away from the crowd. Before she knew what was happening, her bag had been flung into an auto, and she had been pushed in after it. The driver bent and yanked its starter. It would not start. Two of the other auto drivers ran toward him and shouted, "Sisterfucker, bastard, she's ours."

The man who had grabbed Charu yanked the engine handle again. This time the engine held and he swiveled the auto in a sharp circle and accelerated, charging past the men still yelling after him. Charu cowered in the seat, rigid with terror. She clutched her bag and began to pray in a fast mumble to Jhoola Devi. "I will tie a bell if you keep me safe," she said, again and again. "I'll tie a big fifty-rupee bell."

When they were well away from the bus terminus and on a wide road, a traffic light forced them to stop at an intersection. Small children ran from car to car, begging for change. Charu turned away, afraid they would demand money from her when she had nothing to give them. She studied the rough black hair on the back of the auto driver's head, and noticed that his ears were pierced. On the panel above his head were three words in Hindi, painted in red. She stared at the line and tried, letter by letter, to see what the phrase added up to. "Ga," she mouthed, "Oh-lah Uuh" She understood at length that the letters made up the words: "Jai Golu Devta." All hill drivers prayed to Golu Devta for safe journeys. She began to feel a flutter of hope. The man driving her turned around. As soon as she saw his face, relief surged through her. But still, she could not be absolutely sure.

She asked him, "Are you a Pahari?" She could see from his facial features that he might be from the hills.

"What did you think? That I run to rescue every girl those guys harass this way?"

She said nothing, but could not stop a radiant smile. So he said, "Why alone? They would have made you vanish and robbed you before you knew what was happening."

"I am visiting a relative," she said. And partly to change the subject, and partly out of curiosity, added, "Where are you from? Kumaon or Garhwal?"

The light turned green and the auto tooted and puttered through the huge din of moving cars, buses, Tempos, scooters. Charu shrank behind its fluttering window shades each time a car tore past them as if it would run them over if the flimsy little three-wheeler dared stand in its way. Buses towered over them, honking at their slowness. With the breeze sweeping through the two open sides of the auto and the noise from the road, she could hardly hear one word in ten of what the man was saying, but his reply, which he shouted, was: "I'm from a village near Almora. And you? Where are you from?"

She could have cried or danced with joy. Almora! The town closest to her own, where so many people she knew had been. To which she had often been told she would be taken. The Almora whose famous Singhori sweets she had eaten, the ones that came individually wrapped in fresh green leaves.

"Ranikhet," she breathed, her voice caressing the familiar name. "I am from Ranikhet."

SEVENTEEN

Diwan Sahib came home from hospital at the end of October, after more than a month there. Veer, who had just come back from the Valley of Flowers, wrapped him in a thick blanket and carried him for the few steps Diwan Sahib would have had to walk to reach the jeep parked at the hospital's entrance. And whereas it was Veer's habit to drive on twisting hill roads as if he was on an arrow-straight highway, today he eased the jeep watchfully over every bump and pothole, and took the loops at a crawl.

Some of the joyousness of our earlier days was restored. Diwan Sahib was as fragile as a dry leaf, but revived enough to go back to a gin in the morning and his evening rum. He was hungry for all the news of the hillside. When he heard how Charu had eloped and married, he laughed until he coughed and laughed again, telling me I had done my life's one good deed. He insisted on hearing the story from Ama as well, chuckling at her embellishments. His durbar and our newspaper sessions resumed. Mr. Qureshi once more became a fixture at the Light House, cradling his steel glass, and shaking his head when he thought back to the day he had taken Diwan Sahib to the hospital. "I never thought I would reach the hospital in time," he said. "Truly, I thought Diwan Sahib would—"

Diwan Sahib wanted us near him all the time as if he could not afford to lose a minute. "Why do you go home to that cottage of yours?" he would say to me. "Just colonize one of the bedrooms in this house." Veer did not look up from his computer, but he added in an undertone: "Take mine." Aloud, he said to Diwan Sahib: "The cantonment sent a notice that the lease for this house needs renewing.

Let's dig out the documents and I'll get that done while I'm here. You might lose the house if we don't get down to it now."

"Such efficiency," Diwan Sahib said. "You make me feel old and tired. Why would I need to renew the lease? There are still a few years left of it, and if I can prevent Qureshi carting me off to the hospital again if I so much as cough, I hope I'll never need to renew anything."

The General now came to visit Diwan Sahib much more often than before. He said he had realized during Diwan Sahib's illness that nobody else in Ranikhet was as close to him in years, although at a mere eighty-seven Diwan Sahib was but a stripling in the General's eyes. "Still, Diwan Sahib," he said, "who but you and I remember firsthand the accession of the princely states to India? The way Nehru wrested Junagadh, Hyderabad, Goa from the jaws of the enemy—all with the help of the Indian army. How men of our generation have built this country, the sacrifices we have made. Only you and I know, Diwan Sahib."

Reminiscing made the General gloomier than ever about the present and he poured out larger measures of rum than before. What he observed did not please him. "No, sir, there is nothing to smile about," he said of the elections that were now only a few weeks away. "On one side there is a boy still wet behind the ears. On the other an old rogue who thinks the only way to get votes is to make Hindus hate everyone else. There are no statesmen now. None that you or I would be willing to work for and die for, isn't it, Diwan Sahib? I would have died willingly if Nehru had sent me off to fight. But now? What is the reason for this decay, Diwan Sahib? Tell me, what is the *reason*?" Bozo, lying at his feet, would whine as he heard the familiar inquiry and the General would pat him down murmuring, "Not you, my boy, you are my only hope."

In the bazaar, Ankit Rawat walked around like a man who had already won. He spoke of the things he would do in his first hundred days in parliament. It was clear from the adoring crowds his meetings mustered that there was a good chance of his defeating the Nainital veteran, who had never lost an election. Umed Singh's party was trying everything to deflect attention from Ankit's triumphal march toward Delhi and parliament. It organized singing competitions. It set up a tent where food was being distributed free to the poor. It was giving away cheap sweaters to village children.

It was not long before someone from our neck of the woods got wind of that meal tent.

Charu's childhood friends Beena and Mitu, the blue-eyed twins, had been charity students of our school. Their father was a drunk who could not pay their fees. Their deaf-mute mother barely managed two meals a day from cleaning houses and washing people's clothes. Earlier that year, when the twins turned fifteen, they had been sent off at the church's cost to a convent in Varanasi, where destitute, disabled girls were schooled and trained in vocational skills. They had gone that March with three new sets of clothes, and new books, largely paid for by Diwan Sahib.

They had returned to Ranikhet for their first vacation that October. The girls had got used to more food at the convent and were hungry all the time at home, where there was one sparse morning meal and another at sundown. One Sunday, wandering in the bazaar, they smelled poori-aloo and followed the scent like a spell.

The General, who believed in firsthand reconnaissance of the enemy, was at the tent at that time, waiting for Umed Singh's next speech. He observed the girls enter the tent and sit in a corner, eating in quick, single-minded gulps. "The way to a poor man's heart," he reported later to Diwan Sahib, "is through his hungry stomach, of course." To those unused to them, they were a fascinating spectacle. They were immediately noticed in the crowd. People stared. The girls looked the same, and their facial expressions reflected each other's. Braids of almost identical length framed their faces. Their mixed parentage had given their skin a lighter tint than most, and their hair was more chestnut than black. And there were those bright blue eyes.

The politician noticed them too. He stopped to pat their heads and speak to them as they ate. He rejoiced when he found they could only smile or nod in reply or gesture in a way nobody in that tent understood. He would help them, he announced in his speech. It was precisely the cause of the helpless poor in rural areas that his party was devoted to. His voice echoed down the street from loudspeakers fixed to lampposts. He commanded a worker to go and find the girls' parents and bring them to his meal tent. "We will let them know their worries are over. Victory or defeat, our good work will start right now, and carry on forever. We will take charge of them from this moment." At that point, someone took him aside and told him in a hurried whisper about the convent in Varanasi.

In his next speech, Umed Singh said St. Hilda's was trying to convert two illiterate, disabled girls who could not know better. At worst, he hinted between portentous pauses, the school authorities were perhaps trafficking girls. "Who knows what these girls are being trained in?" the politician thundered. "Why are the children of Hindu parents being sent to convents far away where nobody knows if they are being used as servants or slaves or worse? They will become Christian converts—this is an international conspiracy. They must be rescued."

Soon after that speech, we received a circular from Miss Wilson summoning us to an extraordinary staff meeting. She stood at the head of the table and made a sign of the cross before she began. Her voice was low and grave. The time had come, she said, for us to be tested. It was our turn to prove how we would cope with the provocation and adversity we were facing. Her students and teachers were at risk of physical harm. She could not rest as long as this threat persisted. The school was her child, she said, and we were her family, she had given her life for the Lord and for us, we were all she cared for.

At this several of the teachers looked at each other in disbelief. Behind her back, the younger teachers called her the Great Dictator, and someone had once painted a mustache onto the portrait of Miss Wilson that hung on the staff room wall next to a laminated poster of the Vatican's Pietà. It had needed nail polish remover to clear it from the glass. Her latest pet, Joyce, the senior school's newest teacher, had begun to mimic the way she ticked us off for our lapses: "Don't make *ex-kewses*! I accept no *ex-kewse* but *death*!"

For Joyce and for the other teachers at our school, Beena and Mitu were two among the numberless children who had passed through our classes. For Miss Wilson it was a larger administrative anxiety. It was different for me. I remembered those desolate early years in Ranikhet when I would wait for them to arrive with Charu for our games of gitti, for the sound of their clinking pebbles to fill my empty house. The games always ended with Bisht Bakery's cake or the tea and boiled eggs I made for them, which they finished in seconds, hardly pausing to chew or breathe for hunger. They would never again go through such hunger and deprivation. I was determined they would not. The Brigadier was too high up in the pecking order for me to be able to get an appointment with, so I went to see Mr. Chauhan about it. Could he provide protection for the school until the elections were over? And could he ask the politician to tone down his speeches?

Mr. Chauhan had given me a four o'clock appointment, but when I arrived, he was not there. I found his wife instead. She was a pretty woman, with a very straight back, neat braid, chiffon sari, and fixed smile. She sat in her garden under a pergola of roses, at times shouting a reprimand to her two children, who were playing nearby. Butterflies rose and fell from the flowers around us, and her maids, one of them a cowgirl I encountered on my walks, served us tea and chocolate cream biscuits. Mr. Chauhan would be a little late, she said. "He is so busy these days. Today, he has gone out with the Brigadier. The Brigadier wants to see the work my husband has been getting done for the Regimental Reunion." She reached for my hand. Hers felt as soft as a petal when it briefly cradled my own, hardened with work. "This gives us women a chance to talk in peace, doesn't it?" she said with a mischievous smile. "I have a dull married woman's life. You tell me about yours! So many things happen in it!"

After a pause in which I discovered nothing to say about myself, she began to speak again.

Her husband remained preoccupied, she said. He had much to do: the entire administration of the cantonment. Had I noticed how much better the power supply and water supply had become? That was all because of Mr. Chauhan's untiring efforts to make our town the Switzerland of India. He was getting roads relaid and parapets painted—oh, all sorts of things—and there was this terrible deadline of the reunion, about which the Brigadier was so anxious. To top it all, the sign painters kept making spelling mistakes. The Brigadier had noticed one the other day that said "Streaking Route." Actually, said Mrs. Chauhan, the sign painter had written "Trekking" as "Treaking," and then some mischief-maker—"who likes to see another man succeed, tell me?"—had gone and added the "S." Still Mr. Chauhan worked on, writing improving slogans, thinking up new ways to better people's lives. "Just like Mr. Lee Kuan Yew in Singapore, my husband tells me. He says Lee Kuan Yew is an Asian hero."

It was difficult, she said, living with a writer. Mornings, Mr. Chauhan remained closeted in his room. If the gardener came in to ask, "Sa'ab, should I order more manure?" Mr. Chauhan waved him away, not replying, and the gardener's work came to a halt. Sometimes the telephone rang, and Mr. Chauhan snapped a surly "Yes?" into it, not even bothering to find out who it was at the other end. Once it was the Brigadier and he had been offended at Mr. Chauhan's tone, not aware that Mr. Chauhan was in the grip of inspiration at that moment. The Brigadier had said in a curt voice that he wanted his fences painted and orange trees planted at the back. "Order some saplings, I believe this is the right time," he had said, and hung up. Mr. Chauhan had had to call back to explain.

My mind was wandering. I stared at Mrs. Chauhan's face in an effort to focus on her words, and instead began to imagine her head topped by the mysterious wig Mr. Qureshi had found in the trunk of a car. There she sat, in a daring frock of the kind the General's late wife had favored, in that curling red-haired wig with its two blue clips. She was smoking a cigarette. She had a thin mustache. At times she gargled with a gulp of hot rum that she drank from a teacup.

Mrs. Chauhan noticed my faraway look and laughed, "Maya-ji, where have you wandered off to, lost in your thoughts? Tell me too?"

"Oh no, I was listening," I said. "You were saying the Brigadier keeps interrupting Mr. Chauhan's writing?"

Her husband was infuriated by interruptions, but how was Mrs. Chauhan to know they had taken place? When she had called him for lunch a little after the Brigadier's telephone call, he had been curt with her. "Can't you see I'm writing? Can't a writer get some peace in this house?" Alongside the signs he was working on a book. "His memories," said Mrs. Chauhan, lowering her voice. This took up a lot of his time. Mrs. Chauhan waited, the servants idled, the food went cold. "So you must not take it wrong, Maya, that he is late today," she said, reaching out for my hand again. "He makes me wait also," she said with her smile. "Maybe that is a woman's fate!"

Forty long minutes had passed before he came down for lunch that day, and found Mrs. Chauhan at the table, surrounded by congealing food, steel plates, bowls, tablespoons, and red napkins. She had not eaten either. "I cannot eat before him," she said. "Unless he is out of town." He took her out for a drive to the golf course that evening to watch the sun set and make up. "People say I am very lucky." She smiled. "He is still romantic after all these years, and two children."

She came to an abrupt halt as if realizing the impropriety of discussing conjugal happiness with a widow. She stood up, restless all of a sudden, and said, "Maybe you can tell me what you came to discuss with him. I don't think he'll have the time to see you in the next weeks, when he has so much work. Or you can write an application and I will send it to his office."

I came back and told Diwan Sahib about my misfired attempts at helping Miss Wilson, and he said, "There you are, a man of many talents. If Corbett had picked Chauhan as his biographer the book would have been written and published many times over by now."

Then he said, "I had a visitor too, while you were gone. The General—again. He hasn't visited me as many times in all our past years combined."

That afternoon, Diwan Sahib said, the General had come over and sent Himmat Singh off to make him tea. He had at last found Diwan Sahib free of minders: Veer had gone to Dehra Dun, Mr. Qureshi had not reappeared after his morning gins, and I was at Chauhan's. He had waited for Himmat Singh to leave the room before speaking.

At first the conversation followed the beaten paths, Diwan Sahib said, the General giving news of the latest developments in Ranikhet's elections, mourning the state of the country. It surprised him, Diwan Sahib said, that a man who earlier boasted he never read the newspaper beyond the headlines should have become so concerned about matters political. When Diwan Sahib had remarked on this, the General had explained in despairing tones that in the past months, watching the way the election campaign was degenerating, he had been overtaken by a sense of impending catastrophe. Something was very rotten in the state of India. In Rudrapur, down in the plains, not far away, a mullah had given a hate-filled speech, and then a pig had been slaughtered and thrown into the mosque. Now the town had curfew from dusk to dawn, in spite of which people were managing to kill each other. There had never been riots here in Ranikhet, but anything could happen now: hatred and anarchy were viruses that spread fast. The country was in the hands of immoral ruffians who would stop at nothing, absolutely nothing, for their own gain. The only worthwhile institution that remained in the country was the army. Did Diwan Sahib not agree?

The General grew more loquacious as he held forth. Ever more, he felt, it was the duty of the old guard—of whom the oldest in Ranikhet were he and Diwan Sahib—to do what they could for the nation. Nobody else was bothered. The nation relied on them.

For what, precisely? Diwan Sahib had asked him. What was he to do for the country, wheezing and coughing, just back from the dead—and perhaps not back for very long?

Social service had to begin close to home, the General said. They could start by giving over their own possessions, as in the glorious nationalist days. His old uniforms, those were museum pieces now. Old photographs. All his money of course, and his medals—he would bequeath them all to the army. After all, how many military men now alive had served under the British as well as under Nehru? He had much that would prove invaluable for military historians. Such things would be a worthy reminder of more idealistic times for the cynical youth of today.

"That's a noble thought," Diwan Sahib had said, and then waved his arm around his shabby living room. "Not much your brigadiers and generals would want for their museums among this shambles, you know."

"But that is exactly where you're wrong, Diwan Sahib!" The General had pounced in triumph. It was the Diwan, more than anyone else, who possessed what truly belonged to the entire nation. Historical documents. Letters to do with the accession of Surajgarh to India. Minutes of meetings between the Nawab of Surajgarh and officials of the Indian government. Diwan Sahib's own old diaries, appointment books, and manuscripts. And of course, Nehru's letters, and Edwina's. The General had tacked this on almost as an afterthought, and hinted at the danger of such sensitive letters falling into the wrong hands—then being used to score grubby political points. It was the Diwan's duty, the General said, to hand over what he had.

Hearing the word "duty," Diwan Sahib confessed, he had lost his temper. "I told the General a thing or two. There was a time when I was important for the army, because they knew I had friends in high places. Even the General then—I recall him as a colonel, then a brigadier—was forever calling on me, pumping me for information, begging me to put in a word for him here and there. Now he's back because he wants my papers. But in between? His army did not think it fit to trust me with anything. Maulana Bhashani was here for weeks on end and I had no idea. Apparently the ex–Diwan of Kashmir took refuge here for a time and I was never told. They forgot me as a has-been, an irrelevant old fool, and now they're preaching at me to do my duty. I had to press my lips together to stop myself laughing at his continued peevishness over that same little thing. I frowned hard in an effort to appear as outraged as he was.

"Anyway, when I calmed down," Diwan Sahib continued, "I was almost persuaded. Then he played his trump card. What a fool! Well-meaning, but a fool. Do you know what he hinted at after much humming and hawing? He had been *given to understand,* he said, by the *highest* authorities—not that he expected this would influence me *in the least*—that a gift of the letters might ease the way for renewing the Light House's lease from the army."

Diwan Sahib's laughter made him choke on his rum and I ran to him to thump his shoulders. "Whatever next? Maybe they'll offer me a full military funeral too as a reward. A twenty-one-gun salute when I join Corbett in his happy hunting grounds, provided I hand over his papers too?" he wheezed, smiling through his spasms. "Some people can't wait for that to happen. But you have to admire the man's sense of public purpose. At his age, soldiering on to serve the army still! Would you care, Maya, in your early hundreds? I don't give a damn even at my youthful eighty-seven what happens to the nation. As long as the nation leaves me in peace, that ass Chauhan can destroy it at leisure for all I care."

EIGHTEEN

One week later, what Miss Wilson and the whole school feared came to pass. Umed Singh had come back to campaign and had begun in the market, at the marquee where the Baba now held court several days a week. Many of the politician's henchmen spoke before him. Bhajans were sung, set to the tune of popular movie songs. When the main man stood up to speak, all chatter stopped. He began with municipal issues, then went on to the environment, and then to religion: "Why doesn't the government subsidize pilgrimages to Deo Bhoomi to help the hill economy? These hills are the abode of Hindu gods, and India is the Hindus' last refuge in a new world order dominated by Islamic terrorism and Christian missionaries. There is soft war and there is hard war." Here Umed Singh paused for a long while before continuing, "While the Taliban plans attacks on our cities with bombs and guns, the pure, untouched tribal parts of India are being bombed by Bibles." From there Umed Singh went on to the threats Hindus faced worldwide. They were in danger of being wiped out, decimated, outnumbered, converted. From this to the conversions at St. Hilda's was but a step. "The threat is here, in this very town. It has to be investigated."

They rushed to their motorbikes and cars and roared off in a procession. The politician had told the crowds that there were deaf-mute students whom the school had converted into Christian dancing girls, and they played hymns at the factory all day: "We must find out for ourselves what the truth about all this is."

The cavalcade went to the school in the bazaar first, but it was a holiday. Without students, it was no more than a hill cottage with bright red tin roofs and ocher walls, all its blue doors and windows locked. It stood on a patch of earth drummed by children's feet into a square of dust, which was being swept by our chowkidar, who gaped speechless at the campaigners' cavalcade. The politician and his henchmen turned away disappointed. Then they remembered the factory. Their cars and motorbikes sped away toward the cantonment.

From up the hill, one of the girls working in the factory heard the noise of the motorbikes and ran out to see what was happening. I was sitting at a desk in the inner room, punching numbers into a calculator, with half an ear toward the Hindi version of "Swing Low, Sweet Chariot," which had just started playing on our tape recorder. I was adding up columns of expenses, trying to work on the figures so that they made sense for our annual report. In the outer room, half a dozen girls were fixing labels onto the hundreds of bottles of apricot, peach, and plum jam we had made that summer. The labels, which were printed in Delhi, had arrived late, and we were in a hurry now to get the bottles ready for dispatch. I had asked for workers—anyone possible. Beena and Mitu came every day, and sat working for hours, getting up only to munch roasted peanuts at times, or to make tea and stretch aching shoulders.

I heard the music change and pushed my papers aside to get up and reprimand the girls. It was really too much, the way they flouted my authority. They had started a song from a film featuring a girl lost to promiscuity and drugs because of befriending hippies. Her brother in the film scoured the country for her and, after many diversions, located her somewhere near Darjeeling, dancing with other hippies, to a song she sang through lips that were renowned for being the sexiest of the seventies. The song had a mesmeric, incantatory melody. It was an old song by the time even I came to it, but it still played at college parties Michael and I went to. Now it had been remixed and was pepped up with a thumping beat. I returned to my chair and sat down. My feet, which had traveled away to a dance floor of my memories, tapped in time to the rhythm of "Dum Maro Dum." Michael's hands were on my waist, he was whirling me round the room. I was saying, "You're making me dizzy," and he was saying, "That's exactly what I want to do."

Umed Singh and his cohorts reached the factory and found a roomful of girls hard at work. Beena and Mitu had just made tea and, in a shy show of hospitality, were smiling and nodding to the visitors, pointing at the row of little glasses on their tray. I recognized Deepak in the group, and the man who was with him when Miss Wilson tried to get them to take their cars away from the school playground all those months ago. The second man was short and thickset, with a weightlifter's shoulders. He kept his reflecting glasses on, even inside the room, and turned them toward the twins when one of them bent over him with the tea tray and the other brought around the glucose cookies. The reflections on his glasses followed the girls about as they took the tray from person to person. The other girls did their namastes and returned to work, suppressing giggles of complicity. The song continued to play. Its refrain was "Harey Krishna Harey Ram." Umed Singh left disappointed. His henchmen followed, pretending they had come for a regular canvassing visit rather than to catch us out playing "missionary hymns." Despite the drugged, seductive voice of the singer, they could not deny that the singer was chanting the names of two of the holiest Hindu gods.

That afternoon, when the jam was all bottled, labeled, and packed away in boxes, and the room's floor empty, the girls put the song on again. The more daring among them danced to it, while the other village girls, screaming with laughter, joined in sometimes or hid behind dekchis and dupattas in embarrassment. When I entered the room, they tugged my hand, and begged me to join in. "You have to, Maya Mam, we do everything you tell us to. Now it's your turn."

I tied my dupatta in a knot at my hips, and danced too. It had been five years or more since I had felt as lighthearted. Diwan Sahib was well again, Charu was united with Kundan, we had bottled our jam in time, and the goons had gone away without doing us any harm. My loose bun came undone and my hair flew around my face. Someone came and plucked my glasses off and threw them aside. The girls exclaimed, "Without her glasses, Maya Mam looks exactly like a film star!" Beena and Mitu gestured with their hands to show me the steps, teaching me how to dance the way they did—shoulder shrugs, hip wiggles, hands that sliced the air like blades. Our clothes were drenched in sweat by the time we stopped, and I was breathless and buzzing with happiness.

It was only a few hours later that Beena tore up from the valley below to the clearing outside their hut, which I could see from my house. Her teeth were bared and her mouth gaped in a silent scream. Her clothes were half ripped off her shoulders, revealing yellow, frayed bra straps. Her mother, scrubbing a pan with sand outside their hut, looked up, and Mitu started up from the stairs on which she had been sitting and daydreaming. Beena squatted in the middle of the courtyard speaking with her hands to her mother and sister, too fast and frantic for me to try making sense of it. Her talk was mute shadow play, her cries more terrifying for being noiseless. When she had finished, the mother swooped at Beena and pulled her head by a handful of her hair. She slapped her again and again, on her face, or wherever her hands could reach. Mitu tried to prise them apart, but her mother was too strong for her. Beena managed to bend, picked up a handful of dust, and flung it into her mother's eyes, then scrambled away as her mother's face warped with pain and her hands flew to her streaming eyes.

I had no way of reading their gestures and could not tell what was wrong, but as I looked on in horror, I heard Ama's voice at my ear. "Beena says she was coming back from the bazaar through the forest, and a man molested her. She says it was one of the men from Nainital who came to the factory today. He had been ogling her in the afternoon also, she says, when she was serving them tea. Her mother says it's her fault, she wears tight clothes and goes wandering in the market, and giggles at boys."

Ama turned back to the spectacle with a grin, and said, "That Beena's a wildcat. Just look how they're fighting, mother and daughter." She cackled and stuffed some tobacco into her mouth. "It's like watching a TV with the sound off. Whenever they fight, I run out to see."

She noticed the disgust on my face and said, "Why are you so worried? Nothing happened to the girl. She's very tough. She bit his cheek, and kicked him in the stomach and he ran away. And the mother is a loose woman anyway, she doesn't care, really."

"I'm going to take her to the police," I said. "She has to report it right away. They can catch the man before he disappears."

"Teacher-ni," Ama said in a resigned voice, "Lati will never let you take her daughter to the police, and Beena won't go. It'll just add to their troubles. The less this news travels, the better for the girl." She assumed her knowing expression and said, "There is so much I don't talk about. If I revealed all the secrets I've digested and stored in my stomach, half this hillside's people would have to go and drown themselves in a pail of water." She gave me a long, pregnant look.

* * *

That night I dreamed my familiar dream of the dead lake at Roopkund, only this time, Beena's and Mitu's heads had joined the other skulls and they were scratching with their dead nails at an ice floe, trying to escape the water. I woke in a sweat and saw that the branch of a tree had stooped so close to one of my windows that I could see its black claws tapping the glass pane as the wind gathered and buffeted the trees. The house creaked and muttered, and the first drops of rain quickly turned into a steady drumming on the roof. The wind chime I had hung on my peach tree tinkled with such insistence that I wanted to run out into the rain and pull it off to stop the noise. All the happiness of the afternoon had disappeared, as if it had never been.

I curled my body into a tight ball of aloneness. Diwan Sahib had been world-weary when I told him I wanted to go to the police about Beena. "Nothing's ever going to change," he had said. "No policeman will be interested, no new politician, no elections, nothing will ever make a difference." He had slumped into his chair and dozed off after a while as he often did nowadays, even midway through conversations. Veer was in Dehra Dun, from where he would leave on another long trek with a new lot of clients. We had not been able to find the space or time for days to be together. He had not appeared remotely regretful at our parting, and when I had announced with blithe nonchalance that I would go to Dehra Dun with him, we had had another quarrel. "You in Dehra Dun with me? Forget it," he had said. "I'll be at work. It's not a vacation for me." He had shoved things into his rucksack, hoisted it into his jeep, and driven off without a proper good-bye. He had not telephoned since.

NINETEEN

In winter the barbet calls all day from its lonely perch high in a leafless tree. Its plaintive, monotonous cry is the distillation of solitude and sadness. The tourists have gone, and the summer visitors with them. Only now does our town feel truly ours, as if it has been rescued from intruders and returned to us. The earth is hard with cold; the air stings ears and eyes and makes noses water. The tree-darkened roads looping the hillsides are deserted; there is no fear of tourists' cars careering round the bends. The big old houses in the cantonment area are empty again. Waiters and cooks are playing cricket on the lawns of their hotels. They have planted three somewhat straight sticks as wickets. One of the waiters, Chandan, is teaching himself to ride a bicycle and he lurches dangerously as he lets go of the handlebars to join his palms and say, "Namaste, Maya Mam," as he passes me. I taught him when he was a boy of twelve or fourteen. Another of my relative failures, but at least he mastered the alphabet, and he learned to add, though he never managed multiplying or dividing.

Mall Road in this season has a lazy air. In the morning when the sun bakes the other side of the road, every shopkeeper at the row of cupboard-sized shops below Meghdoot Hotel deserts his post, and customers have to seek them out on the opposite parapet. Men slurp tea at Negi's shack. Next to the lamppost, people sit on their haunches at a charcoal brazier munching the warm peanuts roasted on it. Dogs amble around, occasionally snapping and snarling at each other. When the sun starts to go down, swallows knife through the air into their perches at the candlelit grocery shop. A squad of monkeys clambers over the tin roof of Pandey-ji's vegetable shop, dividing into ones and twos to attack the vegetable baskets from many fronts. Pandey-ji's mother, a woman with gold nose studs and a large bun, chases them with a stick, screaming at the top of her voice. Two soldiers polish the already gleaming brass plate that says "Officers' Mess" next to an imposing pair of gates, while dozens of cadets, hair shaved to their ears, file past to their barracks further down.

In winter, the air is clear enough to drink, and your eyes can travel many hundreds of miles until they reach the green of the near hills, the blue-gray beyond them, and then the snow peaks far away, which rise in the sky with the sun, and remain suspended there, higher than imaginable, changing color and shape through the day. Every hour, they come closer, their massive flanks clearly visible, plumes of cloud smoking from their tips. After the last of the daylight is gone, at dusk, the peaks still glimmer in the slow-growing darkness as if jagged pieces of the moon had dropped from sky to earth.

These are secrets hidden from those who escape the Himalaya when it is at its bleakest: the mountains do not reveal themselves to people who come here merely to escape the heat of the plains. Through the summer they veil themselves in a haze. The peaks emerge for those devoted to them through the coldest of winters, the wettest of monsoons. The mountains, Diwan Sahib said in an uncharacteristic rush of sentimentality fueled by a few drinks at his fireplace, believe that love must be tested by adversity.

It was more or less the last thing he said. He got up to poke the fire and go to the bathroom. "Fix me another drink please, Maya," he said, and half stumbled to the door, from where he called in a voice too high to be his own, "Switch on the light, why is it so dark, I can't see." Before I could reach him, he had crumpled over the arm of a chair and was sliding to the floor. He had grown so thin that I thought I would be able to move him easily enough to his bed, but he was too heavy to shift, and I could see there was no need.

* * *

The night Diwan Sahib died, I realized that I had never experienced death at firsthand. The two people closest to me had died far away:

Michael's death happened with a telephone call. My mother's death too had reached me the same way—this time it was a call from my uncle. To prevent my rushing to Hyderabad for her funeral, my father had forbidden anyone from telling me until after she had been cremated.

I had no idea what to do. Ama and the protocols of death took over. She ordered everyone about, even Himmat Singh, who bathed Diwan Sahib's body and laid him out on the living room floor dressed in formal clothes I had never seen before. They were too large for him and his arms disappeared into the sleeves, which the postman folded up so that his long-fingered, square-nailed hands could be seen. They stuffed balls of cotton wool into his nostrils. Someone covered him with a brown and maroon checked sheet and pulled the sheet over his face. Ama placed an incense holder on his chest, and lit half a dozen incense sticks. "Why can't he stay in his bed till the morning?" I asked Ama, but she pronounced: "That is not how we do it here."

People came from everywhere, many I did not recognize, as well as Mr. Qureshi, the General, Puran, Ramesh, even Mr. and Mrs. Chauhan. Ama took up a position right before Diwan Sahib's body, where she sat utterly still, hooded in her sari, as mourner in chief. When someone new came in, where she would normally have erupted into a loud namaste and a volley of questions, not the suggestion of a smile altered her expression of rigid solemnity. We sat in a gloomy circle around Diwan Sahib's body all night, though the men took turns to go outside into the freezing garden, and stood swathed in shawls, warming their hands at a brazier, a firelit cabal that smoked, drank. Diwan Sahib would have joined them, I thought. He never did anything merely because it was expected of him. He would have cracked jokes. He would have finished a whole bottle of his rum.

Halfway through the night we heard a loud creaking, cracking, splintering, groaning sound like a giant's death rattle, and then a huge falling. It was a rotted old tree that woodcutters had been sawing at for the past three days and the sudden gale that struck up after midnight had finally torn the trunk from its base. The men outside marveled at the coincidence and said: "Diwan Sa'ab has taken a whole tree with him. The forest is mourning."

After his cremation early the next day, I occupied myself clearing out Diwan Sahib's room. The unused medicines I threw in a bin. There were empty rum and gin bottles behind curtains, under the table, under Diwan Sahib's bed. Books towered by his bedside in piles that tottered when touched. Anthropology, the folklore of Kumaon, histories of India, hardbound volumes on the flora and fauna of the Himalaya, records of appointments in the princely state of Surajgarh. A set of cassettes with recorded birdcalls. No more performances from Diwan Sahib; the children at the school would have to settle for those tapes now. A ticker tape of thoughts ran relentlessly through my head. His closest relative was probably Veer, but how would we get in touch with him when he was unreachable somewhere in the high Himalaya? In the absence of anyone else, I would have to deal with the pedantic after-death chores. I did not know if he had medical insurance or if he had left instructions for his bank accounts. I probably needed to write to someone about stopping his pension. And what about that lease for the house? It had not been renewed in the end. I would have to find Ama and Puran somewhere to live if the house had to be returned to the cantonment. And where would I live? My mind went over and over the same thoughts, but all of them were punctuated by one question as unending and softly insistent as the scops owl's hooting: where was Diwan Sahib's Rolls-Royce cigarette case? Now that he was gone, it was imperative that I should have it. There was no other object I associated more closely with him. I needed to find it. I would turn the house inside out if I had to.

But first I had to finish with his room. I folded Diwan Sahib's worn-out blankets and put them in a cupboard. Stripped the bed of its sheets. Busily I reached for his pillow. That was when I saw that it still held the hollow of his head and a few white strands of his hair.

I sat down on his sheetless bed. I had not lost my composure when he died, or at his cremation, despite the incongruous cascade of red roses at the cremation ground, and the thrush that insisted on whistling in accompaniment to Mr. Qureshi's noisy tears, or even when the blue-yellow-red paragliders performing for the Regimental Reunion floated past us over the smoke from Diwan Sahib's pyre like two brilliantly-colored birds. At the sight of that pillow and the strands of his hair, I became unjoined.

I left the house and went down to my cottage. A deadening inertia closed its fist around me. I began to feel sleepy all the time. I stopped going to work. I do not know what I did. Things rotted, dust settled, the alarm clock clanged every day at six in the morning, but I did not get out of bed, nor did I bother to change the clock's setting to stop it ringing the next day. Maybe I slept. I think I ate at times. I had no memory of it, nor any recollection of crying, yet when I woke up at odd times in the middle of the day or night, my face was wet with tears. In my dreams, my mother, Michael, and Diwan Sahib were trapped in unlikely, fear-freighted situations. We could not find each other at crowded stations. Someone was left behind on a boat at sea that had glided far out into the water. We were in different rooms of the same house; I called their names but nobody answered. An enormous bird with a curved beak and sharp talons came and sat on my arm in one of my dreams, making me wake up in a panic, rubbing my arm where its claws had been. Sometimes Veer was there, but we were in rooms filled with trekkers, rucksacks, strangers sending us off in two different directions. I heard Ama calling my name or Charu saying, "Did the postman come? Look, here is a letter for me, read it out," but when I unglued my tight-shut eyes, I knew I had dreamed their voices.

One morning I heard a banging sound that went on and on, and struggled awake. I managed to sit up, understood that this time someone really was knocking. I stumbled to the door and found Ama there. She had been calling me for days, she said. "Today I was ready to bang the door down. I thought, 'Teacher-ni will die of starvation if not grief.' Look at yourself: thin as a stick and old, your head like a dry coconut. Why? Is it your father who has died, or your husband?" She stood over me while I washed my face and then thumped a steel plate down on my table. It had three fat, dark madua rotis soaked in ghee, a steaming spoonful of lai saag, the greens I loved, some raw onions, and a green chili. I ate without a word, as if I had never eaten before.

After I had finished eating, Ama and I sat in the veranda, where she settled at her favorite place on the stairs and said, "You were sleeping, but someone's been very busy while you were dead to the world." She tucked a wad of her chewing tobacco into her mouth to create the space for a dramatic pause. Diwan Sahib's house was a mess, she said, every single trunk and cupboard was inside out, the pages between every book had been examined—by Veer. He had scarcely stopped for a minute's rest; he was like a man possessed. He had ransacked the whole house, and then left in his jeep without explaining anything to anyone.

"How long was he here?" I asked her, startled. Did he come to my cottage? I wanted to ask her. Did he not try to find me? Did he ask Ama about me? How could he have left without a word to me? I did not dare ask her the questions I really wanted answers to.

"He came two days after the cremation, looking like something blown here by the wind. He didn't want to know anything about how his uncle had passed away or who had done the cremation or any of that. He kept asking: has anyone been in this house? Has anyone been looking for anything? I told him you had been there, settling Diwan Sahib's room, but for no more than half a day."

"And then?"

"I told him you were down here. I said I had called many times, but you had not come out, so we were worried. But he? He has no time or ears for anything that is not about himself.

"Don't look like that," Ama said after a minute. "You are blinded, you can't see. There he is, swearing love and care for his uncle, but who looked after the old man through his illnesses? Was he here? Oh no, he only turns up when it is all finished, to see what he can get. All these months, he kept leaving cigarettes all over the house, and getting Diwan Sa'ab drunk. Didn't you notice how his health collapsed after his nephew came into his life again?"

"What do you mean? Have you gone off your head? Do you know what you're saying?" I stood up in one violent movement, had to hold on to the chair to steady my spinning head.

Ama had hinted at her suspicions before, but they had been barbed suggestions. Now, with Diwan Sahib dead and Veer having come and gone without even seeing me, she spoke her mind and her words had the unmistakable coloring of the hostility she had long felt toward Veer. Himmat Singh never failed to relay to Ama anything of interest that he overheard in the Light House so she had known for years that Veer wanted her evicted. I wondered what else she knew. I lowered myself carefully into my chair again, still feeling wobbly.

"Look at you," Ama said. "That's what happens when you don't eat for days. And I haven't gone off my head, my head's very clear. Who kept the old man supplied with so many bottles? Who bought all those packets of cigarettes that he found wherever his eyes fell? I had told you then, and I will tell you now, this apple of Diwan Sa'ab's eye came back here only to send him to his death. There are many ways to finish people off, you know."

She heard cowbells close by and hurried away to the edge of the hill to yell at Puran. "Arre O, Puran, can't you see Ratna is eating Sahu-ji's beans? Donkey, good-for-nothing, fool! Lost in his own world and the cattle wander anywhere they please." She was tender-faced as she sat down again. "Everyone says Puran's a madman and he's a crazy fool, there's no doubt about that. See how he's crooning over that pet owl these days. It's like the sun rises when that owl opens its eyes at night. But if I had to trust my life to anyone it would be Puran, not that Veer Singh, who cares only for himself. Your teeth will break on a big black pebble when you eat *that* bowl of dal, take my word for it. I notice everything, nothing escapes me."

She gave me a significant look and repeated, "I notice everything, make no mistake. People may not pay attention to what an old woman thinks. People who are educated and think they know it all."

* * *

That night I again had the nightmare that had visited me from time to time, each time subtly altered. This time I was speaking to someone whose breath I could hear only inches from my ears: wheeze and gurgle, wheeze and gurgle. It was a man—who could not hear me. I could not see his face for the hood of his anorak, but I knew who it was. "Stop," I cried in my dream with a terrible urgency:

Come back. Where are you going?

You force foot after foot. You slide downward even as you move up. The slope shifts. The rock that seemed firm slides and falls a soundless distance away into the black gorge. Your feet are wet and warm. With your own blood—though why should that be when you've left the leeches behind? You look down at your boots. Blood is spilling over their rims. You stop at last, and so does the man with you, who says, You were always a worrier, come on.

Look this way, to the left! Can't you see me begging you to turn back? Why can't you hear me?

Your feet start up the slope again and your heart booms like a drum keeping time. The air is cold and dry, scouring your nostrils. You are pausing every few steps, drooping with weariness. The other man prods the small of your back to urge you on. Around us, all is gray: gray rocks, dirty gray snow, low gray sky. The binocular strap around your neck is a resting noose.

I would scoop you up like a baby and carry you away to safety if I could. I would zip us into a single sleeping bag and wrap myself around you all night so that the warmth of my legs could thaw your legs. I would press your hands into the warmest part of me to unfreeze your fingers.

Just a little further, the other man says. I strain to see his face. I think I have heard his voice before. Your blood-filled boots ooze into the gray snow. They drip slick red onto stones. Can you feel anything but the sticky wetness of your feet? Only exhaustion. What can you hear? The binoculars knocking against your chest. The wind like an ocean wave.

We come to the top. It is not the level top of a plateau or the crest of a hill. It is the rim of a cavernous gray-white bowl within which the wind is swirling, shifting snow dust, tiny pebbles. Far below, at the base of the bowl, we can see water reflecting sky, slabs of ice breaking the reflection into irregular geometries. Steep sides of gray scree slide away from us into the bowl.

The other man says, Have you seen anything like that? Look through your binoculars.

The voice is from far away, the sound of sand scraped with a spade. I have heard this voice before, in another place and time. He puts a hand on your shoulder and it is missing a finger.

You raise the binoculars to your eyes and see what I knew was waiting. The edges of the lake are populated. Human skeletons and bones. Clavicles, skulls. Tibias, fibulas, femurs. Mandibles and ribs, foot and hand phalanges with silver toe rings and gold finger rings on them still. Necklaces of gold beads intertwined with vertebrae. Some skeletons almost intact, frozen into the bed of the lake, others clinging to the slope, trying to claw a way out. A skull floats on the liquid part of the lake.

This is it, you say, hearing your own voice for the first time. Where we all end. A smile of sorts cracks your face, painful in the cold air.

You get no answer. You look to your left; there is no one. Nobody to your right, or behind, or further away, or down toward the lake. You shout a name. I try to reach it, cannot snatch a syllable of it from the wind. Your boots are heavy with blood, you can barely lift them for the weight. A drop falls, and then another, of ice-melt from the low sky. You step back from the rim of the lake and your bloodied feet, now inexplicably bare, lose their grip. You see the water in the lake and the skeletons in it, the ice and the cloud-heavy sky in the water, rushing toward you. You feel a vast weightlessness and vertigo as you fly down through the emptiness.

You cry out, but it is not your friend's name. You are calling, "Maya, Maya."

Maya, illusion, a woman's name, mine.

I woke up with my own name in my ears. Through the uncurtained windows the eastern slopes of Nanda Devi and Trishul, suspended between night and day, were icy blue. It was going to be a clear morning, with beautiful views, but I wanted to run away: push aside the forest, escape the oaks and the darkness of deodars, clear a path to the plains, run down and away from the cold, the damp, the rain and snow, the calls of owls at night. I wanted the mango trees of my childhood, the visible heat of the afternoon sun, the creamy flesh of young green coconuts and their spring-sweet water.

I flung away my mass of blankets and sprang out of bed. I wriggled under it to where I stored things I might never need: suitcases, bags, cartons of books. I dragged a suitcase out and prised at its catches. It would not open. My hair streamed over my face. The dream was still vivid; my heart thudded with the certainty of knowledge. I ran down and brought up my box of old keys, which I tipped onto the floor. Rummaged through the jumble of metal and tried key after key in the rusted locks of the long-unopened suitcase. I flung aside the wrong keys, not caring where they fell. I found my hammer and smashed it against the locks: once, twice, three times, until the locks broke.

I opened the creaking lid of the dusty suitcase and pulled out the heavy, plastic-covered bundle inside it: Michael's rucksack. It had been delivered a week after his death and I had never looked through it. Today, when I opened it, there was the generations-old smell of mildew.

I pulled out the sweatshirts—the blue one with the dolphin that I had bought him days before he left, a red one with John Lennon's face; other clothes that I recognized tumbled out, crushed into tight balls in these five years of storage. And then a carefully folded packet in which I could see a book, a Tibetan good luck charm, and a letter that I had written and sent by courier to wait for him in Dehra Dun as a surprise before he started the trek.

I opened the packet and saw that there were other papers too that Michael had placed in it for safekeeping: a few pages torn from a first-aid manual; two maps; a few typewritten, official-looking sheets from the mountaineering institute with details of the trek: the list of things the trekkers needed to carry, meeting points, train connections. On a separate sheet, there were the names and phone numbers of the trekkers. Three names, as Michael had said—he and two others—one of them an experienced mountaineer, he had told me that night before he left, the other a porter.

I closed my eyes. I was certain I knew what I would see.

The names on the typewritten sheet were:

Michael Secuira
Ranveer Singh Rathore
Shamsher Bahadur Gurung

I went back to a time when I had woken from one of my nightmares gasping for breath. Veer had calmed me with slow whispered reassurances. I had talked to him until the night paled into dawn, about Michael's death, about everything I had gone through that year—things I had never talked about to anyone. Veer had held me close, not once interrupting me. When I finished, he had described the terrain to me with a cartographer's accuracy. But said nothing to suggest he had been Michael's last trekking companion. He did not mull over what might have gone wrong. He did not list the many horrific possibilities—death by frostbite, death by falling, by injury, by brain damage, by pulmonary edema. And not suspecting what his silences hid, I had been grateful for all that he had left unsaid.

He had not told me he even knew of Michael's mountaineering institute.

He had not told me Michael had broken his ankle.

He had not told me he had left Michael to fend for himself in a snowstorm with a broken ankle when they both knew it meant certain death.

I sat on the floor holding the papers, fragments of Michael strewn around me. The bugle at the army barracks trumpeted to wake the cadets as on every morning. Window squares lit up one by one and smoke rose from fires for the morning's hot water. Birds sang to each other across trees and forests. The daily business of mornings that usually made me uncurl from my quilt with a smile now hammered nails into my heart. I felt utterly, absolutely alone. Wrapping my arms around my knees, I held myself as my body shook with sobs. I wept as if Michael had died the day before. I picked up thing after thing from his rucksack and flung them across the room in a rage. How easy to be dead! Everyone had marveled at the way I had made myself a new life in a faraway town after my husband's death. What unnatural composure, what a swift recovery, they had said. Today it was as if I had torn off a dried-up scab with my fingernails and exposed the wound oozing for years beneath.

I had grieved for Michael's death before. Now I would torment myself to the end of my days for my intimacy with the man who had walked away from him when he most needed help. How had I allowed it to happen? When had Veer dropped his last name and shortened his first? Even Diwan Sahib had never called him anything but Veer, and sometimes "Mr. Singh," or, when in a bad temper, "the Great Climber, Mr. Singh."

Where had the Rathore part of his name gone?

Perhaps Veer never used that last name except in formal documents. That was possible, even normal, as was the abbreviation of his first name.

Or maybe he had chosen to lose pieces of his names in the snow after abandoning Michael to his death.

I wanted to scour off my soiled skin with a rough stone. I wanted to tear out the long hair Veer had murmured endearments and promises into, playing on my sympathies with his bitter stories of childhood suffering and homelessness, the search for his identity. I had been held in thrall by the quietness of him—his enigmatic, troubling aura of unknowability. Now I knew his silence was no more than a shroud in which he had tried to bury his connection with Michael's death.

TWENTY

It is December in Ranikhet. A pair of eagles wheel slowly through the sky's ceaseless blue. They are above the golf course, circling the yellow-capped army caddies, the colonels and brigadiers and lesser beings ambling behind white balls, knocking them with misdirected clubs, sending them hurtling down slopes. The caddies look upward as the shadows of eagle wings pass over their faces. They swing golf clubs in their direction and the eagles become faraway dots quicker than the eye can see.

Nearby, a dark olive convoy of army trucks is inching down the road. The line is unable to move fast for the press of people saying their last good-byes to the young, shorn, uniformed boys packed into the trucks. There are reports of infiltrators on the remote icy border with Pakistan, and every day trucks leave with soldiers to be transported to the trouble zone. In one fortnight, everything has changed. The soldiers' daily morning training, their target practice, the camping in the woods in camouflage is no longer playacting. They try not to see every familiar house, barracks, gateway, and shop as if it were for the last time. In his head, Gopal is already somewhere inside one of these trucks winding their way toward trouble. The clerk is too exhausted with anxiety to say to his son, "I told you so."

The eagles fly unconcerned over the trucks filled with young men thinking their somber thoughts. Further down, at Bisht Bakery, the staff are sunning themselves on the courtyard outside the shed with the ovens. They have decided not to bake bread that day because the old bread is still unsold. The tourists will only return next year. Christmas is just over, and Christmas pastries are getting drier and staler in the glass case. The eagles have their eye on a tastier morsel:

they swoop down on the rubbish dump near the bazaar, having seen movement—a rabbit, or a mongoose. People leap away in alarm. The town's local environmentalist takes a picture on his mobile phone's camera and says he will send it to *Hornbill*. "What is *Hornbill*?" the friend asks.

Up the steep Alma Hill and away from the bazaar toward the cantonment, the eagles pass over the church and St. Hilda's school. There are women sitting outside the church in the sun, peeling fruit that has been heaped high, orange and yellow. Music plays; some of them sing. In another corner, women make earrings and bead necklaces. This is their new line of business. The elections are over, Ankit Rawat is installed in Delhi as the first-ever MP from Ranikhet, and nobody is any longer interested in the Christian mission of the school, not until the next elections. Miss Wilson has placed a larger portrait of herself on the wall facing the old one. Next to the laminated Pietà, she has added a portrait of the Pope, whom she dreams of glimpsing one day in the Vatican. She has decided she will not object to the girls playing film music in the factory. She will not admit it, but she enjoys it.

At Mall Road, the eagles pause on the summit of a deodar tree. They look down at the people sunning themselves on the parapet, storing up heat for the long, dark, cold evening ahead. They observe the man roasting peanuts, the shopkeepers chasing monkeys away with sticks, the girls lining up at the water tap, the jeep-taxis coming and going. There is a baby monkey alone by the roadside, tiny, pink-eared, a morsel of flesh, blood, life. The eagles stretch their wings, and think of food. But the monkey's father and mother appear from somewhere; they have sensed danger. They collect the baby in their arms and leap away over rooftops to a place less exposed.

Frustrated, one of the eagles perches low on the arm of the new statue Mr. Chauhan has installed on Mall Road. The first month, it was a statue of B. R. Ambedkar, wearing a suit and round glasses. The second month, overnight, the blue suit was painted olive and given a belt, an army cap was placed on its head, and the very next morning the people of Ranikhet had gasped in collective astonishment, for they had found Subhas Chandra Bose where Ambedkar had been, as if by magic. Mr. Chauhan had seen possibilities that no one before him had seen. He alone had noticed there was no need to change the statue's face, since both men were rotund and wore similar glasses. Now Mr. Chauhan cannot stop himself from telling every passerby that he has invented the world's first transformable statue, ready for any occasion. With a bit of effort, he thinks, it can become Nehru too, though removing the glasses may present a problem. "But where would solutions be if there were no problems?" he says.

One of the eagles pecks at the statue, leaps onto its head, stretches its wings, and takes off. The pair fly further up Mall Road, over the decrepit, rambling colonial houses. They have nested there once and may do so again. They fly over Aspen Lodge and the forest road to the Westview Hotel. They fly over a leopard padding down the dusky ravine near the Rosemount Hotel. Over Gappu Dhobi's house, where lines of clothes are drying and fading in the strong winter sun. They start their descent when they reach an overgrown lawn, and I open my eyes, sensing a shadow sliding over my face. I can see their feathers and talons, they are so low.

I have never seen eagles before, these beautiful and dangerous birds, in my part of the hillside, and I stare at the pair wheeling and circling over me. Where have they come from? Where are they headed? Could they really have come here all the way from Mongolia or Kazakhstan? Diwan Sahib would have told me everything about them; we would have looked at them, together, spellbound. Their wings are immobile in flight, the barest whisper of movement, and they pare the sky in unbroken circular lines, as if it's an orange. I watch them for as long as I can until they become high, black specks swallowed up by the blinding dazzle of the sun. I close my eyes and savor my last few days at the Light House before it is returned to the army. All of us have to look for new places to live in. Ama thinks she will take Puran and return to her ancestral village in the high mountains. She has nobody to live for in Ranikhet any longer, she says.

Charu came once, changed. Married now, bride-like, and not at all disheveled as before. Her arms were covered in red bangles from wrist to elbow, she was still wearing her mother's gold and pearl nose ring, and the parting in her hair was red with sindoor. She looked remote and grown-up, although just eighteen. Ama, practical as ever, scolded her once to show her what was what. After that she reveled in telling the hillside lavishly spiced stories of Charu's brave journey to Delhi. She fed Charu kheer every day, and would not let her do any work—now she was not the daughter anymore, she was a guest who belonged elsewhere.

A month after Charu's visit home ended, I had a letter, which I ran to show Ama, saying, "See! Your daughter can write!"

> *Maya Mam,*
> *Are you well? Are Ama and Puran Chacha well? I am well. He is also well. Singapore is very beautiful. I have seen the sea.*
>
> *With respect,*
> *Charu.*

Ama has proven yet again that there is no woman more shrewd this side of the Nanda Devi. After I read her Charu's letter, she went into her house and reappeared with a brown-toothed smile, holding out a packet wrapped in layers of plastic.

"I have something for you too. This is what Diwan Sa'ab's nephew was looking for, I think," she said. "Now he's gone, it's yours to do with as you please." Her smile broadened and twisted. She said nothing more as she left me holding the packet.

I unpeeled the packet and read its contents with a sense of astonishment mixed with disbelief. For it was clear that in the end, Diwan Sahib's closest, darkest secrets had been biding their time in the care of our town's greatest gossip. The packet was not even sealed. Could Ama have stolen and hidden away those papers to spite Veer? Or had Diwan Sahib given them to her, thinking his papers would be safest with a trusted, unlettered village woman? Even when that woman was Ama?

TWENTY-ONE

I have that packet in my hand this afternoon as I lie in the sun and think about this soon-to-be-deserted house, which will keep its ghosts and stories for its next occupant. All the talk around me is of the future and of plans. I talk of neither. I no longer plan anything. I know nothing but the present, this day, this hour.

I open the thick packet. I have been through it many times these past few days. Now I know that Diwan Sahib was not playing a practical joke when he titillated scholars with rumors of love notes from the past. There they are: three sheets of yellowing paper, with a famous old handwriting that I recognize from signatures I have seen in print a hundred times.

The first letter is written on the back of the menu card at a banquet for a shikar party. Annotated with an "[em to jln]" in Diwan Sahib's hand, it says:

> *We are twelve in our ladies' carriage. It has sliding windowpanes and we had to climb in by a ladder. Does your hunting buggy have a ladder too? Do you know, mine has a secret chamber inside. One of the younger Begums tells me that in case of an animal attack, one must duck and slip into the chamber and make an emergency exit. But my only thought is that I should like to spend this entire shikar in a secret chamber with the one man in the world with whom I feel the deepest sense of peace and happiness.*

The reply to it, marked "[jln to em]," is on a sheet of paper that has a printed line saying, "first published in 1935," above the handwritten lines in ink. This letter is on the back of the title page torn out from a book on the Himalaya.

> *Last evening, I was looking at you across the room, wanting nothing more than to talk to you but unable to be by your side, and I had a moment of piercing clarity about the days ahead, when you will leave India forever. You and Dickie, shaking the hands of a few thousand people, saying good-bye, going further and further away, and I, watching from a distance, and watching that distance grow until you are out of sight and I wander away.*

There is a third note marked "[jln to em]," saying only:

> *There is a dark red rose on the third bush beneath the window of your bedroom. It is so very fragrant, I thought you might want to come down to smell it for yourself tonight, after the banquet.*

There is another sheaf of papers: manuscript pages from Corbett's *Man-eaters of Kumaon,* with editorial markings all over them. There is also a handful of typewritten papers: the notes Corbett's sister Maggie dictated to her friend Ruby Beyts. These are the papers that Diwan Sahib promised me when he was alive, though I did not believe in their existence then.

There are three things still in the packet. I know what to expect, but even so I feel a hollow nausea as I pull them out. There is a photograph, a letter in an envelope, and Diwan Sahib's will.

I have studied the photograph so many times that now I think I know each tiny square of it. It is a black and white photograph of a group. There are men and women dressed in styles popular in the 1960s. They are sitting on easy chairs somewhere in the open. Tennis rackets of the old world, glasses and bottles strewn on the grass. The sun in their eyes is making some of them squint. Diwan Sahib is not squinting: he is looking at the camera, and his chin is raised; his face has a kind of triumphant elation. His eyes have that sparkle I knew so well, but otherwise he looks quite different: no wrinkles and no beard;

short hair brushed back in a widow's peak; a clear-eyed, handsome, young face. He has a toddler in the crook of his arm and his other hand rests on the head of a large golden retriever.

There are three women in the group, all in fashionable chiffon saris and sleeveless blouses. One of the three is not looking at the camera. She is looking at Diwan Sahib and the toddler with a hunger that leaps out from the picture even decades later.

I open the letter that is clipped to the picture. The envelope is addressed to Veer. It is in Diwan Sahib's handwriting and I find it difficult to read despite knowing its words.

Dear Veer, my very dear Veer,

> *What I could not call you in my lifetime, I can say when wiped away by death: my son. I could not own you as my son. I tell myself there were reasons, and many times over these last years I have been on the brink of telling you and begging you, as an adult man, to understand why I did what I did. But I didn't have the nerve—and after such a crime, what forgiveness or reparation? Things happen and deeds are done in a long life for which there are no explanations that will satisfy anyone. Anything beyond is wasted words.*
>
> *I ask your forgiveness nevertheless.*
>
> *In grief,*
>
> *Your father,*
> *Suraj Singh*

The will is clipped to the envelope. Diwan Sahib does not repeat his revelation about his son Veer in the will, but its intention is to make amends, to take a step toward healing with the gift of an ancestral home, his son's rightful inheritance. The will is in Diwan Sahib's handwriting, and the signatures of witnesses flow across the bottom of the page. It has a date, it has everything that makes it legally valid.

It is brief and clear:

RAI BAHADUR SURAJ KISHAN SINGH, EX-DIWAN OF SURAJGARH, HIS LAST WILL AND TESTAMENT. NOW MAY IT BE NOTED AS FOLLOWS THAT CONSEQUENT UPON MY DEATH:

1. Whatever alcohol is left over is to go to Najeeb Qureshi. He is also to get my Rolls-Royce Silver Ghost cigarette case, an object he has longed for all the years we have known each other, and one that, as a lover of motorcars, he considers his by right.
2. My newspaper clippings file must go to General Bisht, so that he begins to read, at whatever age.
3. My tenant, Ms. Maya Secuira, is to inherit the papers pertaining to Edward James Corbett. She is also to have the enclosed letters of Edwina Mountbatten and J. L. Nehru.
4. The money in my bank account is to be divided equally between Himmat Singh and Puran Singh, Charu and Dharma Devi.
5. All my household goods and clothes are to go to Himmat Singh, to sell, dispose of, or keep, as he pleases.
6. The house and all its grounds are to go to Ranveer Singh Rathore, provided he undertakes to allow lifelong rent-free cottages on the estate to Dharma Devi, her son Puran Singh, and her granddaughter Charu Devi; and also allow Maya Secuira to occupy her cottage as long as she pleases. The original deed is enclosed, showing the boundaries of the estate Ranveer Singh Rathore is to inherit from me.

Signed and witnessed.

I hold the will and letter up to shade my eyes and look at the jumbled shadows of the words through the sunlight. I think back to those early conversations with Veer when he told me in bitter tones about the way he was sent from the house of one relative to another as a child, parceled out between them on school vacations. How none of them ever had time for him. How he grew attached to one or two of them, and hoped they would announce all of a sudden that they were his parents. How, by magic, he would know where he belonged and would have a real home. How Diwan Sahib had imitated leopards and thrushes for him sometimes, but returned in five minutes to his gin and his women. How Veer had hungered for affection and never found any.

I put the papers down. How I had yearned to comfort Veer in his loneliness then!

I lie very still and listen to the barbets calling. They sit on the dahlia trees snapping the large flower buds between their beaks, like nuts they are cracking open as a snack. There are big yellow lemons warming and ripening on their stems. Unless the will is made known to the world, all of this—the house, the stream, my cottage, my garden, the spruce, oaks, rhododendrons, and deodars—all these will go to a stranger, some brigadier or colonel we do not know, after being in Diwan Sahib's family for two generations.

But that is how it is with houses, and I have lost too much to care. I will find another and make it a home again.

I read the will once more.

I am balanced on the edge of a knife. I *am* the knife. I can do harm.

Diwan Sahib's face appears before me, his white hair a mess, his beard overgrown, and he says, "Go on, what are you waiting for? You know what I'd do. Revenge is a kind of wild justice."

I remember him at his fireplace, thrusting the pages of his manuscript into it, then throwing the photograph of his dogs into the flames, watching his life burn.

I think of Michael with his broken ankle, on a frozen slope by a lake filled with skulls, watching his friend being whited out in a blizzard, seeing him recede into the distance, calling him back, begging his help, losing his strength with every shout, knowing all the while that there is nothing ahead for him but a slow dying.

Slivers of ice clink in the corners of my heart. If I were turned inside out now, there would be frost and hailstones where blood and muscle were.

I hold the will and Diwan Sahib's letter to Veer tight in both hands, and I rip the pages in half, and then the halves into quarters. The sound of tearing paper lacerates me. I notice the portion that has the words "Ranveer Singh Rathore, provided he undertakes . . ." and rip it into tinier and tinier pieces, until not an alphabet can be distinguished of the name.

I throw the pieces of paper in the air. The shreds that drift over me are almost indistinguishable from the white butterflies dipping over the wildflowers in this garden gone to seed.

The eagles are still watching me from the mile-high crook of a deodar tree. Around them the afternoon has begun its rapid wintertime decline and the sun's long rays slide gently now, and give no warmth. I will need to get up from the grass before the chill seeps into my bones.

The eagles feel the change in air and light. The first of them flexes its talons like an athlete, spreads its wings, and leaves its branch. The other is still looking in my direction. Eventually it turns its basilisk gaze away and follows its mate. The day is over; they have to hunt for a perch to sleep on now. They are lifted higher and higher by air currents as they wheel and arc and sail toward the last hill of the world.

GLOSSARY

arrack	liquor distilled from the fermented sap of toddypalms, or from fermented molasses, rice, etc.
babu	suffix added to men's names to show respect; bureaucrat
barasingha	*Rucervus duvaucelii,* a species of deer with great horns, native to India and Nepal
Batasha	crunchy sugar candy
beedi	cheap cigarette made of tendu leaf and tobacco
beta	affectionate term for male child
bhajan	Hindu devotional song
bhang	preparation from the leaves and flowers (buds) of the female cannabis plant, which grows wild throughout the Himalaya, smoked or consumed as a beverage
Binaca Geet Mala	a popular music program on radio in the 1960s and '70s.
biryani	richly flavored rice cooked with meat, a specialty of Hyderabad

carrom a game similar to billiards, but played without cues on a lacquered plywood board, popular in India, Pakistan, and Bangladesh

chacha uncle (specifically, father's younger brother)

chadar long scarf

chaiwallah man selling tea

charas hashish handmade from cannabis, which grows wild throughout the Himalaya

chikoo *Manilkara zapota,* or *sapota,* a common soft fruit

chootiya strongly abusive word for fool

chota bachha small child

chote sahab young master

chowkidar watchman

coolie porter

darshan holy audience

dekchi a large cooking vessel

Deo Bhoomi land of the gods

Diwali festival of lights celebrated everywhere in India

dosa a pancake native to South India, made from a fermented batter of ground rice and lentil

dupatta	long scarf worn by women
durbar	court
firanghi	foreigner
ghee	clarified butter used in cooking and in rituals; also in cremations
gitti	a game played with five stones, similar to jacks
gongura	a sour, leafy vegetable found in South India
gutka	an addictive mix of crushed betel nut, tobacco, catechu, and lime, sold in foil packets
half sari	a full-length skirt and fitted blouse, combined with a long scarf, commonly worn by girls in South India
hawai chappals	rubber flip-flops
hum	we
jaggery	solid molasses
jalebi	a pretzel-shaped Indian sweet, both crisp and juicy with syrup when freshly fried
jhadu	broom
kheer	creamy rice pudding often flavored with nuts and cardamom
khidmatgar	bearer or valet; a servant

kumkum	colored powder used to decorate or anoint the forehead
kurta	long shirt
kutala	a digging implement with a curved blade
langur	monkeys of the genus *Semnopithecus,* widespread in South Asia
machan	improvised tree loft from which to hunt or watch animals
madua	millet
mandi	wholesale market
murukku	a fried snack from South India
namaste	common Indian way of greeting anyone, by joining the palms
nilgai	literally, "blue bull"; *Boselaphus tragocamelus,* a large antelope
paan	betel leaf folded with areca nut, tobacco, and other condiments, usually consumed after meals
paapam	Telugu expression meaning "You poor thing"
pakoras	vegetable fritters
papad	poppadum; a thin, crisp snack, similar to a cracker

poori-aloo — cheap, streetside meal made up of deep-fried Indian bread and potatoes

pugree — turban

roti — thin whole wheat bread baked every day, a staple food

sadhu — wandering holy man, mendicant

sala — bastard

salwar kameez — combination of a long shirt (*kameez*) and loose trousers (*salwar*) commonly worn by Indian women

samosa — deep-fried, triangular pastry filled with spicy vegetables

sanki — half-witted

shikari — hunter

sindoor — the red coloring in the parting of a married woman's hair

sola topi — pith helmet worn in colonial times

thataiyya — Telugu for "grandfather"

theek — all right/well

tum — you

ACKNOWLEDGMENTS

D. C. Kala, Amit Sen, and Ravi Dayal decoded the hills for me. Their erudition, wit, and individualism, their ability to combine austerity with pleasure, make them a unique Himalayan species now extinct.

Something Arundhati Gupta said started off this book. She also read its first draft, as did Myriam Bellehigue, Sheela Roy, Shruti Debi, and Partho Datta. Rukun Advani suffered countless drafts and demands, and there is a lot of his writing and thinking between the lines. Christopher MacLehose, with his idiosyncratic genius, worked on successive versions as he would on an unmade garden: a space to inhabit, plant ideas in, and over time grow into a book.

Manju Arya's insights have provided much entertainment and education. Mahiraj Mehra's doctoral work on Ranikhet was a rich source of information, as were conversations with S. Ramesh and Akshay Shah. I have benefitted from Janet Morgan's *Edwina Mountbatten: A Life of Her Own,* Martin Booth's *Carpet Sahib,* D. C. Kala's *Jim Corbett of Kumaon,* and P. N. Dhar's *Indira Gandhi, the Emergency and Indian Democracy*. Another delight was *The Social Economy of the Himalayans,* by S. D. Pant, which arrived out of the blue from MacLehose Press. The book is an example of the many overwhelming kindnesses of Christopher, Koukla, and Miska MacLehose, who break every cliché there is about the cruel impersonality of modern publishing. As do many others at MacLehose Press and Quercus, especially Katharina Bielenberg and Nicci Praca. Martha Levin and Millicent Bennett have helped me learn a great deal about publishing by the powerful mix of ideas, energy, and warmth with which they live-wired the U.S. edition.

Ivan Hutnik and Thomas Abraham's involvement in this book are fortuitous culminations of old friendships. Nasreen Kabir, Radhika Prakash, and Manishita Das will as always shelter me through its publication. To each of them I am ever grateful.

READING GROUP GUIDE FOR

THE FOLDED EARTH

by *Anuradha Roy*

Introduction

In a remote town in the Himalaya, a young widow named Maya tries to put her past behind her. By day she teaches in a school and at night she types drafts of a magnum opus by her landlord, an eccentric scholar and a relic of princely India. Her bond with him and her friendship with a village girl, Charu, seem to offer her the chance for a new life in the village of Ranikhet, where lush foothills meet clear skies. As Maya finds out, however, no refuge is remote enough to separate her from her past. The world she has come to love, where people are connected with nature, is endangered by the town's new administration. By turns poetic, elegiac, and comic, *The Folded Earth* is a multilayered narrative about characters struggling with their pasts even as they fight for freedom and clarity in the present.

Topics & Questions for Discussion

1. The setting of *The Folded Earth*, particularly the author's descriptions of nature in the Himalayan foothills, plays a huge role in the book's narrative. In what ways does nature—from the weather in Ranikhet to the landscape—impact the story of *The Folded Earth*?

2. Why does Maya come to the small, isolated village of Ranikhet? Is it to escape her troubled past? Does she succeed? Do you think there's any physical place a person can go to get over the past and begin a new life? If you had to start over, where in the world would you choose to go?

3. Maya's parents formally disowned her when she married outside her faith and caste. How do the residents of the Light House come to be a surrogate family for Maya? What are the problems and rewards of being part of this makeshift family?

4. Roy describes two of her characters, Kundan and Charu, as each being "a child of the hills." What do you think it means to be "a child of the hills"? Does it come with a particular personality or outlook on life? How might a person's hometown come to define him or her?

5. Puran is called half-witted and an imbecile; he's a kind of "holy fool" who creates mayhem, but he has a special gift for communicating with and gaining the trust of animals. What do you think the character of Puran represents in the novel? What important roles does he play?

6. Ama and Diwan Sahib, two central, elderly characters in the book, are from vastly different backgrounds. One is an unread, poor village woman, the other a learned aristocrat. What is the source of their mutual trust and unstated affection?

7. Why do you think Maya first falls in love with Veer? How is he similar to Michael? Is there any indication that he might have ill intentions?

8. Two of the book's prominent characters, Michael and Maya's father, play no direct role in the events, and we meet them only through Maya's thoughts: the past seems as vivid as the present in her life. What does this tell us about the role of memory in the book?

9. Why was Jim Corbett's life so appealing both to Diwan Sahib and to Maya? How do both characters try to live by Corbett's philosophy? What does the act of writing about him say about the personalities of both Diwan Sahib and Maya?

10. Diwan Sahib and the General are relics of an old way of life in India. Do you think the new generation will learn from their mistakes? Can the younger people fully appreciate the old men's glories and struggles?

11. Charu is illiterate when readers are first introduced to her, but she eventually learns to read and write, and she eventually escapes her small village. Did her evolution surprise you? What would have happened to her if she hadn't been able to find Kundan in Delhi? Would she have been able to resume her old way of life?

12. Why do you think Diwan Sahib never shared the letters between Nehru and Edwina?

13. Given the heavy foreshadowing of political and religious unrest in the region, it's a great relief when Ranikhet native Ankit Rawat wins the election. Do you think this victory shows that the village will remain intact? Or will these pockets of unrest cause further problems in the future?

14. For most of the novel, the situation for Miss Wilson and the other teachers and students at Maya's school seems ominous. Do you think they'll continue to be safe?

15. Where do you think Maya will go at the end of the novel? What will happen to Ama and Puran? Did Maya do the right thing in destroying Diwan Sahib's will?

Enhance Your Book Club

1. The author's love of nature is evident on almost every page of *The Folded Earth*. Go for a walk outdoors with the members of your book group—even if it's not quite as majestic as the views that Maya sees every day, find elements of nature that speak most to you in the place where you live.

2. From roti and biryani to mango pickles, *The Folded Earth* features a wide variety of Indian foods. Have each member of your book club bring an Indian dish to your discussion of *The Folded Earth,* and sample some of the delicacies described in the book.

3. Maya has many dreams that mirror her mood or predict future events. Have the members of your book club describe dreams they've recently had, and use a dream book or website to try to interpret the meanings of these dreams.

A Conversation with Anuradha Roy

You currently live in Ranikhet with your husband. What is your experience of the region? What would you like readers of *The Folded Earth* to take away about what life is like in contemporary India?

Young locals in Ranikhet often have the sense that life is elsewhere and leave the town for cities like Delhi looking for the buzz, energy, and opportunities in them. In Ranikhet, by contrast, life is spartan, the weather is often harsh, and the solitude can seem extreme to those unused to it. The pace is very different—everything takes more time—and it has none of a big city's anonymity nor its aggression. If readers went to Ranikhet after being in Delhi or Mumbai they would get to know two very different sides of India.

It's clear from the lush descriptions in the novel that you are deeply enamored of the natural phenomena of the book's setting. How do you think the setting informed the events of the novel? What are some of the defining characteristics of "hill people"?

A big theme of the book is the place of wilderness in our lives—so "nature" in the book is not meant to be decorative, it is central to it. At the level of what happens in the book, many of those things could have happened only in these mountains: Corbett, the wildlife, the climbing.

I can't generalize about hill people, of course, and nobody is isolated from urban influences any more because of TV and the media. But it's striking how generally good-tempered and lighthearted the villagers are there despite leading such hard lives. It's not just a matter of good manners—it's their way of being. Most people there will sacrifice making more money for lying about in the sun in the afternoon for a snooze or chatting with friends. It's as if they've discovered the secret of contentment without a single self-help book.

Maya thinks of Ranikhet as a refuge from her troubled past. Do you think she can ever fully escape? Are you drawn to Ranikhet for any of the same reasons that Maya is? How much of what you've written in the novel is informed by actual circumstances?

Maya and I don't actually share anything but a propensity for long walks. Some things I experience obviously go into my fiction, in the sense that they can trigger a thought process or idea, but they are transformed as I develop the idea. The Ranikhet in the book is not the Ranikhet of real life. Not even the map. Politically, the things that happen in the book reflect disturbing trends in India as a whole, but are not specific to Ranikhet.

You describe Veer's phone and Internet connection, even while characters like Ama and Charu live rather provincial lives. How much has modern technology impacted impoverished villages like Ranikhet? Do you think the divide between the haves and have-nots is increasing?

The divide between haves and have-nots is increasing all over the country. At the same time, modern technology has begun to reach remote places and is accessible to many more people than before. Village women used to be tongue-tied when asked to speak on a telephone; now I see them using their own cell phones. Yet they might still be extremely deprived in their daily lives, doing hard physical labor, eating poor food, walking long distances to fetch drinking water. It's difficult to make any sense of it.

Although many of the themes and subjects you write about in *The Folded Earth* are deeply serious, there's a great deal of humor throughout. How do you balance the two?

I guess what is serious need not be grim, and this is true of fiction as much as it is of life.

You're an editor at Permanent Black, an independent press that specializes in South Asian history, politics, and culture. How does being an editor differ from being a writer? Please tell us more about the press.

We started our press, my husband, Rukun Advani, and I, eleven years ago. It began with one book on our list, our own savings, and no work space but our dining table. We went through huge uncertainty at that time, not knowing if we would survive; gradually the imprint established itself and the list grew into 300 books by the best scholars on South Asia. But we still work at our dining table and are still independent.

Editing needs you to enter another writer's head, see a text as the writer; writing fiction needs you to shut yourself into a world that exists only for you, one that you are creating. Editing needs empathy and outwardness; writing needs a cocoon. I couldn't balance the two. I stopped editing and switched to designing our covers.

You left the ending of *The Folded Earth* ambiguous. Do you have an idea in your head of what might become of Maya after the close of the novel? Or what might happen to the village itself?

I know only as much as the reader does.

***The Folded Earth* is your second novel. What did you learn in the process of publishing your first novel, *An Atlas of Impossible Longing,* and how does this experience compare?**

The publishing process for *Atlas* was long and disheartening because of the number of times it was rejected, and that left me in despair. The excitement, newness, and thrill of it when it did come out were stratospheric, partly because it was so unexpected that from being universally rejected it would end up being translated into so many languages. The writing of *The Folded Earth* was as intense, but fortunately the publication process had more of the highs and fewer lows.

What's next for you? Are you working on a new book?

I'm always writing. But for a long stretch I don't know if what I am writing will shape into a book. That's where it is right now.

ONE

In the warm glow of fires that lit the clearing at the centre of straw-roofed mud huts, palm-leaf cups of toddy flew from hand to hand. Men in loincloths and women in saris had begun to dance barefoot, kicking up dust. Smoke curled from cooking fires and tobacco. The drums, the monotonous twanging of a stringed instrument, and loud singing obliterated the sounds of the forest.

A man with a thin, frown-creviced face topped by dark hair combed back from his high forehead sat as still as a stone image in their midst, in a chair that still had its arms but had lost its backrest. His long nose struck out, arrow-like, beneath deep-set eyes. He had smoked a pipe all evening and held one polite leaf cup of toddy that he had only pretended to sip. His kurta and dhoti were an austere white, his waistcoat a lawyerly black.

He did not appear to hear the singing. But his eyes were on the dancers: wasn't that girl in the red sari the one who had come with baskets of wild hibiscus that she had flung carelessly into a corner of his factory floor? And that man who was dancing with his arm around her waist, wasn't he one of the honey-collectors? It was hard to tell, with their new saris and dhotis, the flowers in their hair, the beads flying out from necks, the firelight. The man leaned forward, trying to tell which of the sweat-gleaming faces he had encountered before in his small workforce.

The brown-suited, toadlike figure sitting on a stool next to him nudged him in the ribs. "Something about these tribal girls, eh, Amulya Babu? Makes long-married men think unholy thoughts! And do you know, they'll sleep with any number of men they like!" He emptied his cup of toddy into his mouth and licked his lips, saying, "Strong stuff! I should sell it in my shop!"

A bare-chested villager refilled the cup, saying, "Come and dance with us, Cowasjee Sahib! And Amulya Babu, you are not drinking at all! This is the first time people from outside the jungle have come as guests to our harvest festival. And because *I insisted*. I said, it's Cowasjee Sahib and Amulya Babu who give us our roti and salt! We must repay them in our humble way!"

A tall, hard-muscled man stood nearby, listening, lips curling with contempt as his relative hovered over the four or five friends Cowasjee had brought with him, radiating obeisance as he refilled their cups. Beyond the pool of firelight, cooking smells, and noise, the forest darkened into shadows. Somewhere, a buffalo let out a mournful, strangled bellow. The drums gathered pace, the girls linked their arms behind each other's waists, swaying to the rhythm, and the men began to sing:

A young girl with a waist so slender that
I can put my finger around it,
Is going down to the well for water.
With swaying hips she goes.

My life yearns with desire.
My bed is painted red.
Red are my blankets.
For these four months of rain and happiness
Stay, stay with me.

Without you I cannot eat,
Without you I cannot drink.
I'll find no joy in anything.
So stay, stay, for the months of rain,
And for happiness with me.

One of the girls in the line of dancers separated herself from her partners. She had noticed Amulya's preoccupied expression, wondered how a man could remain unmoved by the music, not drink their wine. She came forward with a smile, her beads and bangles jingling, her bare shoulders gleaming in the firelight, orange sari wrapped tight over her young body. The toddy made her head spin a little when she bent down to Amulya. As he tried to scramble away, she stroked his cheek and said, "Poor babuji, are you too pining for someone?" She leaned closer and whispered into his ear, "Won't you come and dance? It wipes sorrows away."

Amulya looked up beyond her childish face, framed by curling hair which smelled of a strong, sweet oil, at the flamboyant purple flower pinned into her bun. It had a ring of lighter petals within the purple ones, and a pincushion of stamens. *Passiflora*, of course. Yes, certainly *Passiflora*. But what species?

Despite the haze of alcohol that made her eyes slide from thing to thing, the girl noticed that the man's gaze was not on her face, but on the flower. She unpinned it and held it out to him. A deep dimple pierced her cheek. The drums rolled again, a fresh song started, and she tripped back to her friends with a laugh, looking once over her shoulder.

"Hey, Amulya Babu, the girl likes you!" Cowasjee cried, slapping Amulya's thigh. "You can turn down food and drink, but how can you turn down a lusting woman? Go on, dance with her! That's the done thing in these parts!"

Amulya stood up from his chair and moved away from Cowasjee's hand. "I have to leave now," he said, his tone peremptory. In his left hand he clutched the purple flower. With the other he felt about for his umbrella.

Amulya understood he was an anomaly. When still new in the town adjoining the jungle, he had tried to make himself part of local society by going to a few parties. Songarh's local rich, they too had hopes of him, as a metropolitan dandy perhaps, laden with tales and gossip from the big city, conversant with its fashions, bright with repartee, a tonic for their jaded, small-town appetites. He had had many eager invitations.

After the first few parties, at which he refused offers of whisky and pink gins, and then waited, not talking very much, for dinner to be served and the evening to end, he had realised that perhaps his being there was not serving any purpose. Was he really becoming a bona fide local by attending these parties when his presence emanated obligation?

Today—these festivities at the village whose people were his workforce—he had thought it would be different. He had, for a change, wanted to come. He had only ever seen tribal people at work—what were they like at play, what were their homes like? The opportunity had seemed too good to miss; but Cowasjee, in whom the bare-shouldered village girls seemed to unleash more than his usual loutishness, had ensured that this evening was like all the others.

Amulya looked around for someone to thank, but everywhere people sat on their haunches drinking, or they danced, enclosed in worlds of private rapture. The drums had speeded up, the twanging could scarcely keep pace. Where was his umbrella? And his office bag? Was his tonga waiting for him as instructed? Was anyone sober enough to light his way to the tonga?

"Oh sit, sit, Amulya Babu," Cowasjee said, tugging Amulya's sleeve. "You can't go without eating, they'll be sure their food was too humble for you, they'll feel insulted. The night is young and we have stories to swap! Have you heard this one?" Cowasjee cackled in anticipation of his punchline.

Amulya sat again, annoyed and reluctant, barely able to summon up a strained smile to the yodelled laughs that accompanied the ensuing discussion about why a woman's two holes smelled different despite being geographically proximate. "Just like the difference between Darjeeling tea and Assam!" one of Cowasjee's friends shrieked. "Both in the hills of eastern India, but their aromas worlds apart!" The third said, "You bugger! More like the difference between the stink of a sewage nullah and a water drain!" They nudged each other and pointed at the girls dancing by the fire. "She's for you," giggled one. "How 'bout taking her home and confirming the Assam–Darjeeling hypothesis?"

The tall, muscular villager stepped out from the shadows, one fist clenched around a long bamboo pole. In two rapid strides, he and his weapon were towering over them. Cowasjee shrank back on his stool. The obsequious middleman noticed the threat and scurried out from a corner. He said something over his shoulder to the drummer, then to a woman tending a cooking pot. The drums fell suddenly quiet. Confused, the dancers stopped mid-stride. The woman called out, "We will eat now, before the chickens run out from the rice!"

The stringed instrument played on, its performer too rapt to pause. The man with the bamboo pole stepped aside, not taking his expressionless eyes off Cowasjee.

Far away, Kananbala heard the faint sound of drums, like a pulse in the night. Another night of waiting. At nine-thirty the neighbour's car. Slamming doors. Shouts to the watchman. Ten. The whir of the clock gathering its energies for the long spell of gongs to come. The creaking of trees. A single crow, confused by moonlight. The wind banging a door. Ten-thirty. The owls calling, one to the other, the foxes further away. Then the faint clop of hooves. Closer, the clop of hooves together now with the sound of wheels on tarmac, whip on hide. A tongawallah cursing. Amulya saying, "That's it, no further." His voice too loud.

Kananbala dropped her age-softened copy of the Ramayana and went to the window. She could see her husband hunching to release himself from the shelter of the tonga, too tall for its low bonnet. She turned away and returned to the bed, picking up her Ramayana again. When Amulya entered the room and looked around for his slippers, she did not tell him she had put them under the table. When he asked her, "Have you eaten?" she pretended to be immersed in her book. When he said, "Are the children asleep?" she replied, "Of course. It's so late."

"They only served dinner at ten. They wouldn't let me leave without eating, what do you expect me to do?"

"Nothing," Kananbala said, "I know . . ." Something caught her eye and she stopped.

"What is that?"

"What? That? Oh, it's a flower."

Amulya's voice was muffled beneath the kurta he was pulling off over his head. She could see his vest, striped with ribs, his stomach arcing in. She looked again at the flower, dark purple, wilted. He had placed it under the lamp near the bed. In the light of the lamp she could see one long, black strand of hair stuck to the gummy edge of its stem.

"I know it's a flower," she said. "Why have you brought it home?"

"Just wanted to identify it . . . " he said, leaving the room.

She had often asked him before: were there women at the parties he went to? The host's wife? Her friends or relatives? Why could she, Kananbala, never be taken? He always laughed with condescension or said, exasperated, "I have never met women at these parties, neither do I aspire to." And what of today, the festival at the tribal village—could she not have been taken? If she were a tribal woman herself, she would have needed no man's permission.

Amulya returned to their room with a large, hard-covered book. He sat near the lamp and opened it, then put on his black-framed spectacles. He picked up the flower in one hand, turned the pages of the book with the other, looking once at the pages and once at the flower, saying under his breath, "*Passiflora* of course, but *incarnata*? I've never seen *this* vine in Songarh."

Kananbala turned away, lay back against her pillow and shut her eyes. She could hear pages rustling, Amulya murmuring under his breath. She wished with a sudden flaming urge that she could stamp on his spectacles and smash them.

Amulya laid the flower against an illustration in the book and whispered, "*Incarnata*, yes, it is *incarnata*. Roxburgh has to be right."